SHADOW CHILD

Hardscrabble Books—Fiction of New England

Laurie Alberts, *The Price of Land in Shelby*

Thomas Bailey Aldrich, *The Story of a Bad Boy*

Anne Bernays, *Professor Romeo*

Chris Bohjalian, *Water Witches*

Joseph Bruchac, *The Waters Between: A Novel of the Dawn Land*

Joseph A. Citro, *Shadow Child*

Sean Connolly, *A Great Place to Die*

Dorothy Canfield Fisher (Mark J. Madigan, ed.), *Seasoned Timber*

Joseph Freda, *Suburban Guerrillas*

Castle Freeman, Jr., *Judgment Hill*

Ernest Hebert, *The Dogs of March*

Ernest Hebert, *Live Free or Die*

Sarah Orne Jewett (Sarah Way Sherman, ed.), *The Country of the Pointed Firs and Other Stories*

Lisa MacFarlane, ed., *This World Is Not Conclusion: Faith in Nineteenth-Century New England Fiction*

Kit Reed, *J. Eden*

Rowland E. Robinson (David Budbill, ed.), *Danvis Tales: Selected Stories*

Roxana Robinson, *Summer Light*

Rebecca Rule, *The Best Revenge: Short Stories*

Theodore Weesner, *Novemberfest*

W. D. Wetherell, *The Wisest Man in America*

Edith Wharton (Barbara A. White, ed.), *Wharton's New England: Seven Stories and* Ethan Frome

Thomas Williams, *The Hair of Harold Roux*

Also by Joseph A. Citro

Passing Strange, 1996

Green Mountain Ghosts, 1994

Deus-X, 1994

Dark Twilight, 1991

The Unseen, 1990

Guardian Angels, 1988

Vermont Lifer (writer/editor), 1986

SHADOW CHILD

BY JOSEPH A. CITRO

University Press of New England

HANOVER AND LONDON

UNIVERSITY PRESS OF NEW ENGLAND publishes books under its own imprint and is the publisher for Brandeis University Press, Dartmouth College, Middlebury College Press, University of New Hampshire, Tufts University, and Wesleyan University Press.

Published by University Press of New England, Hanover, NH 03755
© 1998 by Joseph A. Citro
Originally published in 1987 by Kensington Publishing Corp.
All rights reserved
Printed in the United States of America
5 4 3 2 1

LIBRARY OF CONGRESS CATALOGING-IN-PUBLICATION DATA
Citro, Joseph A.
    Shadow child / by Joseph A. Citro.
        p.   cm. — (Hardscrabble books)
    ISBN 0–87451–884–9 (pbk. : alk. paper)
    I. Title. II. Series.
    PS3553.I865S5   1998
    813'.54—dc21   98–24018

This book is for my mother,

who never discouraged

my taste for the bizarre.

CONTENTS

SHADOW CHILD

PROLOGUE

Summer 1952

"Hey, Brian! Wait up!" Eric Nolan called to his brother.

The two look-alike boys, their hair red as apples in the afternoon sunlight, scampered across the farmyard, trying to catch up with their grandfather. The older boy, Brian, aged five, carried a fishing pole. He swished it back and forth in front of him like a whip. It hissed as it cut the air. Squawking chickens dodged clumsily from the boys' path, beating their wings in a feathered flurry of protest.

Eric, the younger brother, giggled. He watched Brian closely, trying to copy the action with the fishing pole. What a wonderful idea it was, using the fishing pole to scare chickens! It was fun. Eric enjoyed watching the white feathers cascade to the ground like summer snow.

It's magic, thought Eric. Snow in the summer is magic. Brian made magic!

It was a kind of envy that Eric frequently felt of his older brother. Eric envied him simply because Brian was older, if only about a year. Sometimes Eric felt like Brian's shadow, a darker, less detailed, less interesting replica of the older boy.

Eric envied the way Brian always saw things in strange, fun ways. He also envied the way his brother seemed always to know about things that hadn't happened yet; like this morning, Brian had announced, "Grampy's gonna take us fishin' today. To a special place. Get your fish pole ready, Eric."

The younger boy had often overheard adults remark about Brian's intuition—"insight," they called it. Eric had come to the conclusion that he himself was somewhat ordinary, unexciting by comparison.

Eric walked behind his brother and their grandfather, following the coarsely pebbled path that led toward the sugar bush, then along the creek to the fishing hole. He was excited about being taken to Grandfather's secret fishing hole, and he wanted to remember everything about the hike. Squinting, eyes nearly shut, he tried to fix everything in his mind. He looked at the maple leaves above his head, tried to memorize their patterns. Across the brook, an early autumn's Midas touch had magically turned some of the trees on Pinnacle Mountain from green to gold.

Eric thought the magic leaves were beautiful, and he called, pointing them out to Brian.

Brian looked at Eric as if about to reveal a great truth. "It means there's gold hidden on the Pinnacle," Brian informed him with great certainty. As he spoke he patted the palm of his hand against the spikes of his crew cut.

Eric had seen the same gesture every time Brian forwarded some similar and equally interesting bit of information. Like the time Brian asked him if he knew what the sun really was. When Eric said no, Brian explained that it was a giant thumbtack for holding up the sky.

And there was the time the two boys were playing by the railroad tracks, leaving pennies on the rails to be flattened to the size of quarters by the next train. Brian told Eric that the track was a long ladder that went on forever and ever. He said it would surely pass Heaven on its way to wherever it went. To Eric this was very possibly so. To Brian there was no doubt.

There was no doubt about the pennies, either. They were flat and wavy as spinners, with only a dull suggestion of Lincoln's profile. Perhaps they too were magic.

Eric felt for the outline of the penny in the pocket of his shorts. Finding it, he knew its twin was in his brother's pocket. It felt good.

By now, Grandfather had outdistanced the two boys and had forged out of sight around the bend where the little stream hugged a towering gray outcropping. Brian and Eric hurried to catch up, but Eric's progress was slowed when he snagged the tip of his fishing pole in some blackberry bushes. Brian stopped to help untangle it, and they rounded the bend together, walking shoulder to shoulder. Together, they saw Grandfather's secret fishing hole for the first time.

It was a special place, just as Brian had promised.

The pool, surrounded by boulders and flat-rock ledges, reflected the vast sky in its tiny surface. The high waters of a million springtimes had eroded a smooth, rounded bowl in a big rock. Grandfather was seated comfortably on this massive stone. Eric thought Grandfather's seat looked as comfortable as a throne.

It was then that Brian told Eric that he had seen the pool before. He patted both sides of his closely cropped hair. He looked nervous.

"When?" said the younger boy, wonder in his voice.

Brian stared at the scene. "I don't know. But I've been here before."

"To this same place?"

"Yes, but don't tell Grampy."

"Oh, no. I won't." Eric was delighted to share this secret with his older brother. He knew it was somehow important, somehow frightening. It never occurred to him that in reality Brian might never have seen the pool before. If Brian said it was true, then of course it was. Eric wanted to know more about it.

Their conspiratorial whispering was lost amid the sounds of the warm afternoon breeze and the rushing water as it merged into a stream that drained from the pool. The sun backlit the deep green leaves of the maple and oak trees bordering the little brook. Grandfather was stretched out on his large rock, baiting his hook, smoking his pipe, heedless of the two boys who watched him.

"See that rock where Grampy's sitting?" asked Brian.

"Umm-hmm ."

"I saw a boy on that rock one time. He jumped right into the water, and the top of the water got all wrinkly like it does when you splash it. When the wrinkles were gone, the boy was gone, too."

Eric could feel his own fear merging with Brian's. He whispered, "Where'd he go?"

"I don't know. He was just gone. I ran to the pool and on the bottom I could see all the rocks. They looked like funny brown faces looking up at me. I even saw some fish. But no boy. He disappeared."

"Did you tell Grampy?"

"No, and don't you."

"How come?"

" 'Cause it's a secret. It's just for you and me."

"What'd he look like?"

"I couldn't see good. But he had red hair like you and me. And I think his eyes were like ours, too. He could have been either of us. He could have been somebody else. He looked right at me and I still couldn't tell for sure."

"Come on, you little rapscallions," called Grandfather. "You better hurry up and get them worms wet!"

Brian touched his brother's arm. "Don't tell anyone, will you, Eric?"

"No," vowed the younger boy. And, in spite of all the things that happened later, he never did.

PART ONE

Vanishing Vermont

These mountains know more than they tell,

And more than you or I ever will.

And there's magic hiding underneath

A country windowsill,

And there's voices in the hills.

—Dick McCormack

From <u>Vanishing Vermont</u>, an unfinished manuscript by Eric Nolan, p. 47:

Certain areas in the state seem especially vulnerable to strange disappearances. There is a "Devil's Triangle" zone near Bennington where, from November 1945 to December 1950, seven people vanished, without a trace, all in the vicinity of Glastonbury Mountain.

The ages of the seven victims range from eight to seventy-five. Four were female, three male. All vanished in the same area during the same season of the year, i.e., from October to December. Four of them vanished in 1950.

Ground and air searches, systematically covering every foot of the forest, revealed nothing.

Not surprisingly, residents theorize about UFOs, demons, and monsters. There has been speculation about people falling through interdimensional trapdoors. Any theory, according to Sheriff's Deputy Lester Prim, seems more probable than coincidence.

1. BREAKFAST

Clint Whitcome took a can of Carnation evaporated milk from the refrigerator and popped it open as he sat down at the kitchen table. He was a big, handsome man, six feet tall in his stocking feet. He had hair the color and sheen of motor oil and wide brown eyes that were alert and cheerful. He looked much younger than his forty-one years. Perhaps that was because of the way he moved; each stride, each turn of the head, each tiny gesture was graceful, full of precision and purpose. Clint Whitcome seemed to glow with pride and a disarming, humble confidence.

He was dressed in a blue flannel shirt and Levi denims bound with a wide leather belt made from a cow collar. Although it was six o'clock in the morning, he was puffing on a corncob pipe. A hazy layer of blue smoke hung like a mist in the sunlight that filled the kitchen.

His wife, Pamela, was at the stove, stirring oatmeal, humming along with a Stan Rogers song on the radio. She watched Clint through the lattice of her fiery red hair. Then she looked over her shoulder and smiled at him.

Clint yawned, belched, ran his hand through his hair, destroying the razor line of the part and the unusually careful job of combing. He left the top of his head looking as if it were the back of a porcupine.

Pamela moved to the table and straightened Clint's hair with a gentle hand before she spooned cereal into his bowl. He smiled back at her and chuckled. Then he put aside his pipe and poured maple syrup over the steaming oatmeal.

"How's the little man?" he asked between a spoonful of oats and a mouthful of coffee.

"He's okay. He's still sleeping. When I went up to bed last night he was standing at the window watching the back yard. He looked so tragic."

"Probably the first friend he ever lost."

"Do you think he's really lost, Clint? I mean really gone?"

"Can't say for sure. He might turn up again. I'm afraid he was out running deer and got lost or something. I always thought a dog couldn't get lost, but then I never knew a dog as dumb as Rusty."

Pamela laughed. "I shouldn't laugh. Luke is miserable."

"He'll get over it. I betcha he'll get over it a lot faster if we get him another dog to take his mind off it." Clint pushed his empty bowl away and gulped the rest of his coffee. Abruptly, he stood up.

"Can I pour you another cup to take with you?"

Clint stopped, as if seriously contemplating the complexity of the question. "Naw," he replied, "I'll get one down to the garage."

"You sure? There's half a pot left."

"Yup." Clint hesitated, then he asked, "What time are you expecting that cousin of yours?"

"Who knows? It's a long drive from Long Island. You may get home before he arrives."

"In that case, I'll bring home a couple of six-packs, and if he's here he can help me drink them. He does drink beer, doesn't he?"

"If he doesn't, I'll help you drink them. How's that?"

"Best offer I've had all day. 'Bye, Sweetie." He kissed her, lingering a moment longer than usual, then dashed out the door.

Stopping on the steps, Clint turned around. "He's still planning to stay for Thanksgiving, ain't he?"

"Yes. I think so."

Clint thought a moment. "Maybe I'll just take an afternoon and see if I can get us a wild turkey for dinner. Think he'd like that?"

"I know he would. So would I."

"Does Eric like hunting? Think he'd want to go out with me?"

Pamela smiled and shrugged.

Clint shrugged too, winked at her, jumped into the green pickup with "Town of Antrim" on the door, and drove off down the hill. The truck disappeared into the bright autumn morning. In its wake, leaves of red, yellow, and brown swirled above the gravel drive.

Pamela held the door open to the chill morning air and watched him go. She had seen the nervousness in her husband; it was almost tangible, hanging in the air like pipe smoke. Yet, she knew better than to acknowledge it, to diminish him by telling him not to worry. The hurried breakfast, the too-long kiss, the offer of the six-pack all were Clint's ways of showing how nervous he was. He was a proud man, a good father, and kind to a fault, but somewhere, locked away behind his solid wall of strength and confidence, there was an uneasiness. It wasn't shame, it wasn't fear. It wasn't anything that Pamela could put a label on. It was something that Clint never spoke about, never acknowledged at all, except during the most private of times. But Pamela knew her husband was uneasy about his lack of education, and about certain responsibilities of his position as a supervisor with the Antrim Highway Department. Clint was especially uncomfortable in the company of highly educated men who taught at colleges. He was nervous about meeting Eric, about what they'd say to each other, about what they'd do. He concealed his apprehension well, but he couldn't hide it from his wife, who understood him better than any woman ever had. When he had asked, "Does Eric like to hunt?" she understood him to mean, he doesn't object to hunting, does he? And, "He does drink beer, doesn't he?" meant, he won't be put off by my drinking beer, will he?

She loved Clint for the awkward consideration that he was showing for Eric; she knew how hospitable and kind he would be when her cousin arrived.

Pamela walked back to the table, gathered the breakfast dishes, and carried them to the sink. She sat down and poured a cup of coffee. Staring absently at her fingertips, she rubbed them over the rings and lines of the finished oak tabletop.

How strange it will be to see Eric again, she thought. She had figured it out last night while waiting for sleep to come: it had been seventeen years. Seventeen. Was that possible?

But Eric was family. More important, she was his family. The only family he had left. He had nowhere else to go.

It had been a surprise to receive his letter, although, really, Eric had never been far from her thoughts. Once Eric and Pamela had been the best of friends, like brother and sister. Seventeen years ago.

She sipped her coffee, looking back across the years to those far-away seasons they had passed as children in this very house. They were young then, innocent, and for them this farm on the top of Tenny's Hill was like a castle on the highest mountain of a fairy-tale kingdom. Once upon a time . . .

The memories of their youth were sweet, gentle, like mother-hood, she thought.

Yes, it would be good to see her cousin again, to try to offer what comfort she could, to share her family and their home. Their life. She should never have allowed herself to lose touch with Eric.

We stopped writing when we had no more to say, thought Pamela. When you write to someone, even if it is rarely, you don't do it out of obligation, but out of need. And, in writing, you define what that need is. The need may not be obvious, but it will be there: the need to be remembered, the need for reassurance, the need for comfort. It will be there, somewhere in the letter.

Pamela reached into the pocket of her apron and fingered her cousin's letter. For some reason, she too, like her husband, felt a little nervous. Maybe she was questioning the nature of Eric's need, but before she could analyze any more she heard a noise from the top of the stairs.

"Mommy," a tiny voice called.

"Down here, Honey."

Luke Whitcome came down the stairs. After briefly detouring to the television set, turning it on and then ignoring it, he entered the kitchen. He was dressed in Jedi pajamas and was dragging Philip, his lanky stuffed monkey, along the floor behind him.

"Was that Daddy?" Luke looked up at his mother, his expression unusually perplexed. He had a way about him that suggested everything was an unfathomable puzzle. Perhaps everything is a puzzle for a four-year-old boy, but Luke wore confusion on his small round face like the paint on the face of a clown. Sometimes it would fade, but he would never be free of it entirely. Clint and Pamela found his expression endlessly amusing. Once, when they got their vacation pictures back from the drugstore, Clint had laughed himself into a state of helplessness at his son's apparent confusion. "Look, here's Luke on the beach, looking puzzled; and here he is on my shoulder, looking puzzled; and here he is on the merry-go-round, looking puzzled."

Pamela was amused too, perhaps more amused because she knew, with a powerful maternal intuition, that their son's confusion was only on his face and not in his heart. He was a loving and happy little boy, perhaps a bit undersized at forty pounds, but healthy, alert, full of questions as the world grew in size and complexity around him.

He looked up at her eagerly, waiting for an answer to his question.

Pamela winked at him. "Of course, it was Daddy. And I bet he saved you some oatmeal. You hungry?"

"Naw. How come Daddy didn't stay home today?"

"Because he had to go to work. Just like every day."

Luke climbed up into one of the ladderback chairs and flopped Philip on top of the table. Pamela put orange juice and a glass of milk in front of him.

"But isn't Uncle Eric coming today?" he asked, a white mustache of milk on his upper lip.

The way Luke picked up on things always amazed Pamela. Although she and Clint had discussed Eric's visit with the boy, it must have been her anticipation and preparations that, in the child's mind, gave the occasion special importance, like a holiday. Clint didn't work on holidays.

"That's right, Uncle Eric will be here later, but Daddy has to work anyway. He'll work just like always, even though Uncle Eric is visiting."

"How come Uncle Eric doesn't work?"

"He does. He works at a school. But he's on vacation for a while."

Luke considered this. Then he asked, "Will he help me find Rusty?"

"I think so, Honey, I think he'll try."

"Mommy, do you think Rusty will come home today?"

"I don't know, Love. I hope so. We'll put some food out for him."

"I'll do it. I'll fill his dish and put it on the porch."

"That would be nice. Rusty is just like your father, really hungry when he gets home."

Luke picked up his glass and drained the last drops of milk from the bottom. He put it down carefully, then sat perfectly still. For a long moment he was quiet.

"What are you thinking about, Honey?"

Luke looked at her. "Do you think somebody coulda took Rusty?"

Pamela blinked. "What do you mean, Hon?"

"It's just that I had a dream. I dreamed some kids took Rusty."

"Dreams aren't real, Luke. They're just make believe. They're stories we tell ourselves when we're sleeping."

"I know. But I heard him barking . . ."

"Maybe you dreamed that, too."

"No."

"Or maybe it was some other dog you heard. Sound carries at night, you know."

Luke thought it over. Pamela could tell that he wasn't satisfied. She felt as if she had cheated him, as if she'd lied. How could she lie if she didn't know the truth? She turned back to the sink and the breakfast dishes.

"Mommy?"

"Hmmm."

"Does Rusty miss us?"

"Of course he does."

"Then why doesn't he come home?"

She smiled, and felt the sting around her eyes that warned her a tear was coming. "I don't know why. Maybe you should put the dish out for him."

Luke brightened. He ran to the refrigerator and reached way up for the handle to pull it open. He put an opened can of Alpo on the floor next to the empty dog dish, ran to the drawer to get a spoon, and with great effort and concentration, began to move scoops of brown meat from can to dish, looking puzzled.

Pamela watched him carefully; with both hands he carried the dish to the porch, letting the door slam behind him. The tear slid down her cheek and she wiped it away with a dish towel.

She moved to the window to watch her son stare down the road and across the fields and into the woods.

2. A CHANGE OF SCENE

Eric Nolan's right hand was shaking. He stared at it helplessly. Tightening his grip on the steering wheel, he tried to control the trembling.

This shouldn't be happening, he thought.

As he watched the twitching hand, his Volvo drifted toward the passing lane. An eighteen-wheeler rocketed past on his left. The blast of its air horn was like a siren signaling the end of the world. Eric's attention snapped back to the highway, the Volvo shuddering in the violent air.

Adrenaline shot through him; his muscles tensed in surprise. The sudden sound and mechanical squall left him holding his breath, sweating. With an effort of will he concentrated on calming just his right hand. He commanded it to be still.

It was no use. The hand seemed to have a life of its own. It shivered and moved at the end of his sleeve like a living thing, making him think of a small white fish impaled on a spear.

The eighteen-wheeler was far ahead now, out of sight. Its demon horn still echoed in his ears as he thought how close he had come. Another yard to the left and—

A brush with death. It can grab us any time. Sneak up on us from behind.

In his rearview mirror he saw exhaust from his downshift. He thought of a metaphor: "Carbon monoxide, the smoke of hell." He thought of a cliché: "Escaping catastrophe, he left death in his wake." Eric would have red-penciled either on a freshman paper.

Yet, he *had* left many deaths in his wake. It was a fact. He didn't want to think about it. He wanted to leave it behind.

Eric passed a sign indicating that a rest area was a mile ahead. Turning on his blinker, he flashed a right turn. Time to stop driving. Now, at three o'clock in the afternoon, with nearly eight hours of traveling behind him, he felt tired, sore. The muscles of his lower back had tightened like a fist; his head throbbed.

Eric pulled into the rest area, shifted into first, and slowed to a stop. He took a deep breath, carefully, as if inhaling might be painful. He didn't want to start hyperventilating again. That, too, was something he wanted to leave behind him, in New York. There were many things he wanted to leave behind.

He flexed his quivering right fingers. The trembling had subsided but thick veins stood out on the back of his hand like blue snakes coiled between his rocky knuckles. It was an ugly thing. He made a fist of his left and jabbed it repeatedly into the cup of his right, as if wanting to punish it. The tension would not pass.

Getting out of the car was painful. Standing up straight was agony as his back muscles strained and stretched.

Eric took more deep breaths. The Vermont air felt cool. It had an edge to it that sliced icily along his nostrils and throat. It was fresh and fragrant; he welcomed it, thinking the drive north had brought him closer to winter.

At last, he was standing on Vermont soil! Somehow, when he crossed that border, that magic line, he had expected a change to come over him, expected a burden to be lifted. The shaking hand warned him that nothing had changed—not yet.

I must be patient.

Eric looked around. To the east, reflecting the afternoon sky, the Connecticut River stretched north and south like a winding bead of solder, welding Vermont and New Hampshire together.

This was the Connecticut River Valley, a belt of rich farmland that comprised the eastern border of the state. From where Eric stood the land rose slowly to the west, where the Green Mountains grew to altitudes of four thousand feet and more. The mountains were the spine of the state, a backbone that stretched from the broad shoulders of the Vermont-Canadian border to the belt that ran below Vernon, Pownal, and the five towns between them, separating Vermont from Massachusetts.

It had been years since Eric had viewed these hills. The slowly flowing river, the dying fall colors, the brittle leaves that fell to earth building insulation against the coming snows, all these things had a calming effect on him. They represented natural cycles. Eric knew these cycles would have altered the things he hoped his return would find intact.

Eyes on the river, he remembered the peace he had known here, so very long ago.

Of course there were bad memories, too—painful memories. He tried not to think of them. Like his death thoughts, they were not important. It was the good thoughts, the beautiful memories, that had called him back, pulled him with the force of a powerful lodestone to the green and gold Vermont hills.

When he had left Vermont things had begun to fall apart. Perhaps by returning he could put the pieces back together, find the ones he had lost. With luck, this drive to Vermont could be the beginning of his new life.

"Things fall apart; the center cannot hold." Yeats's poem, one of Eric's favorites, resounded in his ears. He'd taught it to sophomores just last week. He remembered thinking, perhaps for the first time in his life, that poetry had no real meaning for him. It could not solve his problems, it could not explain the origin of the insidious tension that gripped him at unpredictable times, compelling him to race blindly, foolishly into the night.

Was he running now? Was returning to Antrim just another show of cowardice? After the therapy, after the lonely nights of alcohol and tears, after the anxious drives up and down Long Island's neon-dappled highways, what else could he have done? Where else could he have gone?

"I have seen the eternal Footman hold my coat, and snicker . . ."

The trip to Vermont had appealed to him more than anything else had lately. At least, he thought, he'd be doing something, taking some action to regain control of his life.

He had watched like an outsider as the quality of his classes at Long Island Community College nose-dived with terrifying speed. He became frightened of his students, couldn't face his peers. He just wanted to run, hide, escape.

"And in short, I was afraid."

Vermont was the answer. It had to be. Nothing else offered any comfort. He couldn't lose himself in writing. Tears relieved nothing, they only embarrassed him. The company of his friends reminded him of how alone he felt. It was as though he were losing his identity, destroying himself, combusting from the inside out as he yielded to indefinable passions that were far more powerful than his will to control them.

It was from desperation, real or imagined, that he wrote his letter to Pamela; the last words of a dying man. He reached into the pocket of his coat and took out her reply. The wind tried to snatch it from his hands as he unfolded the paper.

> P. Whitcome
> R.D. #1, Box 188
> Tenny's Hill Road
> Antrim, Vt.

Dear Eric,

I can't tell you how happy I was to hear from you and to know that you'd think of me at such a time. Of course it would be okay for you to come for a visit! You didn't even have to ask.

It really has been too long since we've been in touch. More than fifteen years, I think, since we've actually been together. That's way too long. I think of you often and feel bad that our lives have taken such different directions since we were kids on the farm.

I guess you know that my husband Clint and I moved back into the farmhouse several years ago (My God! Can it be that you didn't even know I was married? I guess not, from the way you addressed the envelope!). The old place is very much as you remember it, I think. We've made some changes, but home improvements are expensive, and Clint has so little time to work around the house. The place will probably never evolve into the showpiece that it could be. But to tell you the truth, neither of us really cares.

But listen to me ramble on. Maybe I'm just trying to cram all the things I want to tell you into one short note. Or maybe I'm trying to avoid getting to the point.

When Clint and I heard about your great loss I can't tell you how we felt. I'm so sorry, Eric. Although I never met Karen, I know she must have been a very special person to win the love of my favorite cousin.

Yes, Eric, please come. Clint and I would like it very much if you'd come to Vermont and spend some time with us! By now you've missed summer (so it won't be just like the old days) and the fall colors have passed their peak. But why not come for Thanksgiving? Stay as long as you can, till Christmas even. It would be nice if we could all be together for Christmas.

I'd like so much for you to meet my husband and, do you know? We have a little boy! His name is Luke. Can you imagine, the old tomboy herself having a son?

Anyway, a change of scene might be just the thing you need. Plan to stay, rest up a while. There's plenty of room, as you probably recall. You can even have your old room back.

Let us know when you'll arrive. I've tried to call you but I guess you're never at home.

Please come, I can't wait to see you again! And please, cousin, take care of yourself.

All my love,
Pamela

P.S. Clint wants to know if you like to hunt and fish.

Eric Nolan put the letter away and got back into the car. He had left it running; the heat felt good. He was optimistic, if only a little bit. Vermont sounded wonderful. It would be great to see Pamela again. She had said it: ". . . just the thing you need."

From the files of Elizabeth McKensie: Letter sent to the town clerk of Chester, Vermont, April 23, 1957, signed Rena LaMotte, apparently an Indian lady:

Fifteen years ago my old daddy was hurt bad by some kids he met in the woods . . . One thing my daddy was good Cathlic and he very little drink likker . . . What happens he say was daddy was with momma picking berries when he went away from others for rest. He say he only look at trees and sky, then two kids comes running from rocks at him, hit old daddy to ground with log, hit him on head and side arm, hit him hard and make grunts. Daddy yell then others come and childrens run away fast. They see childrens running and daddy blood on his head . . . Old daddy scared of woods now, never go anywhere, just stay home.

As Eric drove north his mind was far ahead of him, exploring the hills and houses, the streets and faces, that he had left long ago. Some happy times had been spent in the fire-scented kitchen of the farmhouse, his grandfather sitting by the wood stove, smoking his briar pipe and reading his Bible, while Grandmother stood at the counter, singing Irish songs and making cookies or fudge for her young guests.

As Eric steered the Volvo, a song almost found its way to his lips, but it froze in his mouth when he saw his image in the rear-view mirror. He almost turned away, but decided it was time to begin to face the creature that, in two short months, he had become.

In the glass, he looked himself in the eyes for the first time in weeks. His gaze explored his ruddy, whiskered face.

"You need a shave," he said to his reflection.

His cheeks were an unattractive juxtaposition of red stubble and white runways of skin—the paths cleared by his razor in yesterday's hurried shaving. Yet even in his present state his cheeks were not free of their rosy Irish flush. The red seemed more than normally accentuated against his pale skin and the ink-dark circles under his eyes. Long hair, orange as a pumpkin, lay matted to his head like an oily plastic film. His eyes looked dull and lifeless. Long ago he had taken to wearing tinted glasses to conceal what he considered an unflattering birth defect. His left eye was a darker shade of blue than his right. This imperfection had caused him much embarrassment as a child. Now it merely contributed to his overall disheveled appearance. He stared contemptuously at his image in the mirror. "I look like hell," he said.

His thoughts returned to his destination as he moved his attention from mirror to road. It was as if the tension that had been growing inside him for several months were now encouraging him, pushing him toward Antrim, toward Tenny's Hill. Back to Pamela.

He tried to focus on the tension, understand something about it. Maybe in this more comfortable environment he would be able to analyze it fully, face it head on, get rid of it forever before it made him feel any more scattered and afraid.

Afraid. That was as close as he could ever come to labeling it. Fear. Fear of . . . ?

Eric tried not to think about that last night with Karen. He could hardly remember what they had argued about. Only fragments and phrases lingered in his mind. It was the sound that he couldn't forget: shrill, accusing screams. She'd let loose a fury that left him frozen and speechless.

He'd been practically pleading with her. "Karen, for God's sake, what's wrong?"

She'd looked him right in the eyes, her face contorted and slick with tears. "It's you, you son of a bitch. You're what's wrong. Don't you realize that? Don't you know that I've got to get away from you?"

The door slammed. Her feet pounded down the stairs. The car started with a roar and squealed out of the yard. Eric's eyes were riveted to the closed door. He was stunned, trembling.

Exactly what had happened next he could only imagine. Or, rather, he couldn't stop imagining.

How many times must he play the scene over in his mind?

It was raining hard, it was dark. Karen had turned left after leaving the yard, driving on the back roads heading toward Hawksville.

Eric pictured Karen's eyelids fighting tears. Rivulets of mascara swirled along her cheeks, giving her alabaster skin the look of rough marble. The wipers did what they could to keep her vision clear. But she was mad, burning fever mad. She was speeding. And there were no gates on those rural railroad crossings.

The crash exploded in his imagination for the millionth time. Eric pounded his right palm against the stickshift. He clenched his teeth.

The whole thing had been a sinister plan by whomever it is that designs our lives. If she had turned right instead of left, if she had been going faster, or slower. Christ, if she had only been watching . . .

Any time. It can take us at any time.

The big green sign that said "Springfield, Chester, Antrim—1 mile" brought Eric back to the present. He shuddered again at his memory and thanked that sinister designer that he had not been summoned to the scene of the crash.

Officer Justin Hurd stood before the bathroom mirror straightening his tie. Work was going to be boring tonight and he was trying to think of something to bring with him that might help pass the time.

A thought came to him. "Gimme a pack of cigarettes, will you, Brenda?"

From where she reclined on the bed, Brenda, his wife, tossed him a pack of Marlboros. Hurd grabbed for it, missed, and watched it plop into the sink, floating amid the whiskers and lather of his shaving water.

"Damn."

Brenda, dark-haired and plump as a bonbon, giggled. She walked into the bathroom and stood next to Justin. He stared at the floating pack as if he were standing on a bridge, watching a body.

Brenda snatched up the packet, dried it on a towel and handed it to her husband. "You gotta act quick in these emergency situations," she told him. "See, no harm done, it's waterproof."

Justin kissed her on the lips. "Between the instructions I get from you and the chief, maybe someday I'll make a good cop."

"I just did," said Brenda, leering playfully.

"God," said Justin, "Only one thing on your mind. Speaking of the chief, what shall I tell him about Thanksgiving?"

"Tell him we'll be there. I'll make a pie or something."

"Most likely, 'or something,'" he said, with pseudo-indignation. "See you about midnight, Babe." He kissed her again and headed for the door.

"The witching hour," she called after him in a seductive, breathy voice.

At thirty-five miles per hour, Eric drove along the main street of Antrim. Wide-eyed behind his tinted glasses, he looked right and left. The stores and houses were like familiar faces watching silently as he passed. Late-afternoon light reflected dully from second-story windows, making the buildings look sleepy and old. There was no traffic on the street and no one on the sidewalks or in front of the stores. The only movement was of dry leaves tossed in the wind, and of dark birds, perched on telephone wires, stretching their wings in the cool air.

A calm settled over Eric Nolan. He breathed more deeply, more easily. The tightness in his stomach and back had dissipated, flowed out of his body like smoke through a screen door. His right hand was now as steady as a surgeon's. The electric tremors that had coursed up and down his spine sought ground and discharged. He felt at peace as he slowed to a stop at the roadside in the middle of town. He turned off his engine in front of the drugstore.

A green pickup truck passed him on the left. A uniformed policeman walked out of the old railroad station. A shaggy mongrel dog darted across the green, stopped to sniff at the roots of a dark-trunked maple tree, turned up its nose, uninterested, and moved on.

Eric rolled down the window. The fresh air felt medicinal. He filled his lungs and exhaled slowly through smiling lips.

As the cool Vermont air massaged the dry skin of his face, Eric surveyed the town. The village green to his left was lightly dusted with a covering of multicolored leaves from the lofty maple, oak, and elm trees that grew in the town's center. Overlooking the green, as a cliff overlooks the sea, was the Medford Inn. The inn, Eric's grandfather had told him, had been named after its founder. Its black-lettered sign led many uninitiated tourists to believe they had arrived in the wrong town, a town that appears nowhere on Vermont maps. The monstrous three-story structure had a wide porch all around. Eric remembered when the building was as white as winter snow. Now it had weathered to a dirty gray and was badly in need of a paint job. Here and there the faded paint peeled in six-inch strips that curled like scrolls of ancient parchment.

To his right was the general store; he had often stopped in with his grandfather, many years before. The smells of coffee, leather, and a wood fire wafted across his memory. Beside the general store he saw the new single-story post office. Shiny blue metal mailboxes stood out against its red brick front. When he was a boy the post office had been a six-by-eight-foot cubicle at the rear of the general store, right next to the magazine rack.

House after house of neat colonial design lined the main street. Most were painted white, each stood at a dignified distance from the road, leaving plenty of room in front for lush green lawns. A comfortable space separated the houses; many property lines were marked by white picket fences. Something about the layout of the street—the intervals between the dwellings, the decorative, functional fences—made Eric think about the character of their builders: taciturn, standoffish Yankees, just like Grandfather, who were independent even living in a community and who truly believed that "Good fences make good neighbors."

He looked at the railroad station. Attached to its front he noticed a trim, black-lettered sign that said "Town Offices." Perhaps it was fitting that the town should regain railroad property. Grandfather had often said that more than anything else the railroad was responsible for the downfall of Vermont farming. Trains brought rich folks from the city. They liked the looks of the land and purchased greedily. Land prices soared beyond the means of the locals. The ski developers weren't far behind. It was the train that brought the money, and the money separated Vermonters from acres and traditions the like of which could never be recovered. Eric smiled as he thought of his grandfather.

Now the town had the railroad station back; Eric had come back to the town. Maybe it's an optimistic sign, he thought. Grandfather would have been pleased.

There was still no evidence of industry in Antrim. It was a bedroom community of Springfield, where the machine-tool business supplied income for resident commuters. Years ago farms and logging had been income-producing businesses for the locals. Until the sixties, Grandfather's had been one of the very few working farms left, and he had had to supplement his income by leasing woodland to the lumber companies. Eric wondered if any real farms were still operating.

He took his keys and got out of the car. Although he was eager to see his cousin and her family, he was not yet ready to interrupt his reunion with the town. Besides, he recalled his face in the rearview mirror and knew that he looked pretty unsavory, though he was feeling better than he had for a long time. He would take a room at the Medford Inn, rest, clean up. Perhaps he'd buy some wine and something for the boy so he wouldn't arrive at the Whitcome house empty-handed. He'd phone Pamela and tell her to expect him in the morning, when he would be better prepared for their reunion. He wanted to get off to a fresh start.

He set out on foot across the green toward the inn. The brisk wind tangled his copper hair and animated the dry leaves that scurried and danced around his feet.

3. NIGHT WATCH

In the parked car, Officer Justin Hurd sat quietly, hidden by the bushes and by the night. The engine purred softly, like a dreaming kitten. The defroster breathed streams of warm air into the car, keeping Hurd comfortable and the windows clear. He watched the road, a black vein in the flesh of the evening, and thought about lighting a cigarette. His passing fear that the flare of the match might give away his location made him feel foolish, inexperienced. There was nothing to worry about. No one could see him.

The radio below the dash hissed and scratched. The sound irritated him, but he wouldn't turn it off; that wouldn't be right. He had adjusted it to the lowest volume hours ago.

Hurd had known the shift would be boring, but this was torture. There was nothing to occupy his mind. Too bad he couldn't read, at least. He wanted to finish that Joseph Wambaugh book, *The Onion Field*. Boy, that guy could really write; he knew what cops were all about.

Justin's reverie changed direction as he thought about going home to his wife, Brenda. His shift wasn't over until midnight; all he had to do in the meantime was sit and think. Mostly sit . . .

Brenda hated it when he had to work nights, but she was getting used to it—maybe faster than he was. He recalled how important he had felt when, before their marriage three short months ago, he had told her of all the trials and tensions she could expect as the wife of a policeman. She had accepted the whole package with obvious excitement. Remembering that excitement, his hand moved to his groin. He fantasized about the pleasures that would be waiting for him when he got home.

A scratching sound brought him to immediate attention. His muscles tensed, his ears felt as if they were growing, taking inventory of the sounds of the darkness.

The scratch again. It came from behind him, on his side of the car. Turning his head, he heard it clearly, and relaxed. It was the wind moving bushes against the cruiser.

Justin looked around, feeling foolish at his alarm. I'd better tend to business, he thought.

On either side of him the highway stretched black and empty. There had been no traffic for nearly half an hour. What the hell, why not light the cigarette? It would help him kill the last few minutes of his watch. He groped for his pocket, his hand trembling just a bit.

The flare of the match stung him with its unexpected brightness. His eyes blinked against the sudden flame and took a moment to readjust. It made him aware of how dark it really was.

This is shitty duty, he thought, but the higher-ups were antsy about a bunch of antique thefts, and the citizens of Antrim were forever phoning the chief about hot rodders on this back road from Springfield. The main concern was the thefts, and this backwoods nothing of a road had been carefully targeted by his chief, Dick Bates, as a probable source of illegal activity. Bates had decided to stake out the road. And Bates was probably safely home in bed right now.

Justin couldn't fault Bates though, not really. In fact, he considered himself lucky to have Bates as his chief. Many of his classmates from the Brandon Police Academy had gotten stuck with much more dangerous assignments and much tougher, less reasonable bosses.

No, Bates was okay. He was easy to work for. He didn't lord it over Officer Hurd, didn't ride him about his rookie status, and always spoke well of him to the town manager. If he wanted to, the chief of a two-man force could make life more than miserable for a young officer, especially one who was new in town. Bates was a good man. He'd take his turn at the roadside tomorrow or the next night.

Bates's fairness, however, didn't make Justin's shift go any faster.

So there he sat, three days before Thanksgiving, by the side of Old Factory Road. Bates always called it Olfactory Road because it passed the town dump, or landfill, as the town's newer residents insisted on calling it. One thing about Chief Bates, he had a sense of humor.

Justin smiled as he thought about his rotund and good-natured boss. Then his mind jumped to his wife's warm flesh, her faded tan ending at the tuck of her buttocks. In his mind she was stretched out on the warm sheets of their bed. The thought brought moisture to his lips.

This pleasurable image contrasted with his boredom, emphasized it. Twenty-three thirty hours, the last half hour of his shift; not enough time to want to tackle anything serious, but enough time to go stir crazy from boredom.

He drew deeply on his cigarette and exhaled through his nose. Smoke swirled lazily in the cruiser.

Through the smoke, in the darkness to the north, he could just make out a faint light on the road. It was moving slowly toward him; he watched it with unblinking eyes.

He pinched the cigarette out between his fingertips, never turning his eyes from what he now recognized as the single headlight of a slow-moving vehicle. The light was dim, flickering, like the flame of a candle. Must be an old one, he thought, recognizing the dull pulsing of a six-volt system.

Officer Hurd needed to see no more to conclude that the vehicle was in violation: only one working headlight, defective equipment.

"Shit," he said, rolling down the window and snapping the cigarette out. A torrent of cold November air filled the car.

He waited for the truck to pass in front of him so he could get a good look at it. It was, indeed, an old one, with headlights contained in those bullet-like enclosures mounted on the fenders.

That thing's older than I am, he thought. Must be something

out of the thirties, or maybe even the twenties. Probably some old fart from one of the local farms on his way home after an evening of applejack. It's certainly not the getaway vehicle for an antique heist.

But the driver's equipment was defective, and in spite of the late hour, it wasn't like Officer Hurd to ignore his duty. He had vowed to himself when he finished at the academy that he would never get sloppy like some of the old-timers. Besides, he didn't want to let Dick Bates down, not in any way at all. A bit of late-night activity would make it clear to the chief that Justin Hurd was tending to business. Anyway, an old coot in a broken-down pickup would be a lot easier to deal with than some speeding punk or shit-faced businessman.

Brenda, and their warm bed, would have to wait.

As the shadowy form of the old truck rattled past in front of the police car, its one fiery eye pointed toward Antrim, Hurd hit the button. A blue brilliance strobed the landscape and the howl of his siren assaulted the quiet night.

The truck, which wasn't moving fast anyway, obediently pulled over to the side of the road. The police car stopped a safe distance behind. Dim lights on the waiting vehicle blinked off as Hurd observed the tarp-covered bed. He squinted at the dark machine, trying to identify it.

God, he thought, I can't get a make on it; too old, an antique in itself. By association Hurd's mind began to construct a cycle of possibilities: stolen antiques, drunken fugitives, marijuana smuggled in from Canada and moved to Massachusetts across the back roads of Vermont. Even the antique vehicle itself could have been stolen!

In the bright twin beams of his own headlights he could see no registration on the truck.

I'd better call this one in after all, just to be on the safe side, he decided.

The Antrim police office would be closed at this hour, so he'd have to radio the state police barracks in Rockingham—something he didn't like to do. He tried to avoid the troopers whenever he could. He always felt like a rookie when he compared himself to them. Yet he still had the desire that had been with him since he was a boy in St. Albans—someday he wanted to be a Vermont State Trooper.

Picking up the microphone, he felt a tickle of embarrassment because he had no idea of the make or year of the waiting vehicle.

He pushed the button and spoke. "Eight twenty-two."

"Eight twenty-two, go ahead," came back immediately in a crackling whisper.

"Eight twenty-two. Ten-thirty-eight. Older model black faded truck. Stake body. Old Factory Road. Approximately two miles from Antrim."

"Ten-four, eight twenty-two. No plates?" crackled the radio.

"Negative. None in the rear. I'll advise."

Hurd straightened his tie and got out of the cruiser. His Kel-lite was in his left hand. The beam explored the back of the closed tarp that hung like a drape across the bed of the truck.

Approaching the driver's door from the rear of the vehicle, he felt an odd shiver pass along his spine. Almost without thinking he removed the strap, making sure the .357 was loose in its holster. One of his instructors at the academy had told him that some day this precaution might give him the extra second that would save his ass.

Keeping the beam of his flashlight aimed at the ground, Hurd tapped his knuckle on the driver's window. He was surprised that the window wasn't already open. Most drivers would nervously roll it down as an officer approached.

"Open up, please," he said.

The man inside did not respond. Now Hurd moved the light upward to the bearded face of the driver. The face was old, like wrinkled leather, with a thick crop of white, greasy hair tangled around the ears, across his forehead, and under his chin. There was a mound of knobby flesh, about the size of a Ping-Pong ball, above the left eye. The old man squinted and turned his face away from the light. He massaged the knob of flesh with fidgety fingers, but he didn't open the window.

This time Hurd tapped the glass with the rim of his light. "Police officer, open up," he said. Immediately he felt embarrassed by the melodramatic sound of the phrase.

The man seemed to pay no attention.

Speculation confused Hurd, uncertainty pissed him off. Was this man resisting an officer? Was he drunk? Could he be physically ill, having some kind of attack? What the hell was going on?

The policeman grabbed the ancient door handle and pulled. The door, heavy-metaled and rusty-hinged, opened slowly, loudly.

"Let me see your license and registration," said Hurd, his light hard and bright on the old man's face.

Again the eyes flinched from the bright beam, but the driver made no move for his wallet and made no sound in reply.

Officer Hurd looked at the interior of the truck. The dash was plain, its only instrument, a speedometer, illuminated by a dull orange bulb. The windshield wipers were hand-powered by a small crank at the top of the window. A stickshift with a worn wooden knob on top reached up from the floor. The old man's hand began to move toward it.

"Just a minute, Sir, I want to ask you a few questions. Let me see your license and registration. Right now, please, Sir." Hurd tried to emphasize the authority in his voice.

The gnarled, liver-spotted hand, hideous as a chicken's claw, paused before touching the gearshift, then withdrew. It hovered over the old man's hip, then plunged into the pocket of his dirty overalls with the speed of a diving hawk.

Hurd jumped backward, startled by the unexpected motion. The heat of fright brought perspiration to his forehead. He found that his hand was on his magnum.

Now the old man was looking him square in the face, a twisted smile nearly lost among the other wrinkles of his skin. The mound of flesh on his forehead shone in the light like a third eye.

Hurd froze. There was something frightening about the time-scarred countenance, about the toothless slash of a grin, about the unfocused mania in the wide, staring eyes.

He's too old and feeble to hurt me, thought the policeman.

Unless he brings a gun out of that pocket . . .

When the hand emerged Hurd recoiled as he saw a flash of metal. He relaxed a bit when he realized that the man was holding a small silver flask. The old man, his eyes never leaving Officer Hurd's, lifted the flask to his lips and drank. The polished metal was oddly incongruous in the dirty hand, its surface reflected like a mirror.

Then he extended the flask to the policeman.

Hurd wasn't sure just what was happening. He wondered what Chief Bates would do in this situation. He felt with some certainty that he was faced with a case of a drunken driver. And he felt equally certain that the problem was somehow greater than that. Somehow much greater.

He had always prided himself on his sense of intuition, his gut reactions. Chief Bates had told him many times that gut-sense was a policeman's most prized possession. The same instinct was valuable to gamblers and reporters, Bates assured him, but to a cop it could mean the difference between life and death. "Always use your mind and your gut," the chief had said with a wink, patting his overfed abdomen.

As Hurd stared in surprise at the proffered flask, he heard kind of a choking sound coming from the old man's throat. The face contorted uncomfortably as the dry, leathery lips moved, trying to form words.

"Ye . . . ye . . . yer a policeman?" The wheezing syllables stretched painfully from the toothless mouth. The rheumy eyes seemed to be filled with pain. Tears formed like jewels at their corners. "M . . . mebbe you can help me. Mebbe y . . . y . . . you can . . ."

The hideous old face looked plaintively at Hurd.

The policeman didn't need his sixth sense to hear the faint sound that came from the back of the pickup. It was a tiny, squealing sound, almost inaudible, almost nonexistent, almost to be dismissed as mere imagination.

But he heard it.

So did the old man, who looked toward the back of his truck

with an expression that rearranged his many wrinkles into a tight mask of fear.

The sound, whatever it was, came from the tarp-covered bed of the pickup.

Officer Hurd strained his ears to listen. He could hear nothing.

"What you got back there?" he asked the old man, who was now visibly shaking.

"I . . . I . . . I . . ." It was more a choking spasm than a word.

The noise came again, high-pitched, staccato, rising and falling like air bubbling through water. It was an animal noise. A sheep, maybe?

But it sounded almost human. Almost like—Officer Hurd had it now—almost like a giggle, almost like a child giggling.

Without hesitation the policeman walked around to the back of the truck. The lights of his cruiser beat back the darkness and cast his shadow, long and heavy, on the tarpaulin that hung over the rear of the pickup, covering the tail end like curtains in a movie theater. He disregarded the fact that, technically, he needed a warrant to lift those curtains. His only thought was that something was very wrong; no kid should be out at this time of night, riding in the back of an unregistered vehicle driven by this crazy old drunk.

"Who's in there?" he demanded, and the giggle came again.

"Come out of there."

He waited a moment, alternating his glance from the old man to the back of the truck. No one responded to him.

"Come out of there, I said!"

A fleeting sensation of cold made him shiver. He ignored the feeling, giving his full attention to the tarp. With his right hand on the grip of his weapon, Hurd pushed the canvas aside with the flashlight.

The dark bed of the pickup was exposed, but Justin Hurd never saw a thing. Everything happened too quickly. His eyes went first; stabbing columns of pain pushed with the force of pistons into their sockets, blinding him, hurting more than anything he had ever felt. He snapped off his feet, jerked into the bed of the truck. His scream stopped short when a wet and furry object squeezed into his open mouth. His senses fragmented. Pain seared where his eyes had been, a feculent taste polluted his tongue; he smelled sweat and urine—was it his own? Cold things grabbed at his body, things that felt like tight metal coils, one around his calf, another around his bicep. Something seized his ear. And tore. And all the time the chorus of squeals rose and fell as his consciousness ebbed, and drained away to nothing.

And his sixth sense? It failed him now. He died never knowing what had killed him; his last crazy thought was of his wife, and how she would be angry when he didn't get home on time.

He never felt his limp, battered torso getting dragged the rest of the way into the back of the pickup, nor the edges of the canvas tarpaulin closing around him like the corners of a hungry mouth.

From "Vermonters, and the Odd State that They're In" (Yankee Tales magazine, February 1979) by Diane E. Foulds:

Little Annie Bowen lived on the mountainside in Rochester, about two miles from the log schoolhouse that she attended. Annie was timid and very fearful of the big woods and the frightening perils, real or imaginary, that it contained. She had to walk to school alone, and she often wept and pleaded to stay home. Her father, a stern and often violent man, would beat her to force Annie to leave for school.

She met with such a beating on October 11, 1879, after crying uncontrollably, saying that she feared the "bad children" who waited for her in the forest.

When Annie failed to appear at home after school, neighbors were summoned and a search commenced.

The next morning a shout of horror was heard from a little glade just off the path. There, in all its gory details, was the unmistakable evidence of what had happened to poor little Annie. All about were signs of a terrific struggle, with blood on the trampled grass and weeds. There was a shawl, shoes, and the remains of her dinner basket. A few human bones were all that was left of Annie.

It's the work of wolves, everyone said. But of course, in 1879, there were no wolves in Vermont. There are none now.

4. REUNION

On Tuesday afternoon, November 22, Eric Nolan made the short drive from the center of Antrim to Tenny's Hill Road. He was feeling better, things were more in perspective, his fears in a healthier proportion. The swaybacked bed at the Medford Inn had provided him with the best night's sleep he'd had in months.

As he drove, he began to think about his cousin Pamela. He wondered how the years had treated her, and if she was as happy as her letter implied.

He knew his feelings were typical of those preceding a reunion; he was eager for the meeting yet a little afraid of it, recognizing shyness among his emotions. Was he having second thoughts? The Whitcomes owed him nothing. After all, he and Pamela had been strangers for more than a decade.

Eric recalled Pamela as he had known her many years before. There had been a softness about her, an attentive, quiet interest that had made him feel that he was the most engaging person in the world. She listened, she understood, and she'd never judged him. When she smiled her face lit up like a Christmas tree, the proliferation of freckles on her white skin stood out like jimmies on an ice cream cone. At sixteen, in her Levi's and flannel shirt, this tomboy had given Eric his first idea of what femininity was all about.

Remembering how good he had felt when she'd answered his letter, Eric was sure that Pamela could still be a comfort to him. Just as before, she was there when he needed her. But now she was with another man. Now she had a son.

Eric had no right to feel that he was coming home.

He took a deep breath to control his growing nervousness, but, before he could consider turning back, the lines of his grandparents' farm came into view as he rounded the bend at the end of Tenny's Hill Road.

The farmhouse, newly painted white, shone brightly in the afternoon sun. The barn was gone, its boards rearranged into a two-car garage. In the distance, behind the garage, the rusted metal skeleton of a windmill, blades long gone, was topped with a TV antenna. All was as he remembered, but changed, revitalized.

Beyond the farm there was pastureland and acres of the rolling hills that Vermonters call mountains. To this day, Eric was sure, those hills had seen little of contemporary civilization. They were unsettled and untraveled, uninterrupted but for the occasional logging road, uninhabited but for the wildlife, and unexplored but for the efforts of the most ambitious of hunters and the most curious of small boys.

Eric imagined himself and his brother, Brian, playing among the fat chickens in the yard. Seeing the farm again was like glimpsing the past.

Beneath him the wheels of the car turned noisily on the stony drive. Eric saw the porch door open.

"He's got hair just like Rusty's," Luke Whitcome whispered to his mother from his perch upon her hip. Her strong left arm was around his waist, supporting his forty pounds.

"Sssshh," Pamela laughed, holding her free hand out to Eric as he crossed the stony yard.

This was the moment she had both feared and eagerly anticipated. Eric's extra night on the road had only allowed more time for her anxiety to build. Now her cousin faced her, smiling boyishly. "Eric, Eric, it's so good to see you."

He looked at her long and hard. Like her, she guessed, he was trying to sort through reams of memories. She tried to separate her youthful image of Eric from the near-stranger who stood before her. Her cousin was dressed handsomely in tan slacks, brown sweater, and Harris tweed jacket. His long hair was styled, care-fully combed, looking as if each strand had been individually groomed. He wore slightly tinted glasses, and, overall, looked distinguished and scholarly. Pamela suddenly became aware of her faded jeans and sweatshirt. A twinge of embarrassment left her momentarily tongue-tied.

As if experiencing similar uncertainty, Eric said, "I'm at a loss for words." A blush rose through his neck and filled his cheeks with color. "I . . . I mean, it's so good to see you again."

They kissed each other on the cheek, hands locked together. Pamela moved her smile from Eric to Luke. "This is our son. Luke, this is your Uncle Eric."

Luke hid his face in his mother's hair, hugging her so tightly around the neck that she had to loosen his grip. "He's a little shy. Won't talk. We'd better take advantage of it while we can. Come on, let's go inside."

"I know how he feels," said Eric, following her across the porch and into the kitchen.

When they had settled around the kitchen table, each with a cup of hot coffee, Luke on the floor playing with his trucks, an awk-ward silence crowded the room. Pamela felt a little foolish just smiling at her cousin, but words did not come easily. They didn't tumble out unbidden as she had expected.

"Where do we start?" Eric laughed, extending his hand across the table to her. She took it and shrugged.

"Clint should be home soon," she blurted. "He's really anxious to meet you. All week he's been just like a kid, pestering me with all kinds of questions about you: do you like to hunt, do you drink beer, what kind of music do you listen to, dozens of questions about your job. He was nearly heartbroken when you called yester-day to say you'd be a day late. He spent most of last night asking me all the questions he's been saving up for you. I could hardly an-swer any of them, it's been so long since we've been together."

"Grandparents' funeral."

"I think so, yes. Such a long time, cousin."

"It took another funeral."

Pamela looked at him, then down at her coffee cup.

"I'm sorry, Pam. My first social blunder. "

"It's okay." She squeezed his hand reassuringly, then sat back, hands on her lap. "Eric, you don't need to be careful here. Talk when you want. Don't say anything. It's up to you. Please don't think I'm pressuring you. I don't want to pry."

She felt her face explode into a mischievous grin. "But you better tell me all about yourself so I can answer my husband's questions."

"I don't know what to tell you. I've got a few things that I want to find out about you too, you know."

"You go first."

"Well, how should I begin? After I finished college I stayed at the university another year to get my master's, then taught high school a while. Back in '75 a friend recommended me for the position at Long Island Community College. I settled in, got married, thought things would quiet down enough for me to finish writing my book, the same book, by the way, that was to have been my master's thesis, and then my doctoral dissertation, and then my 'private scholarly endeavor.' Maybe someday I'll finish it."

Pamela watched a faraway look darken her cousin's features. Then he snapped out of his momentary melancholia, eyes sparkling as if matches had been struck behind his glasses. "You know, it's really good to be here, Pam. The old place never looked better. I keep expecting to see Grandpa walk in from the living room. I never thought I'd see this house again. You're lucky to have it."

"Grandpa willed it to me. But I couldn't live here until I finished secretarial school. He had set things up so some lawyer from Springfield took care of renting out the place for me. The money helped with school. I moved in, gosh, it must have been around 1970. Maybe a little after that. Clint and I got married in '75. I never did finish school, either."

"Where'd you go?"

"Katherine Gibbs. I hated it."

Eric chuckled. "At least you knew enough to quit. I can't seem to work up the courage. Karen used to kid me. She'd say, 'Why don't you quit school and go to work?'" Eric's next chuckle seemed forced.

"Don't you like teaching?"

"Yeah, sure. I guess so. I mean one has to do something, you know." Eric's gaze wandered to Luke. "Actually I've been thinking a lot about changing careers lately. Maybe I can get serious about writing. I feel like I'm about due for a new start on just about everything."

"Are you on vacation now?"

"I took a leave. I'm at half salary. They were pretty good about it."

"What are you writing? Something weird, I bet. I remember how you always had your nose in a book. You read some pretty strange stuff."

"You got me pegged."

"So what are you writing about?"

Eric smiled. "It's called *Vanishing Vermont*. My brother inspired the idea. But I'm not getting too far with it. Right now it's mostly research, and that's boring." Eric's eyes found Luke again. "You know something, Luke reminds me a lot of Brian. He's about the same age and . . ."

Eric stopped as if he had run into a stone wall. Pamela watched as he fidgeted, changing the subject again. "And Clint? Where does he work?"

She was determined to answer without hesitation. "He works for the town. The Highway Department, they call it. It's just him and a couple other guys. Clint's the foreman. He wants to get a job with the state, someday. Clint says State Highways is the only department that still hires native Vermonters."

"Is he a native?"

"With a vengeance. He used to be a farmer, but he gave it up. I think that's what he'll always be, at heart."

"Why'd he quit?"

Pamela looked down at her coffee cup. She swirled the fragrant liquid and gazed at it as if it were a crystal ball. She thought of her husband, how he had stayed behind and helped his father work the farm while his two brothers and their sister went away to college, careers, and marriages. As old Mr. Whitcome's health declined Clint had worked harder and harder. Almost single-handedly he had built a fifty-thousand-dollar operation into a three-hundred-thousand-dollar enterprise. Then the father had died, and the brothers and sister had reappeared, as if by magic. The absence of a will allowed them to make easy claim to three-quarters of the business. Clint had been angry. He'd sold them his share and turned his back on the family and on the farm. It took a funeral to tear the Whitcomes apart, Pamela thought. "I guess farming didn't give him the rewards he wanted."

Eric finished his coffee. "Well, I can't wait to meet him. Maybe he can give me some advice on changing careers."

As if on cue the sound of truck wheels on the gravel driveway sounded in the kitchen. Luke jumped up, forklift in hand, and ran to the door. He threw it open and it banged against the counter.

"Daddy, Uncle Ear-ache's here!"

Two solid steps crossed the porch and Clint Whitcome entered the kitchen, a case of Black Label under his arm. Scooping Luke up into his other arm, he smiled, stiff-lipped, nodded to the adults, and kissed his son. "How's my little man?"

"I'm good. We got comp'ny."

"An' so we do." He lowered the beer to the kitchen table.

"Clint, this is my cousin Eric."

"Good to know you, Sir," Clint offered his hand. The two men shook and Pamela watched them look each other up and down, appraising, gauging. The contrast was dramatic: Clint in his coarse work clothes, his heavy boots, his hands hard and dirty; Eric in his cotton and tweed with city-soft skin and professionally groomed hair. The country and the city.

"I want you to know you're welcome here, Mr. Nolan," said Clint. "Hope you can drink a beer. I got more here than I can manage."

"I think I can handle one or two. And it's Eric."

"Sounds like you boys are going to need some help with those. I'd better have one with you."

"Me, too," said Luke and laughed along with the grown-ups at his own joke.

Pamela heard something in the laughter, saw something in the tight smile on her husband's face. It was a wisp of shadow across his eyes, a hollow echo buried below the sound of his mirth. She could tell, by the arrangement of these subtle clues, that something was on her husband's mind. Something was wrong.

Chief Richard G. Bates was worried.

He paced heavy-footed around the desk of his small office in the old railroad station. Sometimes he stopped at the window and looked out, surveying the quiet main street of Antrim. He felt as if he should be out on that street doing something. Anything. But what could he do?

He could pace, he could drive aimlessly around, he could ask the state police the same questions he had asked them over and over again. And he could listen impatiently to the same answers. In short, he could do nothing.

It infuriated Bates when anything happened in Antrim, anything serious, that is. And what could happen, he asked himself, that was more serious than the disappearance of a police officer?

Bates had liked Justin Hurd. The lad had been a hard worker. He was honest, conscientious. And, more important, Hurd liked the townspeople. He would have made a good cop.

"Damn it!" said Bates to the empty office. He slapped his fleshy palm on the desktop. "I'm thinking about him like he's dead."

From the day he'd hired Justin Hurd, Bates had felt a fondness for the rookie that went a little beyond the call of duty.

Bates had been pleased at the way their private and professional lives had meshed. He and his wife often had Justin and Brenda over for dinner. They'd even invited the young couple for Thanksgiving.

If I don't do something fast, Bates thought, Brenda will be coming to Thanksgiving dinner alone.

The two men were too similar in age for Bates to see the younger man as a son. He'd begun to think of Justin more as a younger brother, someone with whom to share his knowledge and experience, someone to guide and advise, someone to groom for the eventual responsibility of accepting the position of police chief of Antrim.

And now he was gone, vanished, his cruiser abandoned, still running, by the side of Old Factory Road.

What had happened?

The state boys had hauled Bates out of bed at one o'clock this morning with the news.

As Bates sat at his desk he reviewed his notes for the fiftieth time: Last night at twenty-three forty hours Hurd had radioed the Rockingham barracks. He'd reported an old black pickup truck in violation for defective equipment. He wasn't able to identify the year or make. That would make it a very old vehicle, reasoned Bates. Hurd then got out to question the driver, saying he'd advise Rockingham momentarily. He never checked back. The state police dispatcher was Corporal Al Hutchins. Hutchins had radioed Hurd after fifteen minutes, but Hurd didn't acknowledge. Hutchins had tried again, and then ordered a backup to the scene. Troopers Holden and Spooner found the empty cruiser, the engine running, headlights and radio on. The two men carefully inspected the scene, but found nothing.

At two o'clock in the morning, Bates himself had checked the scene. He'd returned and examined it again at first light. The soft gravel shoulder of the road made it impossible to tell exactly where the pickup had come to a stop. Bates had paced the area for fifty yards in front of the empty police car. There was no sign of a struggle, and, thank God, no blood. Then he examined the bushes on either side of the road. His careful search revealed no evidence. Nothing. Bates had feared finding the boy's body. He knew it was not unusual for a police officer to get blown away when stopping some psycho for a minor violation.

The chief's only conclusion was that Officer Hurd, alive or dead, had left the scene with the driver of the pickup. If he had been abducted, then perhaps he could still be found. Bates, with the state police as backup, would begin an investigation. Bates resolved to spend the remainder of the day questioning people at random. He'd follow Clint Whitcome's suggestion and start with the local garages; somebody must have the lowdown on old trucks.

Wish Clint had agreed to give me a hand, thought Bates. I gotta do it alone.

The chief prepared himself for a long and frustrating process.

By nine o'clock Luke was in bed. The adults sat in the living room drinking beer while discussing plans for Thanksgiving Day. It was the first opportunity they'd had to sit down and really get to know each other.

Pamela had set out a plate of crackers and cheddar, but the men left it untouched, apparently full from multiple helpings of pot roast, mashed potatoes, and brown gravy.

A fire in the wood stove heated the room. On top of the stove a cast-iron pan of evaporating water moistened the dry air. Everyone seemed relaxed.

After Eric had finished two or three Black Labels, Pamela watched him become more at ease. Perhaps the familiarity of his surroundings helped. She knew the house was full of memories for him, as it was for her. It seemed only to lack the presence of their grandparents.

Many times as children they had relaxed in this very room, often discussing their visions of the future.

Pamela was sure that neither she nor Eric had ever expected the shape their futures would take. Remembering long-ago conversations, she recalled how each of them had expected to end up far from Vermont, living romantic dreams inspired by adolescent ambition.

The realization of her own dreams was most obvious in her son and in her husband. She wanted Eric to take a liking to Clint.

How could anyone help but admire Clint, his quick, easy movements, his quiet confidence, his devotion to his family and his life? There was something simple and substantial about her husband, something basic. His identity had never been challenged by school-inspired questions about reality and meaning. Clint's values were almost tangible, buried deep in the Vermont soil like the roots of a majestic maple tree that grew tall and old because the land was rich and enduring. The name of Whitcome, her name now, was as much a part of the Antrim landscape as the maple tree. There was Whitcome Hill, and Whitcome Creek, and a vast population of Whitcomes whose names adorned slate and granite markers in the village cemetery. Clint belonged here, and Pamela knew that she belonged at his side.

She hoped that in time Eric, too, could develop a sense of belonging, hoped that he could feel as if he'd come home.

Pamela sparkled in the presence of the two men. Although she sat close to her husband on the sofa, she was careful to smile at Eric to show him that he was a part of the family. She rose every time one of them finished a beer, replacing it with a fresh one.

Whatever had been worrying Clint seemed to have passed. It must have been trouble at work, or in town, she reasoned. Surely nothing to do with Eric.

Clint seemed totally involved in the conversation, telling humorous stories about town government and local characters. Eric laughed readily at Clint's dry wit and storytelling skills.

Yet, in spite of the laughter, it was difficult for Pamela to focus her thoughts on the here and now. She recalled how, as a boy, Eric had been eager to escape his summers at the farm. He was bored by the slow pace of the days, the lack of friends, the sameness. During those long-ago summers Pamela had been his only friend. She thought of a time long ago, when she had helped him through an earlier loss.

At sixteen they had passed hours in the old barn, lately torn down by Clint. She and Eric would sit in the loft looking down at the mound of soft, yellow hay. Its fragrance had filled the barn to the rafters.

That summer, their last summer together, they had been a little more than cousins, a little more than friends. They'd begun to experiment with each other, giving voice to newly emerging feelings that were frightening to both of them, but not enough so that either turned away.

"Put your head here," Pam had said, and when Eric's head was settled comfortably on her lap she watched his blue eyes search for something important to tell her. It was a time for important thoughts. She had wondered if she would ever be able to take the place of Eric's brother.

"Do you mind talking about him?" she asked.

"No, I guess not. I don't remember him too well. I was very young when it happened, five years old; he was six."

"What do you think it was? What do you think happened to him?"

"I don't know. My mother told me he wandered off. We were playing in the yard, not too far from the house. I went inside to get something, then I got sidetracked and didn't go back out. I forget why. Gram said, where's Brian? And I told her. She went out and called him. He didn't come so she tried again, using that noisy old triangle she had hanging on the porch, the one she used to call Grandpa for supper. Brian still didn't come, so we went out looking for him. We thought he was hiding, playing a joke or something. We called and called, spent hours searching. Grandpa even called the neighbors for help, and later the police. He was just . . . gone."

"Where'd he go?"

Eric's mismatched eyes looked up at her in wonder. "We never found out. Crews of men from town searched for him all weekend. There were police, firemen, lots of people. They had dogs, and at night they had bright lights. Of course, they kept me away from all the commotion. They kept saying everything would be all right, tried to keep me from knowing something was wrong. But the more they tried to cover up, the more I knew something really bad was going on. They never found my brother. Not alive. Not dead."

Pam began to stroke his hair with gentle, timid fingers. "What did they think happened?"

"They talked about a lot of things, but never around me. Sometimes I listened from the top of the stairs as my parents went over it with my grandparents. They thought maybe he fell down some old, lost well, or something, like that old well behind the barn. Or maybe he hid somewhere as a joke and then got trapped. They mentioned kidnapping, and there was talk of wolves and other things, said in low voices, that I couldn't make out no matter how hard I strained my ears. But one thing's for sure, he's never turned up. There's never even been a clue. It was a couple of summers before my parents would let me come back here."

"It must have been awful for you."

"It was bad. It still is, even though it's been a long time since it happened. It was worse for my folks, of course, and I think even worse for Grampy and Grammy. They felt responsible. When I finally came back to the farm they'd never let me out of their sight."

"Eric, what do you believe really happened to your brother?"

The boy thought for a long, silent moment. Pamela could remember her hand on his forehead, her fingertips felt the blood throb in his temple.

"I don't know what happened to him. It scares me to think about it. I remember something he told me once, a long time ago . . . it was almost as if he knew it was going to happen. Brian was funny like that; sometimes he'd know when something was going to happen. Someday I'll know where he went. I'll read and study. I'll find out why things like this happen."

Clint's laughter intruded on Pamela's reverie. She felt the sting of a tear behind her eyes. Poor Eric, she thought, he's had a difficult life, so many tragedies, so many deaths. Before her melancholic mood could take over completely, she tried to redirect her thoughts. Clint was telling a story about Billy Newton, one of the local characters.

He finished his story and the last beer at the same time. "Anybody want another round?"

Pamela stood up too, motioning her husband to sit down. "I'll get it," she said. "I've got something kind of weird I want to show you guys."

5. THE HERMIT

From the small window of his cabin, Perly Greer watched the shadows of clouds changing position on the mountain. The process was slow, but time was not a valuable commodity to Perly, not something he needed to worry about wasting, like money, or food, or even affection.

For Perly Greer, time was a constant companion, like a wife, or like family. It was something he had learned to be comfortable with, to tolerate, something that he could not escape. And so he and time had learned to cohabit.

Today, for some reason, Perly was more aware of time than he liked to be. It seemed more like a nagging wife than a gentle companion. Was there something he was forgetting? Was he supposed to do something?

The only obligation he could think of had been met just yesterday. Whether the outcome had been okay or not, he really didn't know. Why fret about it? He had done everything he could, under the circumstances. He would leave the checking to someone else and think no more about it.

Now, as night began to fall, he could turn his mind to other things. The hours were once again his own; he didn't have to be any particular place at any particular time.

So why was he worried?

For the first time in years he wished he had a watch, or maybe a clock. He did have a calendar by the door, but it hadn't been changed since 1963. He left it there because he was used to it, and because he liked the picture it displayed, a leggy girl, with her skirt blowing high in the wind.

"Skirts," said Perly. He turned and relieved himself against a beech tree in his yard. Two of the buttons of his fly were missing. For Perly, this was a convenience, not a sign of sloppiness.

He had no one he had to dress up for, so his wardrobe was ill kept and limited; he had two pairs of pants, three shirts, and some overalls. He had no mirror, no television, and no subscriptions to newspapers or magazines—no means at all of judging how eccentric he looked when compared to the rest of the citizens of Antrim.

Perly was a hermit, but it was not a term he used to describe himself. If he had been of a more philosophical nature, he might have explained his existence by simply saying, "I mind my own business."

To practice his philosophy, indeed, to live according to its precepts, he had found it necessary to remove himself from the company of his fellow man. This he had done many years ago, how many years, exactly, it was impossible for him to say.

Perly remembered things that had frightened him so greatly that he had resolved to separate himself from further fears, things like a Japanese war, and a bomb so powerful that it destroyed a whole city, leaving human shadows printed on the walls of ruins even after the sun went down.

These and other things had told Perly that he wasn't safe with men, had led him far back into the forests of Antrim, or Chester, or was it Springfield? It was far enough into the wilds so that borders made no difference and roads led neither into, nor away from, his sanctuary.

So why was he afraid?

In the beginning, certain things had attracted him to the wilderness. There were stories of lost gold mines, the promise of uninterrupted privacy, and lessons for a simpler life. These lessons, he was sure, could be learned only from the endless forest and the wild things that walked among the trees.

In the solitary years that passed, Perly's mind had lost much of its sensitivity to human speech. At one time, perhaps, he'd thought in words and structured his thinking with the familiar building blocks of language, but over the years impressions and sensations had become much more real to him than phonetics.

He responded to hunger. He responded to cold. He knew from the character of the shadows, the length of the days, the color of the trees, and the clarity of the air that soon snow would be coming. He would have to make his prewinter trek to the village to pick up supplies for his annual hibernation. His tobacco was running short, and beans, flour, matches, and other essentials would have to be set in for the months ahead. It had never occurred to Perly to combine these chores with yesterday's venture into civilization. That was one thing, this was another.

Perly walked toward the open door of his cabin and gave a whistle. Ned, his old collie dog, came bounding through the brush that separated the unkempt dooryard from the forest. Ned looked up at Perly with eager eyes, panting open-mouthed, his long pink tongue dangling like a snake.

Perly grunted and patted the dog's head. Somehow, the hermit knew, he had communicated to the animal that when the sun rose on the new day they would make their walk to town.

The fleas that they shared caused them both to scratch at the same time. Perly thought this was quite a joke. He laughed out loud, pushing the dog affectionately with his foot. Ned staggered back a few steps, then bounded toward his master, licking Perly's hand with the snakelike tongue. "Goo'boy," Perly grunted.

Together they entered the cabin. Ned went directly to his blanket in the corner, and Perly to his rocking chair. He dipped two nicotine-stained fingers into his pound can of Bugler, spread the tobacco on a paper and rolled a cigarette with mechanical precision. He brought it to his mouth, licked it, lighted it with a wooden match. Billows of thick gray smoke poured into the air, adding to the pungent aroma of the one-room dwelling. Perly closed his eyes and thought of long ago when he had lived among other men. He pictured the town of Antrim, the store where he would purchase his supplies, the women, wearing dresses, who would pass him on the street without looking at him, as if he wasn't there.

"Dresses," he said, contempt heavy in his voice.

It was always the same, time after time, year after year. Perly knew that his one-day ordeal, difficult as it was, would show him how much safer he was in his seclusion—safer, that was, as long as the wilderness was happy with him.

"I din wanna git mixed up with no little kids, no sir. An' that's one thing for sure," Perly explained to Ned. "If them fellas don't like it, well that's jes' too bad."

Nervously, he ran his fingers through his thick, shoulder-length hair. He did it again, more slowly this time, enjoying the sensual tingle of his nails on his scalp. Distracted by the pleasurable sensations, he pulled at his long beard, massaged the bunch on his forehead and scratched under his chin with closed-eyed delight. A primitive longing tugged at his mind. It was a desire too long unsatisfied, hideously deformed from years of misuse, that began to work its way into Perly's consciousness. He knew that this night there was something he'd have to do before he could leave in the morning. It was a kind of preparation for the trip, and it would help to pass the time, make it a shorter wait until sunup.

Through his open door, Perly watched the sun dip below the tops of the distant trees. The interior of the cabin took on a dreamy quality as soft half-light diffused through the thick tobacco smoke.

Perly dropped his cigarette butt into an empty Bugler can and began to prepare for his ritual. "Ned, you ol' whore, I need me a little privacy."

He prodded Ned with his foot and coaxed the protesting animal out the door. Ned whined forlornly as Perly closed the door and latched it.

He removed his heavy woolen shirt and pulled down his rough denim trousers. Standing naked and white, he methodically scratched his body all over. His ragged fingernails left puffy, red welts on his dough-soft skin, making every inch of him tingle.

From under his bed he slid his old army foot locker and opened it. He stroked its silken contents; a low rumbling moan escaped from his dry throat. He began to hum a song, the words of which he had long forgotten, the name of which, strangely, he remembered—"Greensleeves."

He gently lifted the faded print dress from the trunk, ran his callused palm across its delicate texture. He rubbed the fabric across his chest and over his stiffening genitals. After opening the dress like a huge bag, he pulled it over his head, buttoned it in front to the collar. He smoothed its surface and enjoyed the pleasure of his hands along his body.

Again, he dipped into the locker, brought out an opera-length string of pearls, and, lifting his long gray hair, placed them around his neck.

Then he reached for the perfume.

The notes of "Greensleeves," reconstructed from a failing memory, grew louder and louder. The hands on his body grew more frenzied. He moved haltingly around the cabin in a kind of dance, swaying with a lumbering grace, singing and moaning.

Outside, as if he knew all was not right, Ned howled and jumped repeatedly against the cabin door.

Then he was still.

Perly, oblivious to the sudden quiet, continued with his dance. He was in a private place, away from society and man, away from the forest and his isolation. He was in a secret rapture, an ecstasy that was not bound by rules or definition.

"Gree . . . gree . . . green," he sang to the forest and to the night. And, because his eyes were closed, he could not see the silent silhouetted faces that watched him from the window.

From the <u>Springfield Reformer</u>, Springfield, Vermont.
August 12, 1953:

The organized search for five-year-old Brian Nolan
was called off at dusk tonight, after a National Guard
helicopter made a futile all-day search over the area of
Pinnacle Mountain, where the boy disappeared Tuesday
afternoon.

The boy has been the object of a three-day search in-
volving an estimated 500 persons. No clues, not even a
piece of the boy's clothing, have been found in the triple-
combed area.

William Allen, a special state investigator from Montpelier, and Police Chief Edward Whalen, believe that
there is nothing to substantiate foul play, although it
has not been ruled out.

Bloodhounds, on loan from the Sheriff's Department
in Keene, New Hampshire, lost the boy's trail about one
thousand yards off Tenny's Hill Road. Authorities blame
heavy rains for this.

6. A CAIRN OF STONES

On the day before Thanksgiving, the sky was the color of pewter and the air was cold. A dense growth of evergreen trees surrounding the path made the forest seem unnaturally dark at nine o'clock in the morning. The two men walked side by side when the undergrowth permitted, and single file when they had to. Clint Whitcome, dressed in a red hunting coat and hat, automatically took the lead. He puffed his pipe, sending gray smoke mixed with the vapor of his breath into the chill morning air. With the hatchet that he carried, Clint chopped at occasional trees as he passed, marking a trail. If Clint forgot his visitor for a moment, he would find that Eric had fallen far behind. Eric moved with difficulty in the woods, especially when the path grew steep. Clint saw that Eric was winded and red-faced. He slowed down, waiting for his companion to catch up.

"Ever been up here before?" Clint asked.

"No. Our grandparents warned us away from the Pinnacle. They said there was nothing up here, and they told us it would be too easy to get lost. I'm beginning to see what they meant."

"They were right, there is nothing up here." Clint slowed his pace again, realizing that he was still going too fast. "Let's stop here a minute. I need a rest. It gets steep as a stepladder from here to the top."

The men sat down on a large rock. Clint slipped a pint of apricot brandy from under his coat. He passed it to Eric, who accepted it gratefully.

"My property, but I never come up here. 'Cept maybe to go

53

huntin'. The quality of the land sort of peters out after this. It's all waste, for my money. I like it though, 'cause it keeps anyone from movin' in next to me, if you know what I mean."

"You mean you like your privacy."

"That I do." Fearing he might have offended Eric, he quickly added, " 'Course family's part of privacy, you understand."

"I appreciate that." Eric smiled at him and returned the brandy.

"But you know, there's one thing I don't understand. Why whoever built it would put a root cellar—or whatever the hell it is —way the Christ up here. I don't think there was ever a house any-wheres near it. There's no foundation, far as I can see, and not even a trace of a road. A man would be stupid to build a house, or root cellar, or anything, up there on the Pinnacle. The ground ain't fit to grow on, so he'd have to carry the potatoes, or what have you, up-hill to store 'em. Don't make sense. You'll see." He slipped the flask back under his coat.

Clint was preparing Eric to lead Dr. Carl Sayer to the site. Last night, before they had gone to bed, Pamela had shown Clint and Eric the letter that had arrived from the Ancient Vermont Histori-cal Association in Montpelier. She had read it to the men as they sipped Black Label in front of the warm wood fire.

Dear Mr. and Mrs. Whitcome:

It has been brought to our attention by your town clerk, Mrs. Hattie Wiggins, that your property contains a stone struc-ture that may be of vast historical importance.

It is the structure identified on your deed as a "colonial root cellar" and we have reason to believe that it, like fifty-one simi-lar sites around the state, is of pre-colonial origin, possibly dat-ing back several thousand years.

With your permission I would like to come to Antrim to examine and photograph the site.

I will be happy to explain in more detail if we may get to-gether. Please write, or phone collect at the above number. In the meantime, if you would like some information on the type of investigation we plan to conduct, I refer you to *America, B.C.* by Barry Fell or *The Search for Lost America* by S. M. Trento. Both should be available at your local library.

I hope to hear from you soon, and thank you in advance for your interest in the prehistory of our state.

Sincerely,
Carl F. Sayer, Ph.D.

Clint recalled with a smile how, after hearing Sayer's letter, Eric had become very curious about the stone formation and its historical importance. He had asked a thousand questions. Clint was so happy to see Eric take such an interest in something that he'd decided to take today off. Previously, he'd planned to spend the afternoon of the day before Thanksgiving out turkey hunting. Instead, he'd taken the whole day, using the morning to show Eric the root cellar.

Clint had offered to turn the responsibility of dealing with the archaeologist over to Eric, who had accepted willingly. Certainly Eric was far more interested in the root cellar, and would probably do a better job of discussing it with Sayer. To Clint, the transfer of responsibility seemed fitting.

Clint wanted to satisfy Eric's immediate curiosity about the site. A morning hike would give the two men an opportunity to spend some time together. Clint invited Eric for a preview of the cellar, so they could mark a trail to make the return trip easier for the two college men.

"Well, I'm ready to go have a look," said Eric, standing up. "Lead on, Macduff."

The land beyond was rocky and dry. Fallen trees littered the ground. Crisp leaves crackled underfoot, and moved in erratic patterns, chasing each other in the strengthening wind. Hardwood trees, growing farther apart on the steep slope, looked unhealthy, spindly, like starving shadows.

Clint led Eric up a rocky incline where gray outcroppings protruded, as though the spine of the earth were breaking through the fleshy soil. Soon Clint too was winded and puffing; Eric had fallen fifty feet behind.

"Almost there," called Clint as he stood at the top of a rise where the land leveled out for a few yards and then dipped to form a shallow natural bowl at the peak of the mountain. This bowl was about one hundred yards across, and it looked strangely out of place amid the barrens.

Eric joined Clint on the rim of the bowl, and together they looked at the odd sight in front of them.

"There's your colonial root cellar," said Clint with a sweeping gesture.

"Isn't that weird," said Eric, his voice hushed.

"I never thought so. Not really. To tell you the truth, I never thought much of anything about it. I always guessed maybe it was a shelter for sheep or something like that. I'd never consider using it as a root cellar, no matter what it says on the deed—too far away from anything."

"It's really odd. Creepy." Eric continued to stare in amazement.

"Lots of weird stuff in these hills."

Eric looked around uneasily.

The two men studied the stone wall that partially outlined the rim of the natural bowl. The wall was broken to the south, and the divisions led back from the break, like a set of parentheses, to where they met again on either side of the structure. From any angle but due south, the cellar appeared to be nothing more than a dirt mound that rose eight feet from a twenty-five-foot base. It was covered with shrubs, brown leaves, fieldstones, and twisted saplings. But from the southern perspective, where the men stood, a dark opening in the mound was visible. A doorway.

This time Eric led the way. Clint noted the expression of determined curiosity on his face.

"What the hell is it?" he asked, more to himself than to Clint.

"Beats the b'Jesus out of me. You can haul that guy from the historical society up here and let him tell you."

"Let's look inside."

Clint took the three-cell flashlight from his pocket and handed it to Eric.

The opening was a rectangle about five feet high by three and a half feet wide. Stonework framed the door, and a huge flat rock slab, probably weighing several tons, crossed the top. Eric moved to the opening, flashing the light into the cavelike interior. Clint stepped up beside him, looking over his shoulder. At a glance, they noted the stone floor, the stone walls, the heavy slabs of the stone ceiling. It was like an igloo made not of ice but of stone, then covered with soil. The inside was as cold as a freezer; moisture had turned to ice on the floor. There was the rich smell of earth.

The circle of light rippled over the interior masonry. The men noted the careful placement of the individual blocks, which, without mortar, had stood for . . .

"How old do you think this place is, Clint?"

"I guess that's another question for Mr. Sayer when he comes."

Bending deeply at the waist, Clint followed Eric through the narrow opening. At first the sensation was similar to that of entering a cave. The dampness was palpable, cold. Breath rose from the men's mouths like conjured spirits, and vanished into the darkness. Somehow, Clint knew, things didn't feel just right.

It was the sound that bothered Clint—rather, the lack of sound. When he passed the entranceway all sound from the outside world was cut off, as if a door had been closed. He listened for birds, wind in the trees, tiny animals scratching in the underbrush, and heard nothing. An uncomfortable shiver crawled along his spine; he felt as if he were trapped, cut off from the outside world.

He was sure Eric hadn't noticed him slip back outside. When he realized that he was sweating, he felt embarrassed.

Eric's voice came from within, "This is amazing. I've never seen anything like it."

A red head appeared at the opening of the formation. The grin transformed to a look of concern. "You all right, Clint?"

Clint forced a grin in return. "Yup, sure am. Little touch of the claustrophobia, I guess." Clint enjoyed the other man's excitement, didn't want to put a damper on it. "Just goes to show, even a hole in the ground can be interesting."

Eric emerged completely from the opening. "Is there anything else around here?"

"Not's I know of. We can scout around a bit, if you want."

"Do you think Indians could have built it?"

"Dunno. Never heard of 'em buildin' anything out of stone around here."

"I wonder if my grandparents knew about this place."

"Couldn't say. Pam don't remember them mentionin' it." Clint was beginning to feel uncomfortable with his lack of information. He wanted to have more to tell Eric. But Eric had stopped asking him questions.

"I wish I'd brought my camera. I'll bet some of my associates back at L.I.C.C. would like to have a look at this."

"Things keep goin' the way they have been, they'll have to make an appointment."

Eric chuckled. "Let's scout around a little."

Clint smiled to himself, delighted with Eric's enthusiasm. His own feelings of discomfort were nearly gone. "Why don't you call Sayer first thing Monday and give him the go-ahead? Think you'll be able to find your way back up here?"

"Sure, now that Natty Bumppo has marked the trail."

Clint remembered the James Fenimore Cooper character from his high school days. Somehow the recollection made him feel closer to Eric. He nodded stiffly.

The two men smiled at each other. Clint patted Eric on the shoulder and they were in motion, moving away from the cellar. Something deep inside Clint relaxed a little.

Together they walked the perimeter of the bowl and found nothing unusual, except several round stones about the size of basketballs. The two men separated, and without pattern or purpose, searched the edge of the forest, each never getting too far out of the other's sight. Clint couldn't totally shake his feeling of uneasiness. He wanted to keep Eric in view; he wasn't sure why.

They made their way slowly toward a spot where their paths would intersect, south of the cellar's entrance.

Clint looked to the east. From this altitude, he could have watched the sunrise from above. On the slopes below, bare trunks of trees and circles of evergreens covered the mountainside. The land tapered downward to the blue-green thread far in the hazy distance—the Connecticut River. Clint thought how beautiful the world appeared from up here. He was about to point it out to Eric, but stopped, noticing that Eric had seen it on his own.

Clint's mind returned to the task at hand, and he continued his walk around the woodland perimeter.

When less than twenty feet separated him from Eric, Clint spotted something on the ground. "Jesus Christ, who in the name of God would do a sick fuckin' thing like that?"

He heard Eric move quickly to his side, but he could not move his eyes from the object less than ten feet in front of him. Eric followed silently as Clint moved closer to it.

Both men looked down at the thing on the ground. Eric's mouth opened, then he turned away.

"Fuckin' sick," said Clint. "Somebody's fuckin' sick." He turned to Eric. "Don't tell Pamela about this. But especially don't say nothin' to Luke. I'm askin' ya."

Eric shook his head. He moved his fingertips to his mouth. Then he looked back at the object that froze Clint's gaze.

There, on the ground, bound to a pine tree by a leather cord, was the body of a young Irish Setter. It had been dead for several days. The mouth was open, pieces of leaves and twigs clung to its dry and swollen tongue. Its eyes were gone.

Clint knelt by the animal, stroked its blood-matted coat with a gloved hand.

As he looked carefully at the body, his first thought was that the dog had been shot. It was not unusual for hunters to shoot dogs in the woods—in the forest, dogs went wild quickly, they ran deer, bit at them savagely, tore them apart.

But there was no evidence of a bullet wound on the animal.

Instead the corpse was battered. It appeared to have been clubbed, repeatedly. The two front legs were broken, twisted at impossible angles. Fragments of bone bit through the crushed skull like teeth. The stomach was split open, not cleanly, as it might have been with a knife, but brutally, as if the soft flesh of the belly had been probed with a sharp stick and then torn. The flesh had been ripped back, baring white bones. This was not the work of animals. What Clint Whitcome saw before him could only be the savagery of something else. Could it be the sickness of men?

Clint felt his stomach churn. An ugly taste formed at the base of his tongue; he swallowed rapidly, trying not to be sick.

"This is Rusty," whispered Clint. "This is Lukey's dog."

"Christ," said Eric.

Clint looked up at the other man. "I'm going to bury him."

Eric nodded.

The two men scooped out a shallow grave for the animal, then covered him with cold earth and a small mound of stones.

7. BILLY'S PLACE

"Okay, bring her in," yelled Billy Newton as he limped to the side of the sliding door, clearing the way for the bright red Firebird to glide swiftly into the garage.

"Turn her off," he shouted to the driver. As the powerful engine died, the sound of a barking dog echoed in the distance. Billy closed the heavy door behind the car and hobbled around to the front, groping for the hood-latch.

Billy Newton's property was on Old Town Road, not far from Antrim center. It consisted of his house, which was a ramshackle bungalow that he always called "headquarters," the one-car garage that he referred to as "my place," and a shed at the edge of his land. The house and garage were the result of an agreement that Billy and his wife, Lillian, had made very early in their thirty-year marriage. Perhaps more than anything else, this agreement had been responsible for the length of their relationship.

Shortly after their wedding, the missus, Lillian, laid down the law about a number of her husband's habits, among them smoking, drinking, and cussing. Smoke was a sure sign of the devil's presence, alcohol his sustenance, and vulgarity his native tongue. And there was no place for any of the three in a good Christian home.

So Billy had obligingly moved himself and his habits to the garage, where, at any time he wanted, he was able to indulge in his lifelong preoccupation—working on cars.

For many years his routine had been the same: nine hours a day at the machine shop in Springfield, to headquarters for a quick supper, and then to his place for an evening of smoking, drinking, and cussing with his friends. Since the time he'd retired, three years ago, his only change of lifestyle was to eliminate the daily nine hours of factory work.

Billy had taken an early retirement at age fifty-nine, because the arthritis in his legs had grown so bad that he could no longer stand at a machine. At his place, however, he could work as fast or as slow as he wanted, could sit or recline as needed, and, if a job required too much painful bending or stretching, he could assign the task to one of the more limber men who continued to seek his company, his mechanical expertise, and the privacy of his masculine retreat.

In the garage, Billy could always be seen wearing his green, oil-darkened cap, with matching green pants and shirt. There was, at all times, a resin-coated pipe in his mouth, which was always lit and smoking, although no one ever saw him fill or light it.

When he was not working on "the boss's car," his wife's 1969 Plymouth Fury (which had only twenty-eight thousand miles on it and was still "cherry"), he was tinkering with his pride and joy, a 1935 Ford pickup that he kept, for special occasions, in the shed at the side of his property. He hadn't had it on the road for years, but when he finally brought it out, unveiled it, as he liked to say, he planned for it to be a real showpiece. Restoration work was slow. He rarely had a chance to tinker on the Ford, because there was never any shortage of engines to tune, or carburetors to rebuild, or brakes to reline. People were forever bringing him their automotive problems, then paying for his labor and advice with fifths of Jim Beam, which they would help him drink.

In short, Billy Newton's place was a hangout for the men who, as boys, had hung out at the local gas station.

On Wednesday morning the driveway in front of Newton's garage was crowded with big, American-made cars, road-worn pickup trucks (each with a gun rack in the window), and four-wheel-drive vehicles.

Inside a group of whiskered and warmly dressed villagers crowded around Andy Potvin's new Firebird. A hose extended from the exhaust pipe of the car to a three-inch hole Billy had long ago cut in the garage door.

Billy walked to his workbench, picked up some pliers, then went back to the front of the Firebird. He moved with a painful, rolling gait that made him look like a sailor. As he bent into the engine compartment, he unconsciously maneuvered his pipe to the side of his mouth so it wouldn't collide with the air filter.

"Turn her on again," he commanded, and the engine roared. He reached into the engine compartment, jiggled some wires, removed one, crimped the end with pliers, and put it back.

"Light still on?"

"Yup," said Andy Potvin from behind the wheel.

"Com'ere a minute."

Billy's head was practically hidden within the engine compartment. He spoke loud enough to be heard over the roaring V-eight. "Looky here."

Andy looked.

Billy had the oil cap in his hand and was pointing down the hole. "Oil's drippin' off the rocker arms. See? If it's gettin' up there it's goin' everywhere. That's all that matters."

Billy carefully replaced the cap, then wiped the pliers on a shop rag. "Y'hear anythin'?" he asked Andy.

"Like what?"

"Like anythin'?"

"Nope. Nope, I don't."

"Me neither. And that sounds good enough to me. Your oil pump is pumpin' but the oil light's still on. Problem's gotta be in the sendin' unit. Probably cost you five bucks. You go pick one up. I'll put her in for ya."

"So it's safe to drive?"

"Car's no more safe than its driver."

"Thanks, Billy. I'll be right back."

Before Andy got into his car, one of the other men, Spike Naylor, disconnected the hose from the tail pipe and pulled open the garage door. Naylor, a gaunt and sinewy old man with a face like a rooster, looked up and noticed somebody walking along the road toward town. Naylor found the approaching man an excellent subject to bring to everyone's attention.

"Jesus Christ, if it ain't ol' Pearly Gates hisself." That's what they called Perly Greer, the solitary figure who was approaching on Old Town Road. Perly and Billy Newton had known each other for many years, and Perly, on his infrequent trips to town, would sometimes stop in and pay his respects to Billy. More often than not, the hermit would run into a crowd at the garage, and forget his visit. Billy understood Perly's shyness and would not try to detain him. Billy would simply wave, and Perly'd wave, and then continue on his way.

Watching the strange character, the men made no attempt to hide their amused stares. Perly was dressed in a faded red logging shirt and a filthy pair of bib overalls. He had a rope belt around his waist from which hung the leather pouch where he carried his money. A blazing red hunting cap, too small to fit over his massive thatch of yellowish-white hair, seemed to float upon his head. His thick beard had been hacked away to an uneven stubble. On his back he carried an empty army surplus knapsack.

"Who the hell's that?" asked Andy Potvin.

"That, my boy, is a real live hermit," said Pud Summers.

"Hi, Perly," called Billy Newton.

"Hi, Perly," the men in the garage chimed in, waving and whistling and laughing. Perly caught his hand just before it completed its wave. Then he hurried on, as a young girl might if hooted at by a bunch of leering boys.

Before he had taken ten steps, Perly paused suddenly and looked back, as if he'd remembered something. He turned and took an uncertain step toward the garage, then another.

The men watched him from the wide garage door. It was as if he were coming to join them. Perly's jaw moved up and down. He might have been chewing something, but Billy was sure he was about to speak. The grizzled face, a nest of hair and wrinkles, twisted into a pained expression. The eyes moved from face to face.

Billy pushed his way between Cy Stoddard and Spike Naylor, raising his arm to invite Perly to come forward. The hermit looked

Billy's Place ■ 65

at the ground, took another faltering step, turned, and scurried away.

"You boys oughtta take it easy on ol' Perly," said Billy Newton, opening the sliding boards of the wall, behind which he kept his bottle.

"Little laughin' don' mean nothin,'" said Cy Stoddard.

"Means somethin' to Perly. That's why he took to the hills, to get away from the likes of you."

"Where's he live, anyway?" asked Andy.

"Somewhere way the hell up on Pinnacle Mountain. Can't tell you where exactly. Never been to his place. Don't know anybody has."

"Live alone, does he?"

"Yup. Except for—" Billy hesitated, a look of concern deepening the lines around his eyes. "You know, it's a funny thing. This is the first time I've ever seen Perly without his dog."

8. SOLITARY PURSUITS

A little before noon, when Eric and Clint returned from their hike, everyone sat down for a quick lunch of soup and sandwiches. Pamela told the men how she and Luke had spent the morning doing the first of the Thanksgiving preparations.

"Looks like you two have been pretty busy," said Eric, admiring the apple and pumpkin pies that were cooling on the counter.

"That's just the beginning," Pamela replied. "We've got to drive into town to pick up a few things at the store."

"We still got any of that zucchini relish and them homemade pickles you put up last year? Eric oughtta have a chance to try them," said Clint.

"I think I've got a jar or two in the cellar. I've been saving them for a special occasion."

Eric couldn't seem to get his mind off the stone structure he had just examined. As he ate, it occurred to him that Dartmouth College was just a short trip north on Route 91. He decided to drive up there in the afternoon, maybe check the library for the works of Fell and Trento that Dr. Sayer had mentioned in his letter. He offered to drop Clint off at Billy Newton's garage on the way.

Billy Newton had a contract with the town to do most of the maintenance work on their vehicles. Clint's truck had been misfiring lately, so he'd left it with Billy to be checked.

When Eric let Clint off at twelve-thirty, Billy was alone in the garage. His friends had gone home for lunch.

Clint found him by the wood stove, reclining in an aluminum

and plastic chaise longue, his pipe blowing smoke signals into the air, his bottle by his side.

After sliding the door open only enough to get in, Clint closed it quickly behind him, conscious of the cold air at his back.

"What'd'ya say Billy?"

"'Lo Clint. Fixed her for ya. No problem."

"Points?"

"Yup. Filed 'em a little. Cleaned the plugs and gapped 'em. That's all. No big deal. Sit down a minute, Clint, why don'cha. Drink?"

"No thanks, Billy, I'm in kind of a hurry. Goin' after a wild turkey for dinner tomorrow."

Billy smiled wistfully. "That's somethin' I haven't tasted for a long while. Since I give up huntin', I guess. Little out of season, ain't you?"

Clint knew that wild turkey season had officially ended on November 6. He grinned at Billy. "I'm always a little behind the times."

"Yup. Jest like me. You got a call, have ya?"

"Sure. So damn good, every time I use it somebody takes a shot at me. Either that or I get attacked by a horny bird. Gotta shoot it to protect myself."

Billy laughed and took a swig from his paper cup. "Clint, I want to ask you somethin'. Now I don't like to ask a man a favor. And I wouldn't if it was somethin' I could do myself. But Christ, I'm so lamed-up I can hardly make it back and forth to the house. 'Course sometimes that's a blessin'." Billy winked at Clint.

"What can I do for you, Billy?" Now Clint's attitude was free of humor. He was giving the older man his full attention. Clint had known him a long time. It wasn't Billy Newton's way to ask for anything.

"Well, I been thinkin' about ol' Perly lately . . ."

"Perly Greer?"

"Yup. Perly an' me go way back. I'm worried about him. He ain't gettin' what ya might call any more clearheaded in his old age. Some might say he's a little tetched. But he still remembers me, usually stops in for a shot when he gets to town. Talks a little in that funny way of his. Kind of jabbers on till he runs out of steam, then he clams up tighter'n a drum and heads out. Usually it's kinda crazy talk, too. I think he's made hisself up some imaginary friends to keep him company. Knows enough not to talk about 'em; and when he starts he knows enough to clam up. I guess prob'ly he gets pretty lonesome up there.

"Anyway, this mornin' I seen him walk right by. 'Course I had a crowd with me, and that mighta scairt him off. Usually does. But the thing that worried me—well, Perly was actin' kinda funny, like he had somethin' to say. And he was all by hisself. Ol' Ned weren't taggin' along like normal. Ned's all he's got. Perly never goes nowheres without that dog. And . . . well . . ."

"I'll look in on him, Billy, don't you worry."

"I'd do it myself, Clint, but—"

"But nothin'. I'm goin' out huntin' pretty quick. I'll just walk up his way, make sure everything's okay."

"I'd appreciate it, Clint. Here, let me pour you a shot."

"Okay, thanks. But just one. I gotta get to the woods. Not much sunlight left."

"Well, I don't want to keep ya. I guess I'm just a little nervy about all the things goin' on around town."

"Lotta folks are, Billy. D'I tell you Dick Bates offered me a job?"

"On the police force?"

"That's right."

"Nope. Nope, you didn't. But Dick was around here yesterday, askin' a lot of questions about old trucks. Figgered jest 'cause I got one I must be an expert on everybody else who owns 'em." Billy shook his head, blew smoke into the air. "Come to think about it, though, you'd be a good man for the job. Terrible thing about young Hurd. Don't think it would be right to congratulate you, seein's what happened."

"No congratulations would be in order. I turned him down. I don't think I was cut out to be a cop. You got any idea what happened to the boy?"

Billy held his paper cup by his nose and inhaled deeply. He studied the cup's rim and finished its contents in a gulp. Then he sucked on his pipe, and, sighing heavily, filled the air with a gray cloud. "I got no idea, not really. Funny things happen now and again. There's no stoppin' 'em. Some of the boys figure young Hurd pulled over some pretty filly for speedin' and then took off with her in the bargain."

"That what you figure?"

"Christ, Clint, maybe you should've took that job, you sound just like Bates! But I'll tell ya, I got no idea what to figure. I like the kid. I like that little wife of his, Brenda, bless her heart. It's nothin' I can really do no guessin' on. I wouldn't be knowin' what I was talkin' about. Not for sure. As it is, most folks do too much talkin' when they got nothin' to say."

"I guess you're right, Billy, guessin' ain't gonna help." Clint stood up. "But don't you be worried about ol' Perly. I'll look in on him for you."

Billy nodded. "'Preciate the favor."

"And what do the people of Antrim owe you for the work on the truck?"

"Not a goddamn thing." The mechanic smiled, pleased to have something to offer in return.

Clint Whitcome grabbed his shotgun, filled his pockets with shells, and rushed to the door.

"Sorry I couldn't talk Eric into comin' with me," he said to his wife. "He might enjoy it. Guess he's doin' what he likes though, up to the library."

"You'll get him into the woods yet." Pamela smiled.

Clint kissed her perfunctorily and picked Luke up with one arm. "I'm goin' to go get us a turkey for Thanksgiving dinner." He beamed at the child.

"An' get some cookies for dessert, too."

Clint laughed. "You'll have to bargain with your mother about that." In a moment he was off the porch, making for the trail that led between the house and garage, into the woods.

Pamela stepped quickly back into the house and out of the cold.

Luke stood on the porch and watched his father walking away. Then he took a few steps after him.

Eric spent most of the afternoon looking over the works of Fell and Trento, then he thumbed through books by Warren Cook and David Potter.

It turned out that there was more to Vermont's ancient stone structures than he had at first suspected. Because of rules about residency, he wasn't permitted to check out any of the books, but he was able to photocopy sections of a monograph by Dr. Carl Sayer. It was called *Vermont's Celtic Heritage,* and it dealt with the notion that over fifty ancient stone structures in Vermont were actually of Celtic origin. They'd been built perhaps two thousand years before Columbus discovered America. Although Eric found the treatise highly speculative, he believed that it put forth some arguments that an open-minded scholar could not ignore. For example, the majority of the Vermont structures (as well as those in New Hampshire and other New England states) were found near navigable rivers that connected to the sea. Ancient script—long believed to be glacial markings or scrapings from colonial plows—had been found to be identical to a pre-Roman writing called Ogam, found in Europe. The New England script, like the European, could be translated.

A marked stone found in central Vermont was recently translated by Dr. Fell to proclaim, "Precincts of the Gods of the Land Beyond the Sunset." Eric couldn't wait to tell Clint that he had learned what was probably the earliest name for Vermont!

As Eric read, the possibility that the Whitcomes' root cellar was in fact an ancient Celtic ruin became more and more believable. Now he was more eager than ever for his meeting with Dr. Sayer. He wanted to discuss the fascinating subject at length. With the photocopied pages under his arm, he left the library. Later he would study them at home. He would be far more prepared for meeting Sayer than he'd expected.

Eric felt charged, full of purpose. He was thankful that Clint had given him the responsibility of dealing with Sayer. It was a job he could handle, it gave him a role in the household.

Eric left the library whistling, looking forward to spending time with his thoughts on the thirty-five minute drive back to Antrim.

On the gentle slopes of Pinnacle Mountain, the fresh, chill air was as clear as glass. As he hiked through a stand of poplar trees, Clint Whitcome's mind was on Eric—Eric's library, his books, and his college. Clint was trying to understand his new friend, make sense of their differences and similarities.

For Clint, Eric lived in a world of words, a world having very little to do with the realities of life in the rural town of Antrim. Clint thought that Eric's life's work was made up of reading books full of words, and teaching youngsters complicated ways of saying simple things. Words are important, thought Clint, but the words must always come after the doing. For Clint it was a simple truth.

Clint breathed the mountain air. It had an invigorating quality that made him want to smile when he exhaled. He felt like whistling, but knew he had to remain quiet so as not to frighten his quarry. Sundown was more than three hours away; there was ample time to get his turkey, either on the way to Perly's cabin or afterward. That was enough to think about for now. Eric was a puzzle to him, but now was not a time for puzzles.

The hermit's cabin was at least a mile away. There were no paths to follow on the crow-flies route that Clint took through the bushy undergrowth. Bent twigs and grasses tugged at his trousers and crackled under his boots.

The memory of Rusty's battered corpse intruded for a moment. Perhaps he should have discussed it with Billy. But Billy hadn't been in a talkative mood, especially when the topic of Hurd's disappearance came up. Billy was completely unwilling to speculate. Then again, it wasn't Billy's way to speak loosely.

Clint stood still and let the ugly thoughts run their course, knowing the cool November air would carry them away with the wind. Good thing me and Eric found the body, he thought. Not

Luke. Sure, the little man's got to understand about such things, but maybe not yet. Probably Luke still figures the dog ran away. That's okay, at least he gets to hold on to a little hope while he's suffering. But the boy's got to learn about loss at some point. Better a dog than a parent. Luke'll be a little tougher now. He'll be stronger for when the hard stuff comes along.

At least here in Vermont, Clint thought, the family can usually be protected from such things. Imagine being like Eric, living downcountry where senseless violence goes on almost every day. Not just to dogs, to people! Clint felt bad for Eric, coming all the way up here and seeing such a horrible sight.

Walking beside a stone wall that separated the woodland from an overgrown pasture, Clint began to move with a practiced caution. He tuned his ears for the sound of a turkey's rustle or squawk. Long shadows of leafless trees snaked over the stone wall and stretched across the brown grass, twisting into a complex of random patterns. With a mild shudder, Clint saw the patterns as the vast web of a giant spider. He thought, Spider's gonna snare us a turkey.

He sat on the cold stone wall, stood his gun beside him, and removed the turkey call from his jacket pocket. The rasping cackle of the wooden pieces rubbing together lied to any birds within hearing distance, hinting at fatal pleasures. Bet that kind of sexy talk's gonna bring 'em running, Clint mused. Then, placing the call on the rock beside him, Clint eyed the bushes, scanned the trees. Slowly, without looking, he reached for his shotgun. His fingers found the cold steel of the barrel and he pulled it to him.

Wish I could've got Eric to come out here with me, he thought. Clint was convinced that the forest had something to offer his wife's cousin. He was sure there were lessons for everyone in country ways.

In his heart Clint believed that there were really only two types of people in this world: Vermonters, and those who wished they were. He wasn't sure which group Eric fit into. Eric had been born in Vermont. His youth had been spent in the Green Mountains, but he had been away for so long . . . Clint hoped that Eric's trip to Hanover didn't mean he had retreated permanently to his books.

Clint marveled at Eric's interest in things intangible. The hours Eric planned to spend researching that damned root cellar were hours wasted as far as Clint was concerned. What difference could it possibly make, really, if the structure was made by ancient Irish monks or colonial potato farmers? The plain fact was that the structure existed, as the trees and mountains existed. If Pam's grandfather or old man Tenny had not been the first stewards of the land, so what? What real difference did it make? The land had been there for a long, long time. Even the hundred acres around Clint's house held too much history for him, or anyone else, ever to learn. Why bother?

The root cellar was nothing to Clint. Sometime after he'd received the letter from Carl Sayer, he'd mentioned the mystery of the cellar's origin to Billy Newton. Billy had said, without much interest, "Y'ever been in a cave in the summertime? Good place to keep food from spoilin', right? Unless o'course you ain't got a cave on your property. Don't have to be too damn smart to make one. Fill her with snow in the winter, keep stuff cold durin' the summer. Hell of a way to spend my tax dollar, paying some guy to come all the way from Montpelier for trackin' down homemade caves. I'd tell him to stay the hell away, if I was you."

At the same time, Clint thought, I suppose it's good that Eric's found something to be interested in. Must be hell to lose your wife.

He couldn't begin to think of what he'd do without Pam. Without Luke.

All at once Clint felt as if he understood Eric very well, understood him, admired him for the strength he was showing. It wasn't important that Eric didn't want to hunt. Maybe the thought of death in any form upset him now in ways that Clint couldn't understand. Clint recalled the uncanny pallor, the painful silence that surrounded Eric when he saw Rusty's body.

He needs more time, Clint decided. Maybe for now it's better he stay home with Pam and the boy.

Since no turkey had answered his mechanical call, he pocketed it, picked up his gun, and followed his sense of direction toward the hermit's cabin. The confidence that he would bring home tomorrow's dinner was beginning to wane, just slightly. There were only a couple of hours of daylight left. Clint was starting to get discouraged.

One at a time, the sounds of the forest captured his attention. Bluejays squawked, bitching at the presence of the human intruder. A chipmunk scrambled up a birch tree, its tiny claws made scratching sounds on the parchment-bark. Two gray squirrels chased each other along the branch of an elm, chattering, jumping to a lower limb, like somersaulting acrobats. An owl in the distance hooted and was still. Above Clint's head the afternoon wind rubbed evergreen boughs together; the rustling sound soothed him, reminded him to be patient.

Suddenly, to the right, his ever-moving eyes caught a flicker in the underbrush. Shotgun ready, he concentrated on the thick bushes. His senses were keen, waiting, alert for any noise or motion. He remained calm, stood still as a deer in a headlight beam.

A patch of brown flashed between bush and tree trunk. Clint turned and instinctively fired. The roar of the blast rolled like a fierce wave over the hills and valleys for miles around him. It was counterpointed with a horrified cry from the creature he had not yet seen. He knew instantly that it was not a turkey. From the thick, shot-torn bushes, indistinct among the camouflage of shadows, Clint saw a child lurch and stumble.

"Hey," Clint shouted, panic sharp in his voice.

Seventy-five yards away the tiny figure got to its feet, wailing painfully. It held its shoulder and ran screaming into the forest.

Clint chased after it, a dreadful recognition forming in his mind.

"Luke," he cried. "Luke, stop! Stop!"

Clutching his shotgun as if it were a useless limb, Clint raced into the confusion of the trees.

"Where's Lukey?" asked Pamela, coming into the living room.

Eric shrugged, momentarily distracted. "Outside, I guess. I

wasn't paying any attention." He put the photocopy of Dr. Sayer's treatise on the table beside him. "I'll help you find him. I should have been watching, I'm sorry."

As Eric and Pamela approached the kitchen door, it burst open. Clint Whitcome, looking breathless and terrified, filled the door-frame. Red-faced, his eyes darted wildly around the room. His chest heaved like something inside was fighting to get out.

"Clint!" Pamela stared at him in surprise. "Clint, what's wrong?"

"Where's Luke?" he wheezed, clutching her by the shoulders. He looked expectantly at Eric.

"I don't know. We were just looking . . ."

"You don't know!" He pushed his wife aside and moved quickly toward the stairs, heading for Luke's room.

"Luke," he shouted ahead of him.

There was the sound of a toilet flushing, and Luke stepped timidly from the bathroom. Clint fell to his knees before his son and hugged him tightly, trying to catch his breath against the boy's tiny shoulder. Arms around his father's neck, Luke looked at his mother and Eric, a puzzled frown on his face. Frightened tears quickly followed.

Stepping forward, Pamela put her hand on Clint's back. "What's wrong, Clint? Tell me."

Clint got to his feet, lifting his son in his arms. "It's okay, Luke. I guess the both of us got quite a scare."

The child sobbed quietly, looking over Clint's shoulder at Pamela. The boy reached out to her and she took him. His crying stopped almost at once as his mother held him. "Why don't you go upstairs with your Uncle Eric?" she said softly to the confused child.

Clint Whitcome hugged his wife. He breathed easier now, but his black eyes blazed with desperation. "I think I shot a kid. I thought it was Luke."

"Oh, Clint, no!"

"I looked all over for him. I couldn't find anything. No blood, nothin'. I yelled to him. I ran after him, but he musta hid. He musta thought I was tryin' to kill him."

"Oh, Clint, what are we gonna do?"

"I'm afraid I gotta call Dick Bates."

"The police! Oh God . . ."

They embraced long and hard, knowing that when they stopped, more unpleasantness would follow, then a long, sleepless night.

9. WAITING

The blazing wood stove in the cabin didn't seem to warm the place, though the flue was wide open and the draft was excellent. On the side nearest the wall, the cast iron glowed red like a fiery coal. Perly Greer felt the heat against the arms of the wooden rocker in which he sat, yet he shivered, unable to take in enough heat to warm his frozen insides. His feet, in sweat-drenched wool socks, were propped up on an inverted bucket, too close to the stove. The socks steamed, drying stiff and uncomfortable around his toes.

His muscles ached; he shook with a violence that made his head throb. Turning, he looked at the window and at the night outside, dark as a crow's wing. On the glass, beads of condensation formed like rain inside the room. The beads sparkled like laughing eyes, reflecting the golden light of the kerosene lamp on the table.

Perly had a bottle of cheap brandy that he had bought in town. He fetched it from the shelf over the dry sink and poured a good five ounces down his throat. It felt like sandpaper against his palate. Instead of warming him, it tightened his guts into a cramped, painful knot that folded him in half, bringing his arms involuntarily across his abdomen. He retched dryly.

Sweat poured from his skin and slid across his cheeks in icy rivulets. The flesh on his face and back felt as if it were stretched too tight, as if parts of it were hardening, turning to stone.

Holding his gut with shaking hands, he staggered back to his chair by the fire.

Sick, he thought. *Sick.*

It was the only word his fevered mind could locate to describe his condition. But the word he wanted was "terrified." He felt little security in knowing that the door to his cabin was firmly bolted, and the familiar form of his twelve-gauge on the table gave him no comfort.

He strained to hear every sound in the air. The crackle and roar of the fire, the hum of wind across the chimney, the sounds of the old boards creaking from the contrasting temperatures, seemed to fill the air with confusion. But there was no single sound that he feared, no warning in their persistent cacophony.

He feared there would be no warning at all. If Ned were at his feet, the slightest stirring in the yard would cause a growl, sure indication that there was something in the shadows, something close enough to the cabin to be heard, or smelled, or otherwise detected by the dog's acute senses.

His own senses were inferior at their best, and now, dulled by the years, were nearly useless to him.

Earlier, he had paced from window to window, peering into the darkening woods. His memory roamed for miles in those acres of unsettled woodland surrounding the cabin, but found no one who might be able to offer him help, no one who could hear him if he called or if he fired his shotgun as a signal.

The solitude that he had chosen many years ago was now his prison. Only the thin walls of his cabin separated him from the darkness, and from whatever it was that waited for him out there.

Sometimes, briefly, he'd forget that Ned was not with him. He'd speak to the dog, as he had for so many years, just to hear the sound of his own voice. Tonight he spoke in a whisper. "I don't know where they git off bein' so goddamn pissed. I didn't get the fuckin' bottle, why should they care?"

Perhaps, Perly thought, he shouldn't have returned from the village when he'd failed at what he'd tried to do. Perhaps it would have been better to have sought help, or to have traveled far away from Antrim. But these thoughts were too complicated for Perly to sustain. His mind was locked into simple routines—for him a trip to town was always followed by a trip back to the cabin. He had nowhere else to go.

He'd done almost everything they'd asked, he was sure of that. He'd even agreed, just this once, to do things that he really couldn't abide.

"I ain't gonna hev no part of no little kids. That jest ain't right."

It was a good thing that policeman came along when he did. That put a stop to the whole mess.

"Them fellas ain't likely to try that again for a while. I got plenty a time to get the Christly bottle."

He really had wanted to do the simple errand. From the beginning he was able to visualize the consequence of failure, both to himself and to Ned. Perly looked at the empty blanket in the corner. Ned was gone. They'd taken him. It wasn't fair.

It was the people! It was the people who'd made it impossible. He had gone right to Billy Newton's place, just like he was supposed to. He had gone over and over in his mind what he would say to Billy. He had fished around in the depths of his memory to catch all the words that he would need, and if the word he caught was not correct, he tossed it back and fished for another one.

Billy Newton's yard had been full of cars, more cars than Perly had seen for a long time. There were so many men crowded at the door, framed like too many people bunched into a photograph. They seemed to be crawling all over themselves to get a look at him. They were laughing at him, calling obscenely to him, their faces cruel and menacing. He couldn't even see Billy, so how could he ask him? How could he have done what was required of him?

Instead, he did what he had to do. He left, drifted away from the crowd at Billy Newton's place as he had drifted away from all society. It was the only thing he could do. It was necessary, just as it had been necessary to return home with his few provisions, his tobacco, and his brandy.

And yesterday nothing had happened.

And last night nothing had happened. And maybe tonight nothing would happen, either. But what about tomorrow, and after that?

Each day would be full of horrid anticipation, each night would hold its own terror. Perhaps the coming of the policemen was all that he had to fear. So why worry, they couldn't find him here in the woods, wouldn't know where to look . . .

But if they did, then what? Would they hurt him? Tear him away from his mountain home? Make him trade his freedom for a lifetime in a cage?

Would they make him talk? He imagined tortures, rubber hoses and hard fists. He saw his face, bleeding, raw, and heard himself blubbering like a beaten child.

If they did make him talk, what then? What would he say? Would he confess to all his mistakes? Tell what had happened to the policeman? Would he admit what he had been planning to do?

Then it came to him. There was more than the bottle. He had spoken to the policeman, had asked for help. That was when things had really started to go wrong.

Perly knew for certain, in one of the few coldly logical parts of his failing mind, that he'd actually made more than one mistake. His problems were very, very serious.

If only he could have talked to Billy. Billy would have known what to do. Billy was his only friend, his only link with the civilization that he had forsaken for a lifetime alone on Pinnacle Mountain.

Perly knew that his other friends were gone now; he was sure they had rejected him because of his mistakes. They wouldn't give him a second chance, it was not their way.

Perly realized with a seizure of dread that they would never allow him to talk to the police. It would be far too dangerous.

With this realization, a new suspense came into his life, a suspense that would intensify each time the sun went down. Each night would be an agonizing vigil until morning. He could think of no way to force the situation to a crisis, to get it over with once and for all.

Impatiently, he marched again to the window. He could see nothing beyond the glass; it might as well have been a moisture-covered mirror. In it his face was a mask of tangled hair and wrinkles.

A quiet thump brought his breathing to a standstill. Eyes shifting back and forth, he sought the source of the noise. A squirrel on the roof? A crazed bird slamming against the wall of the cabin? A pesky porcupine gnawing on the log foundation?

The sounds of the night had never panicked him like this before. The protective forest that insulated him from the people had never before been so oppressive.

Thump . . . Thump . . .

Reflexively, Perly's eyes went to the ceiling. Something on the roof! Delicate footfalls progressing up the slanted roof toward the top of the cabin.

Perly's white-knuckled hands gripped the shotgun and pulled it to his shoulder. He could hear motion near the spot where his stovepipe penetrated the ceiling.

"Gi'dow dayuh!" he shouted.

The movement stopped. In his mind Perly built images of what sort of creature could be up there. The sounds were too heavy, too slow for a squirrel or a coon.

He listened and they started again.

Thump . . . Thump . . .

Perly banged the stovepipe with the stock of his weapon. From above, the intruder banged it in return.

Fear hit Perly like a bucket of cold spring water. His eyes, wide with anticipation, were glued to the spot above him. He fired the shotgun. The deafening blast jarred his ears and shook the walls of the building.

There was a flurry of motion above him. Pieces of sawdust and splinters rained down upon his upturned face.

He heard what sounded like a laugh. Something solid smacked the ground on the other side of the wall. Perly ran to the window, trying to clear his eyes of wood particles in hopes of getting a glimpse of what was outside. The sound of running feet trailed off into the darkness.

The air had changed. An odd odor, a warning scent, hung heavy in the room. Painfully blinking his watering eyes, Perly looked around his cabin. Smoke poured from the stove. It streamed in thick billows from the cracks around the metal door. It flowed from the vent, from the seam where the stovepipe connected, and from the fittings where segments of pipe joined each other. Relentlessly, the gray tide filled the cabin like water flooding a sinking ship.

The smoke seemed to ignite the wood fibers in his eyes. They stung with searing, hot pain. Perly took an uncertain step toward the stove.

Something's pluggin' the chimney, he thought.

His instinct was to put out the fire before the cabin filled with smoke. He lurched toward his water bucket and found he had neglected to fill it. There was less than a quart in the bottom. He lugged it to the stove and opened the door with a poker. Smoke and flames jumped at him as if from a jack-in-the-box designed for a devil. In defense, he splashed the water in the direction of the open door. He heard some of it sizzle as it vaporized against the hot metal. The water that found its way to the fire was ineffectual, producing only steam and more acrid smoke.

By now the smoke was a thick, black smog in the tiny cabin. Perly's eyes burned like hot coals. They were useless in the noxious haze. His scorched lungs pumped like a bellows, but could not find enough oxygen.

Instinct took over. Gun in hand he groped for the bolted door. Moving too quickly, he slammed into the wooden table and knocked it over. The kerosene lamp smashed to the floor, exploding into a slick of liquid fire.

Another few blind steps brought him to the door. He wrestled with the bolt. His gun ready, he staggered into the cooling air and charged toward the forest, bellowing an unintelligible war cry into the black autumn sky.

Something tripped him. He pitched face forward into the damp weeds, accidentally discharging the shotgun's second barrel. Pellets tore through the tall, sapless grass, making a rustling sound. Unseen hands grabbed him by the hair on the back of his head and ground his face into the dirt. The fleshy bunch above his eye tore away like a finger wrenched from its socket. Stones dug mercilessly into his stinging eyes. He cried out, inhaling particles of earth and filling his mouth with bitter vegetation.

A squirming mass flopped against his back, holding him down, pushing brutally. The pressure made him gasp. It felt like his bones were penetrating the muscles along his spine, snapping through the fabric of his clothing. His sightless eyes filled with specks of gritty black soil. All his muscles tensed; the arteries on his forehead stood out like bloated worms. The pain in his back was so great that it flooded every part of his body.

Now a grip as strong as metal pliers pulled the thick hair of his scalp. It forced his head backwards while his chest remained flat on the ground. His throat stretched so much that he could no longer take in air. Trying a painful breath, he heard and felt a sickening series of muted snaps under the folds of skin at the nape of his neck. It hurt him so much that he died, a scream half expelled from his smoke-tortured lungs.

The last thing he heard, from someplace far behind him, was the muffled and meaningless sound of smoke-shrouded figures working doggedly to put out the fire in the deserted cabin.

From <u>The Chittenden Chronicle</u>, November 15, 1982:

FRIARS ISLAND—Ken Mitchell, resident state policeman in the Champlain Islands, said yesterday that a
search has been instituted for Mr. and Mrs. Gaston
Pelletier and their son Roger, of Montreal, Quebec.

The Pelletiers, who have a summer camp on Friars
Island, were last seen by island storekeeper Abner Mott
when Mr. Pelletier stopped at the store before leaving for
home. He had just closed the camp for the season.

The family was reported missing when Mr. Pelletier
failed to report for work on Monday morning.

"Funny thing, a whole family like that," Mitchell
stated. "I mean, you could see if it was just the guy, or
just the wife. But both of them, and the kid, too."

10. THANKSGIVING DAY

Thursday,
November 24, 1983

Chief Richard G. Bates stood six feet tall and was broad of shoulder and broader of waist. He wasn't exactly fat. He was a man who had been in good shape, but, because of a comfortably soft job, had begun to get out of condition. He had grown self-conscious about the strain his expanding physique placed on his carefully tailored uniforms, so he chose to work out of uniform during off-duty hours.

He drove up Tenny's Hill Road toward the Whitcome house a little after seven o'clock on Thanksgiving morning. He was dressed in loose-fitting dungarees, a baggy sweatshirt, and his heavy uniform coat. Bates always had a tired look about him, dark circles under his eyes and a powdery-white pallor that even the summer sun could not alter. He was known for his caustic sense of humor, which he often directed at himself, with quips intended to camouflage sensitivity about his corpulence.

Bates knew most of Antrim's fifteen hundred residents by name. He was liked by everyone, even those he had to caution about speeding or rowdy behavior. He saw his popularity as evidence of effective public relations, and took it as an indication that he was doing a good job. The town manager seemed to agree; year after year Bates received glowing performance evaluations.

Because they both worked for the town, it was easy for Chief Bates and Clint Whitcome to continue a friendship that had started in grammar school.

As Bates parked his station wagon in the Whitcomes' yard, he noticed Clint on the eastern side of the house wrestling with a roll

85

of tarpaper. Clint was covering the foundation with the paper and securing it in place with pieces of lath and nails.

Bates rolled down the window of his wagon. "Kinda late to start your winterizin', ain't it, Clint?"

Clint put down his tools, walked around the car, and got in. He removed his pocket watch and flipped it open. "I'd have to disagree with you, Dick. Seven o'clock seems a little early to be doin' it. Kinda early for you to be out too, don't you think?"

"Thought I'd get out here early so we can get this thing cleaned up, get home, and have us a nice dinner."

"Appreciate you comin' out."

Bates rolled up his window. The inside of the station wagon was hot. Clint unzipped his parka. He pulled his corncob pipe from his pocket and filled it from a wrinkled packet of tobacco.

"Tarpaper's kind of an expensive way to insulate, ain't it? My pa always used to use spruce boughs and then bank 'em with snow."

"Mine done the same thing. I figure I can get two, three years out of a roll of paper if I don't rip it up too bad. In the long run it's quicker'n gatherin' boughs."

"I guess it would be at that." Bates paused, lit a Camel. "Well, Clint, why don't you fill me in on what's been goin' on up here?"

It was Bates's technique, even when talking to a friend, to open an investigation with small talk and then follow up with questions that were deliberately vague.

Clint lit his pipe as he explained the details of yesterday's shooting. He also mentioned finding Rusty's battered carcass while hiking on the Pinnacle with Eric, within two miles of the scene of the shooting.

Bates tried to put Clint's mind at ease by telling him there had been no reports of injured or missing children. Still, he asked Clint to take him to the spot where it had happened, all the time grumping about the exercise that would be involved in the hike up the side of the mountain. "The only exercise I like this time of year is shivering," he muttered.

Clint ran to the door to tell Pamela where they were going, and the two men drove off down the road.

. . .

In the kitchen, Pamela was preparing for the feast. She had taken the precaution of buying a fifteen-pound turkey more than a week ago, in case her husband's hunting expedition didn't produce as planned. She had stored the bird in the freezer in the mudroom, swearing Luke and Eric to secrecy about its being there.

She mixed stuffing in a big aluminum bowl, her hands kneading bread crumbs, pieces of apple, and pork sausage into a lumpy paste.

Eric sat in the living room reading yesterday's edition of the *Tri-Town Tribune*, the weekly newspaper for Springfield, Antrim, and Chester. Luke sat in front of the fireplace near Eric's feet. He made noises like a truck as he moved his toys in random patterns that obviously made perfect sense to him.

Suddenly Eric began to chuckle. Pamela came in from the kitchen, wiping her greasy hands on several paper towels.

"What's so funny?"

He folded the newspaper onto his lap and looked at her. "You ever read the poetry in here?"

"Sure." Everyone who read the *Tri-Town Tribune* looked forward to the column "Voice of the Mountains" by Mrs. Elizabeth McKensie. She was the local poet, whose verse appeared at least two out of every four Wednesdays.

"Listen to this," said Eric, still smiling, "just the last verse.

> "The Connecticut flows
> Near Antrim's nose
> Down to the ocean's well,
> Past the stony dell
> Where wee folks dwell
> Safe from the winter snows."

Eric could not contain his laughter. "'Near Antrim's nose,' honest to God. Sounds like Julia Moore, 'The Sweet Singer of Michigan,' or something. People like her?"

"Or get a kick out of her." Pamela wasn't too sure what he was laughing at.

"This stuff must be deep. I don't have any idea what she's talking about."

Pamela looked over Eric's shoulder and scanned the poem. "She almost always writes about hometown stuff, or something about Vermont. She had a book of her poetry published last year."

"I can't believe it. In New York, writers are starving in the street!"

Pamela sat down on the couch across from Eric. "You don't like it, huh?"

"I love it! It makes Grandma Moses look like Mondrian. I want her book. But I still don't know what she's talking about."

"What do you mean?"

"Well, what's this about 'wee folks,' for example. Where'd they come from?"

"Beats me."

"Between Mr. Sayer and his Celtic root cellars, and Mrs. McKensie and her 'wee folk,' I get the feeling we've stepped into the *Twilight Zone* and back to medieval Ireland or something."

"She probably just means kids. She's always writing about children. You could ask her if you want. I hear she's a very nice lady."

"I don't know, maybe. I take it she lives in town."

"She lives in Chester. I think she's pretty rich. She's a local historian, and president of the Connecticut Valley Historical Society. Actually, she'd be a good one to ask about the root cellar."

Luke looked up at Eric, tugged on his pant leg, and informed him, "The backhoe has a broke motor."

"What happened to it?"

"Broke." Luke handed him the yellow toy. "Gotta stop at Billy Newton's to fix the motor."

"Okay," said Eric, placing the toy back on the braided rug. He gave it a little push and it rolled back to Luke. "All fixed." Then to Pamela, "Maybe I'll give her a call on Monday. I want to do all my homework before Mr. Sayer shows up."

"When's he coming, anyway?"

"I'm going to call him and set up a time. I'd like to get him down here next week. I'm eager to get started checking out that site."

. . .

Bates handed the discharged plastic and brass shotgun shell to Clint.

"Yup. That's mine. Winchester number eight shot." He pointed to a bush growing near a beech tree. "That's where I fired it."

The two men walked up the short incline to the spot. Above their heads, thick rolls of black clouds were breeding rain.

Bates, puffing like a gasoline generator, cleared his throat and spat on the ground. "Let's have a look around and get the hell out of here before we get drenched."

Bates observed the way Clint examined the bushes. He was looking at where his shotgun blast had torn through the dry stalks and dead leaves.

He'd make a good cop, thought Bates.

The policeman knelt beside his friend. He noted how three stalks had been snapped nearly in half by the pellets, their tops, bowing low, scratched at the cold earth. Slowly, Bates examined the earth itself.

"What do you think, Clint?"

Clint shook his head.

"I don't see nothin' here to worry you," Bates concluded. He stood up, stretched, spat again, then looked at the sky. "You say whatever you seen run off? Which way?"

Clint pointed at the dense forest.

The men walked the line from the bush to the edge of the woods. Their eyes scanned the ground.

"Forget it. Let's go back," said Bates. Abruptly he turned, walked downhill, his bulk adding momentum. Clint hurried to follow.

"So what's the verdict, Dick?"

"You didn't shoot nothin'. There's no blood on the ground, no tracks, nothin'. If you'd winged a kid, we'd find both, along with a scrap of cloth, if we were lucky. Same thing with an animal. If it was a bird, maybe he'd fly off and not leave no tracks, but he might leave us some feathers. Then again, if you shot a bird, or scared one, that's no crime, and it's certainly not worth gettin' soaked for. My verdict is, you ain't as good a shot as you think you are."

Clint chuckled. Both men looked at the darkening sky.

"Musta been windy up here," Bates said.

"Always," Clint agreed.

"Look here," said the chief, standing a little downwind of the torn bushes. Bending like an obese troll, the policeman picked something off the ground and extended his hand toward Clint. His fingers held a scrap of fur that had been lodged against a boulder.

Clint took the fur.

"Suppose that's your doing?" asked the chief.

"Could be. I can't tell if it's coon or squirrel. Don't think it's fox."

"Don't matter which it is, doesn't look like you killed it. And if you had, there's no crime in it. You're a free man, Whitcome. Now let's get the hell out of here."

Rain splattered against the policeman's sweating forehead.

Billy Newton was expecting company.

For most of the men in Antrim, a day off, even Thanksgiving Day, could be a pretty boring time. The boys, as Billy called them, were accustomed to the structure that the work week provided. Although a vacation day offered many folks an opportunity for creativity, household chores, or visiting relatives, most of Billy's friends didn't take advantage of their free time. Instead, they devoted themselves to idleness and sloth, activity enough following their huge Thanksgiving feeds. No doubt the November rain had inspired some of them to stay inside napping. But, with the exception of Spike Naylor, who had already arrived, most would start showing up at any moment, one or two at a time.

Billy had a comfortable fire in the stove, and the interior of the garage was bright with neon lights hanging on chains from the hand-hewn beams overhead. The smell of pipe smoke, heavy in the air, mixed with the less pungent odors of grease and gasoline.

Around noon, Billy had been presented with a half gallon of Black Velvet as a down payment for work to be done on Dick Bates's station wagon. With it, he'd received the scoop on the troubles the Whitcomes were having up on Tenny's Hill.

Billy often said he had his finger on the pulse beat of the town. It was for this reason that he never bought newspapers. The important stuff in print was rarely news to him, and news on the state or national scene didn't interest him. Like many of the men in Antrim, his political opinions had very little to do with a knowledge of current events. His central political-economic philosophy was to vote against anything that might raise taxes. His rationale was simple: the less money you spend, the more you have to use your head. No one visiting his place ever disagreed with him; the consensus was that Billy Newton was a pretty clever fella.

Since Thanksgiving was a special occasion, and because the troops hadn't begun to assemble, the center of attention in the garage was Billy's 1935 Ford truck. He had brought his twenty-five-hundred-pound pride and joy in from the back shed and planned to spend some time with it. Renovating the old machine was a long and loving task, not something he wanted to hurry. Billy wasn't one to rush and risk making a mistake. His goal was to restore the truck to its original condition, using only authentic parts if possible. Although most knew about it, few of his associates had ever seen the machine. He was saving it to unveil when he had brought it back to showroom condition.

He had just received a new headlight assembly, in its original packaging. Billy lifted the equipment lovingly from the box and held it up, admiring it as if it were a shiny brass trophy. "It's a beauty, ain't it?"

"That it is," answered Spike Naylor, helping himself to another Dixie cup full of Black Velvet and stretching out comfortably on Billy Newton's chaise longue.

Billy was seated on a wooden box near the right fender of the truck. He had removed the old, battered lamp and was sanding the fender before he began to fit the new assembly in place.

"Don't think we'll be seein' Clint Whitcome stop by today," Billy said matter-of-factly.

"Why's zat?"

"Guess he had a little trouble over his place, yest'dee, day before."

Spike Naylor came to immediate attention. He had more than

a passing interest in the Whitcomes. Clint was a nice fella and all that, but it was Pamela Whitcome that really made his pulse quicken. To Spike she was about the finest piece of woman-flesh that he'd ever laid eyes on. He always got a sense of satisfaction from talking about her, and on many occasions had admired her from a distance when he had seen her in the store or post office. He admired especially her ample bosom and full, moist lips. Once he had said, "Christ, I bet she could suck the brass right off a bedpost." Billy had shot him such a withering look that he never spoke about Mrs. Whitcome again.

"What happened?" asked Spike, feigning indifference.

"Maybe nothin' from the sound of it. But I guess ol' Clint got quite a scare." Billy liked working up a story slowly, building suspense. He puffed his pipe a few times, a kind of dramatic pause, and rubbed the sandpaper on the fender with slow circular motions.

"Dick Bates was over here earlier this mornin' on his way back from the Whitcome place. Tells me he got a call out there yest'dee. It seems Clint was out huntin' turkey. Seen somethin' and shot. Says he seen a kid runnin' away. At first he thought it was his own kid, but it turned out not to be. Dick an' Clint, and maybe that fella they got stayin' up there, went out to look around. Didn't find nothin', no blood, no sign of footprints. Nothin'. Dick says he ain't heard no reports of no kids gettin' hurt in the woods. Figures Clint made a mistake. But I don't know . . ."

"What d'ya mean?"

"Well, always seemed to me Clint was a pretty levelheaded fella. Don't seem like the type to be seein' things. Dick says Clint's pretty upset about it."

"What's the story on that guy they got livin' up there with 'em?" asked Spike, obviously hoping for a bit of juicy gossip.

"A cousin of the missus. Comes from New York. Just lost his wife. I remember him when he was just a kid. Him and his brother used to come by with their granddaddy now and again. Cute little fellas, red hair, always grinnin' . . ."

"Plannin' on movin' in up there, is he?"

"Dunno."

"Must be somethin' for the missus havin' two men around, don-cha think? How's Clint takin' to that?"

"Dunno, Spike," said Billy, unhappy with the turn of the conversation. "Why don't you ask him?"

"Just wonderin'," said Spike innocently, pausing for a sip from the Dixie cup. "I mean, I don't think I'd much relish the idea of workin' all day and leavin' my wife to home with some other guy."

Billy didn't rise to the bait. "I know what you mean, Spike. Course you got nothin' to worry about, not havin' a wife. Or a job."

"You're right about that, Billy. You're right about that." Spike Naylor took the hint.

Billy briefly ignored his friend, allowing time for his gentle reprimand to sink in. He hobbled over to the driver's door of the Ford and climbed in. He flicked on the ignition switch and pulled the knob that controlled the lights.

"Spike, you wanna check and see that they're all on but the busted one?"

Spike, projecting monumental effort, rose from the chaise and checked the front and rear of the vehicle.

"Workin' as good as they're gonna."

Billy turned off the switches and placed his hands on the seat, preparing to use the strength in his arms to push himself out. In the tight pocket between the seat and the back, his right fingertips touched something hard. He fished around until he could get a grip on the object and pulled it out for inspection. It was a silver flask.

Turning it over in his hand, he stared at it as if he were holding a dead rat. This time the discomfort that he felt came not from the pains in his joints, but from the recognition of the article he held.

"God damn it! That old fart's had the truck out again," he concluded. With the realization, a feeling of dread sliced through him like the blade of a razor and fear welled up inside him like blood from a wound.

On Tenny's Hill the Thanksgiving feast was in progress. Clint had smiled broadly when he had gotten home and smelled the turkey roasting in the oven. He slapped Pamela on the bottom and told her that from now on he'd leave the turkey hunting to her.

She was relieved to see his change of mood. Knowing Clint as she did, she guessed he was still a bit worried, though not letting on. Clearly, the time he'd spent in the woods with Dick Bates had eased his mind. She could tell that the men had found nothing to be alarmed about.

Luke was already at the table, arranging his silverware in various formations on his plate and sneaking black olives when he was sure Eric and Pam weren't watching.

Clint brought a bottle of homemade hard cider from the basement. The men took seats around the table waiting to be served. Pamela brought in trays and dishes with turkey and stuffing, mashed potatoes, carrots, squash, and a selection of relishes.

Luke had ventured to the kitchen to help and returned with a dish of cranberry sauce in one hand and a bowl of creamed onions in the other. With his father's assistance he got both on the table with no mishap.

"Well, as of right now," said Clint, "we got a lot to be thankful for." He raised his glass of hard cider in a toast.

The four touched glasses. Luke had to lean way over the table, kneeling on his chair, to clink his glass of milk against the others.

Platters were passed, and plates were filled. Stuffing and mashed potatoes with gravy buried Luke's dish. Eric leaned over to cut Luke's turkey into bite-sized pieces, and in doing so pushed some stuffing onto the clean linen tablecloth.

"Who gets credit for first mess, Eric or Luke?" Clint asked with mock sternness.

Pamela felt warm and content surrounded by her three men. She watched her son, who, in deep concentration, attacked his plate with his fork in quick, precise jabs, as if he were stabbing fish in a bowl. She smiled inwardly as Clint and Eric discussed the theories of Dr. Carl Sayer.

She hoped that, finally, everything would be all right. With the eager expectancy of a mother about to give birth, she tried to feel certain that life was starting fresh and right for all of them. Clint was obviously feeling better, Eric would be staying at least until Christmas, and they'd conspired to get Luke a new puppy.

Their futures should be as bright as the November sunset that filled the evening sky, after the rain.

Clint Whitcome glanced at the bedroom door to make sure it was tightly closed. "Can I get you anything?" he asked his wife.

"No thanks." Her voice was muffled by layers of blankets and a heavy patchwork quilt.

"That was really quite some feed." Clint was loosening his belt and unbuttoning his green chamois shirt. Pamela watched him peel his shirt down over his broad shoulders. The muscles in his back looked hard as a maple log. He hung the shirt on the doorknob.

Turning to her, he shed his jeans and underwear in two graceful steps. She admired his body. He was solid and lean. His firm chest was covered with a thatch of gray and black hair. His hips were straight and tight.

Clint pulled back the covers and got in beside her.

"Brrr," she shivered, "warm me up."

He took her in his strong arms and she snuggled her head against his shoulder. In the soft light from the bedside lamp she admired his face—the dark, boyish eyes that made her feel protective when he was sad, that gave her boundless happiness when they sparkled with humor or passion; the straight, perfect nose and strong proud chin that gave him the look of poise and confidence.

She hugged him, smiled against the skin of his chest.

"He gets along good with Luke, don't he?"

Pamela could tell their minds were not on the same thing. She had anticipated this discussion, but she wasn't prepared for it now, didn't expect it to come so soon. She had feared from the beginning that it would be just a matter of time before Eric's presence began to bother Clint. She knew her husband was a man who liked his privacy, and anyone, neighbor, friend, or out-of-stater, no matter how well liked, would sooner or later become a burden to him.

She had dreaded this moment. "He likes Luke," she replied non-committally.

"And Luke likes him. Can't say's I blame him."

Pamela looked up at his dark eyes. "You like Eric too, don't you?"

"Damn it, just said I did." The twinkle in Clint's eyes contradicted the tone of his voice. "I mean, he's okay for a city fella. You think he's doin' all right?"

"I think he's better. I think it's hard for him. I know he's lonely."

"You think he's plannin' on stayin' here? After the holidays, I mean?"

"Here at the house?" Here it comes, she thought.

"Well, maybe not at the house, but here in town."

"He hasn't talked about it. Do you want me to ask him?"

"I can ask him. I just wondered if he's said anything."

"No, not yet. I don't think he knows what he wants to do. He's got his teaching job to go back to when he's ready."

"Figure he could teach around here? Maybe at the high school or at the community college in Springfield?"

"Clint, I think you want him to stay."

"Mebbe." He grew quiet, stared at the ceiling. A thought seemed to be forming in front of his eyes. "His wife. Does he talk about her?"

"He has, a little. I almost think he's given up on talking. He's had a hard life. More than his share of loss. I almost think loss is normal for him. That sounds mean, doesn't it?"

"Nope. Not from you. You say what's on your mind. But I got a feelin' he's got somethin' on his mind, and he ain't sayin'. Sometimes when him an' me are out together, like after dinner when we put up the rest of that tarpaper, it was like he was about to explode. Like he wanted real bad to get somethin' out. I don't know what's eatin' him."

"You'd like to help, wouldn't you? You'd like to be his friend."

"Mebbe."

"Are you worried about him, Clint?"

Clint nodded. It was brief and stiff, almost imperceptible. "He's different than me. He's put together different. I ain't sure what I got to offer him."

Pamela moved closer to her husband, placing her right leg over his and stretching her neck to kiss him on the cheek. She felt her breast flatten against his chest as she hugged him tighter, scratching the hairs on his chest with her fingertips. "I love you, Clint," she whispered.

She remained like this for a moment, then rolled over onto her back, holding tightly to her husband's hand. "I always felt close to Eric. Even though we lost touch for years, what we had when we were kids never left us. We grew up together, summer after summer. Eric always had a kind of tragedy about him. A kind of sadness. But I admire him because he tries not to let it show. He lost his brother when he was very young. I told you about that, Brian, remember?"

"He got lost, right?"

"Yes, and then when our grandparents died Eric was the one who found their bodies. Gram was dead on the floor, I guess her heart gave out. Gramp's did, too, when he saw her. Anyway, Eric found them and ran for the doctor. Later his parents died, now his wife. I don't know how he stands it. No wonder he's so terrified of death."

"It's like he's supposed to be alone. Like he's not supposed to have no one."

Pamela looked strangely at Clint. She thought that was an odd thing for her husband to say, but she knew how it made Clint uncomfortable to have to explain himself, so she let it go. Instead, she said, "You can see why I feel for him. Why I wanted him to come here."

"You done right, Pamela."

He took her in his arms and held her tightly. She liked the feel of his hard muscles against her, liked the way she felt weak and powerless in his embrace. He didn't have to speak; she could tell, just by the way he held her, that he was proud of her. But surely his pride in her was nothing compared with the way she felt toward him.

She coaxed him on top of her, directing the position of his shoulders with her hands. Then she moved her fingers to his head, grasping his hair and pulling him closer to her. They kissed softly, and again with more passion.

Pamela moaned quietly as her husband's hand moved to her breast. Clint carefully changed position then, fitting himself between her legs. She hugged him tightly around the neck, pulling him closer still. The coarse hair on his legs excited her as it scratched her smooth skin. As they made love, she shuddered, moving reflexively. She felt weightless.

"I love you, Pamela," he whispered.

"Ah, Clint," she sighed, "I love you so much."

"I'd be lost without you."

"Never worry about that, Lover."

PART TWO

Hungry Night

The earth hath bubbles, as the water has,

And these are of them.

Macbeth I.iii

11. SUMMER 1963

After supper, on a warm August evening, the fifteen-year-old Eric Nolan led his cousin Pamela down the road toward town. A paperback of H. P. Lovecraft's short stories bulged from his back pocket. He removed the book to make walking easier.

At the place where Tenny's Hill Road intersected with the highway between Chester and Springfield, there was a concrete bridge over the Williams River. Eric enjoyed sitting under the bridge. He would read or contemplate the pool of water that collected there. He liked to watch the fat suckers floating in the pool, like zeppelins in a crystal sky.

The water fascinated him. It reminded him of long ago, when he and his brother had gone fishing with their grandfather. He wanted to tell Pamela about those days, but feared sounding corny.

Sitting side by side on the bridge's cement foundation, Eric and Pamela talked about unimportant things. Tossing pebbles into the water below, Eric thought about how soon his summer at the farm would end and he'd have to return to school. He was glad. Vermont summers had lost their excitement since Brian went away. Now the days passed all too slowly. He guessed it was like doing time in jail. He wondered how Pamela could stand it all year round.

"What do you do here in the winter?" he asked.

"Same thing you do, I suppose. I go to school and do homework. I spend time with my girlfriends. Nothing too exciting."

Eric remembered when Pammy Nolan had begun spending summers at the farm, back when he was ten years old. When her mom and dad started having "their trouble," the grandparents had offered to care for Pamela while her parents tried to improve their marriage. When the failing marriage had led to divorce, her grandparents took Pamela in for good.

"But don't you get, you know, bored on the farm?" Eric asked.

"I don't think so. Not really. I guess I don't really mind it. I help Gram around the house."

"I'd go nuts here all the time. I like spending time alone and everything, but up here you don't even have a choice."

"I never think of it like that. There's always something to do. I read, and write letters. Gram and me are trying to get Gramp to buy a TV, now that we've got the electricity hooked up."

"TV, huh? That would be something, at least."

Eric became quiet. He stretched out on his stomach with his head hanging over the ledge. He looked down the ten feet to his reflection in the water. His thoughts drifted to his cousin, how she had changed since last summer, and of how he had changed to notice it.

"Do you . . . ah . . . have any . . . boyfriends or anything like that?"

She blushed, as she did so easily. "No, not really, I mean I've been out a couple of times. I don't know how Gram and Gramp would like it."

"I guess not . . ."

"Do you have a girlfriend?"

Eric wrestled with an unfamiliar pride that tried to make him boastful, make him lie. But he couldn't lie to Pamela.

"No. No, I don't. I don't think girls would like me very much. I don't know."

Pamela seemed startled. "Why do you say that?"

Eric shrugged. "I guess I'm not very good-looking."

"You are too good-looking. Oh, Eric, you are too."

"I don't know. My hair, you know." He ran his hand through his crew cut.

"You have beautiful hair. I wish my hair was as red as yours."

"Well, maybe it's okay for a girl. But red hair! I mean it's not very . . . sexy."

"It is too, Eric, come on."

"And my eyes are stupid lookin'. I should wear sunglasses."

"What's wrong with your eyes?"

"You know what's wrong with 'em. They're different colors, that's what."

"You can hardly tell. You probably notice it more than anyone else. Besides, I think it looks distinguished."

"You're just saying that."

"Of course, I'm saying it. Because I mean it."

Eric sat up and looked at her. There was a plaintive expression on her face. Eric could tell it was important to Pamela that he believe what she was saying. He looked away from her eyes, and down at the cement platform between them. He stole a glimpse at the way her well-developed breasts pushed at the front of her blouse and then, out of modesty, looked back at the concrete.

"I believe you like the way I look," he told her.

"And do you like how I look?"

"Sure, 'course I do. If you weren't my cousin I'd . . . you'd . . . I mean, you'd be a girl I'd like to go out with, or something."

"Thank you, Eric," she said softly.

Another silence followed. Eric felt pleased with himself; at the same time uncomfortably shy. He stood up and stretched, faking a yawn. Pamela stood up, too.

"Don't forget your book," she said, as Eric started to move away. Picking it up from the concrete, she studied the lurid cover.

"Why do you read this stuff, anyway?" she asked with a little shudder.

Eric shrugged, embarrassed. He took the paperback from her and returned it to the pocket of his jeans. "I guess it helps to keep life interesting around here. I mean, who knows what breed of loathsome creature prowls these haunted woods?"

He looked around mysteriously, squinting at the forest. Then he started to laugh.

Pamela laughed too, blushing, as if for a moment she'd really been frightened.

"Look at that big ol' sucker down there." Eric pointed to where the water flowed from the narrow end of the pool.

"What's that over there?" Pamela pointed at a spot farther downstream.

"I don't know. Let's have a look."

They climbed down from the concrete foundation and onto the dirt path, worn grassless by novice fishermen who believed the too accessible and overfished pool below might promise a good catch.

From behind him, Pamela put her hands on Eric's shoulders to steady herself on the steep walkway. On the riverbank below, they changed places and Pam led the way, jumping from stone to stone toward the mysterious object in the water.

They found a partly submerged burlap sack lodged against a rock in the swift current. A lather of white water, a miniature rapid, partially veiled the bag with a rainbow spray. The top of the sack was tied with a length of clothesline.

"What is it?" asked Pamela, childlike wonder in her voice.

"I don't know. But it's full of something. Let's open it up."

Eric dragged the waterlogged bag to the gravel bank of the river. It was difficult for him to untie the wet cord, so he cut it away with his Swiss Army knife. Then he grabbed it by the bottom and tipped its contents out onto the ground.

He winced in disgust, and looked at Pamela's face to see it change from puzzlement to horror. Then to outrage.

"How can people do that!" she cried.

On the ground, in a soggy heap, were six baby kittens, their silky fur matted and dull. Torn flesh showed where their undeveloped claws had ripped at each other in their dying frenzy.

"Someone must have tossed them off the bridge," said Eric, stepping away. "Come on, let's get out of here."

"No," said Pamela, tears rolling down her pale cheeks. "Let's bury them."

They dragged the bag with the tiny bodies on top to a place above the high water line where the grass grew in sparse patches.

There with the aid of an old license plate, they scooped out a shallow grave. Eric tumbled the kittens into the hole and covered them with the burlap. Together they replaced the dirt and marked the grave with a pile of stones from the riverbank.

They stood looking helplessly at each other until the sobs behind Pamela's tears died away into the darkening evening. Without knowing what else to do, Eric held out his arms to her and she collapsed into his embrace, crying like a small child.

"How can people do that?" she asked again.

"I told you there were monsters in these woods," said Eric. "Come on, let's go home now."

From the <u>Newport Messenger</u>, July 7, 1954:

A young Canadian farmer is insisting he saw a group of "miniature people" while he was fishing on the shores of Lake Memphremagog, just south of the Canadian border.

Roger LaChance, twenty-five, told his story yesterday to Royal Canadian Air Force authorities. The RCAF declined to investigate because the sighting was in U.S. territory. They refused further comment.

LaChance claimed he saw four little men moving field-stones last Friday—the day on which the planet Mars was nearest to the earth's orbit. He describes them as "more than a meter in height, with large heads and small piggish eyes."

He says he thought they might be from a flying saucer, and addressed them, from a distance, in both French and English.

"They fixed me with a hypnotic stare and ran away," LaChance said.

U.S. Coast Guard officials on the lake have no comment.

12. THE OTHERS

Thursday,
December 1, 1983

"I'm not suggesting that it's true," repeated Mrs. Elizabeth McKensie, putting her teacup down and staring over the top of her spectacles at Carl Sayer, who sat across the table, "but suppose— just suppose—there was such a thing."

"It is difficult for me even to suppose such a thing without supposing first that it would be impossible for it, or them, to have remained undiscovered for so long." There was a mocking quality in Sayer's voice and a defiant twinkle in his eyes. It was as if the subject were not worthy of him, so, rather than discuss it, he smiled and chose to view it as amusing.

The three people were meeting for the first time. They had been talking for nearly an hour around the oak table in Mrs. McKensie's kitchen.

Their meeting had been organized when Eric phoned Sayer on Monday morning to set up an appointment to examine the root cellar. Sayer mentioned that part of his agenda for the trip to Antrim was to interview Elizabeth McKensie. Even in Montpelier, Vermont's capital, Mrs. McKensie's reputation as a local historian was known. Since Eric also wanted to meet her, they decided to rendezvous at her house in Chester.

Elizabeth McKensie was seventy-five years old. Although she was confined to a wheelchair, she appeared otherwise healthy— spry even—with an intellectual alertness that stimulated her two guests, challenged them. Her clear eyes sparkled in conversation, her good-natured smile told the visitors that she was genuinely happy to have them with her. She had a prevailing sense of hospitality that made Eric feel completely at home.

She pushed a tray of molasses cookies, which Eric noticed were slightly burned around the edges, toward Dr. Sayer. The doctor ignored them.

Carl Sayer sipped tea so diluted with milk and sugar that it looked syrupy. He was a quiet, officious man, with a smooth, bald head and thick horn-rimmed glasses. The lenses were so thick that his eyes appeared unnaturally wide. Sayer seemed silently impatient with the direction the conversation was taking. He fidgeted in his seat like a bored child.

Eric looked closely at Dr. Sayer, trying to guess his age. The doctor was of indeterminate years. Eric guessed he was somewhere between thirty-five and fifty. It was impossible to be more precise.

Actually, it was during his last two years of graduate school in Cultural Resources Management at Idaho State University that Dr. Sayer's hair had begun to fall. It had frightened him at the start, and he quickly sought, first, the aid of barbers, then cosmetologists, and ultimately, dermatologists. He was even fitted for a wig after learning that his hair loss was hereditary and unpreventable.

Since he'd always worried more about his health than his appearance, he had decided to ignore the hair loss, and he'd never bought the wig.

His fish-eye glasses, however, were something he could not do without. He needed them for his studies and research, the things that gave meaning to his life.

Sayer had first heard about Vermont's stone chambers in 1975 from a fellow graduate student, David Potter, who later became a writer and head of the Department of Vermont Archaeological Studies at UVM in Burlington.

When Sayer heard about the chambers, something inside him ignited. He found the possibility of ancient Celtic settlements in New England so thought-provoking that he had offered his services to the State of Vermont without pay. His credentials and enthusiasm quickly won him the offer of a paid position that would be created for him when he finished his studies.

This waiting placement gave him an enviable advantage among college graduates in the year 1976. The prospect heightened Sayer's sense of self-importance, and he felt special, perhaps for the first time in his quiet and studious life. Whether he was envied or ridiculed by his classmates for his new confidence he never knew; he was too preoccupied to think about it. Besides, he was used to it; people had always joked about him. But when he announced publicly that he would soon be doing research that was likely to rewrite the pages of American history, his colleagues began to scoff in a self-righteous, academic manner. They began to refer to him as "Sooth," in recognition of his ambitious and boastful prediction.

Perhaps it was the ridicule of his peers that made him so eager for success, or so secretive about his opinions. Whatever his motive, he pressed to redirect the conversation in Mrs. McKensie's kitchen to the root cellar on Pinnacle Mountain. It was in those cellars that he planned to establish, and then build, his reputation.

Eric, who had introduced the unimportant topic of "wee folks" with questions about Mrs. McKensie's poetry, was interested in the old woman's speculations. He was an English instructor and a sometime student of legend and myth; he had never before realized that New England folklore included little people. Also, with a feeling of perverse satisfaction, he wanted to press Sayer by playing devil's advocate. There was something vulnerable about Sayer, something that invited teasing. Eric responded to it. Obviously, Mrs. McKensie did too. It seemed that people always wanted to get Carl to "loosen up."

"I don't know," Eric began, "the explorers in the Himalayas keep seeing that elusive snowman; and the Irish have their leprechauns—even though now they're probably toting guns. And North America has some oddities of its own. What about Bigfoot? And the Lake Champlain monster? I don't think it's unreasonable to think that maybe, just maybe, here in New England, in fact right here in Vermont, we have our own—what shall I call it?—subrace, perhaps? Possibly their stronghold is right over there in Antrim."

"How can you say that, Mr. Nolan?" Sayer's voice rose, "It's far too speculative. Unscientific. There's nothing at all, anywhere, to support such claims. The idea is as fanciful as UFOs, or ESP, or even religion. You can't really expect these imaginary mountain men to actually start showing up."

Mrs. McKensie smiled. "Sometimes the most scientific minds are capable of the most unscientific thought. Does your science exclude everything that it doesn't yet include, Mr. Sayer? Sounds a bit silly when I put it like that, doesn't it? And you're clouding the issue by bringing in religion. We're not discussing mysticism here. Unless, of course, these folks have something better to offer than Christianity. Personally, my faith isn't as fragile as yours seems to be. Honestly, Mr. Sayer, for a scientist you show a dangerous lack of imagination. All I'm asking, for the moment, is that you suppose they exist. Suppose. That's what God gave you your imagination for."

Sayer couldn't help chuckling in spite of himself, and Eric felt a release of tension when he heard it. Both men were surprised at the outspokenness of their hostess. She was not in the least intimidated in the presence of two younger people.

"Let me show you something." Mrs. McKensie wheeled herself to the counter by the sink, placed a book and a folder on her lap, and returned to the table. "You're from around Montpelier, is that right, Mr. Sayer?"

"I work out of Montpelier. Actually, I live in Duxbury."

"Well, no matter. Listen to this." She prepared to read from the book on her lap. "This is a biography of Rudyard Kipling, who, as you know, lived for a while near Brattleboro, not far from here. In 1894, I think it was, he was visited by Sir Arthur Conan Doyle, who was touring America at the time. Doyle, you may recall, was an interested and devoted researcher, and a tireless investigator of psychic phenomena: all things in the realm of the mysterious and strange, including the little folk. I can just picture these two dignified old gentlemen, sitting in rocking chairs, overlooking the Connecticut River in the distance, puffing their pipes and telling each other stories. One of the stories Kipling told Doyle takes place up in your neck of the woods, Mr. Sayer. Listen . . ."

She read from the book: " 'One tale told on a pleasant autumn evening upon the gazebo at Naulahka involved fairies, the little folks whose existence Doyle would later come to accept as factual. In his carriage, traveling to Montpelier, the Reverend Baring-Gould had an encounter that, for the rest of his life, troubled him greatly. A group of dwarfs, less than three feet high, ran from the nearby woods and accompanied the carriage. Some laughed and pointed, some tried to climb upon the wagon or tried to mount the horses by way of the leather harness. They followed the carriage for some distance and then, one by one, returned to the shelter of the woodland.'"

Mrs. McKensie lowered the book, looking over her glasses at Sayer. He fidgeted as he spoke. "Your 'history book' doesn't say where the reverend was traveling from. My guess would be a tavern. The reverend, most probably, was drunk!"

"Perhaps so," the old woman said patiently. "That need not change what he saw, only how he interpreted it. Perhaps that's why he saw them as playful and carefree, missing altogether the true nature of those little people."

"Midgets," protested Sayer. "Midgets and drunks. Nothing so damned unusual about either."

"But there's more," said Mrs. McKensie and handed Sayer the folder full of newspaper clippings. "Here's a whole collection of sightings dating all the way back to 1860. You'll notice that many clippings describe the same thing, and always in one of two ways: they either see what they think is a child, or a small, stocky man, between two and four feet tall, always sighted in some wooded area, usually about sunset. Some are reported as being grotesquely wrinkled, often with a hunched back."

"Really, Mrs. McKensie," Sayer pushed the folder away. He was beginning to look angry, as if he thought Eric and Mrs. McKensie were enjoying a joke at his expense. "Your fairy tales are having the same effect on me that my mother's used to. They're putting me to sleep. I wonder if we could change the topic and get back to the business of the root cellars."

"I wonder if it's really a change of topic at all," ventured Eric, the devil's advocate again. He wondered why the scientist was being so obtuse, so disagreeable.

Mrs. McKensie smiled tolerantly at Sayer. "As you wish, Mr. Sayer. Could I offer either of you gentlemen some more tea?"

Eric listened quietly as the conversation continued for about an hour. The old woman had little information to offer about the stone structure on the Whitcomes' land. She had known about it since she was a little girl, and she seemed to remember its being used as a shelter for sheep many years before. She was aware of the controversy surrounding similar structures throughout the state, and had read about the research going on at Mystery Hill in Salem, New Hampshire.

As a historian, she acknowledged the possibility that the Whitcomes' stone structure could have been built three thousand years ago by Celtic explorers who settled in the Connecticut River Valley. It was possible. She guessed the evidence was buried in the remote past; it was likely the proof would come long after she had passed on.

Eric realized she was much more interested in evidence about the existence of the little people, who apparently were more a part of today than of history. He vowed to talk to her again about this subject. But for now, he would leave with Sayer.

Mrs. McKensie seemed genuinely grateful for the company and for the conversation. She seemed disappointed when the men left.

"I'd like to stop by again, if I may," Eric said as he was leaving.

"I was going to suggest it myself. Perhaps for dinner. It's been a month of Sundays since I've had a chance to cook for a handsome young man."

Eric felt himself blushing. He knew that he had something to learn from this old woman—perhaps something about life, or loneliness. He knew he would be back.

In his car, leading Sayer to the turnoff where they would park and walk to the site, Eric thought a lot about the conversation that had just taken place. He was left a little unsettled by the new ideas he had been forced to consider. His mind worked rapidly to weave the threads of the discussion into a coherent and believable pattern. The notion of outdated knowledge, beliefs made obsolete by modern revision and contemporary science, was nothing new to him. Indeed, he'd always had an appetite for the bizarre, even as a child. He recalled his own research on the mysticism of William Butler Yeats, and chuckled as he remembered that Stevenson had jokingly credited little people with assisting him in his writing.

But then again, on the serious side, what if all of a sudden something he had habitually dismissed as superstition did an about-face—reasserted itself with new strength? The possibility was frightening, the idea unnerving, the whole concept exciting. Best of all, the thoughts were not painful to him; his mind made no effort to turn away from them. It felt good to have something to ponder.

Still, it disturbed him to think he might have to change his concept of reality. Could another race actually exist; a lost race, possibly similar to, possibly totally different from our own?

I'm taking this too seriously, he thought. Sayer had a good point —how could they have remained undiscovered for so long? Especially if they were living peacefully in the wilderness of Vermont. Peacefully? Maybe not. What would they be like? Where could they have come from? How could they have come to be? It gave the whole notion of human evolution a new slant. Suppose the first ape who lifted his front paws and called himself a man had taken his first human step on his left foot while his brother had begun with the right? The two might have walked off in entirely different directions, to become totally different creatures. Eric could not dismiss these speculative thoughts as easily as Sayer seemed to. Rejecting or ignoring anything that might challenge or conflict with his philosophy of life and truth was against all the academic principles that he tried to live by. To reject would be to forfeit discovery, to cease to grow.

Still, on another level, the whole subject had overtones of lunacy about it. He had to admit it. He had been doubting his own sanity altogether too much lately. Perhaps his interest in this topic was not healthy. He wondered how it would be perceived. Most people he knew on Long Island would have listened to Mrs. Mc-Kensie with an attitude of bemused tolerance, later laughing about the ravings of a crazy old woman.

She wasn't crazy, though. Eric knew that. She had a razor-sharp mind, a scholar's urgency to communicate, and an educator's gift for inspiring thoughtful discussion. Again, Sayer had dismissed her more easily than Eric could.

In his excitement about the new ideas, Eric, too, felt an urgency to communicate. But who could he talk to about the little people? He thought of Clint. Clint was down-to-earth, not given to fanciful contemplation. Eric worried about sabotaging their growing friendship by appearing to be too much of an eccentric. And yet— the memory returned to him with the force of an avalanche— might not Clint have actually seen a little man? What, or whom, had he shot at when he thought he had wounded Luke? Eric shuddered at how perfectly this piece of the puzzle seemed to fit. Perhaps he should talk to Clint.

In any event, he would talk to Pam. She would not think less of him, and he knew her well enough to believe she'd be fascinated by the possibility.

If not, he concluded with a smile, tales of the "wee folk" would make excellent bedtime stories for Luke.

The stone site came into view a short distance beyond the last marked poplar tree. Eric was puffing from the exertion of the climb, but he was pleased that he was able to lead Sayer so effortlessly through the forest maze. He had carefully pointed out each of Clint's marks so that the archaeologist could later reconstruct the route.

Sayer became visibly excited when he saw the stone mound. "That's the real thing. No doubt of it." He handed Eric his nylon backpack and lifted his camera to his eye.

The men approached the dark rectangular opening in the stone mound. Sayer was looking at the compass that rested flat on his palm. "Most of them are like this," he said. "They open to the south. The theory is that they have astronomical and possibly religious significance."

The archaeologist hunkered down and duck-walked through the opening. He reached behind him, took the backpack from Eric, and quickly removed a flashlight. From outside the structure's opening, Eric watched Sayer move the beam of light across the wall. Slowly, pausing briefly on each stone, the white circle explored the rough interior walls. Occasionally, bright flashes lit the opening as Sayer took pictures.

"Find anything interesting?"

Sayer didn't reply. Eric moved partially through the doorway to get a better view of the process.

"Look here." Sayer pointed to a spot on the left, just inside the opening. Eric shifted his position, kneeling beside the other man to see what was revealed in the light. He felt dampness from the stone floor soak coldly through the knees of his pants.

One of the stones was scored with a series of short vertical lines that grew out of, and sometimes bisected, a longer horizontal marking.

"Is that the so-called Ogam script?"

Sayer nodded.

"Can you translate it?"

"It isn't clear. I'll come back tomorrow and do some rubbings and sketches. The interior warrants closer examination." Sayer pointed to a concentration of strokes. "That's the symbol for Bel, the Celtic sun god. The inscription probably dedicates this structure to Bel. If I can reproduce the markings, I can get them translated."

The two men left the structure and stood up. Eric felt the muscles in his lower back stretch and pull. He watched Sayer poking through the backpack. Inside it, he caught sight of a tape measure and a ball of knotted string. Sayer removed a notebook and closed the pack, quickly moving it from Eric's view.

"Well," he said with great finality, extending his right hand to Eric. "I certainly appreciate your bringing me up here, Mr. Nolan. As a matter of fact, I appreciate all the cooperation you and the

Whitcomes have given me. What remains, at least for today, is paperwork. I have to take measurements, do computations, readings, that sort of thing. None of it will be very interesting, I'm afraid, and—I mean no offense by this—it is nothing that an untrained person can really help with. I hate to inconvenience you by asking you to remain up here in the cold while I go about my work. I believe I can find my way down alone. The trail is clearly marked and your directions have been excellent. If you'd like to go back by yourself, I'm sure I can find my way down after a few hours."

Eric was surprised. There was something in the finality of Sayer's tone that communicated that there was no room for discussion. Eric had been dismissed.

He stammered, "Well, if you're sure you don't mind . . ."

He encouraged Sayer not to remain after dark, remembering Clint's warning, "Be careful in them woods."

Within minutes, feeling embarrassed and uncomfortable, Eric found himself making his way down the mountainside alone.

13. THE ARTIST

Within seconds after the redheaded man disappeared among the trees, Carl Sayer began to remove things from his backpack. He was alone now, just as he liked it, and eager to start his research.

Research, he thought, is a lonely art. When he was by himself, engaged in an important project, he was surely an artist. For Sayer, research was the only true blending of art and science.

Sayer was glad to be rid of Nolan. The man's silly questions, like the old woman's chatter about fairies, were difficult for him to tolerate. Unschooled minds, like primitives viewing an eclipse, were most imaginative in the dark.

He chuckled, delighted with his analysis of Nolan and McKensie.

In Sayer's research there was little place for imagination. He wanted evidence, facts. He had no intention of sharing his search, or his discovery, with a folklore-crazed English teacher, or a superannuated relic in a wheelchair.

Now there was no need to guard against Nolan's prying eyes. Sayer had Nolan figured out. He'd seen the type before: a failed scholar, hungry for an idea. In his questions about "little people" and his nosiness about Sayer's research, Nolan had displayed all the scientific integrity of a Von Daniken, or a Velikovsky. Sayer didn't want any part of him.

Placing the compass next to his tape measure and slide rule, he carefully removed his camera and reattached the electronic flash.

Standing up, he faced the mound of stones. To Sayer, it was an adversary, something to be conquered, tamed, compelled to give up its secrets.

As he regarded the mound he couldn't help thinking how strange it looked. He wondered if its alien appearance had inspired Nolan and McKensie's talk about "little people." They should know better; they were adults, who shouldn't engage in the magical thinking of children, or psychotics.

He wondered if he was being too closed-minded. Maybe he should have taken a look at the old woman's collection of clippings. If people thought they were seeing "little people" in Vermont, what, in reality, could be the basis for the illusions?

The structure in front of him was a hump in the rocky carpet of earth. It resembled a grass-covered beehive, less than ten feet high. The doorway beneath the massive stone lintel was about four feet tall. He remembered stooping to enter. The size of the opening made him think of Professor Leakey's discovery, in 1961, of *homo habilis*, the remains of an early race of human beings, even smaller than pygmies.

Sayer wondered what the builders of the mound might have looked like; surely, they had been much shorter than modern man.

Of course, the ancient Celts were a small race . . .

When they were violently displaced by Saxons and other invaders, many of them had fled into the hills of the British Isles. There they had lived in isolation, occupying woodland caves.

Perhaps some of them had traveled to the New World. If so, most researchers agreed, they would have bred with the indigenous population, eventually losing their racial identity and leaving no trace of themselves but the monuments they had built and the influence of their language on the speech of American Indians.

If they hadn't mixed, reasoned Sayer, they would have kept to themselves, reclusive, necessarily interdependent for their own survival.

Then the idea came to him. It shot into his brain like a rifle bullet: Could a small group of Celts still exist today?

For some reason the notion seemed logical. Perhaps the Vermont sightings of "little people" grew from the same inspiration as British folklore. Sayer imagined ancient Celts hiding from savage invaders. He pictured their furtive sorties at dusk, their unexpected daylight appearances in isolated spots. Surely this could have given rise to the belief that curious little beings inhabited the endless wilderness of old England, or modern Vermont.

Sayer looked around him, scanned the edge of the forest, the trees, the darkness within their branches. Squirrels chattered. A bird called. A few maverick flurries of snow were beginning to fall. They moved in loops and arcs as the wind strengthened.

Sayer stumbled on a small round stone and caught himself against a spindly oak. He put the strap of his camera around his neck.

If he could only prove, irrefutably, that the stone structures were built by ancient Celts, he'd have his reputation made! If he could also prove that a limited number of their descendants still survived in the Vermont hills, hopefully right here on Pinnacle Mountain . . .

What a grand discovery it would be! Far more important than the discovery of the mountain gorilla back in 1901. He'd have more than a reputation, he'd have fame!

As he stepped eagerly into the mound, Sayer became immediately aware of how quiet everything had become. He couldn't hear the birds or the sound of the wind in the trees. Even with the afternoon light pouring in through the rectangular doorway, the site's interior seemed very dark. It was cold, as damp as a crypt.

Sayer's senses were fine-tuned. For some reason he felt edgy. Why was he thinking this way? It wasn't his habit to entertain such fanciful notions. Impatient with his speculation and thoughts of fame, he struggled to get his mind back on his work.

He flicked on his flashlight. Again he studied the walls. The individual stones were moist, the floor was a frozen puddle. On the northern side, a scarred slab stopped the searching beam.

Sayer looked closely at the organized markings. His thick glasses magnified the grooves and slashes. Scrutinizing them carefully, he recognized the strokes for "Bel," and the mark for "heed," or, as it was sometimes translated, "beware."

Some of his colleagues had insisted that none of these markings were pre-Christian Ogam script; they were all attributable to glaciation, erosion, or, as was often asserted by his most skeptical contemporaries, the work of pranksters.

Sayer had to admit the markings revealed in his light did look comparatively new. They were too distinct to be as much as one thousand years old. But did that mean they were the work of colonial, or even modern, pranksters?

Not necessarily.

Again the speculation: the markings could be the work of living Celts. It was possible.

By God, he decided, I'll try to prove it!

He'd go back, talk to that old woman again, have a look at her collection of clippings.

From memory he was able to make a tentative translation of the script in his flashlight beam: "Take heed of Bel, his eye is the sun."

Sayer removed the lens cap from his camera and framed the inscription in the viewer. He inched back a little to include all the pits and grooves within the frame.

As he was preparing to flash the picture, the chamber was plunged into darkness.

Sayer's head jerked to face the door. Something indistinct covered it, shutting out the sun.

As a reflex, he snapped the picture.

14. THE WARNING

Snowflakes fell gently across the graying evening. To the west, a ribbon of crimson light joined the mountains to the sky. A delicate whiteness veiled the balsam firs surrounding the Whitcomes' yard. Near the porch, a fleet of Luke's Tonka trucks lay abandoned in the snow. Eric's car, partially obscured, had been in the yard since the first flakes fell.

Eric and Luke were out in the yard getting a closer look at the snowfall. After his early-afternoon hike to the top of the Pinnacle, Eric concluded that he preferred his nephew's company to that of the stuffy scientist. He smiled as he watched the boy playing amid the falling snow.

God, Eric thought, he looks just like Brian . . .

Luke, squealing happily, chased the biggest flakes, trying to catch them on his hand.

Eric enjoyed watching him. Pointing at Luke, Eric turned around, smiling his approval at Pamela, who watched proudly from the window.

The boy realized quickly that he could keep the flakes longer if he caught them on his mitten instead of in his hand. He brought one to show Eric, moving cautiously as if he were carrying a too-full glass of milk.

"Look," he said, with a hint of wonder in his voice.

"It's pretty," replied Eric. "And did you know that no two snow-flakes are alike? A man from right here in Vermont proved it."

Luke looked around at the expanse of white that had formed over everything. There was an expression of total bafflement on his round, apple-cheeked face. As he stood thinking, clouds of breath puffed from his tiny nose like smoke signals. Eric could tell that Luke was pondering the idea, confused because all the snowflakes looked pretty much the same to him.

"Have you ever seen snow before?" asked Eric, fully aware that he was falling into the familiar grown-up habit of asking children questions to which they most assuredly knew the answers.

"Yup."

"Where, can you remember?"

"Yup. In the 'fridgerater." Luke laughed merrily, delighted with his joke. Eric laughed too, a little embarrassed, but impressed with his nephew.

"If this snow keeps up, maybe later we can make a snowman, how'd you like that?"

"Okay," Luke responded halfheartedly, apparently not interested at all in changing activities. Distracted by a snowflake the size of a silver dollar, he darted off after it.

"Wise-ass kid," grumbled Eric as he stepped into the warm kitchen. Immediately, his tinted glasses fogged-up. He removed them, polished them with his handkerchief, and put them back on. All the while he was explaining to Pamela how Luke had suckered him. "In the 'fridgerater,' indeed . . ." Eric said with mock indignation.

Clint was expected home from work shortly. Pamela was getting things ready so that the family could sit down for dinner. She stood at the stove adding red wine to a fragrant beef stew. "I might have known that we'd get snow on the first day of December, it's just like clockwork. Clint'll probably be out half the night plowing."

"That's his job too, huh?"

"Yup. That and a hundred other things. He works hard."

"That he does. I don't think I could keep up with him."

Pamela tasted the stew from a wooden spoon. "You haven't said too much about your meeting with Mr. Sayer."

"*Doctor* Sayer, if you please. And I can see that Clint had the right idea, not wanting to talk to him."

"You two didn't hit it off, I guess."

"He's about as likable as a toadstool. He acted like he thought I was going to steal all his professional secrets, whatever they might be. He practically ordered me to leave, after I hiked all the way up there to show him the cellar."

Pamela smirked. "My husband won't like hearing about that. It'd be just like Clint to go right up there and kick him off the property."

"That would be amusing." Eric took a seat at the kitchen table. "How's he doing, anyway?"

"Clint?" Pamela looked distractedly from the stew pot.

Eric nodded as she sat beside him at the table. "He's better now, I think. He knows he didn't hurt anybody. But it worries him because he still feels he saw something in the woods. Clint's proud of his ability as a woodsman. It bothers him to think that he was careless, shooting when he wasn't absolutely sure of his target. Of course, he also doesn't like to think that he might have been seeing things."

"Maybe he wasn't seeing things."

Pamela looked at him, startled. "What do you mean?"

Eric told her about discussing "little people" with Mrs. McKensie and Sayer.

Pamela listened attentively, nodding encouragement. She never scoffed or laughed. Indeed, it was clear that she took the whole matter quite seriously. "It's hard to believe. Of course, it is. And I can't say that I do believe it. But I won't say it can't be so."

She walked back to the stove and removed the cover from the stew pot. Then, from a bowl on the counter, she placed spoonfuls of dumpling batter into the boiling stock.

"I remember once, maybe five or six years ago, before Clint tore down the barn and built the garage. I was looking out that window over there. I think it was about sundown. Yup, just about this time of day. But it was in the summer, so it was probably after supper. Right beyond the barn I saw three or four kids, little kids. They were out there in the field, just in front of the woods. I thought it was strange, because they were all alone. I mean I couldn't see any adults with them or anything. They were going around in a ring, as if maybe they were playing a game. I went to the bottom of the stairs to call Clint, and when we got back here to take a look they were gone. He thought I'd probably seen a couple of deer or something. I mean the light wasn't that good, and they were pretty far away. But I was sure, at least, that it wasn't deer, so I sent Clint out to check. He was good about it. He's always good that way. He doesn't like me to worry. As you might expect, he didn't find anything, though. I guess I became less sure of what I saw and actually forgot about it until right now."

Pamela's eyes took on a faraway look as she replayed the twilight scene in her memory. She spoke, as if to no one, "It was kind of creepy, now that I think about it. Really makes me wonder, you know?"

"Wouldn't it be something to see one of them?" said Eric. "I'll have to start spending more time in the woods, just in case they really exist. I think it would be great having a bunch of little guys wandering around."

"One's enough for me," said Pamela glancing at the opening door.

Luke walked in carefully, his mittened hand outstretched. He headed toward his mother. "Look," he commanded, and when they both were looking at his hand he said, with great and profound disappointment, "Oh, melted."

Pamela helped him out of his snowsuit and told him to go get cleaned up before his father got home. Luke insisted on a glass of milk first, then headed toward the bathroom. Moments later they heard Clint's truck arrive.

Clint didn't come directly into the house. It was several minutes before they heard him stomp across the porch and into the kitchen. Anger hung around him like a dark cloud.

"Goddamnedest thing," he muttered.

"What's the matter, Hon?"

"Some damn fool's been writin' on the garage."

Eric and Pamela both went to the window, looked at the barnboard garage, but saw nothing.

"Ya can't see it from here. It's on the side near the woods."

"What'd they write?"

"Nothin' that makes any sense."

Without putting on jackets, Pam and Eric went outside. Clint followed. They walked through the deepening snow toward the garage.

"Around back," Clint directed. "Musta been done 'fore the snow started. Whoever done it didn't leave no tracks."

The three stood in a row looking at the windowless side of the garage. Scratched into the barnboard with a knife or a sharp stone were letters about six inches high. They were about five feet off the ground and printed in a blocky, nondescript style. They said: AN I FOR AN I.

Clint had been both angry and mystified by the writing on the garage. It could have been scrawled by some God-minded but illiterate hunter, Eric suggested.

"Or somebody with a beef against me," Clint ventured. Pamela wondered aloud if Perly Greer might be inclined to do such a thing, if he had walked by. She then apologized for the groundless suspicion.

No one had an answer. Jokingly, Eric said, "Everyone is a suspect. Only Luke gets off the hook, because he can't write."

A bit of laughter eased the tension.

After dinner everyone was quiet and more relaxed about the strange message on the garage. For a while Clint and Eric stood at the bay window watching the snowfall as Pamela cleaned the kitchen. Luke took no interest in either of these activities. By seven-thirty he was asleep on the floor amid his collection of Star Wars figurines and toy trucks.

Clint was certain that the quickly accumulating snow would necessitate an unusually early start in the morning, and a full day of plowing. At eight o'clock, he said goodnight to Eric, kissed Pamela, and scooped Luke up into his arms. Clint carried his son into the bathroom, an often unsuccessful measure to keep the boy from wetting the bed. Then he brought Luke to Pamela and Eric for kisses.

Luke sat on his father's forearm as if he were on a ski lift. He rode up the stairs with one hand on Clint's shoulder and the other in his father's dark hair, grasping it tightly like the mane of a horse. Luke looked puzzled.

Luke's bedroom faced the back of the house and the forest beyond. His stuffed monkey, Philip, waited for him on the bed. A plastic clown, suspended by one hand from an illuminated balloon, hung from the top of the window frame. It revolved slowly in the currents of warm air from the vent. The walls were colorfully decorated with pictures of Sesame Street characters. Tacked over the bed was a big poster of Mickey Mouse reading in an overstuffed chair beside a cheery fireplace. Pluto slept contentedly at his feet. In a nearby poster, Snow White smiled under a rainbow of flowers and birds.

Clint, making a noise like a revving truck engine, dumped Luke on the bed. The boy was wide awake now. He bounced and squealed with delight.

Clint laughed too. "Need some help getting into your pj's?"

Luke held up his arms, a signal that Clint was to pull off his jersey.

"What you gonna dream about tonight, Lukey?"

"Dream?" The puzzled face again. Luke was giving careful thought to his answer.

"You're gonna grow up to be just like your pa, son. Always thinkin' before you speak. That's good."

Luke looked his father in the eyes and squinted a little. "Maybe tonight I won't dream."

Clint smiled and sat on the bed. "Don't you like to dream at night? You can dream about your trucks and all the snow you and me got to plow tomorrow. Or maybe you can dream about what you want to do when you're as big as your old man. You can dream about all the things you like. Special things."

"Maybe I can dream about Rusty."

Clint kept the smile on his face, but the ugly image of the dead dog flashed across his mind. He helped Luke with the buttons of his pajama top, stood up, and pulled back the bed covers.

"You gonna be warm enough, son?"

"Umm-hmm." Luke snuggled into the bedclothes.

"Need a drink of water or anything?"

"No, thank you."

Again Clint sat on the edge of the bed and molded the blankets around his son's tiny body. The boy was so very small. So frail looking. Clint bent forward and kissed Luke on the forehead.

"Daddy?"

"Yes."

"Will Uncle Eric come to my window again tonight?"

"What do you mean, son?"

"I like to see him at my window. Like the other time."

"This window?" asked Clint, indicating the only window in the room.

"Umm-hmm."

Clint walked to the window and looked out, then down. The night was so black that he could hardly see the snow. He knew there was nothing out there but the ground, twelve or more feet below. "Maybe you were dreamin', Lukey."

Luke giggled. Clint walked to the bed. "Settle down now and close your eyes. You and Uncle Eric can do a little more work outside with your trucks tomorrow, okay?"

"Yup. G'night."

"Goodnight, son."

"Daddy . . ."

"Yes."

"You be sure to leave the night light on, okay. Because I'm afraid of the dark, you know."

Luke said it with such a stern, serious expression, that Clint had to leave quickly to control his laughter.

From the <u>St. Johnsbury Journal</u>, September 4, 1970:

Authorities in charge of the search for five-year-old Rodney Congdon are very anxious that anyone who was in the Lyndon State Forest district on August 27 contact State's Attorney James Duzak. Those conducting the investigation are very anxious that any hikers, campers, or residents who have any information should at this time make it known.

15. WORRIES

After a quick lunch at the drugstore, Clint Whitcome stopped at Billy Newton's place on the way home.

Clint had started work at five that morning, plowing the roads to make them safe for school buses, parents, and early-morning commuters. By noon he was tired and feeling weak, fearing his first cold of the season. But his mind was racing, uncomfortable thoughts spinning violently in his head. Because of his confusion he couldn't tell exactly what was bothering him.

In spite of his fatigue, he was not relaxed. He was on edge, keyed-up from so many hours on Antrim's snowy roads. In his mind, Clint could still hear the metallic grind of his plow on the surface of the road, see the massive wave of snow churning to the roadside in the plow's wake. He had nailed Mrs. Perkins's mailbox again this year, sent it sailing into the bushes like a surfer riding a tidal wave. And again, just like last winter, he could expect a call from the town manager—something else to worry about.

He was in the mood for some conversation, and he knew he owed Billy an explanation about why he'd never looked in on Perly Greer. Yes, a good talk might help calm him down before he went home. He always felt good after a visit with Billy.

Because it was a work day for most of his cohorts, Billy Newton was alone in the garage. A quick smile announced his delight at seeing Clint. Billy's tone of voice, however, would never betray that he was happy to see anyone.

"How's it goin', Clint?" was the greeting delivered from his position on a stool behind the workbench. Pieces of a disassembled transmission were arranged like chessmen in front of him.

"Wha'd'ya say, Billy."

The mechanic stood up and hobbled stiffly to his chaise longue beside the stove. He pushed his cap back on his head, exposing a band of oily black grime around his brow.

"Come on in and set down. Like a shot?"

Clint thought for a moment, about to decline, then, "Best idea I've heard all day."

Billy placed the fifth on a wooden crate between them, then tossed a paper cup to Clint.

"Kinda surprised to see you at this hour. Bringin' me some repair work, are you?"

"Naw, on my way home. Been plowin'."

"Helluva storm, eh?"

"Gonna be a hell of a winter. Wanted to tell ya I never got a chance to check in on Perly for you. He been back to town, has he?"

"Ain't seen him. That ain't unusual, though. Prob'ly won't come out of hibernation till spring."

"I meant to get up there like I told you, but I've had the damnedest bunch of luck lately. One thing after another. I'll get up there, though, I promise you that, before the snow gets too deep."

"No big deal, Clint. I guess prob'ly it'll keep till spring. I don't know what I was so worried about. It's just that Perly ain't got nobody up there to look after him, I s'pose. That was his choice, though, there's no arguin' that."

The two men sat in silence, sipping their rye. Clint's eyes darted nervously around the garage, his foot tapped rapidly in time to an unheard beat. Finally he blurted out, "Weird fuckin' stuff goin' on up to my place."

Billy responded with immediate concern. He leaned forward in his seat, silently encouraging Clint to continue.

"Lemme ask you about it, Billy. Maybe you can make some sense of it."

"You go right ahead. Just help yourself to the bottle there, when you want to."

"Well, the day before Thanksgiving, when I was headed up to see Perly, I got off a shot at what I thought was a turkey. Somethin' ran out of the bushes and into the woods, but it weren't no turkey. More'n anything else it looked like somebody's kid. I thought I'd winged a kid sure as hell. Got Dick Bates in on it. The both of us looked around, but we didn't find nothin' but fur."

"And you ain't heard nothin' since?"

"Nothing."

"Well, I guess you didn't shoot no kid . . ."

"But that ain't all. Me an' the wife's cousin—he's stayin' with us for a while—we was goin' up to look at that old root cellar on the top of the hill, and we found my kid's dog. He was tied to a tree, dead. Somebody tore him up, Billy. Done a hell of a job on him. That's why I got to thinkin' when you said Perly didn't have his dog with him. I wondered if somebody's killin' dogs around here. I mean, I can see it if they're runnin' deer or something. I've shot a couple myself. But Christ, they'd tied Rusty to a tree. He wasn't runnin' nothin'. Never did, far as I know.

"Then, yesterday, I found somebody'd written something on my barn. Carved it right in with a knife."

"What was that?"

" 'An I for an I.' "

" 'An eye for an eye'?"

"They spelt it capital 'I,' not like E-Y-E."

"That's passin' strange." A look of deep concentration covered the mechanic's whiskered face. "Sounds to me like you got somebody after you. You got somebody pissed off at you?"

"I gave that some thought. Somebody's always pissed about somethin'. I had to fire a guy at work a couple months back. Lou Bennett. Lou'd never kill a dog. I can't believe he would, anyway. I can't make no sense of it, Billy."

"A crazy man don't make no sense. I had a guy once worked for me over to the shop in Springfield. Had to let him go, drinkin' on the job. Son of a bitch brung vodka to work in his thermos. I fired him after he stumbled into me, almost knocked me into a band saw. Told him to take his toolbox and punch out. Next night he come over here—prob'ly really tied one on—anyway, he stands right out there on the road and chucks every one of his wrenches through every one of my windows. Didn't miss a one. Son of a bitch."

"Lou Bennett'd never do nothin' like that. If somebody's got it in for me, I can't figure who. It's kinda scary."

"'Course it is. And I'll bet your mind rests easier knowin' that fella's up there to look after Pam and Luke when you ain't to home."

"I guess so. Eric's a pretty good man. But he's having a time. Lost his wife a while back."

"So I heard. He's a college teacher, right?"

Clint nodded.

"You get along with him okay?"

"Oh hell, yes. Sometimes we ain't got too much to talk about, though. Know what I mean?"

"Tell me somethin', any of this funny stuff go on before he showed up?"

Clint bolted up straight. "Hold it there, Billy. Eric's family. He wouldn't do nothin' crazy like I been talkin' about."

"I ain't sayin' he would. But did ya ever stop to think maybe somebody's out to get him?"

Clint thought it over.

"Naw. What's it to him if my dog gets killed?"

"I'm just supposin'. Somebody pissed at your wife?"

"Naw. I think we're headed in the wrong direction, Billy."

"Mebbe so." The mechanic rubbed his head, the green cap sliding back and forth on his scalp. "Anything else goin' on?"

"Just the stuff with the root cellar. I told you about that guy from the historical society out of Montpelier. He's all fired up about the root cellar. He was up there lookin' it over, yesterday and again today. I seen his car while I was plowin'."

"I still can't see what's the big deal with that root cellar."

"I don't know. Can't say it makes much difference to me how old the place is."

"Me neither, if you want the truth. People are always dreamin' up all kinds of crazy things. As if there weren't already enough foolishness in this world . . ." Billy seemed to want to say more. Instead, he returned to the topic at hand. "Looks to me like you got yourself a puzzle, my friend. I'll do some thinkin' on it. Ask some of the boys, see what I can find out."

"I'd appreciate it, Billy. I guess all this stuff, back to back with Justin Hurd's disappearance, makes me feel kinda, well . . . nervous." Clint crushed his empty cup and tossed it toward the kindling pile. "Anyway, I'll get up there to check on Perly for you pretty quick. That's a promise."

"Mind doin' me another favor while you're at it?"

"Sure thing."

Billy hobbled over to his workbench and brought out the silver flask that he'd found tucked into the seat of his truck. "Perly left this here one time and he ain't been back to pick it up. Mind givin' it to him? I'll fill her up for you to take along when you go."

"I'll be glad to take it to him. But I'll take it empty. If I drink any more I'm afraid I'll fall asleep." Clint put the flask in his jacket pocket.

Billy smiled. "I thank you, Clint. My best to the missus and to the little fella."

Clint slipped out of the garage through a narrow slit in the door, trying not to let the heat leave with him. He quickly slid the door shut behind him.

Chief Bates was walking from his station wagon toward the garage. Both men nodded a greeting. For an instant Clint thought he should tell Bates about the writing on his barn. Then he thought better of it. He'd been bothering the policeman too much lately. Bates had more important things to think about.

"How's it goin', Dick?"

"Same old shit."

What was said by way of greeting was simple and informal. What was meant was clear to both men: Anything new on Justin Hurd?

No, nothing.

Nothing at all.

. . .

On his way home, Clint was surprised to see Carl Sayer's snow-covered Toyota still parked at the turnoff near the trail that led to the root cellar. He had noticed it that morning while plowing. Could Sayer have camped out at the site? No, Clint didn't figure Sayer for the type to camp out, even in good weather. In fact, he seemed to remember Eric saying that Sayer had taken a room at the inn.

Concerned, Clint pulled his truck up behind Sayer's car. He noted the accumulation of undisturbed snow on and around the vehicle.

"Ah, shit, I suppose I'd better have a look," he said wearily. He climbed down from the truck, checked the Toyota, and plodded through the foot-high snow into the woods.

Under the protection of the evergreens the snow was not so deep. It was piled thickly on the branches and tumbled at the slightest touch, sending icy dampness under Clint's collar and down his back.

Even at three o'clock in the afternoon it was beginning to get dark. Snow sparkled in the dim afternoon light. Hardwood trees, black and abrupt in contrast to the white ground, grew closer and closer together as Clint made progress up the mountainside. The slope grew steeper; the effort of climbing in his heavy boots reminded Clint of how weary he felt. His legs ached more with each step. The white uniformity hid familiar landmarks, making him pause frequently to seek his direction. He watched the ground for tracks, hoping to see indications of where Sayer might have walked.

Hadn't Eric warned the man to be careful in the woods? He shouldn't blame Eric. Anything could have happened. Possibly Sayer had made his way out of the woods yesterday afternoon, only to find that his car wouldn't start. He might have hitchhiked back to town. Clint feared his climb up the mountain would turn out to be a waste of time.

Still, Clint felt a sense of responsibility. It was his property and he'd given the man permission to visit the root cellar. Clint had thought the directional markings back to the road were adequate.

All Sayer would have to do was walk downhill, following the markers until he came to the road, then follow the road to his car. Should be simple enough, even for a city fella. Could Sayer have gotten himself lost? Maybe he had tried to find similar stone structures nearby, even though Eric certainly would have assured him that there were none.

God damn it, thought Clint, always something to worry about lately. He remembered the one thing he hadn't discussed with Billy. It was a tiny, nagging uncertainty that was underlying all the concerns he had discussed. Perhaps it was the center of the uneasy thoughts that had been rattling around inside his head all morning. Perhaps it was nothing at all. Just a dream, like he'd told his son.

Still, it was unnerving to think that Eric might have been at Luke's bedroom window. It was impossible, of course. There was nothing but a twelve-foot drop out there. If Luke hadn't been dreaming, what he must have seen would have to have been an optical illusion: Eric's reflection in the dark glass. And for his reflection to have been there, he must have been in the boy's room. Why? What could he want there?

Billy's question echoed in Clint's ears: ". . . any of this funny stuff go on before he showed up?"

Naw, thought Clint, this is foolishness. I'm thinkin' funny because I'm tired. I'm gettin' suspicious, and suspicion's just like a truck skidding on ice. Once it gets started, you can't stop it, can't control it, and there's no tellin' where it'll end up with you when it's done.

No. Luke was dreamin' and I'm dreamin'. There's nothin' to worry about. Nothin' at all.

Except Sayer.

Looking around to get his bearings, Clint began to feel a little lost. He suddenly became fearful that the way out of the woods was not as simple as Eric might have led Sayer to believe. Clint started to move more rapidly, oblivious to the throbbing in his leg muscles.

His fatigue reasserted itself when he started to feel as if the surrounding trees were closing in on him. Their black trunks, like

dark-uniformed soldiers of an enemy army, seemed to move toward him, crowding him, making him feel an inexplicable urgency
to get away.

He had never felt claustrophobic in the woods before. The new
feeling was uncomfortable. He took a deep, cold breath, trying to
calm himself.

Watching the surface of the snow for a trail to follow, he moved
steadily upward, tripping over logs and stones hidden beneath the
blanket of white. His boots felt as if they weighed ten pounds each,
and the cramps of protest in his tired legs slowed his progress.

"What's goin' on?" Clint muttered, realizing that he was genuinely frightened for no good reason. He wanted to call out to
Sayer, but something locked the cry in his throat. He felt dis-
oriented—as if the clear and darkening mountain air were a sheet
of nearly transparent glass that was bending, distorting everything
around him. The features of the surrounding woods seemed unreal, unfamiliar. He had been here many times before, but somehow he didn't know the place at all. Clint looked around in confusion, his eyes scanning the bushes and trees, peering at stones and
logs as if searching for an unseen enemy.

Then he remembered the trees he had marked for Eric. Those
marks could help him now. To his left his searching eyes found a
white notch in the trunk of an ancient oak. Beside it a smaller oak
was marked as well. Quickly scanning tree after tree, he saw that
many were notched, pointing to trails in random directions.

I never made all those marks, he thought.

A rustling sound behind him!

He spun to face the noise. Again he heard something to his left,
and his eyes flashed to the source. He saw nothing.

An all-encompassing fear settled over him like a falling shroud.
Everything around him appeared menacing, strange. The white
earth, the black trunks, the evil cobweb of branches intertwined
above his head, all seemed designed to trap him in a sinister net. A
chill wind was beginning to blow. It whined in the treetops and
rustled the snow-laden branches above his head.

All his life he had been at home in the woods, but now he was a stranger, his woods an alien landscape. It was almost as if the army of trees had done something to Sayer, something frightening, and were now planning to turn their attention to Clint.

Clint Whitcome had never felt like a coward in his life, but now, for the first time, something in him, some subtle, long-buried instinct told him to run, to get away. Quickly.

The force of this sudden intuition allowed no time for thought or analysis. He bolted, mindless of the pain in his legs, mindless of his heavy boots and the resistance of the ankle-deep snow. With no thought to direction, he forged to his right, kicking waves of snow out in front of him. Sounds filled the air and assaulted his ears— scrapings, scratchings, the creak of tree limbs moving in the windy air. The dying sun gave a blood-red cast to the snow, making tree trunks and their shadows inseparable in his hazy vision. Sweat covered his face. His hands in their leather gloves felt like dead things, useless attachments to his arms, weighing him down, slowing his progress. His heart pounded like the piston in an overworked engine, pumping blood that throbbed painfully in his temples. On either side he seemed to see motion in the underbrush, as if the bushes themselves were moving. Above him, tree limbs groaned and swayed. The icy wind seemed to grow teeth and tear at his face.

He had no idea where he was going, no idea why he ran. He forced his sore and tired body to escape some unseen threat, to find some unknown sanctuary.

Faster and faster he ran, until he almost collided with a man standing in his path. No, not standing—Clint looked up—the man was floating—no *hanging*—in his path.

Clint looked from the distorted face to the shoes suspended two feet off the ground. The grotesque vision was too complicated to take in all at once. Clint's mind fought to make sense of it.

The snow below the suspended man was dark, pitted, melted from the heat of the blood that dripped from the corpse. The face, eyeless and bloody, was contorted in a grimace of agony and horror. A length of barbed wire tied the body to the branch of a maple tree. The end fastened to the neck was lost in a crimson cavity.

And he was naked! The man was naked except for his shoes and socks. He turned slowly to the left and right, dripping blood from the long, clumsy wound that started at his collarbone and divided his chest and abdomen to the indistinct point where it stopped, perhaps just above his genitals.

A smashed 35mm camera, the film trailing like a flattened intestine, was buried in the wound.

Clint staggered back a couple of steps. He felt his gorge rising and struggled not to vomit. Somehow, it seemed vitally important for him to determine if, under the mess of entrails, blood, and feces that collected between the man's legs, the genitals were still intact. Pondering the question seemed important to him only because it allowed him not to think about the identity of the hanged man.

He had seen the face before. It was on one of the pages in Eric's photocopied booklet. The glasses, more than anything else, identified the man. Their thick lenses, strangely clean, had been placed over the gouged-out eyes and sparkled like crystal eggs in a nest of gore.

Sayer's face! The bald head was unmistakable. It hit Clint like a jolt of electricity. Sayer!

Clint whirled and ran again, thinking only of his own safety. Billy Newton's words blasted around in his head. "Sounds to me like you got somebody after you . . . after you . . . after you."

He crashed through the woods as the trees and shadows blended into a chill twilight. His boots, anchors on his feet, slogged through the thick snow as if it were mud. Clouds of steam billowed from his mouth and nostrils, sweat froze on his brow, blurring his vision. Whiplike branches snapped at his face; his heart pounded viciously against the inside of his chest. A cramp stabbed at his right side, making him bend and run awkwardly.

In his frantic memory, the image of Perly's cabin moved in and out of focus. Was he heading in the right direction? He didn't know. Nothing around him seemed familiar. As the darkness deepened he had no hope of spotting landmarks.

He thought he heard sounds on either side of him. And from behind. He couldn't concentrate on them, couldn't make them clear. He just wanted to get away from them, get to Perly's cabin, get home to Pam, to Luke.

Somehow he found more speed. He used it to mount a little ridge that appeared before him, thinking that from its summit he could see the road, or perhaps the cabin.

It was too late to stop. He had gathered too much momentum. The ground crumbled under his feet. Clint waved his arms helplessly, trying to maintain balance. But there was no way to stop, nothing to grab. He gave a powerful thrust with his legs, hoping to get a hold on the other side, but the opening was too wide. Hands grasping air, feet pedaling frantically for purchase, he passed the edge of the hole. And suddenly he was falling . . .

16. MEALTIME

"I think it's about time I was heading back to New York," said Eric Nolan, helping himself to a Black Label from the refrigerator. He sat down across the table from Pamela where she was deboning pieces of chicken.

She looked surprised. "Jeez, Eric, you just arrived. You haven't even been here two weeks. You can't be thinking about going back already."

"I have to go back sometime." He took a swig from the bottle. "I appreciate everything you and Clint are doing for me, but I'm beginning to realize that I can't turn mourning Karen into my life's work."

Pamela seemed a little hurt. A weak smile flexed the corners of her lips.

Eric let the words come. He wanted to say everything that was on his mind. "Listen Pam. I don't want to overstay my welcome. It must be a strain; I know I'm not the best company . . ."

Pamela shook her head. "Eric, please, you're more than welcome here. We want you to be comfortable. Clint and I both. And Lukey loves you."

"That's just it. I'm afraid of getting too comfortable. This is your house, not mine. And your family. I have pieces of a life to put back together on the Island."

"Pieces of your life are here, too."

"I know that, Pam. Since coming here I've felt better than I have in months. I feel stronger now; you've helped me feel that way."

"We were hoping you'd stay at least until Christmas. We don't want you to be alone during the holidays."

"That's good of you, Pam. More than generous. But I've got responsibilities. I've got a job to go back to, my book to work on. I've got to start facing up to things."

She smiled at him, brushing red hair from over her eye with the side of her hand. "I suppose I should say, 'that's good.' And if you're really and truly feeling up to it, that's fine. But if you want to leave because you think you're an imposition on Clint and me, then you're still not thinking too straight. You are welcome here. We enjoy having you with us. We'd all be pleased if you could stay at least until Christmas. Maybe get a fresh start with the new year."

Eric thought it over, challenging his decision to leave. Was he really feeling better, or did he simply want to run again?

No. There was no reason to run. He was essentially happy here. Yet other emotions complicated the picture. He envied the Whitcomes. Never in his life had he experienced the kind of happiness he witnessed here. He was jealous of it.

If he was honest with himself he had to admit that he didn't want to leave at all—he just wanted to hear Pamela ask him to stay. With the realization came anger; how could he be capable of such ignoble emotions?

Eric finished the bottle of beer. He turned it around in his hands, studying the opening in the top. His eyes drifted to Luke, who was sitting on the floor by the stove playing with his Star Wars figures. The boy was stuffing the little men into the back of a toy trailer-truck that he used as a spacecraft.

"I'd like to be with you folks at Christmas. That would be great. Maybe what I'll do is go to New York, try it for a week or two. Then I'll come back for the twenty-fifth."

Luke looked up at the adults. "I'm hungry, can I have a san'wich?"

"It's almost suppertime. Your daddy will be here any minute. Don't you want to wait and eat supper with him?" Pamela looked at her watch.

"Okay. But I'm gonna be real hungry." Singing contentedly, Luke returned his attention to Darth Vader.

Eric looked at his watch, too. It was after six. "Clint's put in a full day today."

"He'll be dead tired when he gets home. He probably ended up with all the plowing himself. That happened to him once last winter. Both guys that work for him were sick and we got a huge snowstorm. He worked all night, came home and slept until noon, then went back out."

"He's a hard worker."

"He is, but he loves it. He loves this town. The only reason he wants to work for State Highways is for the money. But I bet he never makes the change." Pamela rolled the chicken in batter, then placed the pieces in an oval platter of bread crumbs. "Do you want a snack while you're waiting?"

"Like what?" said Luke.

"Not you, Glutton," said Pamela, "I'm talking to Uncle Eric."

"No thanks, I'll wait for Clint." Eric winked at Pamela.

"I'll wait for Clint, too," Luke said grandly, pushing the space truck across the pine floor and to a galaxy far away.

The adults laughed, but Eric caught Pamela stealing another glance at her watch.

At seven o'clock, she fixed a peanut butter and banana sandwich for Luke, which he ate with ravenous appetite. He washed it down with a big glass of milk. At eight o'clock, she put her son to bed and joined Eric in the living room, where he was building a fire in the fireplace and working on another bottle of beer.

"Can I cook you a piece of chicken?" she asked.

"Aren't you hungry?"

"I don't know. I don't think so." Eric could see that his cousin had become quite nervous. He had been watching it build for some time, and marveled at how well she had concealed it in front of the boy.

"Why don't you let me cook the chicken," Eric offered.

"No thanks. Let's wait a bit longer. I'm going to call the garage."

She went to the phone in the kitchen, hesitated, and dialed. She stood with the phone at her ear for a long time, then came back and took her place by the fire.

"No one answers at the garage. That means Clint's on the way home, or he's the only one working."

"Can't you call one of the other men at home?"

"Clint wouldn't like me to do that. He wouldn't want them to think he was married to the kind of woman who'd check up on him. And I wouldn't want Clint to think he was." Pamela was a strong woman, and Eric admired her. Perhaps her deep concern for her family could be traced back to her parents' divorce. Eric knew she'd work hard to keep her own family happy. He wished he could help.

A little after nine o'clock, Pamela broke a long silence and finally admitted to Eric, very emphatically, that she was worried.

"Would you like me to take a drive into town to see if I can spot him?" He didn't know what else to offer.

"Would you?" She thought a moment. "No. That wouldn't be good. You shouldn't be out on those roads, they're too dangerous. Besides, I'd rather have you here so I won't have to wait alone. I don't want to have to worry about both of you."

She wandered to the window and Eric followed. Together they watched the heavy snowflakes fall, almost horizontally, across the light on the garage.

In his bedroom Luke Whitcome stared at the night light on his dresser. It was a small, chubby balloon man. When it was lit the balloons glowed with warm colors.

Luke couldn't understand why his father was not home. Mommy'd said Daddy would be home for supper, but when she made him the sandwich, he knew that that wasn't true. Could it be that Daddy wasn't coming home? When Daddy was going to be late Mommy usually knew it and explained, and sure enough, Daddy would come along just when Luke thought he couldn't go another minute without eating. When Mommy put him to bed she'd said, "Now you go right to sleep and when Daddy gets home I'll send him up to tuck you in, okay?"

"When's he coming?"

"I think he's going to be late tonight, honey." Luke could see that his mother looked a little strange when she said this, like the time she tried to explain to him about Rusty—only Rusty never came home.

Luke listened real hard, hoping to hear the roar of his father's truck in the yard, the stomp of his snow-covered boots on the porch, the sound of his voice in the living room below. Several times he drifted off into a light sleep and heard his father walking up the stairs to tuck him in, but then he'd wake up a little bit only to find he'd been dreaming.

Luke began to feel kind of afraid and a little lonely. He crawled out of bed and tiptoed into his parents' room and over to the window. From there he could look out at the yard and at Tenny's Hill Road. There was nothing to see in the moonlight, nothing but the dark, thick woods and the big snowflakes that fell, white as teeth, in the bright porch light below.

After a while he returned to his bedroom, stopping briefly at his own window. Outside the night made everything seem far away and hidden. When he got into bed he was cold. He pulled the blankets around him and curled into a tight little ball. He hugged Philip the monkey snugly to his chest.

Maybe tomorrow he and Uncle Eric would build a snowman. Luke wondered what the snowman would look like, but all he could picture was his father, standing very still, snow falling all around him, covering him, making him look all white and cold and funny.

The vision of his father was so real that it frightened Luke a little. He rolled over and looked at the dark glass of his window. Maybe Uncle Eric would look in at him again. Maybe he could ask Uncle Eric about Daddy.

He fell asleep staring at the window, waiting for his uncle to tell him that everything was all right.

At eleven o'clock Pamela, with great hesitation, decided to call the police.

17. OLD STORIES

When the telephone rang at a little after eleven, Chief Bates answered it on the second ring, pausing only to clean the last of a piece of apple pie from his mouth by washing it down with a large swallow of milk. The late phone call really didn't bother him since he hadn't been to bed anyway; why bother, he knew he wouldn't be able to sleep. Too many things were going on to allow him to get the kind of night's rest that would clear the fog from his brain and restore the color to his pallid cheeks.

Lately, in the nightly absence of sleep, he relied more and more on eating to keep his energy level up. The consequence of many sleepless nights showed mostly in his dark-circled eyes and his ever-expanding waistline.

When he arrived at the Whitcome house it was a little after midnight. Normally the short drive would have taken only fifteen to twenty minutes, but snow had piled up heavily on the secondary roads. Under the circumstances, though, Bates thought it better not to delay until they were cleared. His station wagon inched along Tenny's Hill Road, fighting the onslaught of white flakes with its wipers and fish-tailing dangerously from side to side. His new studded snow tires fought for purchase, keeping him out of the gutters and heading in the right direction.

If anyone else had called him for a missing person in the middle of the night, he probably would have offered a few reassuring words over the phone and encouraged the caller to wait until morning. When Pamela Whitcome phoned, Bates had come at once. Clint was a friend of his, almost like another cop, working for the town and all. And Bates had uncomfortable memories about the last cop, Justin Hurd, who had vanished in the same general area less than two weeks ago. Perhaps there was cause for alarm. Better to be safe . . .

Eric Nolan and Pamela Whitcome met the policeman at the door. They stood close together under the pale, harsh glow of the porch light. Right away Bates saw that Pamela's eyes were red-rimmed and the skin of her nose was slightly irritated. She had a wad of tissues in her hand.

He watched as she braced her shoulders to greet him. Standing beside her, Nolan appeared ill at ease, awkward in the situation. He seemed unsure whether to stand with his arm around Mrs. Whitcome or to remain at a proper distance until he got some indication of how to fit into the scene that was taking place around him.

Moving rapidly out of the cold, the three people took seats around the kitchen table. Pamela offered coffee, which Bates gratefully accepted. He hoped she would offer something to eat.

After he had gathered routine information about Clint's scheduled activities for the day, Bates's attitude became less formal. "Now Pam, I know how worrisome something like this can be, but I've known Clint a good long time. Christ, him and me were in 4-H and FFA together back in junior high school! He's a responsible man, and a man who can take care of himself. I know how you're feeling right now, but, in my professional judgment, it's a little too soon to be really worried."

"I know Clint pretty well too, Dick. He is responsible, no doubt about it. That's why I can't understand why he hasn't at least called. It's not like him. Not at all. He tries never to worry me."

"Well, tomorrow we're going to find that he has a good reason, even though none of us can guess what it is right now. Officially, we can't report him as a missing person for forty-eight hours, and I betcha he'll be right back here at home before he's officially missing."

"Can't we go out and look for him?"

"Well, of course we can, Mr. Nolan. But he'll be a lot easier to find come mornin'. I know that's not real comforting to hear, but if the three of us head out now we could all get ourselves lost out there, between the darkness and the snowstorm. When I go back I'll check the town garage for his truck, maybe drive around a little, see if he's off the road somewhere. Pretty easy to do in this weather. Maybe I'll even make a few phone calls."

"Phone calls?"

Right away Bates realized his mistake. "Just to be certain," he said noncommittally.

"You mean hospitals, don't you?"

"Well, sure. It's just routine. Let's eliminate them right off quick. Then I'll call the men he works with, John Royce and that other fella."

Eric Nolan spoke up, "Is there anything at all we can do tonight?"

"My advice is to try to get some rest, and leave the other stuff to me. I know how hollow that sounds, but you'll need a lot of energy tomorrow 'cause I'm gonna be right back here just as soon as I finish my breakfast. We'll find Clint, and all of us will probably have a good laugh at whatever mischief he's got himself into. Meantime I think you should keep things as normal as you can for the little fella. No point in getting the lad all upset. I got a boy about the same age to home. Mark, his name is. Believe me, I know how important it is to keep things normal for the young ones."

"I'll try," Pamela said.

"And you can be sure I'll let you know on the double if I hear anything. Okay?"

"Okay. Thanks for coming out, Dick. I'll call you if we hear anything."

"Okee-doke. Now you folks get on to bed. Good meetin' you, Mr. Nolan."

Chief Bates drove home slowly, watching both sides of the road and keeping an eye peeled for car lights or people on foot. He radioed the state police and put in an inquiry, asking them to contact the hospitals.

He had an uneasy feeling. Reaching up under his sweatshirt, he scratched his soft stomach. There was something specific about all this that bothered him. Perhaps it was the lateness of the hour, perhaps the apparent inconsistency with Clint's normal behavior. Perhaps it was the comforting words he had said to Mrs. Whitcome—words he didn't really believe. Bates wanted to call it instinct, more than uneasiness.

He'd always said there was a place for the irrational in police work; most good cops had hunches. Perhaps what Bates called his "hunches" were nothing more than experience—using the collected memories of years of police work unconsciously to evaluate the present situation, checking evidence against a storehouse of subliminally catalogued facts and data.

Whatever the explanation, Bates somehow knew that things were not as optimistic as he had led Mrs. Whitcome to believe.

In the dark cruiser, the wipers working like twin flyrods, Bates thought of old legends, stories he had heard as a child. The whole area of Pinnacle Mountain had always been a setting for ghost stories whispered around the campfire, or tall tales shared among drinking buddies at deer camp. Bates guessed that every town had its haunted house or cursed acre. People seemed to take pride in superstition.

But why think of it now? It had nothing to do with police work.

His most recent conversations with Clint, when taken all together, were rather unsettling: the business with the shooting in the woods; the dead dog; what Billy Newton had told him about the writing on Whitcomes' barn. Why hadn't Pamela, or Clint himself, mentioned the writing? It did, after all, sound like a warning—or a threat. And now Clint was missing. And Justin Hurd was missing. And all this shit was going down in the same general locale—territory for which Bates was responsible.

In the morning I'll have a look at that message on the barn in broad daylight, he decided.

Chief Bates checked off all the people in the picture, one at a time. When he got to Eric Nolan he stopped. He couldn't go any further. Was it instinct again?

Skidding on a patch of tightly packed snow, his car slid toward the edge of Old Factory Road. Skillfully, hands slapping the wheel, he regained control. Almost immediately he noticed what he had missed during his hasty drive to the Whitcomes'. A town truck and a car were parked together on the turnoff near where Old Town and Tenny's Hill roads intersected with Old Factory. The vehicles were far enough off the road to have been easily overlooked. They were coated heavily with snow, which blunted their plastic reflectors, making them nearly invisible. He pulled over, the blue light on his cruiser blinking on and off, turning the snow from white to blue.

Bates got out of his car, flashlight in hand, and examined the area around the abandoned vehicles. He wasn't certain what he was looking for. Snowflakes fell, diffusing the beam of his flashlight as he moved it among the dark trunks of snow-laden trees. Everywhere tiny crystals flashed like diamonds.

After clearing away the snow that had built up on both driver-side windows, he flashed his light around the interiors of each machine. He was certain this was the truck that Clint drove; there was a lunch pail and a thermos on the seat. Inside the Toyota he saw a briefcase.

Bates noticed footprints, nearly filled with snow. They led from the truck to the car, and then into the woods. He could tell that only one man had left the tracks.

He followed the nearly invisible footprints of the truck driver for about twenty yards. The woods were dark; they'd be dangerous at night. Bates decided not to continue. With each step he was persistently aware of the disappearance of his fellow officer, whose cruiser had been found not far from this spot. Bates felt a flicker of fear. The old stories came back to his mind, lurking shadows, hunting for little-boy fears that hid among his rational thoughts. He looked around at the deep forest, kicked at the knee-deep snow.

Without a snow machine, or at least snowshoes, without a trained and reliable backup, it would be crazy to go deeper into the woods. Footprints, by themselves, proved nothing. To follow would be a gamble, a risk. It would be foolish.

Returning to the warmth of the police car, he radioed his discovery to the state boys and asked for a registration check on the

Toyota. It belonged to a man named Carl Sayer from Duxbury, a stranger. Suddenly Bates's curiosity peaked. His mind began to race. Groundless theories piled on top of one another.

When he looked at his watch, he saw it would be another five hours until light. There would be a lot of work to do in the morning. In his present state of mind, going home to bed was out of the question. Instead, he decided to go straight to the office. He never had any trouble sleeping at his desk.

Pamela made hot chocolate with brandy in it, and they sat side by side on the sofa, sipping the steaming, sweet-smelling liquid. They didn't speak for a long time. Each was wrapped tightly in private thoughts, each feared saying something that might upset the other. They had agreed, without discussion, to try to relax enough to get at least part of a night's sleep.

Eric, now more aware of Pamela's situation than his own, knew very well what she was going through. The uncertainty must be maddening. When Karen had been killed at least it was final; there was no room for doubt. He thought of the investigator with the loud voice and the thick, prematurely gray hair who had interviewed him at the Long Island Railroad office. The man's face had showed a touching sympathy, but he had had no consoling words to offer. After the interview Eric watched the man struggle to end on an informal note, to try to make human contact. "Sometimes these things happen," the man said helplessly. "It's crazy, but they do. I'm sorry."

What else could he have said? What else can anyone say in the event of death, natural or accidental? But when somebody vanishes, what the hell can you say then?

Eric placed his mug of cocoa on the coffee table and put his arm around his cousin. In a graceful, fluid motion Pamela put her mug beside his and buried her face against his chest. She sobbed quietly and Eric felt the fabric of his shirt dampen with her tears.

"I'm being so weak," she said softly, her voice muffled by his clothing. "Clint would be ashamed of the way I'm acting."

"No," he said gently, stroking her hair, "No you're not. You're worried about your husband. That's not weak."

He remembered the times when they were young, the experimental embraces that had threatened to go a little beyond proper affection between cousins. Recalling the fragrance of her hair, the softness of her breast, he became angry at himself, forced the sensual thoughts from his mind.

"He's such a good man," she said, more to herself than to Eric. "This is so unlike him. I know there's something wrong. I'm sure of it. If he was okay, he'd be home by now."

"Come on, Pam, you don't know that. A million things could have happened. He might still be working, for all we know." Eric knew he wasn't making much sense, that there wasn't much substance to anything he said, but at the moment poor conversation seemed safer than silence.

"He would have called."

"Pam, we don't even know if the phones were working after the storm. Maybe he tried to call. Please try to relax. The policeman was right. There's not much we can do until morning."

"I know. But I'm scared, Eric. I keep thinking of that policeman who disappeared two weeks ago. It happened right near here, too, you know. Two disappearances in less than a month seems a little weird."

"Clint hasn't disappeared . . ."

"Then how come he's not here?" She bolted upright on the couch, her Irish temper flashing in her eyes, then fading just as suddenly. She took his hand in both of hers. "I'm sorry, Eric. I'm sorry. It's just that I'm so nervous. You can't imagine how scary it is living up here after hearing about Justin Hurd disappearing, and not knowing what happened to him. Clint told me how they found his police car down near the foot of the hill, but no sign of him. Nothing. Not a clue.

"I know Clint would hate to leave Luke and me alone up here if it weren't for you. Thank God you're here with us. But still I keep Luke real close by. And I'll continue to until I know what's going on. It's scary. Real scary. And not the kind of scary you probably feel in the city. It's a scariness that reminds you how alone you are —how alone we are, way the heck up here in the middle of nowhere, so far away from help. It's like when you were a kid and afraid of the dark, and you don't know just why, or just what it is you're afraid of. But you know you're afraid.

"Then you become an adult and it's different, because you know, you honestly know, that there is something to be afraid of. There really is, Eric! There's crazy people, and animals, and weird cults, and all kinds of horrible, awful things going on." She cried harder, her words tinged with hysteria. "I don't know what, but there's something out there, Eric. Something terrible. It's as if the night itself is hungry. Waiting. Looking for a chance to devour us."

Pamela was talking through convulsive sobs, choking out her words. "Oh I don't know why people have to disappear around here . . . I just don't know. What's happening to us, Eric?"

Eric held his cousin closely, listening to her cry like a frightened child. "We'll find Clint . . ."

She ripped herself away. "We never found your brother, did we?" The Irish temper again.

Stunned, Eric realized that it was true. He hadn't associated Brian with what was going on here. How could he have been so obtuse?

They stared at each other, then they embraced with great strength and tenderness. "I'm sorry Eric, I'm so sorry," Pamela cried, her tears falling and vanishing like tiny quantities of hope.

18. SWALLOWS

For a long time he didn't know where he was.

Waking had been a gradual process. First there was a localized sensation of discomfort, as if he'd been lying on his arm for too long and it had gone to sleep. The prickly feeling spread over his chest slowly, like a thick, bubbling oil, until it was joined by an uncomfortable awareness of cold. This he experienced for some time before it occurred to him to open his eyes. That was his first mistake. When he opened them the lids fluttered involuntarily and the headache struck like a hammer blow to the skull.

Initially he couldn't see anything. His first thought was that he was waking in the middle of the night in his bedroom, suffering from a killer hangover. Then random memories began to assert themselves and he knew he wasn't at home.

He had no sense of time or place.

Again he closed his eyes and felt a small relief from the persistent pain that made the back of his neck feel as if it were squeezed in a clamp. Testing the extent of his discomfort, he opened and closed his fists a few times, then moved his arms to his sides and tried to position them to help him sit up. He found his legs were lending no assistance.

His eyes opened wide in alarm, mindless of the resulting pain. He tried to look down at his body, staring in the direction of his feet until his vision cleared.

It was difficult to see. Clammy darkness pressed against him like a wet sponge. Tilting back his head, he looked above him. He could see the winter moon, a frosted mirror in the sky far above.

The opening through which he looked was an oval frame around the mirror. It was shaped like an eye with the moon in its center.

He remembered falling. Running and falling. And he remembered, oddly, how his cry had disturbed a group of bats. They flew up around him as he fell, brushing his skin like dry leaves. He remembered the noisy flutter of their leathery wings, and how, at first, for some strange reason, he had mistaken them for swallows.

He forced himself to study his situation. Concentration brought back a clarity of thought as his predicament came into focus. He had fallen into a hole, perhaps a cave or a well that burrowed deep into the earth. He was on his back below the opening, motionless, dreading the thought of trying his legs again.

With the power of his arms he was able to elevate his head and back a little more. In the dim light that found its way into the cave, he could make out the shadowy outline of his body. His left leg was straight; he could see the bulky form of the Sorel on his foot. His right leg was twisted in a grotesque way—it made a right angle at the knee—and the toe of his boot pointed at his face.

Reaching down to touch the mangled limb, he discovered he had no sensation there. He reached across and touched his left leg, pinched it hard, and felt nothing. Closing his eyes, he settled back into a horizontal position. He felt a helplessness, a frustration that pushed him close to tears. Cold sweat exploded from every pore.

My back's broken, he thought, close to panic. Dear God, I'm stuck here.

He lay that way for a moment, frozen in the horrible realization, not knowing whether to cry out or to remain motionless and quiet.

Trying to stay calm, he began to use what senses and mobility he had to survey his surroundings. With little effort, his arms and hands could explore a circle of about six feet. To his right, he felt only cold stones and dirt. On his left, his hand spidered along similar terrain until his fingers struck something soft. It was hair, or fur.

He withdrew his hand rapidly, turning his head to see what he had touched. There was a black, motionless mass beside him. With all the strength in his arms he inched himself a bit closer and cautiously reached out to touch the thing again. Some kind of animal, a deer, maybe, or a dog. No doubt it had made the same mistake, suffered the same fall, but surely it had not been as lucky. He tugged at the fur, and a clump of it came off in his hand in a stinking tuft. Whatever it was had been dead for a long time. How many similar unfortunates might surround him? He dreaded the thought of waiting until morning to find out.

Feeling a sudden exhaustion, he reclined again. The motion took the considerable pressure off his upper arms. His eyes returned to that awful gray eye above him, with its frost-white pupil moving imperceptibly to the left. When the moon passed across the opening he would be in utter darkness.

Perhaps it was fortunate that he was exhausted, too tired to release the panic that was forming in his nerves and muscles. Control, he thought, must keep in control.

He tested the environment with his other senses. First he listened, holding his breath and lying perfectly still. In the distance, plainly but softly, he heard what sounded like water dripping. There was a rhythmic ping of droplets striking the surface of a pool or puddle. That was all. He took a breath. The sound of air moving through his nostrils and the thumping of his own heart drowned out the dripping water. Above him, as if from the end of a long tunnel, he heard wind moving across the opening of the cave.

He sniffed the air, and the tangle of unfamiliar odors confused him. There was the damp, earthy smell of the cave itself, like the smell of his dirt basement at home, or the smell of the root cellar that he had shown to Eric. Mixed with it was the fetid odor of rotting flesh. How could he have ignored this smell before? It was overpowering, the smell of a slaughterhouse. Having noticed it, he was sure he could never grow accustomed to its foulness. He concluded with certainty that he and the animal beside him were not the only victims of the horrible trapdoor above. The floor of the cave was probably littered with victims, all in various stages of decay.

When the throbbing pain in his head had subsided to a dull irritation, he set his mind to making a plan. There was no point in shouting for help—no one would be in the woods at this hour. In fact, it could be a good long while before anyone passed near enough to the hole to hear him calling. The best thing he could do was to accept that he was stuck here and plan to stay a while. He would make himself as comfortable as possible while he waited. It would only be a matter of time before Pamela and Eric came looking for him. Perhaps they'd call Dick Bates for help. In either case, someone would see his truck and Sayer's car and would search the woods for them. But surely not until morning.

The thought of Sayer's corpse swinging on the wire like a puppet hanging on a string intruded on his planning process. If, right now, there was someone nearby in the woods, it was someone he didn't want to find him.

He began to shiver from cold, and from the fear that surrounded him like the fetid dampness. He fought to control his mind as it began to race. Stay calm, he told himself. Think. Plan.

How would he pass the time until he was found? He suspected that, with difficulty, he could drag himself around the floor of his prison. But even if he had the use of his legs, escape would be impossible without assistance. His impression was that the walls of the cave tapered inward toward the opening. Climbing would be out of the question. Unless there was another escape route, he would have no choice but to remain. That might be okay: there was water in the hole, and there might be food if any of the animal bodies were fresh enough to eat. He might even be able to build a fire. If so, he was uncertain if the draft would be sufficient to take the smoke up through the opening. There would be time to consider these things in the morning.

Looking up, he saw that only a sliver of the moon was visible on the edge of the opening. Soon it would be dark. Maybe the best thing to do right now was to rest, gain strength. He could take a better inventory of his chances for survival in whatever light the new day provided. Yes, rest. He felt so weak; his throbbing head was spinning like the blade of a saw.

A tapping at the window.

Luke tried to open his eyes but found that he couldn't. Groggily, he figured that he must still be asleep, and the tapping part of a dream.

Maybe not. Could Daddy have come home? Was he coming up the stairs to tuck Luke in?

Listening attentively, Luke felt funny—neither awake nor asleep. It was kind of like the time last winter when he had the mumps. Mommy kept putting that glass thing in his mouth. What was it called?

"Thermometer," a voice in his head told him.

That was right, a thermometer. Luke had had a fever and he kept seeing things above his bed, floating in the air, like balloons. He remembered liking them: clown faces and rabbits and dogs. But they had worried Mommy. She'd called the doctor and Luke had to keep taking those terrible-tasting, orange-colored aspirin.

The tapping again.

"Luke," the voice said. "Luke, open your eyes."

This time he could open them, so he was sure he was awake. The faint glow of his night light cast soft shadows in the room, its image reflected distinctly in the glass of his window. The night light seemed to be far out in the back yard, hovering over the snowy fields like the spaceship in *Close Encounters*.

Something was moving outside the glass! It seemed to be floating, like the face in Snow White's mirror. But it wasn't scary. It was like the fever-pictures. Somehow it was good to see the shape. It was familiar.

Luke could see, but not see, the face; hear, but not hear, the voice. He hoped he wasn't sick with the mumps again. But the other time he hadn't heard anything. This time he did. "Luke. I'm going back home, like I told your mother. Do you want to go with me?"

Luke tried to answer—Will Mommy and Daddy come?—but he couldn't.

"No. Just you and me. You and me . . . and Rusty."

Luke knew Rusty would come back, he just knew it. He'd guessed from the start that Uncle Eric would help find him. He wanted to ask where Rusty was, if Rusty was okay.

"Rusty's at my house. He misses you. He wonders why you don't come and play with him."

The night light's reflection seemed to dim. Uncle Eric's voice was getting softer and softer. Luke could see the outline of his uncle's mouth moving outside the window. The shadowy head bobbed like a bottle in the water.

Luke wanted to tell him to speak up, he couldn't hear.

"Come to the window, Lukey, you can hear me better."

The boy tried to get up. He couldn't. His muscles wouldn't work.

"We'll talk again, Luke. You'll get stronger. Maybe next time, when you're stronger, you can come see Rusty. He misses you, Luke. But he can't come to you. You must go to him. He misses you . . ."

The face was gone, the voice, silent. Luke's heavy eyelids closed and he slept without dreaming.

Clint awoke with a start, realizing he wasn't alone in the hole. Something dry and scratchy was inching its way across his right hand. His first thought was of the fleshy tail of a rat. Then he froze. A snake! God, he hoped it wasn't a timber rattler. With all his will he resisted the urge to yank his hand away.

Soon the movement stopped and the unseen creature slithered off into the blackness. A horrible realization came to him: he had no feeling in his legs. If it were a snake, it could crawl up under his cuff and settle near the warmth of his skin. He'd have to try to tie something—the laces from his boots—around his pants legs to prevent such a thing. With a great effort, he bound his cuffs to his senseless ankles. Relentless jolts of pain slowed the process. He didn't have the strength or dexterity to bind his pants tightly, but it would have to do.

When he lifted his head, he was surprised to find that it was not totally dark. The sky through the opening above was black as boot polish, but hovering about two or three feet above the floor of the cave was a blue-green incandescence. It glowed like a dull neon haze. It really didn't provide enough light to see by, but it kept him from being totally in the dark. It must be gas from the rotting bodies, he thought. Methane. He hoped it wouldn't hurt him.

His ears, sensitive to the silence, began to detect another sound besides the dripping water. It was a low, rumbling sound coming from some far corner of the cave, deep within the shadowy blackness. He listened hard, trying to identify it. Somewhat like the hum of a motor, it stopped and started with unpredictable irregularity. It was a low, throaty sound. He had it now. It was a growl. A living sound. An animal sound that assured him that he and the snake were not the only ones who had survived the fall.

Straining his eyes into the blue-tinted darkness, he searched for the source of the growl. Then, over his left shoulder, almost behind him, he saw them. Two shining eyes buried deep in the murky bowels of the hole, like the glowing tips of two cigarettes in a lightless room. Something waited on the perimeter of the cave, something living, something watching him.

He groped around on both sides of his body until he located a rock that was just a little bigger than his fist, his only weapon.

Not knowing for sure if the eyes he saw were those of a friend or an enemy, he brought the rock closer so he could find it easily if he needed to. It was all he had, except for his pocket knife, to use against . . . against what? Could it be just a cat, maybe a dog, or perhaps one of their more fearsome relatives, a mountain lion or a coyote? Surely it had been here longer than he. It watched him, waiting, protected by the shadows. Perhaps it was wild, fierce, crazed with hunger.

He could get no idea of its size or of how far away it was. He had no sense of depth or distance. Was it waiting, with animal patience and cunning, for him to weaken, to die?

He vowed that he would not sleep again until he knew for sure what was with him. How long would it be until morning?

His watch! He remembered his watch! Digging around in his pocket, he first found his jackknife, which he eased out, opened, and placed next to his other weapon. Then he located his pocket watch, the one his father had given him that had belonged to

Grandfather Whitcome. The case was dented, he could feel it. And it didn't spring open as it should. He had to pry it up with the blade of the knife. He felt shards of glass from the shattered crystal. Lifting the watch to his ear, he heard nothing. It had broken in the fall and wouldn't close. He returned the useless timepiece to his pocket. Hopefully it could be repaired.

For a moment he was distracted by a chittering sound, a scramble of motion among the rotting mounds. Rats! He knew the threat of their needle teeth and vicious claws. With rats nearby he knew that sleep would be a dangerous way to pass the time. Possibly more dangerous than . . .

The position of the eyes had changed. They'd moved to where he didn't have to crane his neck so much to see them. And they were closer.

He felt his heart beating faster; he was short of breath. His hands found the rock and the knife. Then, using his elbows for support, he changed the position of his body, made himself more comfortable and better situated to watch whatever it was that was watching him.

Not fully understanding the severity of his injuries, he feared additional movement might do more damage to his nerves, or to his back and leg. In a way he was grateful that he had no feeling from the waist down. Since he hadn't survived the fall intact, at least he didn't have to endure the terrific pain his broken leg would be causing. In either case, broken leg or broken back, he wouldn't be able to walk for a while. At least this was painless. Thank God he had full use of his arms.

The low growling stopped, the orange eyes blinked. Then, slowly, they started to move. He braced himself, clutching the knife and stone. Although he still felt icy cold, sweat filled his pores. The handle of the knife felt slippery in his grip. Random images whirled and cascaded, churned chaotically in his mind; images of Pam and Luke, of swallows and Sayer, and of the blade of his snowplow tossing sheets of white in front of the truck's headlights. Snow, sparks, metal against asphalt. Eyes.

Fearing panic, he watched the eyes approaching him. Slowly

they advanced until they got close enough for him to make out the amorphous form that contained them. Its black outline was vaguely human, yet smaller than a man. There was too little light to tell any more.

Too late he thought of the matches in his pocket. He didn't dare to compromise his defensive posture to search for them.

The thing was close enough now to get a better idea of its size. Most certainly it was bigger than any cat, domestic or wild. He braced himself as the form slowly approached. He wondered if he should throw the rock, maybe wound or scare it. But such an attack would cost him half of his defenses. No, he felt safer with the rock's firmness in his hand. He knew if he didn't throw it he could use it to pummel. The strength in his arm would add to the force and accuracy of the blow. So he waited, holding his breath.

When the shape was within five feet of him, the faint blue glow of light revealed the nature of his enemy. The narrow, pointed head, the floppy ears, the thick, rough coat, belonged to a dog, a collie. Relaxing a little, but not yet willing to lower his weapon, he watched the animal intently. It neared him, one careful step at a time, until he could smell its foul breath. He knew that if it were mad it would have attacked by now, so he waited. Eye to eye, each watched for the other to make the first move.

"It's okay, boy," said Clint in a whisper.

Clint could sense, almost see, its tail wagging. It stepped a foot closer to him and licked his face, its warm, wet tongue rank, but welcome. Clint reached up and patted its neck, scratched behind its ear.

He smiled and chuckled, "I guess we got ourselves in quite a fix, ain't we, boy?"

In a while the dog lay down beside him. In spite of its smell, the warmth felt good. Clint could feel its belly, swollen with carrion, its hair tattered and loosely attached. It was a sickly animal. Clint felt bad for it; he hated to imagine what the beast had been through.

"We'll figure us some way out of here in the mornin', don't you worry. I got a little fella to home who'd be real happy to meet you,"

Clint told his newfound friend. He felt the hardness of the silver flask in his jacket pocket. If only he'd let Billy fill it for him.

The dog pressed closer to Clint, scratched itself, and was still. Soon they slept.

Clint woke to the sound of barking. He opened his eyes and saw the collie, standing up, looking at the opening above. Perhaps they had been found! The dog backed up several steps, growling, and then was silent.

Sunrise had come. Saturday morning. Through the opening above Clint could see blue sky and white clouds streaked with red. Morning colors. He was stiff from sleeping on the rocky ground, but, with little discomfort, was able to turn on to his side and look up at the oval-shaped hole.

He could see the spindly shafts of dry grass hanging down into the opening, and there were cavities where rocks had been dislodged by his, or someone's, fall. As he looked up, the collie pawed at the earth, a low growl rumbled in its throat. Clint was excited to see, far above him, a head peering down over the rim of the opening. He couldn't make out the features, only a silhouette, black against the morning sky.

"Hey," cried Clint, waving and smiling.

The silhouette was joined by another . . . and another. Clint Whitcome watched as five heads silently took position around the rim of the opening, all black as night, all silent, motionless.

Beside him the collie growled, pressing closer against him. It was trembling.

The opening above him looked like a horrible grinning mouth, full of oddly spaced, rotten teeth.

From <u>The Woodstock Weekly</u>, February 5, 1870:

Considerable curiosity is felt in regard to the sudden disappearance of Jasper Rand of Bridgewater, who has lived alone for about two years past. No one can tell of having seen him, or any signs of anyone about his house, since the 23rd of November. His premises have been searched on suspicion that he might be dead, as his kitchen has the appearance of his being about to prepare a meal, there being a chicken in a kettle on the stove and some potatoes washed, on the table. His house was not fastened, and everything has the appearance of his intention of coming back in a short time.

19. WHAT THE MEN SAID

Saturday,
December 3, 1983

When Billy Newton wriggled out of the pit where he had been working under Archie Moulton's '66 Dodge Dart, he had trouble getting to his feet. Archie and Spike Naylor quickly stepped forward to give him a hand. They helped him over to his chair by the stove.

"Jesus Christ," Billy groaned. He eased himself back on the lounge, exhaling a long sigh. He winced, sniffed loudly, and shook his head. "I got them old brake cables off for you, Arch, but the Christly things were rusted on tight. Afraid I'm gonna have to ask you to put the new ones in yourself. I guess I gotta stay put a while. Spike, why don't you see if you can find us a little something to drink?"

Spike moved speedily to the loose boards on the wall behind which Billy hid his bottle-in-progress. He grabbed three paper cups and returned at once to find Billy removing the pipe from his mouth, emptying his lungs of smoke, and reaching out for his portion of whiskey.

"They's no medicine to cure this damned arthritis, but this stuff sure soothes it some."

Spike and Archie sat down in front of Billy, pulling up a wooden crate to share as a footstool. Each lit cigars.

As the three men relaxed, Chief Bates slid open the door to the garage and slipped in through the narrowest possible opening. This was a simple courtesy observed by all local people who recognized the value of conserving heat, but Bates had to open the door wider than most men.

"Good to see you, Dick," said Billy. "Can I offer you a little taste, or you on duty?"

"Nothin' I'd like more right now, Billy, but I am workin'."

"On a Sat'dee?" Spike said, as if he really couldn't believe it.

Bates looked directly at Spike. "Yes sir. I'm short a man, as you probably remember."

"What's the trouble, Dick?" Pipe smoke rolled from Billy's mouth as he spoke.

"I want to know if any of you fellas have seen Clint Whitcome?"

"Clint? Nope, not today." The other men shook their heads, leaving the talking to Billy.

"When'd you see him last, Billy?"

"Yest'day, day before. I guess it was yest'day, the day of the snowstorm. Stopped in on his way home from work. Somethin' wrong, Dick?"

"Might be, Billy. Might be something real wrong. Clint's missin'. Not only that, but another fella, name of Sayer, is missin' too. Found both their cars up a ways on Old Town Road, on the turnoff. Got some of the state boys together this mornin' and we searched the woods up behind where we found the vehicles. Searched that whole stretch of land from the road up to around Greer's cabin. Couldn't find neither man. Found somethin' else, though."

"What's that?"

"I'm afraid I gotta be the one to tell you, Billy. We found Perly Greer. He's dead. I know he was a friend of yours, Billy. Word has it you were his only friend."

Billy settled back in the chaise longue and blew a long, steady stream of smoke through his nostrils. The three other men remained silent, waiting for Billy to speak.

"What happened to him?" Billy asked, his voice far away, his eyes glassy.

"Hard to say, exactly. The medical examiner's looking at him. We found a dead bird in his stove pipe. Crazy sort of accident, from the look of it. But I guess a bird's gotta die someplace. Appears it plugged up the chimney, smoke backed up into the house.

Probably smoked things up in pretty good shape. Looks like Perly knocked over a kerosene lamp tryin' to get out, stopped to put out the fire, and ended up inhalin' too much smoke. Doc says he probably had a heart attack, staggered outside and died. I'm afraid it wasn't an easy death. Looks like he mighta had convulsions, tore up his face pretty bad. He saved his cabin, though. That's all I can tell you right now. I'm sorry, Billy."

Billy Newton blinked a few times in rapid succession, and reached for the bottle. He took a shot. Then another. He needed to say some words for his dead friend, but words didn't come easy. "He was a good old fart. Crazy as shit, but a good man. I liked him. You know, he give me his old truck for twenty-five bucks before he took to the woods. Said he wouldn't be needin' it. Christ, that was twenty, thirty years ago. Used to stop in to see me when he come to town. Liked to say hello, check on his pickup. Even borrowed it once in a while to run errands. Then he'd stop back. Chat a while. Maybe have a drink. Queer ol' duck. Last time I see him I knew there was somethin' wrong."

"What do you mean?"

"Didn't have ol' Ned with him. His ol' collie dog. You find Ned up there, did you?"

"Nope. He must have run off."

Billy told Chief Bates about the visit with Clint Whitcome, and how Clint felt that something strange was going on up on Tenny's Hill. Bates showed some interest in the facts as Billy related them, and made a note that Clint had fired Lou Bennett.

"Either of you fellas got anything to add?" Bates held his notebook ready.

Billy's two sidekicks looked at each other with great interest. Each was waiting for the other to begin speculating about what was going on in town, where things were rarely out of the ordinary.

"Clint Whitcome, disappeared . . ." said Archie Moulton thoughtfully.

Spike Naylor, who always figured human frailty and animal passion were behind most of the affairs of man, offered, "Maybe he found himself a left-hand thread and took off with it." This was

Spike's term for a different sexual partner, one interested in unusual coupling. A normal screw, as all the men realized, has a right-
hand thread.

"Naw," argued Archie, "Not with a wife like his."

"I don't know," said Spike slowly, never quick to give up on his
groundless theories, "I might be inclined to take off myself if my
wife was spendin' so much time with another man. It ain't right."

"What the hell are you talkin' about?" There was a tremor of
anger in Billy Newton's voice.

"That redheaded fella they got livin' with them up there. Don't
you think that's just a mite peculiar?"

"That's Mrs. Whitcome's cousin, for God sake."

"Just the same, I think it's odd."

"Spike, you keep talkin' like a man who don't know Clint Whitcome at all." Billy's voice was stern. "Clint ain't the kind of man
who'd run off. Not with somebody, not from somebody. I think
somethin' happened to him. Like I was tellin' Bates, Clint's been
worried about the strange goin's on up there."

"Jes' the same . . ."

"Jes' the same nothin'. I'm not gonna have you mean-mouth
Clint Whitcome in my garage."

"Spike," said Dick Bates, pocketing his notebook, "I think you're
lettin' your pecker come before your head again."

Billy and Archie laughed. Spike was respectfully, fearfully quiet
in the presence of the law.

"Terrible thing . . ." muttered Archie Moulton.

"Somehow, contrariwise to Spike's thinkin', I don't believe jealousy is at the bottom of this." Billy looked Dick Bates square in the
eyes. "Come on with me, Dick. I want to show you somethin'."

The policeman followed Billy out the door and across the snow-
covered property to the back shed. "I ever show you my rig?"

"Yup, I've never had a good look at it, though."

"Well, it's time you did. And out of earshot of them two boys."

Billy pulled open one side of the double door and they entered
the shed. The inside was crowded, with barely enough room for
the Ford, not to mention the piles of tires, spare engines, transmis-

sions, and assorted pieces of junk that Billy liked to keep in case he ever found a use for them. Billy rested himself against the fender of the truck.

"I just put on that new headlight assembly. Looks pretty good, don't it?"

"Just like new. You ever get this thing running?"

"Been runnin' right along. I told you old Perly borrowed her from time to time."

"I know you did."

"And I know that didn't get by you. I seen you make a note."

"What do you want to tell me, Billy?" Bates's voice was patient, encouraging.

"Well, I don't know if it means nothin', but . . . well, maybe I don't know too awful much about police work, but I can still put one and one together."

"Go on."

"I think Perly borrowed the pickup and didn't tell me. The other day I found a silver flask of his on the seat while I was working on her. That's one. I calculate Perly had this truck out the night your deputy come up missing. That's one. Now, I just fixed that headlight. It weren't workin' the night young Hurd disappeared. Another thing, the other day you told me that the truck Hurd stopped had no plates. That's what he radioed in, am I right?"

Both men looked at the spot where the license plate should have been.

"One and one makes two," said Billy. "Perly had the truck out and Justin Hurd stopped him. Then what happened? Well, that's a bit of cipherin' I don't think I can do."

Chief Bates sat down on the bumper of the truck. "You shoulda told me, Billy."

"I'm tellin' you now. I didn't piece it together before."

"What was Perly doing with the truck?"

"Damned if I know. I didn't even know he'd took it."

"Son of a bitch," Bates said slowly, almost under his breath. "First my deputy, and now Clint Whitcome and the Sayer fella. I never thought of this truck. Never." Bates shook his head. "Weird shit going down, Billy. And I guess Perly Greer's the only one with any answers."

"And right about now the old bastard's prob'ly smokin' a turd in hell, and not sayin' nothin' to nobody."

Without speaking, Bates stood up and left the shed. He walked, head down, across the undisturbed snow of the yard, moving toward his station wagon. His shadow was massive and black on the white, sparkling surface.

From the shed door Billy Newton watched the policeman's slow progress. Billy wiped his eyes with a greasy blue handkerchief.

When the chief returned to the station, the printout from the New York State Police was waiting for him on his desk. He picked it up but didn't read it, knowing full well what it was, and what he expected it would tell him. He sat down heavily on his wooden desk chair and rested his feet on the bottom drawer that he left partially pulled out to use as a footstool.

With his right hand, he held the paper against his chest; with his left, he reached up under his sweatshirt and scratched his belly. He was breathing heavily and felt tired.

Leaning as far back as the springs of the chair would permit, he closed his eyes, trying to relax, trying to clear his mind.

The part-time office clerk had, according to instructions, left him his messages, turned down the thermostat, and gone home at noon.

Alone in the quiet office, Bates had time to think.

What Billy Newton had told him about Perly Greer was probably going to be nothing more than a dead end. If, in fact, Perly had been stopped by Justin Hurd on November 21, then quite possibly Justin's disappearance had become an unsolvable mystery at the moment of the hermit's death.

But the moment of death, the exact time, was yet to be determined. From the appearance of the body, the old man had died prior to Sayer's and Whitcome's vanishing. If so, Perly Greer was not the solution to the puzzle. Instead, he was quite probably another part of it.

And there were still the other loose ends: Whitcome's dog, dead; Perly's dog, missing; the writing on Whitcome's barn; the episode of Clint's shooting at a child who never materialized.

Were all these odd pieces related? If so, what the hell could be going on in Antrim? If not, which of the pieces were unrelated? Even if the end to this cycle of mysteries was not yet in sight, the beginning seemed pretty well established: on or about November 21, 1983, things had started to go crazy in Antrim, Vermont. Everything, it seemed, had begun that Monday.

And that's where I have to start looking, thought Bates. He unfolded the computer printout and started to read.

It began: "Nolan, Eric D.O.B.: 14 March 1948 . . ."

From the <u>Bennington Independent</u>, Friday, October 13, 1950:

RAIN-SOAKED POSSE HUNTS WHITE CHAPEL WOODS
FOR 8-YEAR-OLD PAUL JENNISON, MISSING SINCE LATE
THURSDAY AFTERNOON; BLOODHOUND SEARCH FAILS.

The mystery of Paul's complete disappearance, and
not a single clue to work on, makes the third search for
a missing person in practically the same area during
the past five years. One of these was Middie Brooks, a
hunter, lost five years ago in November. The next, Paula
Wellmen, a Bennington College student, was last seen on
the Long Trail on December 1, four years ago.

20. SYMBOLS

The five days following Clint's disappearance were a painful and difficult time on Tenny's Hill.

For Pamela the nagging uncertainty about her husband's welfare was compounded by the unfamiliar behavior of her son.

Luke had become strangely quiet. He often sat among his toys, but rarely played with them. Even Eric, who usually had an excellent rapport with the boy, couldn't bring him out of his slump. His appetite, normally slight for a child his age, decreased to the point that Pamela had to insist that he eat. Frequently she tried to tempt him with his favorite foods, things she ordinarily wouldn't offer at mealtime—peanut butter and banana sandwiches, hot dogs, spaghetti from a can, and chocolate ice cream. But it was clear that Luke's mind wasn't on food.

Every day, from four to six o'clock in the afternoon, she would find him standing by the kitchen door, looking down the road, as if waiting for some sign of a truck or car.

Evenings he would go to bed early, without protest. He napped in the afternoons, sleeping fitfully, sometimes crying out in words his mother could not understand. On two occasions she had looked in on him while he slept to find his window open two or three inches, cold winter air flooding into the room. When asked, he had no recollection of opening it. Pamela suspected that her son was beginning to walk in his sleep.

It worried her because the boy had asked about his father only a couple of times, and then no more. It was as if he knew Pamela had no honest information for him.

She and Eric tried constantly to project an atmosphere both normal and unthreatening. They'd engage in routine tasks and try to get his mind on the future by reminding him that Christmas was near. Eric gave him colorful catalogs of toys to look at. Pamela gathered spruce boughs, tied them together by the stems and decorated the spray with ribbon and holly. Luke helped her to hang it on the door, then quickly lost interest.

Luke's moroseness pained Pamela in two ways. First, she felt helpless because she could find no way to comfort him. She felt as if she were losing him, too.

The other source of pain came when she realized how much Luke's moods reminded her of Clint.

In his subtle mannerisms, Luke was just like his father. The similarities were so minute that only a person who knew them both very well would notice at all. Pamela saw the resemblances with exaggerated clarity: the way Luke stalked the house, his tiny blue jeans low on his hipless body, looking out the windows or into dark corners as if he believed relief for his troubled mind might be as easy to locate as a misplaced toy or a lost picture book. Also, as with Clint, the depth of his discomfort would be reflected in the degree of his silence.

These were Clint's patterns, Pamela thought. Just like his father, Luke takes things hard. And he takes them quietly. He thinks about them, broods about them—but Clint always snaps out of it in a few hours, a day at the most.

It was as if Luke were almost certain about something, something that Pamela wouldn't allow herself to consider. Perhaps now the only things she really had left of her husband were the mannerisms she saw in their son. This realization awakened in her a sense of tremendous loss.

During the times when Luke was asleep or waiting in his room, Pamela would look to Eric for comfort and strength. Sometimes she would just stare at him, unable to find words, feeling helpless and ashamed. At those times Eric would go to her and hug her. He could say nothing, she realized. They both knew how hollow words of comfort would seem.

She hated to act this way, but couldn't control it any more than she could control her thoughts and feelings. She tried to busy herself to help put her mind on other things. She painted designs on Christmas tree balls, baked cookies and pies, gave the house an unnecessary, but thorough, cleaning.

On Wednesday, in her efforts to maintain a comfortable balance within the household, her cleaning attempts unwittingly tipped the scales, irrevocably altering Luke's frame of mind. For nearly three weeks Rusty's dog dishes had remained on the floor between the counter and the refrigerator. The water in one had long ago evaporated, and the small amount of food left in the other had become dry and crusty. Pamela had picked them up, washed them, put them away.

She cursed herself because she had not realized that for Luke those dishes were a symbol of hope, in the same way that for her Clint's hunting jacket hanging on the peg by the door was a symbol. She hadn't moved the jacket. It would be there the next time Clint needed it. But when Luke came downstairs after his nap, the dishes were gone.

Pamela watched as Luke looked at the pine floor beside the refrigerator. It was scratched, and the finish was worn thin and rough by the dog's claws. Luke looked at his mother as she slid a tray of chocolate chip cookies out of the oven.

Like ripples in a pond, a look of tragic confusion started from his eyes and spread in waves over his round, pale face. Pamela watched the change in her son. She remembered how she and Clint had often laughed at his perpetually puzzled expression. Now she felt as if her heart were about to break.

She closed the oven door and knelt down, opening her arms to him.

Luke didn't move. He only stood, and looked at her, then at the place where the dog dishes had been. "He isn't coming home is he?" Luke's tone was controlled. There was a finality in his words. He was definite. This time his expression was not of confusion, it was of certainty.

Pamela knew she couldn't lie to him, she couldn't mislead him. Somehow, at that moment, he wasn't a child anymore.

The confrontation was more difficult than it might have been. Although she had resolved to be honest with Luke, she really couldn't be sure who he was asking about, Rusty or Clint. Maybe both.

The child's blue eyes watched her. They held honesty captive like a fish on a line. Luke's fixed stare reeled that honesty to the surface, fought with it, tried to pull it out to where he could get a look at it.

"I don't think Rusty is coming home, honey."

"I know. Uncle Eric told me."

Pamela couldn't believe it. Why would Eric do such a thing? And without discussing it with her first. "When did Uncle Eric say that?"

"One night. In my room."

"Are you sure, baby?" She'd have to speak with Eric. Anger, like a sinister worm, started to wriggle in among her other emotions.

"I'm sure," answered Luke. "Rusty's gone. And maybe Daddy's with Rusty. Is he?"

Pamela felt the pressure of tears behind her eyes. Still, Luke looked at her. She knew that if she said the wrong thing, a part of their bond would be broken and her son would begin to lose sight of her, as he had lost sight of his father and his pet. But to speak the truth, to be honest with Luke, she'd have to be honest with herself. They would both hear it at the same time.

"I don't know, honey. I don't know if Daddy's coming back."

"Is he mad at us?"

"Oh, no, Sweetie." She went to him now, took his tiny biceps in her hands. "Your father loves us very much. He loves you very much. He's not angry."

"How do you know he's not?"

"Because I know. When you live with someone, when you love someone, like you and I love your father, you get to know how they feel. Your father isn't angry, Luke. Don't worry."

"Then, if he's not mad, he should come home."

"He will come home. If he can."

"Mommy," Luke's tone was quiet, earnest. "Is Daddy dead?"

This time the tears came. They tumbled down the sides of her nose and slid across her cheeks. They tickled, and the incongruous sensation irritated her. The tears themselves irritated her. The absence of comforting words infuriated her.

"I don't know, Luke. We both pray that he isn't."

Now the little boy hugged her. She felt his warm cheek against hers, felt his delicate hands scratching at her shoulders. His voice was muffled against her sweater and softer than a whisper. "If Daddy doesn't come back, will Uncle Eric be my new Daddy?"

Pamela held him so tightly that she was afraid of hurting him. She had no more words to offer, no more honesty, no more truth. All she had for him was this long, tearful embrace, and a few questions of her own that she dared not ask.

While Pam and Luke were at the store, Eric telephoned his department head to explain why he'd decided to postpone his return to New York. He said he'd call again in two weeks to say whether he planned to return or resign.

He devoted all his energy and thought to trying to make the days easier for the Whitcomes. As he watched them, he feared that something beautiful, something as close to perfection as human interaction could allow, had been irreparably damaged. Eric suffered with them and damned his helplessness.

At night, from the guest bedroom, Eric could hear the muffled sobs of Pamela crying in her room. On Tuesday, she had begun sleeping on the couch downstairs, explaining that the big bed only reminded her that Clint was gone. "The couch is closer to the stove, too," she'd joked, and smiled weakly.

With just Eric and Luke on the second floor, there was no more crying at night. Sometimes Eric heard Luke chattering away in his room. The late-night monologues were a new habit for the little boy, who now rarely spoke in the presence of the adults. Eric wondered if Luke were talking in his sleep. Perhaps Luke talked to his father at night. The thought hurt Eric, troubled him like a pain that wouldn't go away. He chose not to tell Pamela about hearing Luke, and instead decided to listen at the door the next time he heard the voice.

Somehow Eric wasn't worried quite so much about Pamela. She's always been strong, he reasoned. She has the ability to carry her suffering. In time she'll get on the better side of this. But Luke. Eric wasn't so sure about Luke. He was worried about the changes in him.

In his mind, Eric watched his little friend's endearing expression of chronic puzzlement flatten into a white, emotionless mask, with hard, cold eyes.

By Wednesday, Chief Bates's visits and phone calls had become less and less frequent. The two-day search of the woods had turned up nothing but the body of Perly Greer and the two abandoned vehicles belonging to Sayer and Clint. Even the Vermont State Police had contributed nothing that Bates hadn't learned on his own.

Lab tests proved that Billy's truck had been involved in Hurd's disappearance. Traces of blood were found in the truck's bed. These, however, predated the Whitcome and Sayer mystery, and so shed no light on it. At this point, with no connecting evidence, Bates was forced to see Hurd's disappearance, and Clint's, as two different situations.

It was the latter case that troubled him now.

Bates was aware of most of the stories going around town. The idea that Clint and Sayer were in league, that they'd found something of great value in the woods and had run off together, was the most common. A variation was that one man had killed the other, then made off with the imagined booty. Bates laughed at this idea. Although there had always been tales of treasure and lost gold mines in the wilderness of the Pinnacle, the notion seemed the fanciful product of minds trained more in television programming than police procedures.

They were not as fanciful, though, as some of the old legends that were being whispered among certain of the townspeople. Bates joked about the tales of goblins, ghostly Indians, and supernatural creatures, but, he had to admit, they made about as much sense as anything else that was being suggested. In reality, he had no better answers.

Jealousy was a popular explanation. Most people remembered how Clint had turned his back on his brothers and sister when they claimed their share of Old Man Whitcome's farm. Wouldn't he as quickly run out on his wife and child if Pamela was getting sweet on that Nolan character?

This theory brought still more whisperings about murder. If Nolan and Mrs. Whitcome had something going, then, some people reasoned, wouldn't disposing of the husband be a logical and convenient outcome? Bates didn't think so, and dismissed the idea with impatience every time it was hinted at.

Then there was the idea that someone was after Clint. The name of Lou Bennett was most often mentioned in this context. Somehow Bates knew this, too, was not the answer. He checked it out anyway, and filed it along with all the other dead ends.

It's something else, he thought. It's something I'm missing.

On Monday, when Bates had phoned the Whitcome house, Eric Nolan had answered. The chief had been waiting for the opportunity to speak directly to Nolan and he arranged for them to meet at the police station on Friday.

Bates was eager for the meeting. He hated waiting two more days to learn what Nolan had to say when he was out of earshot of Mrs. Whitcome and the boy.

Bates couldn't shake the idea that, somehow, the Whitcome farm was at the center of all the mysterious goings on in Antrim.

As he thought about it, he realized that as of now, the only thing different about the farm, the only thing changed, the only irregularity, was the presence of Eric Nolan.

The chief leaned back in his chair and put his feet up on the desk. He closed his eyes and scratched his belly. Finally, his instinct told him, he was getting somewhere. Something inside him relaxed a little.

From the files of Elizabeth McKensie. Excerpts from a diary kept by Mrs. Laura Grey, Gassetts Rd., No. Springfield:

Sun. July 31, 1870—The Sabboth has commenced. I want to commence right. May the Lord bless and may we try to do good in this world. I been and got a few raspberries, though they're picked sparse, and have been up in the cornfield. I fear I run too much for Sunday.

Wed. Aug. 10—Charley has gone skunk hunting. I worked over my butter this morning, then I went to the Hollow. I carried down 3dz. eggs—20 cts. a doz. I got white sugar 3#2oz. and Willie Nye cheated me in weight. It should be 3#4oz. instead of 2. Coming back I saw those young ones again. Just like before, they were unattended. I don't approve of it.

Sat. Aug. 13—Charley has gone to Springfield tonight to a Templer meeting. I don't think they are temperate for they stay until twelve in the night. I've been up in the woods and got peppermint and spearmint. I saw those children, three of them this time. They look sickly and run when they saw me. I suspect one of them is the Stebins boy. I shall speak to his mother tomorrow at meeting.

Sunday August 14—We've had a cloudy day and its been cloudy to my soul. I fear I've not made a Sabboth's day's journey to the kingdom of heaven. Mrs. Stebins says her boy is poorly and has been abed all week. I think she didn't take kindly to my concerns. Charley says he'll speak directly to the boys next time.

NOTE: On Saturday, August 20, 1870, the home of Charles and Laura Grey burned to the ground. The cause was attributed to a broken kerosene lamp. Both Mr. and Mrs. Grey were killed in the blaze.   —E. McK.

On Friday, December 9, after Clint had been missing for seven days, Eric Nolan drove to the old railroad station where the town offices were located. He entered by the front door and was greeted by Hattie Wiggins, the blue-haired, shrunken-looking woman who was the town clerk.

"Oh," she said, a bit flustered even before Eric had a chance to speak, "You're here to see the chief."

Eric knew right away that the chief had been discussing their meeting.

Mrs. Wiggins led Eric to Chief Bates's office, which in years past had been a ticket booth. It had been enlarged during the station's remodeling, partitioned with plywood, and named "Police Station." Eric noticed that what had been the stationmaster's office was now labeled, "Town Manager."

Bates was sitting behind his wooden desk. He didn't stand when Eric entered the room. With an abrupt motion he pushed a bunch of papers to the side and folded his hands on the ragged green blotter. He smiled, but to Eric it seemed more a mechanical movement of the mouth than a friendly greeting.

"Sit down, Mr. Nolan." Bates made no gesture toward a chair. His fingers remained linked together. Eric saw none of the folksy friendliness and warmth that the chief had displayed in Pamela's kitchen. Bates's black-circled eyes followed Eric to a folding metal chair in front of the window.

"Things keep going the way they have, we're gonna need men enough to fill this whole damn building. That is, if I don't keep losin' 'em fast as I hire 'em. It's like we're runnin' some god-damn Central American country, the way people keep disappearin' around here."

Eric didn't know what to say. He crossed his legs and tried to look comfortable.

"Sorry to hear about your wife, Nolan. Must be a difficult time for you."

"It is. It's not something one gets over too easily." He's playing cat and mouse with me, thought Eric. He wants me to know he's been checking up on me.

"Heard you two had a big fight the night she died. That right?"

Eric stared at the chief, not sure what was happening. Obviously, the policeman had been doing a lot of checking. Eric felt sick to his stomach; he couldn't answer.

"Must be an awful thing for you, Nolan. You must be carryin' around more than your share of guilt. 'Course, in a funny kinda way, I suppose you can say there's a good side to it."

"What do you mean, Mr. Bates?" Eric struggled to control his voice.

"Well, it brings you up here to Vermont so you could be with Mrs. Whitcome durin' her time of need. Funny how things work out, isn't it?"

Eric felt himself becoming angrier by degrees. It was as if the chief were turning up the rheostat that controlled his anger circuits.

He spoke slowly, precisely, through clenched teeth. "Maybe you should come to the point, Mr. Bates."

Bates tipped back in his chair, putting his hands behind his head. To Eric, the policeman's massive gut looked like a gigantic breast under the stretching white sweatshirt.

"What point, Mr. Nolan? I'm just making conversation. I know Pamela and the boy are having a tough time up there. I'm just glad you're 'round to help 'em out. That's all."

"Is it, Chief?"

The chief looked up at the ceiling, then his eyes fastened on Eric's. "Well, to tell you the truth, Nolan, I'm having kind of a tough time myself. Probably to a man from down-country, like yourself, what's going on around Antrim is pretty commonplace. But up here it's big trouble for us, and, I gotta admit it, the whole thing's got me bamboozled. Thought maybe you could shed some light on some of the darker spots for me."

"For instance . . ."

"For instance, the night my deputy disappeared was the night of November twenty-first, the day before you arrived at Clint Whitcome's place."

Eric stared at him. He could almost guess what was coming next. There was a lump forming in his stomach that felt as hard as Vermont marble.

"And?"

"And Pete Medford over to the inn tells me you checked in there the afternoon of the twenty-first. That right?"

It was. Eric nodded stiffly.

"Well that's one of my dark spots, Mr. Nolan. Seems kinda funny to me you'd drive three hundred miles to see your cousin, then check into a hotel when you were ten minutes from her house."

Eric fought the urge to be intimidated. He could feel his cheeks flushing; he rubbed his moist palms on his corduroys.

"I was nervous. I hadn't seen Pamela in years. I'd never met her family and I wanted to make a good impression, not show up dog-tired and dirty from travel. I wanted to get myself together."

"Now, there you go, Mr. Nolan. See. There's no reason to get edgy. That explanation makes perfect sense to me. You wanted to rest up and spruce up before you went out to the Whitcomes'. You go out at all that night?"

"No."

"Stayed right in your room? Number two-fourteen, on the second floor, wasn't it?"

"I stayed in. I had a couple of drinks at the bar at about eight . . ."

"Three bottles of Molson, wasn't it?"

"You've got the answers already, haven't you?"

"Sure. I'm just checkin' to see that they're right. You're the expert."

"Then I went to bed."

"Alone?"

"Jesus Christ!" Eric stood up. The red in his face changed from embarrassment to anger. "That's it. If you want my help, I'll do everything I can. I want to find out what happened to Clint Whitcome just as much as you do. But I didn't even know your goddamn deputy, if that's what you're implying."

Bates stood up, strode heavily around the desk and planted himself squarely in front of Eric. He looked massive and immobile. Involuntarily, Eric took a step backwards, skidding the chair a foot across the tile floor, stumbling a little.

For a while the two men stood eye to eye. Neither spoke. Neither moved. Eric felt his willpower weakening; he fought not to look away from the big man's eyes.

After some seconds—which to Eric ticked by in slow motion—Bates seemed to deflate. The big man's posture slumped as he let out a chestful of air in a whistling, nasal sigh. He backed up and sat on the edge of his desk, then motioned Eric back to the chair.

"I'm sorry, Nolan. I guess I'm kinda edgy myself. My deputy was a damn good man. So's Clint Whitcome. Both of 'em are friends of mine. I'm sorry I came on so strong."

Eric sat, still feeling guarded, off balance, too cautious to relax. Was this another of Bates's strategies? He said nothing, looked impassively at the chief.

Bates continued. "Just about all I been doing lately is looking for a common thread running through all this crap that's been coming down on us since the twenty-first. I'm looking for a thread, and what I'm findin' is you, Mr. Nolan. I want to be honest about that. I'm not saying you're involved. I'm not saying you're holding anything back. I'm not even saying that you know any more than I do, or that you're guilty of anything at all in any way, shape, or manner. All I'm saying—and please don't take this as an accusation—all I'm saying is everywhere I look I see you. I see you in every one of them dark corners I was tellin' you about. It may be a coincidence, but all this crap seems to have started the day you come to Antrim."

Although Eric still felt tight-muscled and nervous, he believed he heard a tone of sincerity in what Chief Bates was saying. Eric could see that the big man was as shaken as he was. The tough-guy role that Bates was trying to play made him as uncomfortable as it made Eric.

"I'll try again," Eric's voice cracked. "But let's try it cooperatively."

"Fair enough," Chief Bates nodded, and sat down behind his desk again. Eric watched the chief's huge hand slip up under his sweatshirt and begin to scratch his belly. "Mr. Nolan, you got any idea why anyone would kill the Whitcomes' dog?"

"Not really."

"Clint ever speculate?"

"He said people sometimes shoot dogs for running deer."

"But his dog wasn't shot."

"No. It was bashed to death. Clint and I saw its body."

"What kind of a man would do something like that?"

Eric thought about it. He wanted to answer, but thoughts were hard to keep in focus. They kept lodging uncomfortably somewhere between his unconscious and conscious mind like a piece of half-chewed meat caught in the throat. He was far too nervous to think clearly, analytically. What he finally said was obvious. "A sick man, I guess."

"But if he weren't sick, if he killed the dog for a reason—what might that reason be?"

Eric turned the question over in his mind. Looked at it from all angles. "To scare us, maybe? Rusty's death was followed by that warning on the barn. That must have been to scare us."

"Let's take one thing at a time. Forget the warning for a minute. If someone killed the dog, and didn't do it to scare you, why else might he have done it?"

Suddenly the answer was as clear as the writing on the Whitcomes' barn. "Sure," Eric blurted, excited by the clarity, "to get close enough to the barn to write the warning. The dog would have alerted us that someone was around!"

"Yup, Rusty would've barked up a storm when someone got close enough to the house to make good on his written warning.

Rusty was a watchdog. All dogs are. Especially when their master is threatened. So our boy, whoever he is, gets rid of the dog, then makes his threat. What do you suppose the threat meant, Mr. Nolan?"

"'An I for an I'? I'm not sure. I'd guess the writer was poorly educated, with some kind of religious mania."

"It's got kind of a vengeful ring to it. Don't you agree?"

"Of course, it was originally stated by a vengeful Old Testament God—"

"Poor education, religious, vengeful. Know anybody fits that description?"

Eric shook his head.

The policeman wrote something on a piece of paper, scratched it out and wrote something else. He looked up at Eric. "Let's sum up what we got so far: Number one—we got two 'protectors,' a cop and a dog, both taken out of the picture; number two—we got a statement of vengeance; then, for number three, we got the men droppin' out of sight. You were the last person to see this Dr. Carl Sayer, you know. You two were in the woods together."

"He sent me away. He wanted to examine the root cellar by himself. He was okay when I left him. I can't prove it, but he was." Just as it had started to relax, the fist in Eric's stomach began to clench again.

"I believe you. But just for the sake of discussion—objectively speaking now—you had the opportunity, you were alone with Sayer in the woods. You had the means, any number of rocks or fallen limbs, maybe even a knife. But you know what lets you off the hook, Mr. Nolan? Motive, that's what . . ."

"I didn't hurt Sayer."

"That's right. We don't even know that Sayer was hurt, do we? We just know he's missing. Just like Clint Whitcome."

"Where are you going with this, Mr. Bates?"

The big man's gaze drifted to the window. He seemed to look at some far-off spot. "I really don't know. I'm just laying out the pieces and hoping you can give me a hand at putting them together. I can't talk this way in front of Mrs. Whitcome and the boy."

"I understand that."

"Now I admit all these pieces don't fit together very well. Not exactly. But you know what I think?"

"No."

"Suppose somebody wanted access to the Whitcomes' house, for whatever reason. How does he do it? First, he does away with the dog. That's just like disconnecting an alarm system. Next, suppose there's two men in the woods, you and Sayer. Our mysterious 'someone' has it in for one of them. We don't know why at this point. We don't even know which one is the target. Suppose our friend gets the wrong one. Then, suppose Clint Whitcome just happened to see what happened. Okay, our boy takes Whitcome out of the picture, too."

Eric felt dread spreading through him; heat prickled at the back of his neck. He waited for Bates to continue.

"I'm not really sure of any of this, Mr. Nolan. Maybe we got more pieces to this puzzle than we need to make the picture. Maybe some of them are there by accident or coincidence and don't really belong. For example, I'm pretty certain what happened to my deputy has nothing whatsoever to do with what's going on up on Tenny's Hill. But I can't be positive. I've gotta keep looking at it. Maybe we'll never be able to fit all the pieces together. That's one of the frustrations of police work.

"But let me tell you something. If I was you, I'd take a cold, hard look at one of them pieces I've been talking about. You, Mr. Nolan. If I was you I'd be asking myself who it is that's got it in for me? Then I'd ask, of them that do, which ones knew I was coming to Vermont. Get the picture?"

Eric felt the blood rush from his head. For the first time in his life he thought he was going to faint. Could someone be after him? Was he the target of some madman? Who? Why?

Eric thought of his wife's parents. They had never really approved of him. He remembered the cemetery, and the cold, accusing stare as Karen's father watched him from across the open grave. There was hatred in that look, maybe more . . .

"So you can see, Mr. Nolan, any way you want to look at it, you see the same thing. You got to. Even if you were a suspect—and you're not, like I told you before—it would be my job to keep an eye on you. But, as it is, I gotta keep an eye on you anyway, for your own protection. That is, until one of us, or somebody, gets to the bottom of this."

When Eric Nolan left the police station he felt exhausted and afraid. It was as if someone had been probing at his insides with a surgical instrument, cutting out a piece here and there, leaving him feeling somehow different, changed. He felt almost like another person, physically ill, mentally timid, fearful and alone. He felt as he had when he had arrived in Antrim.

Could someone actually be trying to kill him? It sounded like something out of some supermarket scandal sheet. More than likely, the whole thing was Bates's trying to frighten him. No doubt Bates had never stopped suspecting him at all.

Could the policeman actually believe I would kill someone? Is he trying to get a confession out of me? Or does he think I know more than I'm letting on? Whatever the case, Eric thought, I'm right in the middle of things whether I like it or not. I'd better put my mind to getting some answers. Some ideas, anyway.

As he drove back to Tenny's Hill he momentarily considered going to the woods by himself to look around, but, in fact, he was too frightened to do so. Things happened out there. That much was for sure. Whether it was Karen's father, some psychopath, or some long-forgotten enemy, it didn't matter. The woods weren't safe.

They hadn't been safe for his brother, thirty years ago, and they weren't safe now.

All Eric could do was continue to think about the problem, help Bates as best he could, and insist that Pamela not allow Luke in the yard unattended.

Driving past the spot where Clint's truck had been found, Eric's own theory started to form as his mind eased. He allowed the theory to shape and grow, knowing all the while that it was too bizarre to discuss with the police or even with Pamela. The only person who might be at all open-minded about it was Mrs. Elizabeth McKensie. But Eric wasn't yet ready to take her into his confidence.

22. AFTERTHOUGHTS

Elizabeth McKensie was worried. Since the day she'd been visited by that policeman from Antrim, she'd realized things were going wrong. First Mr. Sayer and Mr. Nolan had stopped by together, then that policeman, Chief Bates, and finally a man from the state police.

At first, she had wondered what any passersby might think seeing all those people come and go—especially the people in uniforms. If anyone had noticed, perhaps they'd think that she had been robbed. She knew how curious the townspeople could be, how creative in making up information when they had no facts to distort. It was the way with country people, she thought, probably the way of all people. Fortunately, Mrs. McKensie didn't have any neighbors living near enough to keep a close eye on her. With any luck, all the comings and goings of the police would have gone unnoticed.

She worried about all the questions the police had asked. She ran them over and over in her memory, hoping her answers had been helpful and proper. It occurred to her that maybe the police suspected she knew more than she had revealed. Worse yet, suppose that they figured that she was in some way involved with the disappearance of that unimaginative Mr. Sayer. Of course, she didn't even know Mr. Whitcome, and he was gone, too. But, then again, that would be silly. How could a seventy-five-year-old woman in a wheelchair cause two grown men to vanish? Who would believe such a thing? Certainly not the police. They were trained to know better.

After all, Mrs. McKensie was a respected, lifelong member of the community. She had a good reputation from her occasional column in the *Tri-Town Tribune*. She'd often been praised for her work with the Connecticut Valley Historical Society. Surely she could be believed and trusted. Hadn't she answered in great detail all their questions about her meeting with the two men? What more could she do?

At the moment, she was most worried about what the police might think of her because of the answers she had given. She had related to them the discussion of the ancient stone structures, had then gone on to explain Mr. Nolan's interest in local folklore, especially subjects having to do with the little people. She could see the police were not very interested in that topic.

She even admitted how she tried to provoke Mr. Sayer, just for fun, because of his "more-scientific-than-thou" attitude.

What a discussion to precede a disappearance! What might the police think of her? She would hate to be dismissed as just a senile old woman in a wheelchair, telling fairy stories to grown men . . .

She felt uncomfortably self-conscious. She wanted to be of more help, and to show all of them that she was not crazy in the least. Looking down at her lifeless legs wrapped in a faded, multicolored afghan, she realized that she could be of no use at all. Not to anyone.

She wheeled herself over to the phone on her desk, thinking about that nice Mr. Nolan. He looked like a real Irishman, with his red hair and blue eyes. His voice was kind, his smile sympathetic. He'd been genuinely interested in her stories of the history and folklore of the region. What was more important, he had seemed eager to talk to her again.

Maybe she should call him. Maybe they should have another talk. She felt sure that she would be able to tell him everything—not only the facts, but more. So much more.

After his noon meal, when he left headquarters and hobbled out to his place, Billy Newton found himself alone. He'd had a quiet lunch with Lillian, which was normal, but all the while his mind had been elsewhere. He was preoccupied with important thoughts —thoughts so important that he wanted to spend time alone with them, let them run their course. When he found no visitors in the garage he was pleased.

For Billy, it was a problem of conscience. It wasn't as if he was being dishonest with anyone. He was answering everyone's questions to the best of his ability. He'd even implicated his friend Perly. He'd told no lies, fabricated nothing. In fact, he could honestly say he had told Dick Bates everything he knew.

But he had kept to himself what he suspected.

He was sure that the men who hung out at his garage knew nothing, suspected nothing. He had sounded them out, given them every opportunity to speak up. They had no theories, no new information, nothing any more substantial than Spike Naylor's empty-headed gossip about Mrs. Whitcome's being unfaithful to her husband, or Clint's leaving in a fit of jealous rage.

If someone's gonna speak out, thought Billy, *it's gonna hafta be me.*

Billy knew that when a man lived in town as long as he had, he got to hear a lot of things, came to have a pretty good feel for his neighbors and acquaintances. Having the garage as a gathering place for local men and town employees put him in an excellent position to know just about everything going on in Antrim, and a good deal about Springfield, Chester, and Bellows Falls to boot.

There was a time when he had known everybody in town on a first-name basis. Now, he could probably say he knew every face, if not every name. He'd known Clint Whitcome since he was no bigger than his son, Luke. Had known Clint's whole family. And he'd known Clint's wife, and the grandparents who took her in. Maybe it had taken a while to place him, but he even knew that fellow staying with them, Eric Nolan. He remembered him as a small boy—God, it must have been thirty years ago—whose redheaded, freckled face appeared every summer for a while—every summer until . . .

Until his brother disappeared.

Billy blew a thick cloud of undulating smoke into the air. Then he drew deeply on his pipe, biting hard on the stem. He sighed, remembering the searchlights, the bands of men canvassing the woods of the Pinnacle, looking for the missing child. Billy himself had been a member of the search party. They'd worked for days, until all hope was lost.

Perly had been in the woods at that time. Old Chief Whalen had questioned him at length about the missing boy.

Billy felt bad about Perly. He hoped his friend had died naturally, if not by accident. Horrible way to go, though, and nobody up there to help him. Not even old Ned.

Billy took the pipe from his lips, replaced it with a paper cup. The golden liquid flowed along his tongue and into the cavern of his throat like a warm, soothing river. He felt a wave of relaxation pass along his arms and into his coarse, brittle fingers, which, after years of working with oil and grease, after packing hundreds of pounds of tobacco into his pipe, would never come clean. The warmth spread across his pelvis, and down into his legs where it seemed to lubricate them, easing the pain in his joints.

He tossed a couple more logs onto the fire and sat in his chair, making himself as comfortable as possible for some long and serious thinking.

The problem was, of course, that too many things were happening all at once: two men up in smoke the same day; the Whitcomes' dog dead, and maybe Perly's, too; strange writing on the barn; Clint's shooting at a wild turkey that wasn't there.

Too many things at once, and all of them swirling around the Whitcomes like some kind of crazy cyclone.

It wasn't right. Clint Whitcome was a good fellow. One of the best. Maybe it was too late for him, but his family was still up there on the hill. Maybe it wasn't too late for them. Or for Eric Nolan, either.

Billy thought about the police officer, Justin Hurd. That's when it all started, he thought. That's when it started . . . this time. After nearly thirty years.

And now there are too many things happening all at once. Too many bad things.

His thoughts returned to Perly, and the reasons that, so many years ago, he had given up his house, his truck, his job, all his ties with civilization, to take to the woods. To be a hermit. So many years ago . . .

At that time, Billy had thought his friend was crazy to go, and he'd told him so. As the years passed, Perly's infrequent visits had allowed Billy a chance to watch the "insanity" progress. The hermit's futile search for lost gold mines had given way to frustration, then loneliness. Apparently, in his seclusion, Perly'd created imaginary companions, the "Goodpeople," as he'd called them. The Goodpeople did him favors, showed him things, helped him.

If, Billy reasoned, Perly's neighbors were not imaginary, what "favors" had they expected in return? What else had Perly given up between the time he gave up his sanity and the time he gave up his life? Billy Newton didn't know. He only suspected.

As a child, he'd heard tales of the mysterious "hill people" who lived alone in caves and burrows amid the wilderness of the Green Mountains. The tales had been whispered again, thirty years ago, when Nolan's brother disappeared. And now . . .

Billy gulped down another large shot of whiskey, and a shudder passed through him like the rumbling of a train. He was shivering. It was as if something inside him, something small and well hidden, had suddenly turned cold.

He knew the sensation—it was a tiny bit of his humanity, freezing, breaking away, as fear and cowardice grew. It would continue to chip off, bit by bit, until there was no warmth left in him at all. Billy knew that no whiskey in the world could fool him into thinking that there was.

The pain in his legs was something he had learned to live with, but this was something different. It could turn him from a man into something else. Something he could not bear to become.

He'd have to do something about it, because this, unlike the arthritis, was one disease whose progress could be halted. He'd have to tell more than he knew. He'd have to tell what he suspected.

If someone's gonna speak out, it's gonna hafta be me.

Another tremor passed through him as he made up his mind to tell; at the same time, he realized that nobody at all would believe him.

From the files of Elizabeth McKensie. Letter from an eighteen-year-old recent widow to her parents in Salem, New York:

Bush Hill
Wallingford, Vermont
August 6, 1861

dear mother and father, I seat myself to inform you that yours of the second was duly received and read with pleasure. I was glad to hear from you and learn that you are as well as you are. Do not wory yourself into the grave about me for I want for nothing. I have enough to eat and ware. I have a bed and blankets I am all right. Your letters are a comfort and I shall write you often. The baby should arrive in two months and after we should like to come home and stay with you. The neighbors have been kind and generous. Williams sheep have died, all but two and I have seen some children carry three lambs into the woods. I had planned to market them, to raise money for the doctor and the fare home. Mr. Moody has made a just offer on the place and I shall acept. Tell Roderick to be steady and be a good boy. Tell father to keep up courage and stick to the place. Give my best respects to all. Write again. I'll be with you soon. I remain your efectionate daughter,

Ida

23. THE PHANTOM

Monday &
Tuesday,
December 12
and 13, 1983

Clint had been gone for ten days.

With only thirteen days until Christmas, Eric and Pamela felt an urgency to make the coming holiday season as pleasant as possible for Luke.

Eric's own experience with grief had taught him the importance of routines and short-term goals—they helped one to concentrate on the future.

He encouraged Pamela to take a midweek trip to Springfield for Christmas shopping. Meanwhile he would snowshoe to the edge of the forest to cut a small Christmas tree for the living room. The three of them could decorate it together.

Eric felt that he'd found a role for himself in the family. Maybe it was up to him to take more control of the situation.

"Listen Pam," he suggested, "I think the best thing for all of us would be to get away from here for a while. There are too many reminders here, too many memories. We could all take a vacation, go to my house on Long Island. We could even have Christmas there. It might be the best thing . . ."

"I can't, Eric," Pamela said. "Not without knowing. This is our home, at least for now. I think Luke needs that. So do I. You're very good to offer, but I can't."

When she kissed him on the cheek, Eric knew that the discussion had ended.

Despite all their efforts to be festive, Luke became more and more withdrawn. Pamela confessed that he was breaking her heart.

"I know there's something terribly wrong with him, Eric. I just can't seem to reach him, can't seem to thaw him out at all."

The previous Friday, she had taken him to see a doctor at the Chester Clinic. She'd been assured that there was nothing physically wrong with the boy. The only medicines were a lot of time, and much love.

Eric looked on as Pamela tried to comfort her son. Hugs and soft words had no effect; Luke seemed unable to return her affection.

The boy took on an almost mystical calm. He never cried and rarely spoke in the presence of the adults. The child moved about the house like a shadow, surprising the grown-ups with his silent arrivals, confusing them with his sudden retreats.

Eric hadn't told his cousin that while she and Luke were at the doctor's, he had phoned the chairman of the English Department at Long Island Community College to resign. The decision had been building for some time. He no longer had any interest in teaching, but, more important, he felt needed in Antrim. It was a feeling he'd never experienced before. He didn't want to end it.

After lunch on Monday the phone rang. As always, Pamela's face filled with an irrepressible hope. She moved toward the phone, then stopped quickly, uncertainly. Luke drifted silently into the room and stared dully at the ringing instrument. Eric picked it up.

"May I speak to Mr. Nolan, please?"

"This is he."

"Mr. Nolan, this is Elizabeth McKensie."

"Mrs. McKensie! This is a surprise—"

She cut him off. "It's been my intention to phone you for some time now, but I've been worried about intruding. I know you folks are having a difficult time. I do hope things are going tolerably."

"Thank you, Mrs. McKensie . . ."

She went on quickly, not allowing him time to speak. "I want you to know that if there's anything I can do . . ."

"That's very good of you, very kind."

"Tell me, Mr. Nolan, can you speak freely now, or can someone overhear?"

"We're all right here, yes."

"I see. Mr. Nolan, there is something I very much want to discuss with you. It's extremely important. Possibly urgent. Do you think it would be possible for you to pay me another visit?"

"Yes, yes I could do that. I've been wanting to talk to you, too. Actually I'd hoped to have the opportunity before this."

"Well, that's fine. That's just fine. Perhaps tomorrow evening?"

"It would be better if we could make it for an afternoon, if that's all right."

"Yes, of course. You want to be there in the evening, don't you? Very wise. I should have thought of that. Would tomorrow be convenient for you, then? In the afternoon?"

"I think so, yes. We were going to go to Springfield to do some Christmas shopping. I think Pamela could drop me at your house. Would that be all right?"

"Certainly. I appreciate it, Mr. Nolan. I shall be looking forward to seeing you. Good-bye."

The phone went dead in his hand. Eric turned to Pamela and smiled sheepishly. "That was the 'Voice of the Mountains.'"

Elizabeth McKensie wheeled herself over to her desk and sat before her typewriter. She had an uneasy feeling that she had made a mistake, shouldn't have called. What if Mr. Nolan dismissed her as crazy? After all, trying to provoke that peculiar Mr. Sayer was one thing, but to say the same things after removing tongue from cheek, well, that was a horse of a different color. If Mr. Nolan didn't take her seriously, if he spread the word to others, surely that could be —she had to admit it—dangerous.

She felt cold, shivered a little, then tightened the collar of her sweater. The oil furnace in her cellar whined as hot water rattled through the pipes and hissed from the radiators. Perhaps I should turn up the thermostat, she thought. But fuel oil's so dear. And it seems I'm cold all the time these days. I guess that's the price of getting old.

"Oh stuff and nonsense," she said, "Stop being so fussy." She knew the price of oil was not the problem. She'd been letting her mind wander to avoid thinking about unseemly topics.

"I *am* an old woman, though," she said to herself, as if realizing it for the first time.

And as such, she thought, I should have acquired some of the wisdom that's supposed to be thrown in along with the shivers. So why is the choice so difficult?

She smiled, a little sadly, and looked at the framed needlepoint that hung next to the mantel. It had been done by her mother:

> True friendship
> Is a knot
> Which
> Angel hands
> Have tied

She thought about her mother and life on the farm in the olden days, when "help each other" was the rule. It was a rule that hadn't changed in her seventy-five years.

She had led a full life, seen enough changes in her time to have a pretty good idea in what direction humanity was heading. And she had ten years—maybe twenty—left to watch things change some more: advance, complete cycles, or, quite possibly, end entirely. If she spoke out now, she risked spending all of her remaining years branded as a crazy old woman. If she held her tongue, she risked spending those same years knowing she hadn't spoken up when she should have.

So, she asked herself, where's the wisdom that comes with the years? What should I do? Have I done the right thing?

How many times during her life had she asked herself just these questions? She'd asked them about so many different topics, each requiring a moral judgment. But somehow nothing before today had seemed nearly as important, nearly as final.

She looked at her white and wrinkled fingers, then placed them on the keys of her typewriter. Over the years she had learned to play it like a musical instrument. She wrote:

Snow birds call,
In Winter's chill,
And sing their songs,
From hill to hill.

When nighttime comes
Their bodies lie
Beneath the cold moon's
Warning eye.

And when death comes
He's friend or foe
But we're all snow birds
In the snow.

The next day, Tuesday, brought the worst storm of the season. The flint-gray sky worked overtime, producing an unending avalanche of snow. The forest was invisible from the Whitcomes' kitchen window. Warnings on the radio advised travelers to stay home because of extremely hazardous highway conditions. Schools were closed; the governor closed state offices and liquor stores.

Tenny's Hill Road was a low priority for plowing in such a storm. Snowbound and restless, Pamela and Eric had to cancel their afternoon trips. The Christmas shopping in Springfield would have to wait, and Eric phoned to give his apologies to Mrs. McKensie. The day passed slowly.

At six o'clock Pamela prepared a dinner of fish sticks and rice; she had no energy for cooking. She and Eric ate without comment, but Luke, who never fancied fish in any form but tuna sandwiches, requested cereal instead. He didn't even finish his bowl of Cheerios.

Pamela found she couldn't pick up on Eric's attempts at conversation. She responded with monosyllables, chewing her food slowly, feeling far away and inexcusably rude. She was quietly angry about having to cancel their day's activities. Planning and

doing were the only things that kept her thoughts away from uncertainty. Now she was buried in painful speculation. At the same
time she was angry about feeling sorry for herself. Time passed so
slowly with nothing to do, nothing to look forward to.

The grandfather clock in the den ticked with a deafening metro-
nomic regularity. It chimed with the intensity of Big Ben every half
hour. The fire in the wood stove roared. Outside a strengthening
wind rattled the house.

When seven-thirty came around, Luke, with what seemed a tremendous effort, brought his Superman pajamas to Eric. Eric helped
him with the straps of his overalls and carried him up to bed.

Alone in the living room, sitting at the end of the sofa near the
fireplace, Pamela drew her feet up under her and reached for a copy
of *Redbook*. She flipped through the pages, but saw very little.

The isolation caused by the snowstorm reminded her how alone
and helpless she and Luke would be if they had to manage the place
by themselves. Maintaining the house had been so much a cooper-
ative effort. She hadn't completely realized that before.

Perhaps in these modern times of feminine equality, hers and
Clint's had been an unfashionable, even a primitive lifestyle. But
it had worked, and it had arisen naturally out of the things that
needed to be done. Now, Pamela thought, a change was coming—
and she was terrified.

What will we do? She asked herself over and over again. The
question was like a repeating record; she could hear its echo at all
times: in the background behind every conversation, infused into
radio broadcasts, hidden in the soundtrack of television programs.
It seemed to be printed between the lines of books, newspapers,
even in the magazine on her lap. It was as annoying as a persistent,
hungry cat, rubbing itself against her legs, unresponsive to all attempts to make it stop.

Moving to the kitchen, she poured red wine for herself and Eric.
As he was coming back from Luke's room she handed him his
glass. They sat together on the sofa.

She was grateful to have him with her during this time. It's
ironic, she thought, we invited him here to try to ease his suffering.

So quickly the roles have reversed. Pamela smiled at him weakly, feeling the prickly sensation around her eyes that alerted her that tears were imminent. Eric smiled back and extended his hand. She accepted it willingly, eager for its strength and reassurance. They sipped their wine and sat for a long time in silence, bathed in the warmth of the fireplace.

Fighting against the tears and the feeling of desperation, Pamela wondered whether she should discuss the future with Eric. The great comfort that she felt from having him near seemed to still the panicky voices inside her. She had always loved him, in a way. In his eyes she saw the sensitive, confused young man she remembered.

Thoughts of love made her think of her husband: his face, his laugh, the trembling of his hands, and the grateful, timid smile as he spoke their wedding vows. With the memory came fear, and a flash of shame. She pulled her hand from Eric's. Pretending she was cold, she buttoned the collar of her sweater.

"I'm cold," she said. "Let's turn the couch to face the fire."

As they stood up the whole house fell into darkness. In the glow of the fireplace they looked at each other in surprise.

"Power's off," said Eric.

"The storm. Maybe a tree down on the wires. Last time this happened it was two days before they got it fixed. We've got candles and kerosene lamps. It'll be just like the old days."

Eric was alert, standing still, listening. "Luke must be asleep. Guess he didn't notice his night light's off. Should I bring up a lamp for him?"

"If we hear him, I'll go up."

She went to the kitchen for the wine bottle and refilled their glasses. They sat again, facing the dancing flames on the hearth. The house was as still as a church, the only sounds, the clock and the crackling of the fire. Pamela was aware of the comforting, steady rhythm of Eric's breath. She felt a warmth coming from him that was akin to the warmth of the fire. Moving closer, she rested her head on his chest. His arm moved from the back of the couch and settled on her shoulders, pulling her, ever so slightly, toward him.

Sitting quietly, they sipped wine and warmed their faces in the crimson glow of the flames. In the soft firelight Eric's features were strong and kind. Reflected in his gentle eyes, flickering points of light shone like candles. The fire's warmth surrounded her like a protective bubble. In its center they sat safe, hopeful, and, for this comfortable moment, content.

They were cut off from an uninterested world by acres of snow and fathoms of darkness. They were the only people in all creation, secure in their privacy, mindless of the little boy who slept upstairs. The windows, like shiny sheets of black metal, reflected three more fireplaces in the room. But the warmth that Pamela felt came from within.

In the calm that settled over her, it was as if all creation held its breath, paused for a moment, ending all movement, all sound. Pamela was in a dream-state. She felt good, truly at peace for the first time in many days. She began to drift off to sleep.

But something called her back from her dream. It was something loud and irritating, persistent as a dog barking in the night. As if summoned from luxurious sleep by a dreaded alarm clock, she woke a little at a time. Reluctantly, she opened her eyes to see a look of fear on Eric's face. He looked flushed, coldly alert in the fire's glow. She snapped fully awake, realizing that she was hearing a powerful banging.

BAM! BAM! BAM!

"It's the door," Eric whispered.

"But who . . . ?"

"I didn't hear anybody drive up. I didn't see any lights."

"No one could be out there on foot on a night like this." Pamela's voice shook, her stomach tightened.

She followed, three steps behind, as Eric led her through the kitchen to the outside door. The pounding continued. The evenly spaced, solid blows to the wooden door shook the old house.

Taking the brass knob tentatively in his hand, Eric turned the key and slowly opened the door. Cold air rushed into the kitchen. As it did, something vile churned in Pamela's tightening stomach.

Her eyes were glued to the widening gap that exposed the snow-dark night.

The thing revealed in the doorway was more phantom than man. In the darkness, its features were pale and indistinct. Snow coated the scraggly hair and drooping shoulders. The clothing was torn, covered with dirt, streaked with stains of dampness. Thick, black whiskers masked the pallid face. In the clear winter air the smell of earth and fetid odors assaulted Pamela's nostrils. The phantom's black, empty eyes slowly moved from Eric and fastened on Pamela.

Her stomach knotted and heaved.

"Pam . . ." it said in a hoarse, hollow whisper. She recognized the voice faster than its source.

"Clint!" she cried, as he stumbled toward her, falling into her arms. Then he passed out. Pamela bore her husband's full weight until Eric helped move him to the living room.

PART THREE

The Coming of the Gentry

It must be allow'd, that the Blasphemies of an infernall Train of Daemons are Matters of too common Knowledge to be deny'd; the cursed Voices . . . being heard now from under Ground by above a Score of credible Witnesses now living. I my self did not more than a Fortnight ago catch a very plain Discourse of evill Powers in the Hill behind my House; wherein there were a Rattling and Rolling, Groaning, Screeching, and Hissing, such as no Things of this Earth cou'd raise up, and which must needs have come from the Caves that only black Magick can discover, and only the Devil unlock.

—Rev. Abijah Hoadley, circa 1747, quoted by H. P. Lovecraft

THE OLD HOUSE
(for my husband)

An old house has a heart, you know,
It beats within each room.
But if its heart should chance to go
It's empty as a tomb.

I live my days within these walls.
And hear the steady beats
Like memories, once sweet and new,
Of love and work and treats.

Near Christmastime, so long ago,
A young man, hail and hardy,
Brought me to these joy-filled rooms
To start our wedding party.

The years with Kevin slipped away,
My young man aged and passed.
His heart and mine beat in these rooms,
And will until the last.

—Mrs. Elizabeth McKensie
Tri-Town Tribune, December 25, 1983

From the <u>Burlington Banner</u>, December 28, 1982:

UNEXPLAINED NIGHT NOISES PLAGUE ST. ALBANS RESIDENTS
by Roger Newton

ST. ALBANS—Several village residents have reported strange noises that waken them in the nighttime. The source of these sounds is still unknown.

"Around 2 o'clock Wednesday morning, we heard this loud banging," said Polly Nadeau, a resident of Pleasant Street. "Our house actually shook, like in an earthquake. It literally woke us up. I was ready to evacuate."

Mrs. Nadeau reports that a number of her neighbors have heard the noises which began around 7 o'clock Christmas Eve. She said she is convinced the noises are not the work of children or vandals.

Police Chief William Snelling said Tuesday, "Nobody's reported any vandalism so I don't know how to explain it. Weird."

24. THE SEVERED ROOT

Something's wrong, Pamela thought. Something's very wrong.

She stood at her kitchen window, looking out at the rain that smashed and splattered against the dead brown grass near the house. How strange it was to see such a fierce downpour just two days after Christmas.

The specific cause of her unease eluded her. She hated to admit it, but the only conclusion she could reach was that the tension came from her husband.

During the fourteen days since Clint's return, Pamela had done everything she could think of to nurse him back to health. He had come back to her in a state of exhaustion, thin, weak and infested with vermin. An immediate trip to the Chester Clinic had shown him to be in generally good health, but bruised and undernourished. The doctor recommended that Clint have at least ten days of rest before returning to the job. Strangely out of character, Clint told Pamela that he'd take at least a month before deciding if he wanted to go back to work at all.

Although Clint was acting strangely, he insisted that he felt just fine. He wanted to rest, that was all, to spend time with the family. He thanked Eric again and again for taking care of them while he'd been away.

But Pamela wasn't sure that her husband was really all right. She knew Clint too well to be misled. There was, she noticed, a slight limp when he walked; she was positive it had never been there before. When she asked about it he explained that he must have injured his leg when he fell into the hole, probably sprained it. He assured her that it wasn't painful.

On the more positive side, Clint's affection for Luke was stronger than ever before. Pamela's heart warmed when she recalled how her son's eyes had lit up when he came downstairs to find his father had returned.

For Luke and Pamela, the day of Clint's return had been more like Christmas than the holiday itself.

Still watching the rain, Pamela thought that it didn't look like Christmas at all. It was more like spring, mud season. It didn't feel much like Christmas, either. A cloud of tension and silence had hung over the holiday, in spite of everyone's attempt to be festive.

Eric had appeared pleased with the book of Mrs. McKensie's poetry that the Whitcomes had given him. Clint and Pamela had appreciated the case of Chantovert wine, imported by a dealer in Chester, Eric's gift to them. Yet, even with the smiles, the handshakes, and the kisses, Christmas had lacked spirit.

This was particularly evident in Luke. The thrill that the adults had expected to witness when Luke saw his new two-wheeler just never materialized. The little boy had eyed the shiny bike, first with suspicion, next with a momentary flash of pride, and then with no interest at all.

Without taking her eyes off the mud-rutted yard, Pamela shifted her thoughts to this morning's trip home from Chester after Clint's weekly checkup. As she drove, they had watched the vicious downpour through overworked wipers. Shafts of water poured from the churning skies. To the right, the surface of the Connecticut River sizzled and splattered like hot oil in a skillet. Rising waters lapped hungrily at the riverbanks. The earth, still too frozen to absorb much moisture, formed surface mud about two inches deep. Most of the snow was gone, leaving only an ugly scattering of dirty white piles lining the roadside or clinging like plaster to the roots of trees.

On Tenny's Hill Road the wheels of the car had spun as Pamela fish-tailed up the hill. Self-consciously, she'd offered to let Clint drive. He'd refused. "You're doing fine, Pam. Better'n I could right now. You drive."

This unfamiliar caution was typical of the new Clint. Pamela had noted a nervous preoccupation in her husband, one that showed itself in tense silences, aimless wanderings from window to window, and sleepless nights. They had not made love since he'd returned home.

I must be patient, she reminded herself.

No longer fascinated by the rain, Pamela turned from the window and sat at the kitchen table. She flipped through the pages of a cookbook trying to get an idea for dinner.

There was so much that Pamela didn't understand. The cold, faraway look in Clint's eyes troubled her. His pacing, the insomnia, and his inability to be affectionate upset her more than she dared to let on. When she tried to talk to him about it, he cut the discussion short. "I had a bad time, Pam. I need to rest. That's all. Please try not to worry about me."

With great hesitation, she confided her fears to Eric, who always had a sympathetic ear. In this situation even he had no better advice than the doctor's—give it time. It seemed that time was the only thing she ever had to offer.

There were other things that bothered her.

There was the time when Clint announced, "We ain't gonna do no sugarin' this year. Not enough money in it, and besides, I don't want you folks in the woods."

Clint had never done sugaring for the money, he had done it because he enjoyed it and because his father and grandfather had done it. Pamela hoped that by maple sugar season Clint would change his mind.

Perhaps the biggest surprise of all had come just the night before. They were alone in their bedroom when Clint had broken their nightly silence. "When I go back to work I'm gonna stay for a month or so, then quit. We'll save all the money we can. Then we're movin' out of here."

"Moving?" she said in surprise. "Where?"

"Away. I don't know yet. Maybe we'll all go to Eric's place for a while, until I can find a job."

Pamela couldn't picture her husband amid the fashion and frenzy of Long Island. The idea of leaving Antrim, much less Vermont, was contrary to everything she had ever known about Clint. He loved the town, and considered himself a Vermonter with a prideful, stubborn chauvinism. For Clint, a true Vermonter was something that took generations to build. She remembered a happier time, when she'd heard him talking to a relocated salesman from New Jersey. Clint had told the man that even if his son was born in Antrim, he'd never be a real Vermonter. When the man asked why, Clint had explained, "Just because a cat has kittens in the oven, that don't make 'em biscuits." The two men had had a good laugh at that, but Pamela knew that Clint really meant it. She smiled at the memory, and knew at once that the smile was forced.

"Why, Clint?" she'd asked in a voice soft as a whisper.

"I dunno. I can't take the town no more. I want to try something else." He retreated into his silence, and, she thought, pretended to be asleep to discourage further discussion. She dared to say no more in case he was really sleeping. He needed his rest.

Pamela slapped the cookbook closed, having taken no ideas from it. She went to the freezer in the mudroom, removed a package of stew meat and a bag of frozen carrots. Beef stew was a favorite of Clint's.

Yesterday, the day after Christmas, Chief Bates had stopped in to say hello and to again express his happiness that Clint was safe. During an earlier visit, Bates had gently reprimanded her husband for not immediately reporting his return. Obviously looking for more information, Bates had kiddingly repeated the reprimand yesterday. Clint had made no apologies. "I wasn't thinkin' about nothin' but bein' home, Dick."

Chief Bates had said that he could understand that and led the discussion to Carl Sayer, who was still missing. Clint could offer no explanation, although he admitted that he'd been looking for Sayer when he'd fallen down the hole. Sayer had not fallen down the same hole, Clint assured the policeman. And that was all he had to say; end of discussion. Pamela knew her husband was telling the truth. He must be. Why would he lie?

She rolled the frozen cubes of beef in flour and dropped them into hot oil on the bottom of her cast-iron skillet. They sizzled and spat. A hot bead of oil burned her hand, and she bit her lip to keep from crying out.

"How'd you finally get out of the hole?" Chief Bates had asked as he stood at the door, just before leaving.

"I piled stones day after day. They'd fall down, and I'd pile 'em up again. Then I made a rope from my belt and my shirt. It took a God-awful long time."

"How'd you stay alive down there?"

Clint nervously brushed the side of his nose with his right hand and looked at the floor. "I wasn't the only thing that fell into that hole, you know." That was as specific as he would ever be. He did make an offer, however. He said that as soon as he was feeling better he'd try to find the hole again to show Bates. He suggested they bring dynamite and blow it up, close the dangerous trap forever.

Bates allowed as that was a good idea. "You just give me a call when you're ready to go for a hike."

It seemed to Pamela that Bates wanted to say more, but he left, wishing all a happy New Year.

Pamela couldn't help imagining what it must have been like in that awful dungeon. How horribly Clint must have suffered, never knowing if he could escape, fearing he'd never be rescued. If it hadn't been for his resourcefulness, he'd probably have died there. Maybe he'd never have been found. None of the search parties had even located the hole.

Yet, Pamela feared, there was more to the survival story than Clint was telling. She didn't dare ask for more details, and chose not to discuss it with Eric. She suspected that her husband was trying to protect them, and himself, from the grisly details of his survival. The idea of cannibalism crossed her mind, the thought making her shudder. She had read accounts of the Donner party and of the Andes survivors. She realized that people would do what they had to in difficult situations. She could never ask Clint about the things she feared. Even if her suspicions were true, she knew he'd never tell; it wasn't his way.

If the worst things that she suspected had occurred, wouldn't that explain the strange way Clint had been acting? Perhaps her husband was keeping more bottled up inside than any man could reasonably be expected to.

She wished she could stop wondering—stop thinking about it.

Nonetheless, she couldn't help speculating about her cousin's theories. Knowing Eric, she guessed he surely had some ideas. Maybe it was best he didn't share them with her, especially if his ideas were as grisly as her own.

Elizabeth McKensie was thinking about the people up on Tenny's Hill. Because of the snowstorm two weeks before, she'd never had her talk with Mr. Nolan. She wasn't sure if it was fear or indecision that kept her from setting up another time for their meeting.

Now that Mr. Whitcome had come back, she realized how over-due their discussion had become.

She had resolved some time ago to have her say, and wouldn't talk herself out of it just because Mr. Whitcome had come home. She had a responsibility.

Wheeling herself to the telephone, she referred to the pad where she had written the Whitcomes' number. Glancing at her watch, she noted the time: five after eight, surely not too late to call. She dialed. The phone rang several times, and when Mrs. Whitcome answered she asked for Eric Nolan.

Luke Whitcome watched the shadows that his new mobile made on the bedroom wall in the soft glow of his night light. In his own way, Luke knew things were better, but they were not back to normal.

He wondered why Daddy watched him all the time. He liked to have Daddy hug him, but not so often. It seemed like Daddy watched him and hugged him way too much.

And tonight, while Daddy tucked him in, why had there been so many questions about Uncle Eric? What difference did it make if Uncle Eric came into Luke's room or visited at the window? Luke got the feeling Daddy didn't want Uncle Eric in the room. Daddy seemed to feel better when Luke assured him that Uncle Eric had never again come to the window.

Luke was sure he had done right to tell the little lie to his father. It was just like Uncle Eric had told him: "It's better not to tell your folks I've been here."

Luke still couldn't see what difference it made.

But anyway, it was good to have Daddy back. Luke could see how happy Mom was, and he liked that. She looked pretty when she smiled, and he hadn't seen her smile that way for a long time.

But why wouldn't she tell him where Daddy had been?

And why hadn't Daddy brought him a present when he came back? Probably because it was too close to Christmas. Luke remembered a weekend long ago when his father went away to hunting camp with some men from work. When he came back he had brought Luke a Mighty Loader, and it wasn't even Christmas, or his birthday, or anything. For Luke this had been a very special day.

It was funny that he didn't get a present this time. Another funny thing—Daddy seemed to walk a little different, like his feet hurt or something. And he got mad so easy. Maybe not mad exactly, but something like mad. Like the time Luke went out on the porch after supper to look for his Touch 'n' Go Racer. The second Daddy saw him go out the door he ran after him and pulled him back inside by the arm. Hard.

Daddy said, "I don't want you going outdoors alone. Not now, not ever."

It happened so fast, and Daddy looked so angry, that Luke started to cry. He knew he'd been bad, but he didn't know what he'd done. His father had knelt down in front of him and took him gently by the shoulders. "I'm sorry, Luke," he said very seriously. "I didn't mean to scare you. I just think you should stay inside unless one of us is with you, okay? Promise me you will."

Luke had promised because it made his father happy, but that was funny, too. They'd never told him not to go out on the porch before.

Luke looked at his bedroom window, its surface black and shiny as a pool of oil. There were a lot of funny things going on lately. A lot of funny feelings. Maybe if Uncle Eric comes to the window tonight, he'll explain.

"It's 'The Voice of the Mountains' again," whispered Pamela. She winked and handed the phone to Eric. She went back into the living room to find that her husband had disappeared again.

At first the empty room startled her. Clint couldn't have left the house, because to do so he would have had to pass her in the kitchen. The front door was still sealed with plastic to keep out winter drafts. Clint couldn't have left that way. Pamela opened the door to the basement, but the light was off. She checked the den, spare room, mudroom, and back kitchen, then concluded that he must have gone upstairs.

As she climbed the stairs, Pamela could hear Eric in the background, talking on the phone with Mrs. McKensie.

It's too early for Clint to have gone to bed, she thought, nearing the top of the stairs. Walking down the hall, she passed Eric's room, but, respectful of his privacy, left his door closed. Then she looked in on Luke, thinking her husband might have done the same thing. Her son was alone, sleeping peacefully among the shadows from his night light, his stuffed monkey at his side.

She slowed as she approached the door to her own room. If Clint wasn't in their bedroom, where could he be?

Almost too frightened to open the door, she nonetheless had to find out. The brass knob felt cold in her hand and the coldness made her realize that her palm was sweating. As the door creaked noisily inward, she saw the room's dim interior. The pale light of the December moon shone brightly through the two shadeless windows.

A dark form sat on the edge of their queen-size bed. Head in its hands, it did not turn to look at her. Indeed. it hardly seemed to notice that she had entered.

"Clint," she whispered. She felt her voice crack.

The form turned away from her. There was something in the posture, something in the strange sounds that it made, that told her this couldn't be her husband. It was not like Clint to sit alone, sulking in an empty room. And the noises he made, the deep, hollow, chest-wrenching sobs, were something that she had never heard before.

In that moment Pamela realized that the man who had returned to her was nearly a stranger. His behavior had become so alien that possibly she had never really known him at all. She would have believed, formerly, that Clint's makeup, his strength and confidence, would have made him immune to such deep, ongoing grief and suffering. Whatever had happened in those woods had made a powerful impression on him. Maybe—and this thought frightened her more than anything else—it had even changed him forever. Perhaps the Clint she had lost never would return.

Powerful instincts of her own—the wife, the mother—erupted with tremendous intensity. When she saw the man she loved sitting alone in their moonlit bedroom, crying as if he were hopelessly alone, as if he'd lost everything that he'd ever loved, she knew that she must do anything, everything, to ease his suffering.

She went to him quietly, and pulled his contorted terrified face to her breast.

"Your father's going away again." The voice was like a whisper in his sleeping brain. "You heard him talking about it to your mother. What will you do then? What will you do when you're alone?"

Luke found that he could easily open his eyes, but he couldn't bring the face into focus. It looked gray, misty. It hovered outside his window, like a hornets' nest bobbing on the wind-tossed branch of a tree. In the moonlight its tangled hair was like rusty cobwebs.

Try as he might, he couldn't muster the strength to speak, yet, somehow, Uncle Eric could always tell what Luke wanted to say.

"No," the voice said, "They won't take you with them. Why

would they want you? You'll be all alone here, unless you want to come and live with me."

Everything seemed a little strange, a little unreal. Uncle Eric looked funny; his face was closer now, a Halloween pumpkin perched upon the outside of the windowsill. Perhaps Luke was dreaming. He couldn't tell for sure, but he didn't think so. It was impossible to think clearly.

Luke couldn't see the features distinctly enough to be sure if Uncle Eric was kidding or not.

"No. I'm not joking. They'll leave you alone. But you can come with me. You can. See if you can get up. See if you can come to the window."

Luke tried real hard, but he couldn't move.

The head drifted backward, away from the window.

"I'll come back for you, later," the voice said. "You'll become stronger. Don't worry, Luke, I won't leave you alone. I promise. Rest now, sleep."

The shadowy head sank out of sight as Luke's eyes closed. He slept soundly, beyond the reach of the sobs coming from the next room.

25. FINAL JOB

While Clint and Pamela were talking in their bedroom, Billy Newton was sitting on a wooden crate in the pit under his wife's car. He was thinking about the Whitcomes.

When word that Clint was safe had finally reached Billy, he'd felt a great sense of relief. Although he'd been almost ready to break a silence that he had held for many years, he now tried to tell himself that speaking up would be unnecessary. After all, Clint was safe; he had taken a fall, had survived in the woods, and had made his way home to his family. In time for Christmas, too! What a fine Christmas present that must have been!

In spite of its happy ending, Billy knew the story didn't sound just right. But it was Clint's story, and everyone knew Clint Whitcome was an honest man.

There were a bunch of unanswered questions buzzing around inside Billy's head like a swarm of pesky mayflies. Had Clint actually survived for two weeks because of his strength and skills as a woodsman? Or had he received some help? Was there some condition attached to his unexpected return?

Did Clint owe someone a favor?

A small, self-protecting part of Billy hoped that Clint's return would put an end to all the problems in Antrim. Billy wanted to forget about them. Another part of him wanted to know for sure— all the details—even if there was personal risk involved.

He had been privy to most of the investigation so far. Chief Bates had used him as a sounding board more than once. Although Billy had admitted that he didn't have much of a head for

222 ■ THE COMING OF THE GENTRY

police work, he couldn't help trying to link things together in his mind.

Right now, he knew, Bates was operating under the assumption that the disappearance of Justin Hurd was coincidental, not related to the events on Tenny's Hill. Billy wasn't so sure, but he wanted to be damned certain before he spoke up.

He couldn't help thinking of all the old legends he'd been hearing since he was a boy. People weren't discussing legends much anymore; maybe they should be. It might be possible that there were people living in the hills of Antrim, some wild old family that had long ago severed all ties with civilization, more ties than Perly ever needed to cut to win the title of "hermit."

If there really were "hill people," real honest-to-goodness wildfolk, why, after at least thirty years of apparent peace and solitude, did they suddenly decide to break cover? Had years of inbreeding finally led to violent insanity? Or was there another motive?

Billy tried to connect all the links of the chain: Could the hill people, or "Goodpeople," as Perly called them, be responsible for the death of Justin Hurd? Traces of blood found in the truck's bed suggested that they were.

Perhaps they'd killed Perly, as well. It was likely he'd become less useful to them. His infrequent contacts with Billy had shown him that the hermit was getting crazier and crazier.

Billy took a red handkerchief from his pocket. He wiped the perspiration from his forehead, scratched up under his cap.

What detail could connect Hurd's death with the people on Tenny's Hill? The old legends held that the hill people sometimes captured women to be their brides. Could they have been after Mrs. Whitcome? Was she the connecting link?

Had an abduction been in progress the night of Hurd's death? *It don't quite fit,* thought Billy.

There was another confusing detail: Clint had come back. In the final analysis, Billy suspected, a bargain had been struck. He guessed that, in exchange for his life and release, Clint Whitcome was now in someone's debt.

Debts and favors and silences were things Billy didn't like to think about. He'd been thinking about them far too much lately. He feared that the chain of events that had started on November 21 was not soon to end.

He shifted his buttocks on the wooden crate, trying to get his mind back on Lillian's car. He wanted to figure out why the gears were slipping so he could get it roadworthy in order to take a little spin, a test drive, just to be sure everything was working right. Maybe he'd drive up to Tenny's Hill, drop in on the Whitcomes. Wish them a happy New Year. Maybe have a word or two in private with Clint.

Billy wanted to be sure his theory was correct before mentioning it to Bates. He didn't want to appear as crazy as Perly.

From his cramped position under the Plymouth he reached out, groping for his can of tobacco. He pulled it into the pit and dug at it, using his right forefinger to pack his pipe. Then he fished around in the pocket of his green work pants for his pipe lighter.

It seemed darker than usual in the garage, especially here in the pit. Even with his trouble light aimed directly at the transmission box, things didn't seem bright enough. He hoped nobody had switched his hundred-watt bulb for a lesser one. Even more he hoped that on top of everything else, his eyes weren't starting to give out on him.

As if forty years of arthritis weren't bad enough, now his goddamn eyes were going!

He cussed out loud and then felt foolish, knowing he was alone in the garage. To Billy, anyone who talked to himself—even if it was just swearing under your breath—was probably a little tetched. He didn't want to add insanity to his growing list of ailments.

The motionless air in the pit quickly filled up with pipe smoke. Billy watched it curl and wind lazily in the beam of the trouble light. Beyond the light, the crawlspace was dark and slashed with shadows. Cobwebs seemed to stitch support timbers to the joists and plank flooring. After resting a moment, Billy returned to the task of removing the pan from the bottom of the Plymouth's automatic transmission.

These goddamn bolts are turned on tight as welded, Billy cussed silently. He couldn't budge them with the wrench in his hand. Gotta get some goose poop, he thought (his term for penetrating oil).

His bottom was sore from sitting on the wooden box. His cramped and aching legs felt as if sand were grating in the joints of his knees and ankles. It wouldn't be nearly so bad if the pit were deeper; that way he could stand and not have to contort himself so much. But the pit was only as deep as the crawlspace under the garage. Even jacking up the car's front end had only made a little extra headroom. It did not contribute at all to his comfort. The throbbing, scraping pain was getting hard to ignore. Billy dreaded the thought that someday he would no longer be able to work under cars. Then he would be lost. He'd be old.

As Billy started after the oil he noticed something. Feels cold in here, he thought. Might's well check the fire while I'm at it.

He began to wriggle out of the pit, crawling beneath the engine compartment, where, because it was elevated on jacks, he had the most room. He pushed mightily with his hands and forearms, elbows pointing at the tires on either side of him. As he pushed, he felt his back scrape along the unyielding metal drain plug of the oil pan.

Then he heard the giggle. It was faint and fast, like a mischievous schoolboy. *Christ*, he thought, *now I'm hearing things, too . . .*

Suddenly it felt as if his pant-leg had caught on something. He kicked and pushed impatiently, but he couldn't free himself.

"Shit," he said, and tried to turn his head to see what was holding him. He couldn't turn completely around because of the way his shoulders and back were wedged between the underside of the car and the wooden floorboards.

He'd have to back down, free his pant-leg, and start over again.

By pushing with both hands, and with the help of gravity, he slid back a couple of inches. At that moment, whatever had snagged his pants moved, jerking him further backward. He lost his footing, could feel something solid tightening around the calves of his legs.

Panic seared the nerves along his spine. His muscles tensed involuntarily and squeezed him like a sponge, forcing icy perspiration from every pore at once. Someone, or something, was in the pit behind him! It had hold of both his legs, was lifting them off the oil-soaked dirt floor of the crawlspace.

Again it jerked him, this time flipping him brutally onto his back. The side of his face tore against the metal of the car.

In a mindless convulsion, his legs tried to kick themselves free. But they were weak, and a strength greater than his bound them together and held them off the floor.

"Leggo, God damn it. Git offa me," he cried. The corncob pipe dropped from his mouth, spreading fiery tobacco on the floor just inches below his head.

"Cut it out, damn it, this ain't funny!"

And again the giggling—high-pitched, maniacal.

Billy's fingers fought desperately to find something to hold on to. But there was nothing, only the car itself. His groping hands slipped uselessly along the wooden floorboards, filling his palms with slivers, tearing his nails on the cracks between the greasy planks.

He couldn't get out of the pit, and was surprised to find that he was not being pulled back into it. He was suspended, like a teeter-totter, head in the air between the car's engine and the floor, the small of his back resting on the fulcrum of wooden boards at the pit's edge, his feet below. He was helpless.

Something metallic hit the floor and clattered a few inches from his head. Billy rolled his eyes, trying to see what it was—Perly's flask! The one Clint had taken to return!

Suddenly he was aware of the metal drain plug, like the barrel of a gun pressing solidly against his chest. As the strength in his arms gave out, the back of his head slammed to the floor. He fought the brutal force that held his legs. In a seizure of fear, his face smashed against the underside of the car. Inhaling sharply, air bubbled through his nose; he knew that it was bleeding.

"Let go of me, dammit. Stop it now!"

His plea was met by a volley of shrill, mocking laughter.

It's kids, he thought, *it's goddamn kids!*

Again, as he tried to rise, he felt the pressure of the plug against his chest, but this time it was moving. It scraped back and forth between his shoulders, across the brittle firmness of his ribs.

Turning his head to the side he could see the right tire moving ever so slightly toward him . . . then away . . . then toward him again. Good Christ! Someone was rocking the car on its jacks!

"No, no, please."

When it dropped Billy turned his head as far as it would go; he didn't want to see the car's descent. He heard, more than felt, his ribs collapse. Billy's last bloody breath, squeezed explosively from his lungs by the vehicle's weight, blew pipe ashes in a semicircle around his crushed skull.

Rapid footfalls and a chorus of shrill laughter echoed in the black distance.

26. A MEETING

"That's odd," said Eric Nolan to Elizabeth McKensie, as he held the buzzing telephone in his hand.

"They're not answering?"

"No. And the ring sounds strange. I know they weren't planning to go out tonight; I left there less than an hour ago."

He looked at his watch. It was a little after nine o'clock.

A stern look darkened the old woman's face. "Better call the operator. See if the line's out of order."

Eric broke the connection by pushing the phone's cradle and dialed o. He soon asked for a number check and then hung up, feeling anxious and puzzled. "She says it's out of order. I'm not sure why, but that makes me nervous. I don't mean to be rude, Mrs. McKensie, but I think I'd better get back up there. I want to be sure everything is okay."

"Under the circumstances, I think that's very prudent, Mr. Nolan. I wish to come with you."

Eric was momentarily caught off guard. "Certainly, if you like. I don't want to inconvenience—"

"It's not an inconvenience, Mr. Nolan. I asked you to phone them so that I might gain an introduction to the Whitcomes. This way I shall meet them sooner. Perhaps that is best. I'm impatient to talk to them. I have reason to believe they are in danger."

Indeed, it had been the resonance of alarm, of possible danger, in the old woman's voice that had brought Eric Nolan out into the foggy December night to make the short drive to Chester.

He stared evenly at the earnest, wrinkled face. Her gray eyes, framed by spectacles, held his gaze with a quiet insistence. He remained undecided only for a moment.

"Let's go," he said.

When they parked in the Whitcome driveway, Eric removed the wheelchair from the trunk, opened it, and helped Mrs. McKensie into place. He pushed her across the yard to the steps, then, a step at a time, pulled her onto the porch. He wheeled her to the door and opened it. Eric stepped inside, paused by the door, and looked around the quiet interior. The house seemed empty.

"Pam! Clint!" Eric called. There was no response. "Funny," he said. "The car and truck are here."

He helped Mrs. McKensie into the kitchen, then walked alone to the foot of the stairs to call again. This time Pam's voice answered from above. "I'll be right down," she said.

Mrs. McKensie followed Eric to the living room where he took a seat on the sofa. A moment later Pamela entered. Her red and puffy eyes told Eric that she had been crying.

Seeing Mrs. McKensie, Pamela looked surprised, took an almost invisible step backwards. Automatically, her right hand moved to her eyes in a self-conscious attempt to brush away the evidence of tears. When her hand came away a polite smile lit her features.

Before Eric had a chance to introduce her, the old woman said, "Mrs. Whitcome, I'm Elizabeth McKensie. I'm sorry to intrude on you folks this evening. I know an unannounced visit, especially one at this hour, is generally inexcusable, but I have something very important to talk to you and your husband about."

Pamela looked at Eric, who shrugged and then nodded his approval.

"Well, ah . . . Clint's upstairs just now. He's not feeling well . . ."

"I'm sorry to hear that," said the old woman. "It is surely not my intention to overstep the bounds of propriety, but I must ask that you trust me when I say that what I have to tell you is very important. Won't you please ask him if he might join us, if only for a short time?"

"Well, I . . ." she looked to Eric again.

"I'm right here." It was the flat, emphatic voice of Clint Whitcome as he walked down the stairs, his knuckles pale against the banister. His limp was more pronounced and he appeared haggard. His jet-black, oily hair set off his abnormal pallor. He looked ghostly. His eyes, deep-set and dark-circled, were nearly invisible, like the eyeless cavities of a skull. For Eric, this stark vision of Clint contrasted painfully with the healthy, happy husband and father whom he had met when he'd arrived a little more than a month ago. Clint Whitcome had no smile for his guests.

Eric knew at a glance that Clint looked far worse than when he had seen him last—only an hour ago.

On unsteady legs, Clint walked to the chair nearest the fireplace. He sat in it heavily, almost falling. With his back ramrod-straight, he remained silent and immobile. Pamela seated herself on the far end of the sofa, stealing a furtive glance at her husband. An awkward silence fell over the group.

Eric was the first to speak. "Earlier tonight, when Mrs. McKensie phoned, she asked me to her house to discuss her theories about what has been happening around here. She asked me if I would be willing to introduce her to you two. She wondered how she should present what she has to say, was afraid how you might take it."

Mrs. McKensie nodded.

Eric continued, "I tried to phone you before we came, but the phone here is out of order. Did you know that?"

Pamela looked at Clint who kept staring straight ahead. Then to Eric, "Nuh . . ." She cleared her throat. "No," she said.

"When I found that the phone wasn't working, well, I don't know, I thought something might be wrong. I mean, it was working an hour ago, when Mrs. McKensie called. We got in the car and came right up."

"There's nothing wrong here," said Clint Whitcome coldly.

"I hope you're right, Mr. Whitcome." Mrs. McKensie looked doubtfully at Clint. She nervously moved her hands back and forth on the rubber tires of the wheelchair. "As you people may know, I'm something of a local history buff . . ."

"I've read your newspaper articles," offered Pamela. Eric could see his cousin was straining to be cordial. He understood that their arrival had interrupted Clint and Pam at a bad time. Why the old woman was insensitively pushing the issue he could not understand.

"I've been aware of your property here for a good many years. I knew your grandparents, young lady, and I've got distant memories of this land before there was even a house on it. Did you know that a cabin stood here before this house was built?"

No one replied.

"Well, no matter. I guess when you're as old as I am, you don't need to study history half as much as you need to remember it. I've lived through a lot of history right here in Windsor County. Much of what I remember was never important enough to be included in the textbooks. But, important or not, I try not to let it be forgotten. That's why I write my essays and my poems.

"Years ago, when I was a much younger woman, I thought I'd made a discovery that was extremely important. Important enough not only to be included in the history books, but perhaps to be the subject of one or two of them. Since I believed it was my own discovery, I wanted to be the first to investigate it and to write about it. So, I began doing research and gathering information."

Eric was watching the old woman carefully. She seemed to be working up the courage to get to the point. He wondered if the cracks in her voice came from age or nervousness. Glancing at Clint and Pam, he found them to be listening with interest, but he couldn't overlook the apprehension on their faces. It was as if they too dreaded her getting to the point. His eyes moved back to Mrs. McKensie as she continued.

"I wanted to protect what I thought was my discovery, so I kept my research pretty secret. A kind of vanity, I guess. I didn't even take my husband totally into my confidence. Maybe that was my mistake. Anyway, what I have to say concerns the things I learned many years ago about your property here on Tenny's Hill.

"Folks around here have known about that old root cellar up on the plateau for years. That Mr. Sayer, and several other educated men, are starting to believe that your cellar, and others like it around the state, were actually built several thousand years ago. Well, of course, I don't know about that. The history that I do know about doesn't go back that far. All I can say is that cellar of yours has been around as long as I can recall. I'm sure it was there when Mr. Tenny's cabin stood where this house now stands. In those days, it was the only place for miles around. Logic would suggest that either Mr. Tenny built the root cellar, or that it was here long before he built his cabin.

"Personally, it is my belief that Mr. Tenny didn't build it. I think it was here long before he arrived, when this land was nothing more than wilderness. So, I ask you, who did build it?"

The three people looked at each other. Eric noted that whatever the barrier separating them had been, it was now crumbling. Everyone was involved in the old woman's narrative. Their eyes all focused on Mrs. McKensie, encouraging her to go on.

"Well, I have my own theory," she continued, "and now that I think about it, maybe it's not that different from what Mr. Sayer was probably thinking. As a matter of fact, he was so snooty and unwilling to discuss my ideas that I almost suspect his thinking and mine were pretty much the same, even though he wouldn't admit it. I'll bet he was pretending to look for one thing, while actually he was looking for something else. If he'd been more cordial, I'd have taken him into my confidence, shared information . . .

"But I'm getting off the track." Her hands clutched nervously at the blanket over her legs. Her voice seemed weak and shaky, like a frail child about to give a recitation before a jeering class.

"Let's see now, how shall I explain this? I guess I have to ask you to come back with me to the days when I was a little girl. I lived with my parents and my grandparents—that's the way we did it in those days, all together—in a big farmhouse over in Chester. Actually, right on the Chester-Antrim line. Anyway, my grandmother used to tell me stories, as I'm sure all grandmothers do. Her stories were often about what she called, the 'Gentry.' This was her euphemistic name for the 'Daoine Sidhe' or, more commonly, the 'little people.' I always thought, or at least my father told me, that they were stories Grandmother had brought with her from the old country, from Ireland. I remember cold winter nights when we'd all sit around the wood stove, and my grandmother would tell her stories in that lovely brogue of hers. They were charming, frightening stories of the Gentry and how they were the dwindled gods of the earth's first inhabitants: fallen angels, too good for Hell, too cruel for Heaven. She thought they could work magic, thought they had powers far greater than those of human beings. Grandmother said they were powers that we humans should avoid. She used to warn me not to wander off by myself. She said if I got too far from the house I might meet one of the little men. She told me that she herself had seen them on that worthless, rocky land between Chester and Antrim, seen those little people, many of them, dancing and wailing in the summer nights."

Pamela looked at Eric. He could tell she was recalling the dancing children that she had seen, years ago, outside the kitchen window.

Mrs. McKensie noticed the exchange of glances and continued. "My grandmother warned that if I wandered onto that worthless land alone, they would capture me, take me to their caves in the hills, and I would never see my parents again. I guessed she was just trying to scare me so I wouldn't wander off alone and get lost. At least, that's what I thought for a long time."

"That seems like a horrible thing to tell a child," said Pamela. Then she looked timidly at Clint, who did not look back.

Eric noticed that Clint and Pamela had become silent. Clint was looking at his hands on his lap. Pamela stared at the fireplace.

Mrs. McKensie tried to bring Pamela back into the conversation. "It's always a bad thing to lie to a child, and for years that's what I thought my grandmother was doing. But that brings me to my discovery, doesn't it?

"When I was in my twenties, my hobby was bird watching. One of my hobbies, I should say. I also had my own portable Kodak. I'd go on nature walks by myself and take pictures of things, birds mostly. One day, I was walking up somewhere in this neck of the woods. Suddenly, I got the strange feeling that I wasn't alone, that

I was being followed. I got scared, but not in the same way a young girl alone in the woods might get scared nowadays. At that time, rapes and madmen were not so much a part of our day-to-day lives. We were more, what's the word? Naive? Innocent? Something like that.

"Anyway, I just couldn't shake the feeling that I was not alone, that someone, or something, was watching me.

"The only thing around that I could see was a big old owl snoozing on the branch of an oak tree. He was a funny fellow so I took a picture of him." She reached under the blanket that covered her legs and took out a five-by-seven photograph, which she handed to Pamela Whitcome. "Look at this," she said.

Pamela took the picture and looked hard at it. Eric moved across the sofa and sat beside his cousin so he could see, too. Clint joined them on the couch, and they all studied the photograph.

The right side of the picture was taken up by the trunk and thick branches of the tree. A sturdy limb that bisected the photo horizontally supported the dense-looking, barrel-shaped body of a sizable owl, its head turned slightly to the left. The background was a confusion of earth, limbs, tree trunks and sky. Eric looked up at the old woman with an implied question in his eyes. He couldn't see the point of all this.

"Look at the tree trunk on the far left," she directed. "Look carefully."

All eyes did as instructed. Eric was the first to point to an indistinct, faded form in the old photograph. The focus was poor, and the years had dulled the image, but concentration and imagination helped to clarify it. There, seated on the limb of another tree in the background, was a tiny shape. Its face was obscured by leaves, but careful study made the body look more and more like that of a small, chubby child. He sat on the limb, close to the trunk of the tree. His legs, dangling in the air, were crossed at the ankles. He seemed to lean against the tree trunk for support as his head aimed straight at the camera.

"You see it now?" the old woman asked.

They all nodded. "What is it?" Pamela asked.

Clint continued to stare at the picture.

"I think it's one of the little people. I didn't notice him when I was in the woods that day. I didn't see him until I had the picture developed. But when I did notice it, I knew I was onto something. Day after day, I returned to the forest with my Kodak, hoping to get another picture. I realized now that my grandmother had not been telling me lies. Immediately, I began studying Irish folktales of leprechauns and such. I wanted to learn all that I could. It was at that time that I started my collection of newspaper clippings about people in Vermont who've reported seeing mysterious little people.

"By then, of course, my grandparents were dead, and so I couldn't ask them for more details. I did talk to a lot of local folks, but no one had much to say on the subject. I even wrote a letter to Arthur Conan Doyle and sent him a copy of the photograph. As you know, he was a researcher of psychic phenomena, all manner of ghosts, monsters, little people, and the like. He believed in them, you know. Sir Arthur was kind enough to answer my letter, but, rightly, said the photograph was not conclusive.

"Nonetheless, I was determined to continue my research. I knew what I had in that photograph was important. I wanted to write a book, establish a name for myself as having been the first to discover and document the existence of a new race, or tribe, or whatever. Of course, I didn't believe there was anything magic about these people, but I most certainly did believe they were there. I knew they were. I speculated that their legendary magical attributes were given to them by people who glimpsed them briefly and then told and retold the story with new and more imaginative embellishments. After all, isn't that how legends come about and evolve?

"Over the years I did a lot of reading. I discovered that the folklore of the world is rich in stories about little people. We all know about Irish leprechauns and the capricious Scandinavian elves, but closer to home, and predating the arrival of the white man, American Indian legend includes tales of little people. The Penobscot Indians of Maine told of the *wanagemeswak*, who in many ways resemble European little folks. Right here in Vermont, the Abenaki

Indians have had a tradition of little people for ten or twelve thousand years. That's a good, long time.

"An interesting thing to note, though, is the similarity of beliefs among separate peoples. In all cultures, every one, those who believe in the little folk were—and are—very much afraid of them.

"The little people are considered powerful, ill-tempered, and potentially deadly. Although kindness, I've learned, is not always wasted on them, they are thought to be amoral, and should be, it is generally agreed, approached with caution if approached at all.

"People who choose not to believe in them have hundreds of ingenious ways to dismiss the idea. Some folks argue that the Gentry never actually existed, but are simply the lingering folk memory of a long-lost race of pygmies. Some suggest they came about as a result of the way the primitive mind explained such natural aberrations as human dwarfs—the real and perfect human child was swapped for the deformed troll—the enduring changeling concept. Yet, those who consider them imaginary are hard-pressed to explain why they are so widely known, and so similarly perceived by unconnected cultures around the world.

"These explanations may be imaginative, but I'm convinced the Gentry are not imaginary. I know they are real, and I believe, Mr. and Mrs. Whitcome, that a group of them is your nearest neighbor."

The old woman stopped talking and looked at the eyes of each member of her audience, scrutinizing one face at a time. Eric guessed she was assessing the impact of her disclosure. Her eyes moved from Pamela to Eric, from Eric to Clint.

Clint could not hold her gaze. He looked down at his hands and rubbed them together nervously in his lap. When Pamela put her arm around her husband's shoulders and pulled him toward her, Eric felt the motion through the couch. When Eric looked at Clint, he saw that he was shaking.

27. CLINT'S STORY

A pause in the conversation brought Pamela to her feet with an offer of coffee. Eric eagerly accepted; Mrs. McKensie smiled gratefully and nodded. Clint waved his refusal with a tiny flick of his fingers.

Clint leaned forward on the sofa and buried his face in his hands, rubbing his eyes savagely with his palms. Then, looking the old woman in the face, he blinked a couple of times. He appeared groggy, his eyes looked dazed and frightened.

When he spoke his tone was low and raspy until it evened into his normal melodious diction. "I guess it's time for me to talk," he began. "I know about the danger you came to warn us about. And I know about your little people. That's what Pam and I were talking about when you got here. I thank God you know about them, too. For days now I haven't dared tell anyone, but I had to explain it to my wife. I couldn't stand to have her see me the way I am without understanding why.

"I've been real scared that if I told, no one would believe me . . ."

"I know, Mr. Whitcome. I know that fear. I know how it feels to be afraid people will think of you as crazy. It's made me hold my silence for a good many years," encouraged Mrs. McKensie. Her voice was gentle.

"But there's more than that." Clint continued. "I'm also scared of what could happen to me, to my family, if I do speak."

"But you must speak," said the old woman. "We both must. We must put a stop to this."

"I don't know if we can." Again Clint buried his face in his

236

hands. After a pause he went on. "I'm glad you know about 'em. That's something. That's a start, maybe. I'll bet that probably all the people in the world who know about them are all together right here in this room. What do you think?"

"I dare say you and I aren't the only ones who know of them, Mr. Whitcome. But we may be the only ones who'll speak up. I'd appreciate it if you could tell me just what it is you do know."

"I'll tell," said Clint. "I may be sorry, but I'll tell. Maybe you can help me. Help us."

Eric, against all the conditioned reflexes of his educated mind, was near to believing in the little people. Indeed, in his own imagination, he had theorized their involvement for some time. But when he heard them discussed openly, seriously, and as factual, he felt some of the foundation of his conditioned logic beginning to crumble. He was helplessly caught up in the scene that was unfolding around him. He listened with frightened interest to the strange conversation, and wondered how an old woman in a wheelchair could possibly be of help to any of them.

Clint cleared his throat and began again. "I been lying to folks right along; lying about a lot of things. I saw the body of the man who disappeared, Mr. Sayer's body. He was hung up in a tree, and the front of him was cut open like the carcass of a deer. It could be that he was hung up like that just to scare me—to throw me off guard. But no matter. I got scared. I was afraid whoever got him would get me, too. Anyways, I ran off in a direction I didn't know very well. I don't know why I ran, I guess I was in a panic. I wasn't watching where I was going, and I fell into a big pit in the ground. It wasn't a trap. By that I mean it wasn't man-made. It was more like a cave. But the walls were too steep to escape, even if I'd . . . even if I hadn't been hurt."

"You were hurt in the fall?" Eric asked.

"I was."

"You didn't mention that before."

"There's a lot of things I didn't mention. I been keeping so much bottled up I thought I'd burst . . ."

"Please go on," said Mrs. McKensie.

"Well, I think I broke my back. I know I busted my leg. It was twisted around like a crank."

"You couldn't recover from a broken back this quickly." Eric was incredulous.

"Please, Mr. Nolan, kindly let him finish."

The whistling of the teakettle sounded from the other room. Shortly the fragrance of coffee blended with the tension in the air.

"That's just it," said Clint. "They cured me. Somehow, they fuckin' cured me." He shot a guilty look at Mrs. McKensie, who didn't react in the least to his vulgarity.

Eric could tell that what sounded like anger in Clint's voice was really a terrible fear. He watched his friend fidgeting on the couch, sliding his hands back and forth on his pant legs, combing his fingers through his black hair.

Clint took a deep breath. It seemed to calm him. "I lied to you about the time I spent in the hole. I lied to everybody. I wasn't down there for a long time—it was just overnight. When they pulled me out I must've blacked out. I remember dangling from the rope they threw down to me. I remember slamming into the rock walls as they pulled me up. Then they left me hanging there for a minute. I was spinnin' around like a fish on a line. They tumbled Sayer's body, all naked and bloody, right past me and into the pit. It's like they were using the hole for their garbage dump. Down below I could see another dead man, lying face down. I can't say for certain who it was, but he was wearin' a blue uniform. I bet it was Justin Hurd's body. I bet they got him, too. But the worst thing I remember is what they done to the dog. There was an old collie in that pit with me. They chucked rocks down at it. There was no place for it to hide. It just kept yelpin' and runnin' around the cave, tryin' to get out of the way. The bastards stoned it to death, and laughed while they done it. Maybe I passed out when I seen that, or when I heard its awful howling. Jesus."

He took a breath. "While I was knocked out they took me to their camp on the cliffs over on the far side of the mountain. They live in a cave there, way up on them steep cliffs where no one goes."

"You actually saw their camp?" Mrs. McKensie's voice was full of wonder. "There was a time when I would have given anything to be so privileged."

"It was no privilege."

"What was it like? What were they like?"

"They were like nothin' I've ever seen. It's an odd thing, but in all the time I was there I never really got a good look at none of them. They always kept back a ways, in the shadows or partly hidden. I could tell they was real little, less than three foot high; they didn't even come up to my waist. They was dressed in animal skins, I think. Some of 'em was real spindly-looking, others kinda chunky; that's all I can tell ya. And I couldn't understand 'em when they talked, they spoke in their own language. Funny soundin' talk. One of 'em spoke English, but not too good. I didn't meet up with him till later. I figure he must've been the one who wrote on my barn.

"Anyways, for two or three days they kept me tied up and nobody came near me. They drugged me, at least I think they did, because I could never seem to wake up all the way—maybe it was because I was sick and in a fever, I don't know. Every now and then I'd almost wake up and find they'd left me something to eat. Apples, carrots, mushrooms, some kind of weird, funny-tastin' cheese. I ate what I could. I had to.

"All the while I couldn't believe what was happenin' to me. I thought I must be crazy, or out of my head with fever. I kept expectin' I'd wake up and find myself at the bottom of that goddamn hole again. I think that's probably why they left me alone. So I'd get used to the idea of 'em. Besides, with my back, they knew I wasn't goin' anywhere."

Pamela returned with a tray of steaming coffee mugs. She served Mrs. McKensie first, and helped with the cream and sugar. Then she handed a mug to Eric, and one to Clint, saying, "I thought maybe you'd change your mind." He accepted gratefully, taking big swigs from the mug and licking his lips. Pamela sat beside him, her hand resting on his thigh.

"How many of them were there?" asked Eric.

"I don't know, I never got a good look at 'em, like I told ya. Half a dozen I think, no more'n eight. I couldn't tell if they was any females among 'em. Some of 'em had real long hair with kinda bumpy-looking bodies. I think I saw four, maybe five different ones, maybe more."

"Were there any children?" Eric asked.

"Christ, I don't know. To me they all looked like children, if you know what I mean . . ."

Eric nodded. Mrs. McKensie lifted her head, signaling Clint to continue.

"I 'member there was this one fella who kinda hung around way in the background, away from all the others. I never got any kind of look at him, just his outline lurking in the shadows. He might have been a leader or something. I don't know. But I'll tell you this: he gave me the creeps.

"All the while I just wanted to get away from them. Not that they was hurtin' me or nothin'. But it was so strange; it's hard to explain. I tried to talk to them, but they'd just stare at me from way off in the shadows. Or they'd run away, laughin', kinda. I couldn't follow them and I couldn't leave. I was paralyzed from the waist down, that's one thing I'm sure of.

"They kept me warm with furs and hot water in some kind of animal bladder. They fed me, and they brought me leaves and water to clean myself up with. They even kept candles burnin' in the cave so I wouldn't be in the dark. But they stayed clear of me until . . . Well, one day I woke up, and this little guy—the one I jest told you about—was sittin' across the cave from me. He was all covered up with shadows so I couldn't make him out real clear—but he said the first English words I'd heard in a good long time. He says—I don't think I can copy his voice exactly, he was whisperin' and had this funny-soundin' accent. Another thing, he didn't speak real good—he says, 'We know Mr. Whitcome.' That's what he called me, Mr. Whitcome, just like we was doin' business or somethin'. He says, 'We offer him a work. For us.' He was offering me a job, I thought. Well, I was in no condition to do no work for anybody. I think by this time I was half dead, not good for much of anything.

"Anyhow, we worked at trying to talk for a while. He wouldn't answer none of my questions. He was a cagey little bastard—he didn't lay his cards on the table all at once. No. But he did tell me they could cure me. I didn't believe it, of course, but he kept tellin' me, time after time, that they could. Then he asked me what it would be worth to me if they did.

"I asked him if I had anything they wanted. He didn't answer right off. He just told me to think about it. Then he left, only this time he took my candle with him.

"Without the light, it was pitch black in that cave. It felt damper, too. Now and then I could hear them shuffling around and talking in their high, scratchy voices, but I couldn't tell what they were talking about. I don't know how long he left me there to think. It might have been a couple hours, maybe a couple days, I really couldn't tell. I wasn't thinkin' too clear. After a while—I hate to admit it—but I began to look forward to the time he would come back. I was lonely for my family; I was sick and cold. I was as god-awful scared as I'd ever been in my life. Scared all the time. I didn't really know what they wanted from me, what they planned to do with me. I kept tellin' myself that they didn't mean me any harm, but I knew that was probably just wishful thinking.

"I gotta keep remindin' you how dark it was in that cave. So dark it was just like not havin' any eyes at all. I couldn't see nothin', nothin' at all. I got so nervous waitin' there that I thought I'd surely crack up if I wasn't crazy already. Sometimes I'd think I wasn't alone in the cave. I'd think I could hear those little folks in there with me, rustlin' around in the dark, sometimes so close to me I could smell their stinky breath. It's like they could see in the dark. Like they were keepin' an eye on me, waitin' for me to break. And I couldn't see nothin' at all.

"After a long time that one fella come back again. He brings the light in with him, and I can tell you I was damn happy to see that. But he still never got close enough to let me get a good look at him. He told me his name was Goodman, so that's what I called him. He asked if I was ready to talk business. I was, too. I think I'd have agreed to anything at that point."

With that, a dew-soft film covered Clint's eyes. Eric watched them fill with tears, and saw Pamela put an arm around her husband's slumped shoulders. "It's okay," she whispered to him. "You can tell them. Please, Clint, you've got to get it out."

He brushed his eyes with his sleeve, and looked sheepishly at Eric and Mrs. McKensie.

"I think I did agree to anything," he whispered.

"They wanted you to work for them?" asked Mrs. McKensie.

"Yes, that's right. They needed a connection with the outside world. They said they'd had somebody, but he died. They never said who it was, but I figure it must've been old Perly Greer. The hermit.

"Now they needed a new errand boy. They told me they'd cure me, let me go, but in exchange I had to do what they asked—bring them things, transport 'em around, run errands anytime, anyplace. And I agreed. I had to. I had no choice."

Clint stood up abruptly and began to pace. He moved from the fireplace to the window, pulled back the drape and looked out into darkness. Then he let it drop, and returned to the fireplace, where he stood leaning against the mantel.

"Did they threaten you?" Eric asked.

"Not exactly. Not just like that. I mean they never really gave me a choice. They broke me down a little at a time. They understood from the start that eventually I'd do what they asked. Knew it from the start. It's not as if they said, 'Help us or we'll kill you . . .'"

"What did they say?"

"They said that if I didn't help them—or if I ever said a word to anyone that I knew about them—then they'd . . . they'd . . ."

Pamela stood up and went to her husband. "Go on," she whispered.

Clint spoke with his eyes closed, his voice lifeless and weak. "They said they'd take my wife and son."

"Jesus," said Eric.

"And I agreed. God damn them, I agreed."

"You had no choice," said Pamela, taking Clint's hand in both of hers. "Anyone would have done the same. You were crippled and sick. You were terrified half out of your mind." She put her arms around him.

"I *was* out of my mind. I was crazy as hell. I must've been to put you both in danger. I put us all in danger."

Mrs. McKensie broke in, "You did the only sensible thing, Mr. Whitcome. You got yourself well, you got out of there, and you bought yourself some time. They'd have taken your son anyway."

Her final words had the effect of a blast of arctic air. All eyes froze on the old woman, waiting for her to explain.

"I want to tell you something, Mr. Whitcome. You did exactly the best thing. Exactly. I understand that you don't trust your judgment in hindsight. You were sick, tired, sore, and you're probably thinking that if you had been well you'd have handled the whole situation better. Maybe even done something heroic, like sacrificing yourself to protect your family. But you did the right thing, believe me. You can't trust them, not at all. They feel no more obliged to be honest with you than you do to be honest with, I don't know, a cow, or a goat. Whether you work for them or not, they'll have your boy. They've probably been after him from the start.

"As I told you, I've studied them. I've read all the folklore and newspaper clippings I could get hold of, everything I could. I assume that most of the legends are based on some kind of fact. There's one thing that all stories about little people have in common—they steal children, and sometimes young women, for their own disgusting pleasure."

Eric felt his stomach knotting. He was sweating, feeling lightheaded. The things he imagined sickened him.

When he looked at Pamela he saw terror on her face.

"My theory is that they cannot reproduce. So, if one of their number dies, they must kidnap a replacement. It's the old idea of the 'changeling' again: the human child is stolen to repopulate fairy stock. So, Mr. Whitcome, you probably *didn't* see any children among them, at least none of their own. And they're ageless; that is, they can live for hundreds of years. But they can't reproduce, not with each other, not with humans. For that reason their number remains constant. There can't be too many of them—if there were they would be more conspicuous. My guess is that there are only eight of them, no more, and so they're never discovered.

"I suspect there are several groups of them around the state. Maybe they're all over New England, maybe the whole country. Each group is limited to a specified number. They require a full complement to generate their optimum power, whatever that power may be. It could be magic, it could be some kind of mental telepathy. Whatever it is, I think they need a defined number to use the power at its full strength."

"How did you arrive at the number eight?" Eric asked.

"It is only a theory, Mr. Nolan. I think we can presume that their population is small simply because they are so rarely seen. At first I guessed that there might be seven of them. Seven seems to be a magical number. It recurs often in folklore, religion, and mythology: seven-league boots, Seven Gifts of the Spirit, even seven dwarfs in the Snow White story."

"One of my students did a paper on why there were seven dwarfs in Snow White. Apparently the number came from the days of the week, the number of planets known at that time—seven—and the number of metals the dwarfs mined for—seven again. If you're going by the legends, where did you get the number eight?"

"I can't be sure of the number, Mr. Nolan. I'm just guessing. I've studied the derivation of fairy tales, too, and you're right about the old belief that only seven planets circled the sun. But the old beliefs aren't reliable; we wouldn't want to bet our lives on them. What if we include the sun in our count? Then we've got eight planets, not seven.

"We don't want to underestimate what we're up against here. But whether the number is seven or eight, it's secondary to *why* they need a specific number. In witchcraft there is the concept of 'coning power.' That is, when the coven channels the power of all its members through one individual. Supposedly this will focus and amplify the forces of the magic.

"Regardless of how many they require to form a perfect coven —if that's what they call their group—I believe that their number is now down by one."

Eric looked at Clint. "So that cryptic message scrawled on the garage, 'An I for an I,' must mean that you actually shot one of the Gentry, not a child, as you thought."

"Could be."

Eric was excited. "I'll bet you accidentally shot one of them. He probably died, so they warned you that they would have an eye for an eye. They meant Luke! Your falling in that hole just gave them an extra bonus. They'd take Luke and get some work out of you, too. They'd just use you until they were ready to take your son."

Mrs. McKensie held up a wrinkled hand. "Slow down a minute, Mr. Nolan. As you may recall, the trouble in Antrim started before the shooting. A member of the Gentry died—maybe from an accident, possibly of natural causes—sometime before the 'hunting accident.' Don't forget, young Luke's dog disappeared, and there was the policeman who came up missing."

Eric realized that she was right. Mrs. McKensie had apparently thought out the entire puzzle. Taking a sip of his coffee, he decided he would let her finish.

"It is my belief that the abduction of the boy was in progress the moment the dog disappeared. The Gentry, no doubt, took the animal."

Clint and Eric looked at each other.

"And they killed him," Clint said flatly. "Eric and I found Rusty's body."

Pamela gasped.

"Further, I believe the young policeman accidentally interrupted the kidnapping. It cost him his life. I'm sure the body you saw in the pit was that of Justin Hurd, Mr. Whitcome.

"You probably scared one of them with your shotgun, nothing more. They could have cured a gunshot wound as easily as they healed your back and leg. But they know how to capitalize on fear. That's why they wrote on your barn, to frighten you. The Biblical quotation doesn't mean a life for a life—but you're right, it does imply vengeance."

"Are you sure of all this?" asked Pamela.

"Of course not, dear. It's all speculation, but it's the best theory we have to work on. If I'm just right about the numbers, at least we'll know how many enemies we have to worry about. Even if we have doubts, we'd better not take any chances. I assure you, tonight, after this discussion, we'll all have to protect ourselves. We'll have to be on our guard at all times. You see, as of now—having spoken—we're more vulnerable than ever before. It could be that they're listening as we speak, overhearing us right now, with their ears—possibly with their minds. They'll stop at nothing to protect their secret. We can't trust our safety."

"What would they want with Luke? Why he's just a little boy. What would they do with him?" asked Pamela, her voice shaking, her body trembling.

The old woman wheeled herself over to the young couple, adding her hands to theirs. She looked Pamela directly in the eyes and spoke slowly, earnestly. "They'd alter him. I don't know how. They'll make him one of them, fix him so he won't be able to grow up, or get any bigger. Perhaps he'll stay a child forever; perhaps they're all children, arrested in a selfish and evil childhood that will last until judgment day." A shadow seemed to pass over Mrs. Mc-Kensie's face, and her voice lowered as she continued, "They've learned nothing of morality, nothing of conscience. They wallow in whimsy and self-indulgence; inside, they grow foul and distorted as the years pass, leaving them with the faces and physiques of the children they once were."

"Luke would stay a child forever?" Pamela seemed unbelieving.

"I can't say, dear, not with any certainty." The old woman took a breath, closed her eyes briefly. "In any event, he won't age as we do, not as rapidly, not into any kind of maturity of body, mind, or spirit. Remember, it's likely that some of these creatures are centuries old. Possibly, after the equivalent of several human lifetimes, his head will begin to bulge, his limbs will thicken and bend, and his back will curve and stiffen. But, during your lifetime, he won't get any older. He'll outlive you and forget you. He'll stay with them, doing whatever it is that they do. That's all I can tell you."

Pamela and Clint embraced. Her shoulders heaved up and down in silent sobs.

"I'm sorry to have to tell you this so graphically, dear," a look of sympathetic pain was on the old woman's face, "but I must impress upon you how very serious I believe this is. I'm an old woman, Mrs. Whitcome. Sometimes I wonder why the Good Lord has let me live as long as I have. Maybe it was to tell you folks this. To try to help you."

Eric felt his detached fascination with the narrative change to a total, crippling fear. "How could they do that to Luke?"

"I don't know. They have medicine, or magic. They can do it, Mr. Nolan. They can do it just as certain as they cured Mr. Whitcome."

"What did they do to you, Clint?" Eric's doubt was gone, replaced by an icy fear.

"They all crowded around me after they put a kind of muddy paste over my eyes. Then they made me drink a warm, sweet liquid, like honey. It made me real drowsy. They sang and moved in circles around me. I couldn't see them but I could hear them, chanting and moving, their animal skins swishing and their feet scratching. Two of them turned me over on my stomach—I was too weak and groggy to help or to resist—and they pulled my clothes off. One of 'em poured what felt like hot wax along my spine, and all over my leg. Hurt like a son of a bitch, and I think I passed out from the pain. I don't know how long I was out for, but when I woke up—I couldn't believe it—I was cured. Just like that. Even now I can't really believe it. I can't call it a miracle, there's something too foul, too stinkin' evil about it. But I was better. I could walk. I could feel. Oh, I still have a little stiffness in my leg, but you gotta remember, it was pretty mangled."

"So you see," said the old woman, "they can make good on their promises, and on their threats. Believe it."

"What can we do?" asked Pamela, her complexion now as white as Clint's.

"Let's call the police," said Eric. He got to his feet. Mrs. McKensie frowned. "There's not a chance in the world we'll be believed. Not a chance. And, if you remember, the phone here isn't working. No, I think we'll have to handle this ourselves. We'll have to make a plan, first for our own safety. You'd better sit down, Mr. Nolan."

"Dick Bates is a good friend of Clint's. He's a policeman. He'd believe us." Pamela sounded hopeful.

Clint just shook his head.

"Even if the police did listen to us, we have no proof," said Mrs. McKensie. "My photograph wasn't even convincing to Conan Doyle, who actually believed in fairies."

Pamela insisted, "If we could just convince Dick, he could get some men and search the woods."

"They'd never allow themselves to be seen. They'd cover their tracks like they'd never even been there. My husband and I searched for evidence of them for years. I was looking for them when I took the fall that put me in this chair. I remember looking up at the ledge above and seeing an ugly, grinning face looking back at me. Everyone said I was delirious from the fall. Please believe me, Mrs. Whitcome, whatever we do, we have to do it ourselves."

"That's right," said Clint with a determined finality. "By God, that's right!"

Eric looked at the grandfather clock. It was ten after one in the morning.

28. THE SIEGE

The grandfather clock chimed the half hour. One-thirty in the morning.

In the silence that followed, Eric Nolan experienced an overwhelming sense of unreality. It filled the room like a paralyzing mist, seemed to crowd the occupants into tiny invisible compartments, separating one from the other with impenetrable walls built from the horror that comes when reality degenerates.

Although frightened and alone, Eric felt they were all joined together, linked forever by a powerful bond—the secret that they shared. In an uncomfortable, lethargic state resembling intoxication, Eric felt profoundly helpless. He had no way to test the reality of what was going on; he was unable to know what needed to be done.

My mind is going, he thought. *This time, for sure* . . . The notion had a numbing effect on him, made him feel like the butt of some cosmic joke.

Clint, in deep concentration, stared at his hands. Mrs. McKensie fingered the tattered edge of the blanket that covered her legs. Pamela looked at Eric, her eyes filled with confusion. Suddenly she stood up.

"We've got to do something," she said. "We can't just sit here. We've got to make a plan, or something . . ."

"You're right, dear," said Mrs. McKensie. "In fact, I think it would be best if we all leave here and go to my house. We'll be safer there. Perhaps we can even get some sleep."

Clint looked at Pamela. "I think she's right," he said.

"Yes, that's the best idea," offered Eric, snapping out of his reverie. He was eager to have a defined task to perform, a specific action to take. "Let me go warm up the car before we leave."

It was a misty night, the air was chill, moist to the touch. The quarter moon was a murky white crescent suspended in the haze of the sky. To Eric's left, the road glowed like a luminous carpet until it dipped down Tenny's Hill and disappeared. Before him, across the dooryard, the barnboard garage was a fortress beyond which the forest loomed like a sleeping beast. All around him night sounds echoed with unfamiliar intensity. It was as if the character of the atmosphere had changed, had taken on the dreamlike quality of a frightening children's story, a world of make-believe.

The dampness of the night flowed through Eric's body like a winter tide. He shivered from the cold, but more from the alien ideas that were tugging at his mind.

Eric walked quickly to his car, groping in his pocket for the keys. The interior light went out as he slid into the driver's seat and closed the door. In the darkness, locating its position from memory, he pushed the key into the ignition and turned. He heard the solenoid click, and that was all. Again, he tried the key, feeling the muscles in his stomach and neck tighten, feeling the perspiration form on his brow. The car wouldn't fire. It wouldn't even groan.

As he was about to give up, an ear-shattering crash immobilized his nervous system. The windshield fractured. He watched dumbfounded as a spiderweb design formed instantly in front of him. A stone clattered across the metal of the hood and dropped to the ground with a damp thump.

Eric threw the door open, the interior light stinging his eyes. He made a panic-dash to the house. His heavy shoes thundered across the boards of the porch, and he burst into the kitchen, slamming and locking the door behind him. The startled faces of Clint and Pamela looked at him from the living room.

"They're here," Eric said in a monotone, his chest heaving breathlessly.

"What do you mean?" asked Pamela. "What happened?"

"My car won't start. Somebody smashed the windshield while I was trying to start it. They're out there."

No one moved. Everyone exchanged furtive glances, listening for telltale sounds. Eric heard the tick of the grandfather clock, the muted roar of the wood stove, the scratching of the Christmas wreath, still hanging on the door, as it swayed in the wind.

"Shit," Clint said. He hastened to his gun cabinet, pulled out his twelve-gauge and a box of shells.

Pamela started for the stairs. "I'm going to get Luke," she cried.

"No, not yet." Clint commanded. "Just let him sleep. No point in gettin' him all stirred up. Just check on him. Lock him in his room. He'll be safe up there."

She looked back as if to argue, then raced up the stairs and out of sight.

Mrs. McKensie wheeled in from the next room to join the men in the kitchen.

Pamela returned in an instant. She assured the others that Luke was sleeping peacefully. She looked harried and uncertain, her long hair disheveled, her complexion wan. She was short of breath from the exertion of running.

Looking up from her wheelchair, the old woman said, "If they really are out there then they know I'm here, too. I'm sure they've been listening to us."

"Shut all the lights," Clint ordered. "Maybe they won't be able to see in here."

Pamela scurried from room to room turning off light switches. In her rush, she accidentally kicked Luke's Mighty Loader. It rattled across the floor. "Damn," she muttered. Then she began pulling shades and closing drapes. "Is everything locked up?" Her voice was shrill and cracking.

The front entrance was still sealed tight from Clint's winterizing efforts. Hurriedly he locked the doors to the shed and to the basement.

Eric collapsed into a kitchen chair. He felt drained, frightened. Mrs. McKensie rolled over to the table to join him. "Did you see anything?" she asked.

He couldn't respond.

"Mr. Nolan," she said firmly, "did you see anything out there?"

With effort he shook his head, feeling his heart pound in his chest. Pamela stepped up behind him and began massaging his shoulders. "Relax," she whispered. "It's okay now, Eric. Relax."

He felt her strong fingers working at his tense muscles, trying to coax the paralyzing fear from his body. He closed his eyes tightly, breathing deeply. His heart thumped relentlessly against his ribs. Eric felt dissociated, not clear on what was going on around him.

On the periphery of his consciousness, Eric watched Clint move to the kitchen window, pull the shade back, and look out into the yard. Then he moved on to the next window. "Can't see jack shit out there," he muttered.

Pamela turned to her husband. "What about our car? Or the truck?" She sounded hopeful, eager.

"They're both in the garage. I don't know if I should go out there."

"Is the garage locked?" asked Mrs. McKensie.

"We never lock it," Pamela answered.

"Eric and I can try it together, soon's he catches his breath." Clint looked at Eric as he spoke.

"I don't know . . ." Eric could barely hear his own voice. Fear, like prickly heat, coated the inside of his chest, set a fire in his stomach. His legs were boneless flesh, his arms without strength. "I don't know if I can."

Clint seemed to hear something in Eric's voice that brought him to attention. At that moment Clint's entire attention was on his friend. Moving quickly to the cabinet above the refrigerator, he took down a bottle of whiskey and grabbed a glass from the drainer.

"Take this," he said, pouring three fingers' worth. Eric took the glass and downed the amber liquid in a gulp. He reached for the bottle that Clint had set on the table in front of him.

"Better not," cautioned Clint. "Let that one do its job first."

Pamela, moving quickly from behind Eric, said, "I'm going to try the phone again." Without taking his eyes from the empty glass, Eric heard her pick up the receiver, then tap the cradle as if she were sending Morse code. "It's dead," she announced. "The line's dead." She slammed down the receiver and looked at the group. "We're trapped here."

Trapped.

Eric heard the word clearly amid the confusion of his thoughts. We're trapped. We're prisoners. The word buzzed around in his mind like an angry fly in a jar—prisoners . . . prisoners . . . prisoners . . .

He had experienced a similar feeling before. It was after his wife was killed. He remembered how he had felt trapped by his own misery and grief. He especially recalled the inescapable notion that death was at his heels. He had wanted to escape then, but he couldn't; and he couldn't now. He sat motionless but for the shaking of his hands, the chattering of his jaw. He was a shell, without substance, without courage. The horrible vacuum inside might at any moment cause him to implode. Some part of his mind watched Pamela walk back to the table and sit down. He saw Mrs. McKensie reach out and take the younger woman's hand.

"What do they want with us?" he heard Pamela ask.

"I told you what they want," snapped Clint. "They want our son. Maybe they want you."

"Oh, everything's happening so fast. What are we going to do?" Hysteria creeping into Pamela's voice.

"Maybe nothin'. Maybe they've done their bit for tonight. If we can wait 'em out till morning, Eric and I can get one of the vehicles going. We can get the hell out of here." Clint went back to the window and looked out. "I still don't see nothin' out there." He walked over to Pamela, put his hand gently on her shoulder.

"Mrs. McKensie, where do they come from?" Pamela was looking entreatingly at the old woman.

"I don't know that dear. Not for sure, anyway. I've always believed that the little people were in some way connected to those 'root cellars.' Perhaps the cellars were a focal point of their activities until human settlers pushed them further into the hills. But who can say? They might not even be of this earth. Perhaps they're extraterrestrials. Maybe they came here from outer space ages ago . . ."

Pamela cut her off. "Why have they, all of a sudden, started to make so much trouble?"

"Again I can't say for sure. I think the Gentry have only two motives for interacting with people: keeping their number constant, and protecting their privacy. If they had successfully taken your son, perhaps that would have been their only crime. It would have been a rare, tragic, but largely inconspicuous disappearance of a small child. But, as I said, it's my belief that their kidnapping attempt was interrupted, and the young policeman was silenced. Afterwards, other people were coincidentally involved. I think we can equate each death, or disappearance, with the Gentry trying to cover their tracks, protect their secret. As you know, we have more than your son to be concerned about now. I believe we are all targeted. To me it isn't really important why they've suddenly broken cover. What we need to worry about is that they're here —"

As if to emphasize her point, the sound of an explosion interrupted Mrs. McKensie. A hail of broken glass filled the room. Among the sparkling shards, a length of firewood struck the floor, pulling the torn window curtain along with it.

Pamela jumped to her feet as Clint dashed to the broken window, his shotgun ready. Mrs. McKensie rolled back a few feet toward the living room, but Eric didn't move at all.

Around him, Eric could hear a storm of activity: Clint rushing somewhere, his boots loud on the pine floor; Pamela gasping, crying out in alarm.

Eric felt as if he should act, yet he was immobile, a paralysis draining his limbs of strength and filling his mind with dread. Although he had seen nothing in the yard, he somehow knew that he had come face to face with the supernatural, and the experience had left him a physical and emotional cripple. If the creatures outside wanted him, let them take him. If he was a coward, so be it.

"Eric, I need your help." It was Clint's voice, strong, commanding.

With all the strength he could muster, Eric turned his head and faced the other man. Clint was trying to move a heavy china cabinet.

"Help me move this in front of the window. Pam, there's lumber down cellar, all that shelving I put up. Bring some up here. Get my hammer and nails. Be careful."

Eric remained seated at the table. He felt passive, strangely calm, as if he'd decided everything going on around him was unreal, a dream from which he'd soon awaken.

And then Clint was standing above him. The eyes looking down at him were cold and steady. "Get up, Eric. I need your help."

Clint's voice came at him from a long way off, its authority softened by the distance. "Get up," was repeating itself over and over, reverberating in the canals of Eric's ears. Then, Eric was being yanked to his feet, his chair tumbling to the floor behind him. Clint gripped him by the shirtfront, pulled him to where their faces met. He could see the vapid expression on his own face reflected in Clint's angry eyes. Clint shook him, shook him *hard*.

"Come on, Eric, we need you."

"Yeah," he replied, his own voice sounding far away. Then, "Yeah," with more conviction.

Clint let him go. For a moment he was dizzy. His mind reeled as he swayed on his feet, but he stood under his own power. He could feel strength returning to his legs and arms like blood flowing into sleeping limbs. He watched Pamela enter the room with an armload of boards. She let them clatter to the floor. Then she locked the cellar door, and took the hammer from under her arm.

"Come on," said Eric. Stepping across the room, he took one side of the heavy cabinet. The two men easily slid it across the floor and positioned it in front of the broken window.

"Let's board up the rest of the windows," said Clint. "If we make this floor safe we'll be okay. They can't get upstairs."

Eric listened attentively to Clint. Yet, as he replayed the order in his mind, there was something about it that bothered him. There was something he didn't like. He wasn't sure what it was, but the dissatisfaction persisted, even while he helped Clint nail up the boards.

A series of thumps and bangs stopped all activity. Again they heard the sound of breaking glass. The house was being bombarded with stones.

In the dark kitchen, lit only by the light of the wood stove, the four people sat around the table listening to the pounding of the stone shower. "I'm going to check on Luke," Pamela said. "Do you think I should bring him down?"

"No. Just see if he's okay. I don't want him down here with all these guns, and rocks flying around. It's better we keep him locked in. I think he'll be safer up there. They'll have to get through us to get at him."

The nagging doubt returned to Eric as Clint spoke. The plan wasn't right. They were overlooking something. What? He needed time to think. If only he could collect his thoughts.

Mrs. McKensie looked old and helpless in her wheelchair. She sat with her hands tightly folded over her breasts watching the action going on around her. *She looks like a corpse,* Eric thought.

The old woman seemed so alone that Eric wanted to help her. He wanted to say something that would comfort her, but all he could find to say came from his own fear and uncertainty. "What can they do to us if we stay in here?"

Mrs. McKensie shook her head slowly. "I don't know what they can do. Right now I think they're trying to scare us, hoping we'll act foolishly." Then to Clint, "Perhaps, Mr. Whitcome, if you have some more weapons . . . I can handle a gun if need be."

"Right," said Clint and he moved to the gun cabinet. He took out a Winchester 30/06 and a Colt .45. These he put on the table in front of them, along with his twelve-gauge and more ammunition.

Pamela came back into the room, her face tight with a forced smile. "Luke's fast asleep," she reported. "He's chattering away like he's dreaming." Pamela sat down beside Mrs. McKensie. "I can't believe that kid."

Mrs. McKensie returned her smile. She patted Pamela's hand. Then everyone was silent, listening intently.

It was half past two.

In a little while, they heard the unmistakable tattoo of tiny feet running across the wooden porch. Afterward, all was quiet again. Again they waited.

At about three o'clock, Eric asked Clint, "Do you think you and

I should make a try for the garage? If all they've got is stones, we should be able to make it."

Clint shook his head. "There's no point in any of us taking chances. I think we're safe here. And we really don't know what they got. Maybe just stones. Maybe not. Besides, it's dark out there. It ain't safe. Mornin' will be time enough. We'll be able to see what we're up against."

Mrs. McKensie nodded her head in agreement.

Eric felt welcome relief at Clint's mandate. He wouldn't have to go outside. He'd be safe for a while longer. At least he felt cleansed of his cowardice by the offer of bravery.

The ticking of the grandfather clock was echoed by the tapping of Clint's fingers on the tabletop. Sunrise was just three hours away. In Eric's imagination, the sun was already up. He and Clint, armed with rifles, would make their way to the garage. With Eric standing guard, Clint would skillfully repair the damaged car. They'd back it up to the porch, load Pamela, Luke, and Mrs. McKensie, and drive away, safely. They'd drive away and then . . . and then, what?

If they went to the police, what would they say? If they reported what was actually happening would they all appear insane? Mass hysterics? What proof could they offer of what they were going through? The police would probably say they were the victims of juvenile pranksters, or worse yet, pranksters themselves. They had no proof. Nothing. They hadn't even witnessed anything firsthand.

Eric thought long and hard about this. His own system of beliefs had undergone such a dramatic turnaround that he needed to convince others, let them know he hadn't gone over the edge. Establishing proof was imperative. "We've got to capture one of them," he said.

"What?" said Clint and Pamela at once.

"We've got to capture one of the little people. It's the only way we can prove any of this is really happening. It's the only way we can get anybody to do something about this."

"Now how we gonna do that?" Clint drawled.

"I don't know. But we need evidence."

"Why capture it? Why not shoot it?"

"Okay, let's shoot it then. You said there were only six or eight of them. If we could get just one . . ."

Eric searched one face at a time. Pamela looked worried. Mrs. McKensie seemed to see the younger woman's fear. She seemed to know what Pamela was thinking. "They're not human," she assured everyone. "And they have no kindness. They're more merciless than spoiled, self-centered children torturing a helpless animal. They'll try to kill us, and we know they've killed before."

Then to Clint, "But if you kill one, the rest will have to be killed too. We'll have to convince the authorities of that. And we'll have to convince them to act fast. Otherwise, children will start to disappear. They have to keep their population stable, as I told you. That's why we're going through this right now, Mr. Whitcome. Remember?"

At that moment, a thunderous crash came from behind them. Everyone's attention jumped to the door.

Another crash immediately followed. The door shook and buckled. Clint and Eric were on their feet grabbing their weapons. Pamela and Mrs. McKensie backed toward the living room, moving away from the frightening sounds.

When another blow hit the door, the wood started to crack and then to split. Pamela screamed when the next blow came. A jagged line, like lightning, zigzagged along the center of the wood, running top to bottom.

"Jesus Christ, they're comin' in," cried Clint. He positioned his shotgun at his shoulder, pointing it at the weakening barrier. Eric stood beside him, aiming the 30/06.

With the next assault the door split down the middle, like a cracker. Half fell away, the other half swung on its hinges.

The log battering ram thumped to the floor.

Both weapons discharged at he same time, the explosions roaring in the confines of the kitchen. Through the dark opening Eric glimpsed four animated shadows dash off to the sides, into the protection of the night.

Clint stepped quickly to the blasted door and looked out. "We gotta block this up," he commanded, never looking away from the opening.

Before quiet returned, another scream erupted behind the men. Reflexively, they whirled to see Mrs. McKensie's white and wrinkled face contorted in terror. She seemed to be moving her wheelchair, first to the right, then to the left, but her hands were at her open mouth.

As if under its own power, the chair began to move. First it swiveled from side to side, then, unassisted, moved straight ahead.

"Help me!" The old woman cried, stretching out her arms to Pamela.

Perhaps whatever it was that froze Pamela and Clint was the same thing that held Eric. The three of them just stood and dumbly watched as the wheelchair moved, with nothing visible propelling it.

Its motion was erratic, and without apparent control. The chair bashed the old woman into the kitchen table, then whirled to the left, and began to roll her toward the wood stove. When it was about to slam into the stove, Mrs. McKensie extended her arms to prevent the collision that would have sent her headfirst into the hot metal. She screamed as the flesh of her palms sizzled against the cast iron.

It was the pain in that scream that reanimated Pamela. She dove for the old woman as the chair abruptly changed direction, and, with more accurate guidance, rolled toward the open door.

"No!" cried Mrs. McKensie as the speed of the chair increased. Pamela had hold of one of the rubber handles on the chair's back. She pulled hard to slow its progress. Clint made a grab for the old woman, but, when his hand touched her blistered palm, she screamed and pulled away.

"Help me," cried Pamela above the old woman's screams.

Eric watched dumbfounded as the invisible force that powered the chair dragged Pamela across the pine floor and out the door. "Grab the wheels!" he cried.

It's magic, Eric thought. *It has to be magic. What can we do against magic?* Answering his own question with action, he jumped up and headed for the door.

He and Clint moved toward the opening at the same time, and at once they saw a rope drop around Pamela's neck. It tightened with a jerk that pulled her off her feet. A strangled gasp escaped her throat.

The wheelchair bumped down the steps, pitching the old woman face first onto the gravel drive.

Faster than the eye could follow, diminutive forms leaped out of the shadows. One sat heavily on Mrs. McKensie's neck, its hands in her hair, forcing her face into the stony drive. Her screams were muffled and desperate. Another shadow leaped into the air, driving its knees into her back as it came down.

Two other creatures seized Pamela, dragging her, wriggling and screaming, toward the edge of the porch.

Clint and Eric held their weapons ready, but neither could get a clean shot for fear of hitting the women. High-pitched grunts and giggles blended in the air with the women's screams.

"Come on," cried Clint, running to his wife.

Eric watched as two creatures abandoned the motionless body of the old woman and lunged at Clint's legs. Clint fell hard against the porch, and they were on top of him like hungry dogs on a wounded deer. Clint cried out as a bony knee connected with his solar plexus.

Eric didn't know what to do. Thoughts flew haphazardly around in his head like papers in a cyclone. He couldn't focus, couldn't make sense of them. In his confusion, remembered voices carried on a senseless dialogue: Clint's words—"They all gathered around, chanting . . ."; Pam's question, "Eric, were you in Luke's bedroom? Luke says he saw you at his window"; Clint's command, "Lock him in, he'll be safe up there . . ."

The voices built to a screaming, frenzied crescendo, "We're trapped here . . . trapped here . . . trapped here . . ."

Somewhere in the distance Pamela screamed in agony. To his left, Eric watched Clint's head being smashed repeatedly against the wooden step. He heard his friend moaning senselessly.

Turning from the sprawled and struggling bodies, Eric Nolan ran into the house.

. . .

Chief Bates couldn't sleep. In the darkness of the bedroom he turned to look at the glowing numbers of his digital alarm clock. It was three thirty-five. He tossed uncomfortably, trying not to wake his wife.

Lately, it seemed, he'd been having way too many sleepless nights. It was always the same, and he hated it. He'd snap fully awake from a fitful sleep, his muscles taut, his teeth clenched. Sometimes he'd be soaked in a cold sweat. Uncontrollable thoughts would irritate him, like mosquitoes in his ears. This night, a scrap of a song that he hated repeated itself like an endless tape. Sleep seemed far away.

One thing about being a police officer, he thought, you can't help but take your work home with you. Sometimes you even bring it to bed.

Working night and day, thought Bates. Maybe it's time to give up police work.

Tonight, he couldn't get the death of Billy Newton out of his mind. Bates had been very fond of the old man. He knew Billy was a kind and careful person. Very careful. Billy was so meticulous that he even wiped his tools with a rag every time he used them; anyone using Billy's tools was required to do the same thing. "Keep it new and it'll never get old," Billy always said. Never get old . . . never get old—echoed in Bates's mind.

They wrote up Billy's death as an accident, but Billy was too careful for such a thing to have happened. If he had taken a fall, that would be one thing—his legs were weak, unsteady from the arthritis. But it was the car that had fallen, not Billy, and that just didn't sit right.

Too many things had been going on lately—too many to dismiss any of them as an accident. There were the disappearances: Justin Hurd, Carl Sayer, Clint Whitcome. There were the deaths: Perly Greer, Billy Newton. And the dogs, where did they fit in? Whitcome's dog, disemboweled, Perly's dog, gone. Doggone . . . doggone . . . thought Bates.

Everything's got to be connected. Somehow it's all related.

He sensed he was getting close to something, something important. Perhaps it was the very thing that was gnawing at him, the core of this whole rotten mess. Maybe if he thought about something else for a while, something neutral, he could get his mind off these endless conjectures. He'd give his unconscious a chance to attack the real problem, separate it from all the confusing details. Bates had always trusted his intuition, but he had to give it a chance to work.

I guess I'd better get up and have something to eat, maybe get me a drink, he thought.

It would take more than a nightcap to wash the image of Billy's body from his mind.

The silver flask! Of course! Bates had found it near Billy's crushed skull. That flask didn't belong there. It wasn't Billy's—Billy always poured from the bottle.

Whose could it be? Who could have left it?

He remembered Billy's saying that a silver flask belonged to Perly Greer. Billy had given it to Clint Whitcome to return to the hermit. Now it was back in Billy's garage.

So, Clint Whitcome was the last person to have had it. Was he also the last to see Billy alive?

Where did Clint fit into all this? He had vanished. But he'd returned. He was the only one who had returned. He had that vague story about falling down a hole . . . if anyone but Clint had said such a thing, Bates wouldn't have believed him. No good policeman would have.

And that, Bates knew, was one thing that was really eating at him: he knew that he wasn't being a good cop. He hated to admit it to himself, but it was true.

He had too easily believed Clint's story. Not believed it, really —accepted it—because Clint Whitcome was a friend of his. But if Bates was to be honest with himself, really swear-on-a-Bible honest, he would have to admit that the Whitcome house was suspiciously close to the center of all the mysterious happenings. After all, Clint was probably the last person to have seen Carl Sayer, though he wouldn't admit it, and Billy Newton hadn't died until after Clint had returned from wherever it was that he'd gone.

That flask, thought Bates, *it's the thread that ties all this shit together.*

In his mind he traced what he knew of the flask's history: On December 3 Billy had said he'd discovered the flask in his truck, which suggested Perly Greer had been driving it the night Hurd disappeared, November 21. Later, Billy had given the flask to Clint. On the night of December 2, Clint had vanished, along with the flask. Clint had turned up again, on the thirteenth, but apparently without the flask. He couldn't have returned it to Perly, because Perly was dead. Therefore, he'd either lost it in the woods, or he'd brought it back to Billy's garage.

Bates cursed himself. He'd never questioned Clint about the goddamn flask!

And what about Eric Nolan? Where did he fit in? Bates had come down hard on Nolan, but what good had it done? It had just made him feel like shit, and all the while, down deep, he'd known he was grasping at straws.

Nope. Everything points directly at Clint Whitcome. Maybe I ought to go up there right now, get to the bottom of things. It sure beats thrashing around in bed.

Again he looked at the clock—almost four in the morning.

Bates decided to wait until first light; the questions would keep. He vowed to himself that he would get up real early in the morning and drive up to the Whitcomes' place. He'd take a harder line this time, in spite of the friendship. He'd do all in his power to get all the facts, hear the whole story.

But for now, he thought, please God, just let me sleep.

Eric Nolan ran up the dark stairway toward Luke Whitcome's bedroom. He was mindless of the weight that tugged like an anchor at his left arm.

The key was in the outside of the lock, where Pamela had left it. Before he turned it, Eric put his ear against the wooden panel of the door. He could hear nothing inside.

A spark of urgency flashed in his mind—he knew he was wasting time. With a single fluid motion he unlocked the door, threw it open.

The room was dark but for the faint glow of Luke's night light. Eric sensed several things all at once, yet couldn't focus on anything in particular. Trying to slow down the sensual input, he concentrated on the mobile over Luke's dresser. It was spinning in a chill draft from the open window. He saw Luke, a small dark form, standing alone in the middle of the floor. All the commotion downstairs had apparently awakened the boy, and he hadn't been able to get out of his locked room.

Then Eric glanced at the bed. What he saw there confused him.

He slid his trembling right hand along the wall until he found the light switch. He flicked it on. The harsh white light stabbed at his eyes, but he didn't take them away from Luke, who was sleeping peacefully in his bed, the blankets tucked snugly around him.

The other figure, the one standing in the middle of the room, was rubbing his eyes and cringing from the light.

Eric looked the creature up and down, trying to make sense of it.

He had known that sooner or later he'd have to face this moment. Some little-used part of his consciousness had recognized that, eventually, he'd have to see one of the creatures close up. He really hadn't expected something supernatural, not a troll or an elf or a fairy. He'd anticipated something human, a midget, maybe a dwarf. But this thing, this creature in front of him had none of the bumpy, bandy-legged contours of a dwarf.

It's a kid, he thought. But it wasn't—not exactly. It appeared too old, too mature in its bearing.

The thing stood about three feet high. It wore a vest made of animal hide, with coarse woven trousers tucked into dirty leather boots. True, it had the lithe, wiry body of a child, but something about it, something cold, unnatural in its precision, stirred an atavistic revulsion in Eric.

The room was full of the smell of the thing. It was the odor of earth and decaying leaves. Eric thought of the awful smell of a slaughterhouse.

He took a step backward as the little man turned and faced him.

The tiny creature stopped rubbing its eyes and squinted up at Eric. There was an expression of surprise and fear on the pain-distorted face. He studied Eric with a kind of familiar fascination — and Eric studied him.

The body was small enough to have been mistaken for Luke's, but, in the clarity of the bright ceiling light, the face was wrong. It might have appeared youthful but for the crisscrossing of tiny cracks and furrows, visible signs of unnatural aging. From a greater distance the lines would have been invisible.

Red, matted hair dangled in sticky disarray across its mushroom-white skin. It raised a hairy hand and patted its head, almost nervously.

Although it was diminutive, almost harmless-looking, the sight of the creature disabled Eric with a terrible, bone-softening dread. He could not run or move. He could only stare, dumbfounded, at the single hideous attribute that frightened him more than anything else about the little man. The eyes! The horrible eyes!

It wasn't the icy, razor-bright glare beaming from them like a paralyzing ray. It was something more, something that welded Eric helplessly to the spot. The ungodly eyes peered at him, cementing his gaze to theirs. And, as Eric stared, he saw clearly in the bright light of the bedroom that one of the eyes was light blue, the other dark.

They stood like that for a long time, frozen, grotesque statues, looking hard at each other—two alien creatures, fascinated and afraid. This was surely the face that Luke had seen at the window, the face he'd mistaken for Eric's.

Eric's fingers twitched against the metal in his left hand. A recognition, almost a friendliness, passed between the two creatures as they looked face to face, eye to eye.

It was Eric who spoke first. He started by simply mouthing the word until at last he could find enough breath to drive it out. "Brian?" he said in a whisper.

The creature blinked at him, rubbing its eyes with furry, misshapen hands.

"Brian, is that you?" Eric whispered, his tongue as dry as chalk dust.

The creature's lips moved crookedly, its face contorted into an expression of pain. Its voice was like air in an empty pipe. "Er . . . Er-ik . . ."

Although Eric was half smiling, spasms of fear still tugged at his gut.

With a palsied flutter, the little man's hand moved away from his eye and reached out toward him. Eric extended his hand to meet his brother's. He watched Brian's eyes floating in their too-wide sockets, saw the parted fingers advancing like a Hydra's head. On the pine floor, in the corner of his vision, Eric saw the trembling shadow of their moving hands.

Instantly, as their fingers touched, a cold sensation numbed Eric's hand. The feeling radiated up his arm, spreading to his shoulder, weakening it. Fighting the strange anesthesia, Eric jerked away as if from a bee sting. He gasped in surprise.

And he remembered the weight, the Colt .45 that he held. He had grabbed it from the kitchen table as he ran into the house. Now he lifted it, leveled it at the eyes of the thing, the child-demon, that had been his brother.

Brian's eyes moved from the barrel to Eric's face. Eric could feel his hands, braced tightly around the weapon. He was shaking.

Outside, the world was strangely quiet, no birds called, no dogs barked, the wind was still. The soundless night made Eric feel as if he and Brian were isolated, almost unreal, the only two survivors in all creation. It was as if they were the sole representatives of light and dark, poised for an ultimate confrontation.

Beside him, on the bed, Luke moaned in his sleep. Brian looked at the boy, waved his arm, and the child was still.

Eric's finger flirted with the trigger, his arms shaking. This aberration could not be his brother. Its soul is gone, he realized. *It's an evil thing.*

Brian, his hand still outstretched, began to inch away from the gun, backing toward the open window.

I can end this now, Eric thought.

But something kept him from pulling that trigger. Whether it was kinship or cowardice, he could not tell. Perhaps, in a face-off such as this, evil would forever triumph, because goodness, by its very nature, was incapable of destruction.

Eric faltered; he wanted to shoot, but a thousand questions sped through his mind. Before he could articulate the first of them, a shotgun roared outside

The blast seemed to jolt the two creatures in the sleeping child's bedroom. The little man, as if waking from a trance, lunged for the door.

"Brian, stop! Wait!"

Eric threw down the gun in disgust, cursing his lack of resolve. He moved quickly into the hall. Brian was down the steps and gone before Eric reached the head of the stairs.

"Brian!"

Eric pounded down the dark stairway. He wanted to catch his brother, but wanted more to assist his friends. As he ran he flailed his right arm, trying to shake sensation back into his numbed fingers.

With the stairway behind him, Eric flew through the house and onto the porch. The first thing he saw was Mrs. McKensie, exactly where she had fallen, her overturned wheelchair on the ground beside her. Brian was nowhere in sight.

Directly in front of Eric lay Clint Whitcome, two little men pinning each of his shoulders to the earth. Clint's eyes were wide, staring, his teeth chattered, his lips looked blue. He kicked, tried to roll over, his movements convulsive, more mechanical reflex than thought-directed. His arms were ineffectual under the weight of the demon-children. Clint cried out in pain as repeated blows from tiny, tree-knot fists rained down upon his face and neck.

Eric watched as the kicking stopped. Clint shuddered and was still. The only movement was in his eyes; they were wide with a terror bordering on insanity.

The little men gave a push to each of Clint's shoulders, as if applying the final pressure that would glue him to the ground. They rose, stepped away from the prostrate man. Eric saw Clint's eyes swimming in his head, heard his teeth grinding together. Eric knew, could almost feel, the paralyzing cold that left his friend useless and defeated.

"I . . . I can't move," Clint moaned.

The two little men abandoned Clint. They started toward Eric.

Eric stepped backwards. All at once the rage he had failed to summon in Luke's bedroom exploded within him. He noticed that beside Clint, just out of reach, was the twelve-gauge. Without thinking, he dove for it, aware that it was broken open at the breech. A stubby arm shot out at him. He dodged it, snatching the gun by the barrel, wielding it like a club. Swinging at the nearest head, Eric's precision blow sent a gray-haired imp flying into the driveway. The other scampered away.

Clint saw Eric at that moment. Unable to raise his arm, he pointed a finger, crying, "Help Pamela, Eric. For God's sake, help Pamela!"

Eric looked around for his cousin. He could see where two little men had dragged her off the edge of the porch and across the damp lawn toward the forest. In the darkness it was difficult to tell what they were doing to her, but Eric could see her white flesh almost glowing in the pale moonlight. She was naked. Shrunken shapeless shadows moved above and around her in senseless, random motion.

The inhuman, gleeful croaks that filled the moonlit air made him want to run. Eric forced himself to listen, but he could hear no sounds from Pamela.

Raising the shotgun and holding it like a baseball bat, he ran to her. When he got closer, he could hear her moaning in mindless terror as the child-things went about their repulsive ritual.

One of the little men, his head a ball of black hair and oozing sores, looked Eric in the face. Perched on Pamela's stomach, the creature hissed, baring chunky yellow teeth.

The lust-crazed animal fury in that glare repelled Eric with a nearly tangible force. He felt himself staggering backward, as if physically pushed. The thing, apparently satisfied that he had immobilized his attacker, returned his attention to Pamela's white flesh.

"Warm . . ." the creature moaned. Its festering head descended like a falling rock. Teeth like stones sank into Pamela's soft breast. Crimson gushed like lava. Pamela howled.

The suckling obscenity clung to Pamela's abdomen like a bestial infant. Animated by rage, Eric brought the stock of the weapon down against its spine. The imp vaulted forward, landed on Pamela's face, and rolled off into the dirt. Blood trickled from his motionless lips.

Eric grabbed another man under the arms, picked him up, and pulled him clear of Pamela.

Just then something plowed into him from behind. It buckled his legs at the knees, knocking him off balance. Two unseen objects, about the size and weight of sandbags, landed on his back and moved with a vicious, powerful frenzy. Warped voices shouted unfamiliar words while brutal granite fists pummeled him with the energy of madness. "Clint," he cried, feeling the terror ripping at his insides. "Clint, help me."

Someone pushed his face into the ground. His tongue tasted mud. Stretching painfully, he tried to seize the barrel of the gun beside him. Though no one touched it, Eric watched as the shotgun snaked away, beyond his reach.

He then felt an impact like a stone mallet against the back of his skull. Everything blurred. Dazed, nearly sightless, he somehow rose to his knees in a humiliating parody of prayer. Thoughts without clarity moved lazily around in his throbbing head: must save Pamela . . . got to help Clint . . . their life here . . . beautiful life . . . must protect it . . . must protect Luke . . . must help them . . . save them . . .

His vision clouded. In the dark, misty air, the house, his car, and the black forest beyond, moved in and out of focus as if the projectionist were adjusting the lens in a movie theater.

All around him he saw moving silhouettes of the child-things, nearly invisible among the shadows. He counted one, two, three, four of them, circling him, watching him, moving closer—shapes in a nightmare.

His eyes, filled with tears of resignation, began to scan the shadows, looking for somewhere to run.

Slowly he tried to struggle to his feet.

From the direction of the porch, Brian limped haltingly toward him. Some unseen force, like a corporeal wind, struck at Eric's back, pushed him back to his knees.

He was looking his brother in the eyes.

"Brian . . ." Eric implored, sweat and tears mixing on his cheeks. "Brian, make them stop this . . ."

His brother only glared at him. He whispered, "The boy," the words rumbling and wheezing in his throat. Four tiny childlike silhouettes moved into formation behind him.

Brian's arm shot out with the force of a piston. The blow, this time to Eric's temple, sent the freezing, paralyzing numbness throughout his weakened body. The only thing he felt was the crippling coldness. When it passed, everything was black and still. Everything was gone.

Eric Nolan collapsed like an empty sack onto the cold, rocky ground.

29. SNOW BIRDS

At seven o'clock in the morning Chief Bates slowly drove the cruiser up Tenny's Hill Road. A new snowfall had begun a little before dawn. He proceeded carefully, knowing that the prismatic flakes, though beautiful in the dull morning light, concealed ruts in the road and treacherous soft shoulders in the mud below.

In his rearview mirror, Bates watched the parallel slashes made by his tires in the fresh snow. His tracks told him that he was the first person to drive on the hill this Wednesday morning.

The early hour, the snowy road, and the job he had to do, all made him wish he were still home in bed, catching up on his much-needed sleep. *There'll be no sleep until this is done,* he warned himself.

The sky was gray, overcast with a bank of dark storm clouds that signaled a big storm was on the way. So much for December rains, Bates thought, as he felt the cruiser's transmission shift to a lower gear.

Again, looking at the mirror, Bates noticed the reflection of his eyes. They were rimmed with black, raccoonlike circles that darkened the puffy flesh of his cheeks. They were tired eyes, eyes that reminded him of his troubled, sleepless nights.

In his gut, he had the sense of dread he always felt when he had to ask painful or difficult questions of an old friend. Luckily it was a dread he'd rarely experienced in all his years as chief of police.

He reviewed the list of questions he had prepared for Clint Whitcome and Eric Nolan. This time, he resolved, he would have to push Clint, make him tell what he knew about Carl Sayer, about Billy Newton's death, and especially about the silver flask.

When his car reached the top of the hill, the Whitcomes' yard came into view. Bates noted the presence of three vehicles, one in the yard and two in the open garage. Every object in the dooryard was like an island in the undisturbed sea of white.

He parked the cruiser and got out, holding his notebook in his left hand. All was still. A gentle breeze shook the tree limbs, sending snow fluttering to the earth. His weary eyes surveyed his surroundings. Everything he saw contributed to his sense of unease. The side door to the house was open. No—it was broken in. In the yard, Clint lay on his back. He was covered with snow, the ground around his head was thick with viscous, red mud. In front of the porch steps, Bates saw an overturned wheelchair with an old woman's body tangled lifelessly in its metal frame.

He unsnapped the retaining strap from his .357 magnum, and ran his fingers over the grip for security. To his right, and some distance from the house near the edge of the woods, he saw the outline of another corpse. He approached it slowly. The contours showed him that it was female. The snow concealed her nakedness.

Suddenly he felt cold, deathly cold.

His stomach flopped like a landed trout. Finding himself swallowing rapidly, he feared he was about to vomit.

As Bates stepped backward toward Clint, he noticed the white-haired man sitting on the porch steps. The man was so very still that Dick thought he, too, might be dead. Blood spattered his clothing; it stained the skin of his hands and face. Undisturbed snow on the ground around him—and on the steps—quickly told Bates that the man had been sitting there for a long time.

Bates's hand found the handle of his weapon. "What's happened here?" he demanded.

The man didn't move. Bates realized that the man's hair was not white, but red—it was covered with snow.

"Zat you, Mr. Nolan?"

Still no response. Bates walked over to the seated man and stood before him, legs apart, towering above him. He shouted, "MR. NOLAN!"

The red-haired man slowly turned his head and looked up at the police officer. His eyes were half closed. Bates noticed there was something queer about those eyes—not just that they were of two different shades of blue, but they were somehow hollow, vacant.

"What's happened here, Mr. Nolan?" Chief Bates spoke softly this time, but his reflexes were fine-tuned, his hand never far from his weapon.

Nolan's head sagged to his chest.

"Are you all right?" the policeman asked.

When the man didn't respond, Bates bent over the body of Elizabeth McKensie. His hand touched her cold neck, feeling for the pulse he knew he wouldn't find.

He walked to where Clint lay. There was no need to feel for a pulse this time. Clint's head was asymmetrical, dented on the right side and matted with thick blood. Fragments of bone and sickening organic matter bulged from the wound. Bates turned away, and this time he was sick. He watched in disgust as his breakfast polluted the white snow.

Keeping an eye on Nolan, he walked to the cruiser to radio for help. Then he crossed the damp yard to the young woman's body. The redheaded man remained immobile.

Pamela Whitcome retained little evidence of her former beauty. Horrible things had been done to the skin of her face, her eyes had been gouged out, leaving meaty, bone-slashed cavities. Her full breasts had been hideously mutilated, savagely flayed as if by the teeth of some wild creature. The angle of her spread legs suggested that far worse things might have been done to her, things it was well that she hadn't lived to remember.

Looking down at the body, Bates felt an enormous sense of loss, of waste. He removed the heavy coat of his uniform and covered Pamela's mangled remains.

When he straightened up, Nolan was behind him, hovering silently. He jumped when Nolan spoke.

"I killed a few of them, two or three, I think," Nolan said. Bates's hand locked on the grip of his magnum.

"I think they started planning for this when they killed Rusty." The voice was high-pitched and mysterious. It seemed to come from far away, as if Nolan's vocal cords were in the depths of his stomach. "Rusty probably tried to stop them."

Bates listened to the man's strained tones. He heard the same thing in the voice that he saw in the eyes; it was madness. He'd wait for reinforcements before he interrogated this one. For now just keep him calm, Bates thought. Don't provoke him.

Bates knew better than to unholster his weapon. The man might become violent, or worse yet, might not understand the threat of the gun. Bates didn't want to have to shoot him. "Come with me," he said. "Let's check the house."

Nolan followed the policeman to the porch, and through the broken door. He continued to talk in that high, strained voice.

"But of course it was Luke that they wanted. I knew that. They tried to take advantage of the situation, make Clint work for them. But they'd have taken Luke anyway. They needed him to replace the one that died. They were losing strength, you see. Mrs. Mc-Kensie explained all about it. That's why they started all this. I guess they need a certain number for their coven. That's what happened to my brother. But things kept getting in their way, messing up their plans . . . they had to keep killing."

The two men stood in the kitchen now. Bates saw tears streaking the dried blood on Nolan's face. He walked into the shed, and Nolan followed like a shadow.

"But when they came to get us, it took me a while to figure out what was going on. See, to do magic they all have to be together, like when they cured Clint. I mean, I don't know if it's really magic, or some kind of group telekinesis or what. But they all have to do it together. That's how the wheelchair got outside, that's how Brian got in the window. They were trying to get us all to go outside, trying to keep us busy so Brian could get into the house."

Eric Nolan kept talking as they climbed the stairs. His monotone droned on and on. Bates was only half listening, but all the time he was keeping his guard up.

"But I knew something was wrong. It was what Clint said about Luke being safe upstairs. See, I remembered how Luke talked about me looking in his window. Of course, that was impossible. I thought it was just kid stuff, you know. I mean it's a second-story window. But when I saw what they did with that wheelchair . . . well, then I knew it wasn't impossible. They could levitate. And I knew that's why they were trying to lure us outside."

Eric Nolan pointed to the closed door of Luke Whitcome's bedroom. "Right in there," he said. "That's where I saw my brother. They got him too, you know. A long time ago. He still looks the same. I scared him away from Luke. I knew he wouldn't hurt me. I could tell he remembered me."

Bates opened the door. The chatter of the man who followed him made him nervous. He hoped the state boys would get here quick, before this guy flipped out again.

Carefully, his eyes scanned the bedroom. The window was up about an inch, the closet door was wide open. A kind of anger gripped Bates. He turned on Eric Nolan.

"Where's the boy, Nolan?"

Eric looked at him, blinking, as if he didn't know what was being said to him.

"Nolan, God damn it, what have you done with the kid?"

EPILOGUE

Summer 1984

In June the schools let out, releasing tides of youngsters into the soaring ninety-degree heat of summer. The grass on the common was at its greenest, lush as moss on a riverbank. In the weeks to come, it would turn crisp and brown in the relentless sunlight. A crew of sweating high school boys, already turning brown, had been hired to paint the Medford Inn.

John Royce, the new supervisor of the Antrim Highway Department, drove by in his green pickup and sounded his horn in a good-morning greeting to Chief Bates. Bates waved, smiled, and walked from the drugstore to his cruiser. The new issue of the *Tri-Town Tribune* was tucked securely under his arm.

Bates drove to the town offices and parked in the spot reserved for him. He entered, saying an abrupt, "Mornin'," to Hattie Wiggins, the town clerk. Then he retired to his office.

Sitting in his swivel chair, Bates unfolded the newspaper, smoothing it open on the desk in front of him. He scanned the items on the front page: "Medford Inn Gets a Facelift"; "School's Out!"; "Selectmen Consider Summer Recreation Program." His eyes caught a box in the right-hand column: "Mental Patient Attempts Suicide." Bates read a few sentences, folded the paper carelessly and tossed it aside.

That poor son of a bitch, he thought.

Rarely a day passed that he didn't think about the Whitcome family and Eric Nolan. Bates remembered that frightful morning of December 28, when he had made the drive up Tenny's Hill. Although six months had passed, the memory of that morning hadn't faded at all. Bates suspected it never would.

Nolan had followed him downstairs, babbling on about "little people" and magic and that long-lost brother of his. Bates had thought he'd never shut up. It was obvious that he was crazy. The best thing to do was keep him outside, keep him quiet, until the state troopers arrived.

As they stepped onto the porch Nolan cried out, backed up against the wall, cringing and gibbering. His face drained of color, his eyes were wide, staring at the woods.

"There . . . look there . . ." he pointed.

When he looked up, Bates felt his own heart clench like a fist. There, watching them from the edge of the forest, stood a little man, nearly invisible against the trees.

Bates shook his head, not believing. The little man stepped forward, walking unsteadily across the snow-covered yard. The footprints behind him were like erratic follow-the-dots as the tiny figure moved closer.

"Mmm . . . Mommy . . ." it said in a sad, hollow voice, its breath visible in the chill morning air.

Nolan broke away from the porch, charging in the direction of the tiny form. "Luke," he cried. "Oh God, Luke."

Hand on his .357, Bates bolted after him. "Stay clear of him, Nolan! Leave him be!"

When Bates caught up to them, Nolan was kneeling in front of the boy, holding him. Bates stood silently, and watched. Nolan and the boy were crying.

Luke pulled away and held out his fist. His voice was a soft whisper. "This is for you, Uncle Eric." He opened his tiny hand to reveal a flat round piece of copper. Bates knew what it was, he'd made some himself when he was a boy: it was a penny that had been flattened under the wheels of a railroad train.

Nolan took it, examined at it closely, a faraway look in his moist eyes. He said, "Thank you." And then he said something else, one other word that Bates hadn't been able to hear. It had sounded like "Brian."

In any event, those were the last three words Nolan had said.

The state cops took Luke to the hospital in Springfield. Physically he was healthy enough — as well as can be expected, the doctor had said—but he was in shock; his memory . . . the boy had shut out everything that had happened during that awful December night.

Even now, living with Clint Whitcome's brother's family, Luke's memory remained a total blank.

Opening the top drawer of his desk, Bates removed the typed letter that had long awaited a date and his signature. "It is with regret that I submit this notice of resignation from my duties as police chief . . ."

The letter stared at him from the desktop. Bates rubbed his dark-circled eyes and leaned way back in his chair, propping his feet up on the partially extended drawer.

He had some serious thinking to do.

He was happy that the boy was safe, even if Luke was unable to shed any light on the events of December 28. The child's well-being was enough to help Bates rest easier.

Lately, however, it was the blank and battered face of Eric Nolan that most interfered with Bates's sleep. He hadn't had a good night's rest since that morning on Tenny's Hill.

Bates doubted the correctness of everything he had done following his discovery of the bodies. Sure, it looked like Nolan's work, and Nolan was as crazy as a shithouse rat; it didn't take a Ph.D. in psychiatry to see that. But had Nolan flipped out and killed the family, or had he flipped out because he had witnessed— and somehow escaped—the slaughter? There was no way to tell, not really. Luke couldn't remember, and Nolan . . . Nolan had clammed up tighter than a drum the moment Luke reappeared.

It was not as if Nolan *couldn't* talk, it was as if he were refusing to. Why? To protect himself from prosecution?

The scrap of red hair found in Pamela Whitcome's hand didn't prove anything. Hair would never give a positive ID. Everyone knew that. Yet, the strands did match Nolan's hair; the fresh roots suggested a struggle.

Hell, I know there was a struggle!

Nolan's nearly incoherent testimony at the crime scene couldn't be believed. That was why the judge had ordered him to the State Mental Hospital in Waterbury for observation. Since then Nolan had had plenty of opportunity to speak up; he just wouldn't.

In any case, Bates realized, Nolan would never be found guilty. Either he was the perpetrator, and was too crazy to stand trial, or, if brought to trial, would be found not guilty by reason of insanity.

But maybe—and it was just remotely possible—Nolan actually wasn't guilty. Perhaps he had done nothing. Could there have been something to his fanciful ramblings? Perhaps Bates should have paid closer attention when he'd had the chance.

Of course, it really didn't make any difference: that was the tragedy for Nolan. Whatever the outcome, all Nolan had to look forward to was a lifetime in an institution. That is, unless he was more successful the next time he tried suicide.

Funny thing about a paranoid, though. In some cases all their actions were perfectly rational, but it was the motivation for the action that was insane, the original mistaken premise. In Nolan's case, his incoherent babbling about "little people" was crazy talk.

Wasn't it?

Bates shuddered—of course, it was. But what if, maybe—just possibly—it wasn't? He took the brown manila envelope out of the desk drawer and removed the dog-eared five-by-seven photograph of the owl. He squinted at the confusing tangle of blurry branches, leaves, and sky. The images in the background were fuzzy, out of focus, and helped to set off the bulky white bird, sharply defined in the picture's center. The photograph was old, faded, unreliable as evidence. Bates had picked it up from the floor at the crime scene, and had quickly forgotten about it. Nothing important about a picture of a bird. But there was something in the picture, something subliminal that caught his attention, kept drawing him back. There was the suggestion of an object in the background. It was something he couldn't ignore. The branches, leaves, tree trunks, clouds, and sky seemed to merge into the indistinct shape of . . . Bates had to admit it . . . a small man.

Was it trick photography? Optical illusion? Probably nothing but a fantasy of the light and the shadow. But still . . . there was doubt.

Was it *reasonable* doubt?

Surely, it was not the kind of doubt that Bates could communicate to anyone else, not in a court of law—not in a statement to the press. What would the townspeople say about a police chief who believed in little men? Is this the kind of man you want to protect your town? Your family?

But, if there was doubt, any doubt at all, shouldn't he speak up on Nolan's behalf? Maybe. But what difference would it make? Nolan was pretty far over the edge anyway; if Bates wasn't careful, folks would be thinking he was as crazy as Nolan.

The chief turned his mind to the future. Would he have to live out his remaining years plagued by this particular doubt, thinking maybe there were little men in the woods, but never saying so, and never knowing for sure? Even in his own mind it sounded crazy. Perhaps he should go looking for them, try to get to the bottom of things, just to be sure.

He weighed the photograph in one hand, and his unsigned letter of resignation in the other.

Without a job, what would he do? He had a wife and a son to worry about. He couldn't just up and quit. *And*, he thought, *if there really is something in those woods, maybe I'd better stay clear of it. I don't want to turn my wife into one of them single parents.*

Bates stacked the letter, photograph, and manila envelope together and ripped them into hundreds of tiny pieces. He watched them flutter into his wastebasket like flakes of black and white snow.

Then he reached for the telephone.

Luke Whitcome sat on the floor of his bedroom. He had lined up a bunch of tiny plastic men and was preparing to run them over with his Tonka Road Ranger.

Making a revving sound like an engine, he pushed the heavy metal truck. It bumped across the braided rug.

Smash!

Little men tumbled like bowling pins.

Luke giggled.

He picked up the scattered figures and began to set them up for another assault.

Then the phone rang. Luke tiptoed to the door and listened; maybe it was Uncle Eric. He hoped so.

When Aunt Jenn's voice dropped to a whisper, he knew it was either Chief Bates or that doctor from Chester.

Luke didn't want to see the doctor again. He wasn't sick. And all the doctor ever wanted to do was talk. Just talk. He never listened to Luke's heart; he never took his temperature. He never even gave him any pills, just those big red lollipops at the end of every visit. And Luke was getting tired of them.

Since he didn't feel sick he couldn't understand why Aunt Jenn and Uncle Pete kept taking him to the doctor. It just didn't make sense.

Maybe it was because Aunt Jenn thought he was lonely. She kept saying, "You ought to get outside more, Luke. You ought to be playing with kids your own age."

But he wasn't lonely. He could talk to Uncle Eric anytime he liked, inside his head. And if he wanted somebody to play with, there were always those kids who came once in a while at sundown. They watched him from the edge of the forest. Sometimes they called to him in his mind.

Maybe one day he'd go out and play with them.

Luke stood up and walked to the window. *Maybe they're out there now,* he thought.

In the distance he saw black and white cows munching tall grass in the pasture. A little calf, wobbly-legged and spindly, nuzzled his mama's udder. Farther back, between the fence and the forest, Uncle Pete drove his big green tractor. Luke watched him, remembering the time Uncle Pete had taken him for a ride. It was great being way up there in the high seat. It was fun. But Uncle Pete hadn't been smiling.

Luke didn't know why everyone was acting so worried, why everyone was always checking up on him.

He heard Aunt Jenn hang up the phone. Pretty soon she'd come into the room, maybe bring a plate of chocolate chip cookies and a glass of milk. She'd ask him how he was feeling.

Always the same questions.

He was feeling fine. Just fine.

He made the growling engine sound again, and pushed the Road Ranger into the circle of eight plastic men.

THE END

AUTHOR'S NOTE

The controversy surrounding the origin of Vermont's stone structures continues. If the reader is interested in more information on the possibility of Celtic settlement in the New World, I suggest the following nonfiction works:

Cook, Warren L., ed. *Ancient Vermont*. (Rutland, Vt.: Academy Books, 1978)

Dexter, Warren W., and Martin, Donna. *America's Ancient Stone Relics, Vermont's Link to Bronze Age Mariners*. (Rutland, Vt.: Academy Books, 1995)

Fell, Barry. *America, B.C.* (New York: Quadrangle/The New York Times Book Co., 1976)

Neudorfer, Giovanna. *Vermont's Stone Chambers: An Inquiry into Their Past*. (Montpelier, Vt.: Vermont Historical Society, 1980)

Trento, Salvatore Michael. *Search for Lost America*. (Chicago and New York: Contemporary Books, Inc., 1978)

Also, I'd like to thank some of the people who helped me with this project: Edward Whalen, Mike Rogers, Phil Pochoda, and, for rescuing the book from the limbo of CP/M, Tom and Elizabeth Monteleone.

Because I was born and raised in Vermont, I grew up juggling two sets of Green Mountain myths. One group is best typified by the sunny, sweetness-and-light covers of *Vermont Life* magazine. The other set is darker, more gothic, dealing in death, danger, ghost-lore, and decay.

My affection embraces both.

In a trilogy of novels beginning with *Shadow Child*, originally published in 1987, I tried to explore several of the state's "classic" dark mysteries. These were the sorts of tales Yankee yarn-spinners might have told around the fireplace one hundred and more years ago.

I wondered if such stories would work in a modern setting.

With that in mind, I tried to create a Vermont that, at least on the surface, looks very much like a sunny *Vermont Life* cover. I wanted to populate it with the sorts of decent, small-town folks I'd grown up among. But I wanted to peer unflinchingly into the deep shadows that Vermont sunshine creates; I wanted to see what those shadows might conceal.

To some degree, I think, *Shadow Child* works on an allegorical level—a sort of fairy tale for adults. But really it's a "save the farm" story with a twist. Although the menace may seem more super-natural than avaricious bankers or insensitive land developers, it is, after all, perfectly human—as my original title, *Of Woman Born*, might have suggested.